**Praise for *New York Times* bestselling author
Kat Martin**

"Kat Martin is a fast gun when it comes to storytelling, and I love her books."
—*#1 New York Times* bestselling author
Linda Lael Miller

"This is definitely a page-turner full of compassion and love shared by two unlikely souls. This is a 'don't miss' read.… Kat Martin is a very gifted writer who takes you from the beginning to the end in total suspense."
—*Fresh Fiction* on *Against the Wind*

"[Kat] Martin is a terrific storyteller…"
—*Booklist* on *Season of Strangers*

**Praise for *USA TODAY* bestselling author
Delores Fossen**

"Clear off space on your keeper shelf, Fossen has arrived."
—*New York Times* bestselling author Lori Wilde

"It will take your breath away."
—*RT Book Reviews* on *Outlaw Lawman*

Kat Martin is the *New York Times* bestselling author of more than fifty historical and contemporary romance novels. To date she has over fifteen million copies of her books in print in seventeen countries, including Sweden, France, Russia, Spain, Japan, Argentina, Poland and Greece. Kat and her husband, author L. J. Martin, live on their ranch outside Missoula, Montana, and spend winters at their beach house in California. Kat invites you to visit her website at www.katmartin.com.

USA TODAY bestselling author **Delores Fossen** has had more than fifty novels published, with millions of copies of her books in print worldwide. She's received the Booksellers' Best Award and the RT Reviewers' Choice Best Book Award, and was a finalist for the prestigious RITA® Award. In addition, she's had nearly a hundred short stories and articles published in national magazines. Married to an air force colonel, Delores is the mother of four children and has lived in England and all over the United States. She's had a variety of careers and jobs: an air force captain, a special-ed teacher and a rehab counselor. None was as fun or challenging as the time she spent as a stay-at-home mom. You can get updates about Delores's books or contact her through her website at www.deloresfossen.com.

New York Times **Bestselling Author**

KAT MARTIN

AGAINST THE FIRE

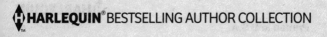

ISBN-13: 978-0-373-28485-6

Against the Fire

Copyright © 2017 by Harlequin Books S.A.

The publisher acknowledges the copyright holders of the individual works as follows:

Against the Fire
Copyright © 2011 by Kat Martin

Outlaw Lawman
Copyright © 2013 by Delores Fossen

Recycling programs
for this product may
not exist in your area.

HARLEQUIN®
www.Harlequin.com

Printed in U.S.A.

CONTENTS

AGAINST THE FIRE

Kat Martin

To Carolyn Pomerene, a longtime friend,
for her help with the psychology in this book,
as well as her work on *Scent of Roses*.

CHAPTER ONE

THE SCREECH OF THE siren didn't reach him at first. Exhausted from a hard day's work, Gabriel Raines slept soundly. But as the shrill cry drew closer and the flashing red lights lit the walls inside his bedroom, something registered in the depths of his mind and he stirred.

Gabe blinked awake, eyes instantly alert as had become his habit during his years as a marine. He'd been out of the corps for years but some things just didn't change.

The wail of the siren grew louder on the street below the window of his downtown Dallas condominium, then the fire truck shot past and the sounds began to dim as the vehicle drove farther away. With a weary sigh, Gabe turned to look at the red neon numbers on his alarm clock. *Three-thirty.*

Running a hand over his face, he lay back against the pillow, hoping like hell he'd be able to get back to sleep.

He might have if his cell phone hadn't started ringing.

The siren's wail had stopped. The fire truck had reached its destination, which meant the fire was nearby, and the sound of a second engine was beginning to fill the night. Gabe reached toward the nightstand and picked up his cell phone, flipped it open and pressed it against his ear.

"Whoever this is," he grumbled, "this had better be important."

"There's a fire at the Dallas Towers." The voice of his foreman, Sam McBride, floated over the line. "Looks like all our hard work is going up in smoke."

Adrenaline jolted through him. Gabe swung his long legs to the side of the bed. "Are you sure it's the Towers?"

"I was on my way home, about a block away when I heard the first fire truck. I saw it turn toward the Towers and decided to see what was going on."

Already off the mattress, Gabe pressed the phone more tightly against his ear. "You see what part of the structure is involved?"

"I could see flames in the lobby."

"Son of a bitch." They were almost finished with the major renovation they were doing on the Tower's soaring marble lobby. *Almost.*

He took a breath to steady himself as he walked toward his closet. "If you were just heading home, you must have had a pretty hot date."

"I didn't spend the night if that tells you anything."

Like Gabe, Sam was a bachelor and both of them lived downtown. An area that formerly consisted of run-down buildings was being revitalized, turned into a chic little district of shops and boutiques. Gabe had built the condos Sam lived in, as well as the Las Posas development that housed his own unit.

"I'm getting dressed. I'll be there in fifteen minutes."

Gabe closed the phone. He should have known things were going too well. In his experience, every time life went a little too smoothly, bad news lurked around the corner.

Naked, he crossed to the oak dresser against the far wall, jerked open his underwear drawer and pulled out briefs and a pair of socks. Dragging on a pair of jeans and a Dallas Cowboys T-shirt, he ignored the row of Western boots sitting on the closet floor and shoved his size-thirteen feet into the heavy leather boots he wore when he was working.

Gabe left the condo and a few minutes later, he was pulling his big white GMC extended cab pickup over to the curb just a little ways down the block from the Towers. Smoke and flame billowed out through the open glass doors leading into the lobby, but the fire boys were at work inside and had three powerful jets of water hitting the building from different angles. With any luck, the blaze would be brought under control before it burned into the offices on the floors above.

The bad news was, the lobby would have to be completely rebuilt.

Son of a bitch.

"At least the building was insured." Sam McBride strode toward him, almost as tall as Gabe's six-foot-two-inch frame, but instead of having Gabe's dark hair, blue eyes and muscular build, Sam was blond and lanky. On top of being a damned good employee, he was Gabe's best friend.

"Well, I guess that's something. It'll sure put us behind schedule, though. I was hoping to finish up here, split the crew up, use the guys to finish our other projects."

"Not gonna happen," Sam said.

Gabe looked up to see one of the firemen walking toward them in full battle gear: fire protection suit, helmet, goggles, high rubber boots.

"Be better if you stepped back a little," the fireman said, "kept out of the way."

"I'm Gabriel Raines. My company's been rebuilding the lobby. A lot of my equipment is still in there."

"Sorry to hear that, Mr. Raines. Most everything in the lobby's completely gone. It was a hot, fast fire. We're lucky we were able to get a handle on it so quickly."

Gabe blew out a breath. "I hope nobody was hurt."

"Not that we know of."

"How'd it start?"

"Too soon to tell. If the lobby was under construction, there was probably a lot of flammable material around. Paint thinner, drop cloths, stuff that really gets a fire going."

"We're really careful to seal everything up at the end of the day, pick up whatever we've been using."

"Like I said, it's too soon to tell. Our investigators will be taking a look at everything, including the security tapes."

Gabe shook his head. "Afraid that won't help. The old cameras are down. New ones aren't up yet."

"How many people knew that?"

"Not many. Replacing the old cameras was kind of a last-minute management decision. Only a few people knew they weren't up and working."

The fireman nodded and headed back toward the fire, pausing for a moment to speak to a second man in a blue uniform, late forties, salt-and-pepper hair. Gabe realized the man had been moving through the crowd that had gathered to watch the blaze, asking onlookers questions. Now he approached Gabe and Sam.

"I'm Captain Daily with the arson investigation squad," he said. "You're Raines?"

"That's right."

"I understand your company's been working on the lobby reconstruction."

"Actually, we were damned near done."

"We've never met but I know who you are. You helped my dad once, Jim Daily? He needed a permit to add a room to his dry-cleaning shop. The building was old and the city was giving him a hard time about it. You put in a good word for him and the permit came through. I appreciate that."

"I liked your dad. I was sorry to hear he passed away."

"He was a good man." Daily straightened, returning to the business at hand. He looked over at the destruction in the lobby of the Towers. "I'll need to ask you a couple of questions."

"No problem. This is my foreman, Sam McBride."

Daily gave Sam a nod and returned his attention to Gabe. "What time did you get here?"

"About twenty minutes ago. We both live in the area. Sam was heading home from a date. He followed the fire trucks and gave me a call."

"You see anyone going in or out of the building?"

"You guys were already here by the time I arrived," Gabe said. "I didn't see anyone else go in or out."

Daily turned to Sam. "How about you?"

Sam glanced over to the crews mopping up the scene. "The first truck was just pulling up. I saw the flames in the lobby and called Gabe. I watched you guys working until he got here. It wasn't long before a crowd started to gather. But no, I didn't see anyone coming or going."

The captain nodded. "The fireman you were talking to…that's Mike Dougherty. He says the cameras are down."

"Didn't seem like a big deal. No one was going in and out of the lobby during the remodeling."

"I'm going to need a list of the people who knew."

"No problem."

"Thanks. We'll be in touch if we have any more questions." Daily started back toward the men working the fire and disappeared among the throng of spectators.

Gabe and Sam stood watching as the fire crews worked. Eventually, the smoke began to thin and one of the water hoses was turned off.

"Anything you can think of we could have done to cause this thing?" Gabe asked.

"I was here at the end of the day. We left the place clean as a whistle." Sam shook his head. "We were so damned close to finished."

"Shit happens," Gabe said.

"I guess."

"At least the fire didn't get too out of control and it doesn't look like anyone got hurt. I'll call Fred Parsons, see what he wants us to do." Parsons managed the building. He had hired Raines Construction to do the remodel. The owner was eager to get the lobby finished and the building running smoothly again. Gabe was sure Parsons would want him to get his crew back on the job as soon as possible.

"I'll talk to Rich Simmons, too," Gabe said. Simmons worked for American Insurance. "We'll need to file a claim." But even if they did, there was a fairly high deductible. Nothing was ever cheap.

Sam slapped him on the back. "Come on. It's damn

near dawn. Neither of us is going to get any more sleep. Let's go get some breakfast."

They might as well. The horizon had begun to turn a pale purple-gray. Gabe's crew started work at seven and though this job was down for a while, there was still work to be done on several other projects they had going in the area.

"You're thinking Mrs. Olson's?" Gabe asked. Mrs. Olson's Café down the block had the best breakfast in the downtown area and the place opened early.

"Yeah. I could really use a cup of coffee."

Gabe checked his heavy stainless-steel wristwatch. "It's after five. Should be open by now."

They both climbed into Gabe's pickup. The company name, Raines Construction, printed on the door in bold black letters, flashed in the early dawn light. He fired up the big, gas-guzzling V-8 he had vowed to replace with a more economical vehicle on his next purchase and pulled off down the street.

His stomach growled. A big plate of bacon and eggs was beginning to sound damned good. Might take his mind off having to rebuild the damnable lobby of the Towers.

GABE SPENT THE morning working away on his favorite project, the reconstruction of an old theater he owned on a street in Deep Ellum. The brick building had once been a local cinema, back in the days when they were extravagantly decorated and elegant. The ceiling was handpainted in bright colors with lots of gold leaf. At least it was back in its heyday. The doors leading into the seating area were guarded by huge gilt Egyptian statues.

Wasn't much of anything left when Gabe had first started. The red velvet seats were completely destroyed, turned into rust and mold by a hole in the roof that had let in years of rain. But the structure itself was still sound, the brick walls sturdy, once he'd had them reinforced.

He'd bought the place for a song, and a barrel of determination. He wanted to see the Egyptian restored and put back into use. He had already made deals with several local theater groups and the Deep Ellum Arts Festival folks. He had no doubt, once the elegant interior was restored, the theater would again be in great demand.

Besides, he had a personal love for the past that had started when he was a kid growing up in Wyoming. Wind Canyon was a true Western town and though he and his two brothers had been raised in a dumpy, run-down house near a set of abandoned narrow-gauge railroad tracks, the wooden boardwalks, long bar saloons and surrounding ranches had instilled in him a love of the West.

All three Raines boys had left Wind Canyon as soon as they had graduated high school, but a few years back his older brother, Jackson, had returned. He'd made a boatload of money in the oil business, bought himself twelve thousand acres of prime cattle land and renamed the old homestead Raintree Ranch.

Gabe had left Wind Canyon to join the marines. After a four-year stint, he had moved to Dallas and started working in the construction business. With Jackson's help, he bought his first fixer-upper house, remodeled and sold it. He'd liked the work and the money he made and began doing a second one.

The real estate market was hot and Gabe was a hard

worker. He made enough money to start his own company and the business had been growing ever since. Along with that, at Jackson's advice, he'd invested some of his hard-earned dollars in Wildcat Oil, where his brother had worked as a geologist, and that had made money, too.

He been smart enough to see the recession coming and made changes that kept him from going broke like so many in the construction business had. There were a lot of opportunities, tax credits and incentives, he'd discovered, for doing downtown renovation and area redevelopment. So for the last couple of years he'd shifted his focus to that type of restoration and found he liked that work even more. Liked seeing a near-dead place come back to life, liked what it did for the people who lived in the area.

Gabe went to work with the nail gun, securing the floor of the stage. He didn't do a lot of his own carpentry these days, but if he wasn't too busy with meetings or solving problems at different job sites, he often lent a hand, doing what had gotten him started in the business in the first place.

The buzz of a nearby saw went silent and Gabe looked up to see two uniformed policemen sauntering down the aisle in his direction. Setting the nail gun aside, he rose to his feet, jumped off the stage, and strode up the aisle to intercept them.

"You Gabriel Raines?" the first patrolman asked, Gonzales, his name plate said.

"That's me. What can I do for you?"

"The fire at the Towers was definitely arson. We've got a suspect in custody. We'd like you to come down and take a look, see if you might have seen him in the area last night."

Arson. He'd been hoping it was just some kind of electrical problem. "Sure thing, I can do that."

Officer Gonzales, with the hard-edged features of a seasoned policeman, and Delaney, the baby-faced cub of the pair, walked him back up the aisle.

"You can come with us or drive down on your own if you prefer," Gonzales said as they stepped into the warm, humid early September air.

Gabe eyed the white-and-blue patrol car and shook his head. "I'll meet you there." In his younger years, he had ridden in the backseat of a police car more than once. In high school, all three Raines brothers had been hell on wheels. At the rate they were going back then, half the town figured one or more of them would wind up in prison.

Then Steve Whitelaw, the school's boxing coach, had recognized a talent in Jackson. Gabe's older brother had been street fighting for years and he was good. Whitelaw taught him how to stop brawling and start boxing, showed him that boxing could mean a way out of the poverty the boys lived in, and Jackson began to change.

Once that happened, he made sure Gabe and Devlin gave up their wild ways, too. Which they did. Mostly.

Gabe arrived at the police station a few minutes later and shoved through the glass front doors. A female officer behind the desk announced his arrival to someone in the back room, and a few minutes later the fire investigator with the silver-threaded hair he remembered from last night walked into the waiting room.

"Thanks for coming," Captain Daily said. Gabe

knew the arson squad worked with the Dallas Fire Rescue Department, but figured now that there had been an arrest, the police were also involved.

"No problem."

"We think we may have found the kid who set the fire at the Towers."

"Kid?"

"He's seventeen. He was pulled over in the vicinity on a routine traffic stop—broken taillight. One of the guys remembered him from the fire he set a couple of years ago."

"And you want to know if I saw him last night."

"He's in a lineup. Let's see if you can pick him out."

"All right, but I wasn't paying that much attention. I was mostly watching the crew work the fire."

"It's worth a try."

"Sure." Gabe followed the investigator down a long stark-white hallway into a small room with a glass window on one side that looked into a staging area. Five men of varying sizes and ethnicities stood on a platform against the far wall. All of them were fairly young. One looked vaguely familiar.

An image popped into his head of a boy, short and muscular, with dark skin and coarse black hair. He'd been standing next to another Hispanic kid about the same age.

"Number three," Gabe said as the image formed clearly in his mind. "I saw him last night. He was talking to another boy. They were standing on the sidewalk when I drove up."

Daily nodded. "Your friend, McBride, was down here a couple of hours ago. Picked out the same kid. Name's Angel Ramirez. Looks like we've got our perp."

Gabe's gaze returned to the boy who was being led away. "What's the kid have to say?"

"Said he was nowhere near the fire last night. Be interesting to see what he has to say now."

"You say he's done this before?"

Daily nodded as he pulled open the door leading out of the viewing room. "Three years ago. Set an old abandoned building on fire. Fortunately no one was hurt, but the building was mostly destroyed. Kid was sentenced to two years in juvenile detention for that little trick. Got out in twelve months for good behavior. Makes you wonder."

Daily walked Gabe back down the hall.

"As I said, thanks for coming in." The captain extended a hand and Gabe shook it.

"Good luck with the investigation." Gabe turned and started for the door. He was halfway across the waiting room when a redheaded whirlwind raced through the glass doors and bolted toward the desk.

"Excuse me. My name is Mattie Baker. I need to talk to whoever is in charge of the fire investigation at the Dallas Towers."

Gabe paused as the information sank in. She was there about the fire. Pausing, he gave the woman a more thorough inspection. About five-foot-four. Late twenties, maybe early thirties. Slender but nicely curved, though it was hard to tell for sure in the conservative brown suit and pale yellow blouse she wore. A great pair of legs, though, and that hair. It wasn't just auburn; it was warmer, hotter, reminding him of the flames last night.

Gabe inwardly smiled. The lady was a looker. The splash of freckles across her nose and the high cheek bones only seemed to emphasize the fact. And yet the clothes she wore and the way she had drawn all that glorious hair into a tight knot at the nape of her neck made him wonder at the sort of woman she was.

Curious now, Gabe waited patiently as the older blond officer behind the desk looked down at her computer and finally came up with the answer to the lady's question.

"The man in charge…that would be Captain Thomas Daily. I assume you have information in regard to the fire."

"Yes, I do."

"The captain's here. I'll tell him you wish to see him."

When it came to women, Gabe was usually more the pursued than the pursuer, but there was something about this particular female that intrigued him.

He crossed the several feet between them, used the name he had overheard. "Ms. Baker?"

She turned at the sound of his voice. "Yes?"

"I'm Gabriel Raines. My company was working on the remodel of the Towers. I couldn't help overhearing. I gather you have information on the case."

"Actually, I'm here for a friend." She flicked an anxious glance toward the long white hallway where Gabe had viewed the lineup. "The police believe he is somehow involved in setting the fire."

"And you don't?"

"No. Angel wouldn't do a thing like that."

"From what I understand, he set another fire a few years back. And I saw him at the Towers last night. If he didn't set the fire, why was he there?"

Huge blue eyes a softer shade than his own stared

up at him in disbelief. "You…you *saw* Angel there? At the fire?"

"That's right. He and another kid were standing on the sidewalk when I got out of my truck. It was still very early. Not too many people had shown up yet. That's the reason I remember seeing him."

Her shoulders drooped, then subtly straightened. "I need to talk to him. There has to be some other explanation."

"Excuse me, Ms. Baker," the desk clerk said. "Captain Daily will see you now."

Gabe reached into the back pocket of his jeans and pulled out his wallet. He drew out a business card and handed it to Mattie Baker. "This has my address and phone number. If there's anything I can do, let me know."

Mattie took the card. "Thank you. I will."

"Good luck," he said, figuring she would need it if she planned to help the kid.

The desk clerk pointed toward the hallway and Captain Daily appeared at the entrance. Mattie started hurrying in that direction, strands of fiery hair flying out from the tidy knot at the nape of her neck. Gabe headed for the door, wondering if he would ever see Mattie Baker again.

And hoping like hell he would.

CHAPTER TWO

"I DIDN'T DO IT, MATTIE." Angel fidgeted on the seat across from her. He was smaller than other kids his age, only five-foot-five, with a stocky build and wide-set brown eyes, but he was a handsome boy, and smart. At least most of the time.

"I learned my lesson three years ago," he continued. "I would never do anything like that again." He looked up at her and she could see the fear in his eyes. "You believe me, don't you?"

Mattie sighed. "If you say you didn't set the fire, I believe you. Just tell me what you were doing downtown last night."

Angel glanced away.

"Angel, look at me." His troubled gaze returned to her face. "You live in central Oak Cliff. You were seen last night at the fire. I need to know what you were doing all the way down at the Towers."

His blunt brown fingers twitched on the top of the table. "I was just driving around. I saw the fire and I stopped to watch, just like everyone else. That isn't a crime, is it?"

Mattie ignored the remark. "The police say you may have been there with someone else. Who was it?"

Angel shook his head. "It was just me. And I didn't set the fire."

"All right, you didn't set the fire, but I can see by the way you're behaving you aren't telling me everything that happened. I can't help you unless you're honest with me."

He swallowed and for an instant his eyes glistened. "I didn't set the fire."

Mattie sighed in frustration. "Then tell me—"

"Time's up, Ms. Baker." A policeman stood in the doorway. "I'm afraid you'll have to leave."

She was surprised they had let her see him at all, since she wasn't a member of his family or his attorney, but Captain Daily seemed moved by her staunch defense of the boy and her obvious concern.

"I'll get you a lawyer," she told him as she walked out the door. "And I'll be back to see you as soon as I can."

Mattie left the small room and was crossing the waiting area when the front door swung open and a familiar black-haired woman rushed in. Angel's mother, Rosa Ramirez, spotted her instantly and ran forward, her ten-year-old daughter, Elena, and her seven-year-old son, Manny, hurrying along, trying to keep up with her.

"Mattie! I am so glad you are here. The police came to the house this morning. They have arrested Angel. They think he set a fire in some building downtown."

"The Dallas Towers. Yes, I know. Angel called me."

Rosa's thick black eyebrows shot up. "You talked to him?" She was a large, big-busted woman, but short like her son. "Did you tell the police he is innocent?"

"I spoke to Angel just a few minutes ago. Unfortunately, someone saw him at the fire last night. That doesn't look good for him."

"Dios mio." Rosa crossed herself. "He didn't do it. I know he didn't. The fire he set before… He was just a boy acting out against his father. But he learned his lesson. He is getting good grades in school. He wants to go to college. He wouldn't do it, Mattie."

"I don't think he did it, either. But I need to know why he was there and who was with him. Can you help me?"

Rosa shook her head, moving the braid hanging down her back. "I thought he was home. I did not know he left the house."

"What about the friend he may have been with? Any idea who that might have been?"

"Angel has lots of friends." She looked down at her children. "Do either of you know who your brother might have been out with last night?"

They solemnly shook their heads, their attention focused on the uniformed policemen walking around inside the building and the people being led into the back of the station.

"I want to see him," Rosa said.

"Talk to the lady at the desk. She'll be able to help you. I told Angel I would get him an attorney. As soon as bail is posted, we'll be able to get him out of here."

"Bail? I have no money for bail."

"It shouldn't be too high. I'll take care of it, Rosa."

Rose grabbed hold of her hand and pressed it against her lips. "*Gracias.* Thank you, Mattie. You have always been good to our family."

Mattie nudged the stout woman toward the counter. "Go on now, tell them you want to see your son."

Turning away, Rosa herded her children toward the desk. Mattie was convinced that she had been right and Angel was innocent, yet certain there was more to the story.

Was he covering for the person who actually set the fire? If so, who was it?

And why would Angel risk himself that way for an arsonist?

MATTIE WAS STILL pondering the boy's predicament as she arrived at her downtown office building. She crossed the lobby to the bank of elevators and pushed the button for the fifteenth floor. She couldn't help thinking of the sullen teenager Angel had been when she had met him three years ago at the Family Recovery Center, a nonprofit organization that dealt with domestic violence.

When she wasn't working long hours as an architect at Dewalt, Greeley and Associates Design, a job she loved, Mattie spent her spare time volunteering at the center. Though she had been raised in a happy home, her friend Tracy Spencer had been a victim of family violence. Mattie had discovered her best friend's secret, but Tracy had begged her to keep silent and ten-year-old Mattie had agreed.

It was a mistake she had always regretted. Mattie's work with the FRC was a way of making up for that mistake.

She had been working at the center when Angel and his family had first come in for help. The next day, Angel had suffered another of his father's vicious beatings. Setting fire to the old empty building was his way of fighting back.

A year later, after Angel got out of juvenile detention, Mattie had been one of the volunteers assigned to his case. He was a sweet boy, and determined to turn his life around. He studied hard at school and volunteered to help other boys his age at the center.

They wound up spending a good deal of time together at the center, and Mattie had even helped him get a part-time job that summer in the mail room at her office. He used the money he earned to help his family.

There was a goodness in Angel Ramirez. Mattie didn't believe the teenager had set the fire at the Towers and she was determined to prove it.

The elevator opened with a *ding*. She walked out into the hallway. She pushed open the glass doors etched with the name Dewalt, Greeley and Associates Design, and made her way into the reception area of the busy architectural firm.

"Mr. Brewer called about the gallery," the pretty receptionist, Shirley Mack, said. "And your mother called."

Mattie took the messages from Shirley's outstretched hand. "Thanks."

"How's she doin'? Your mom, I mean. Didn't she just get remarried?"

"Believe it or not, it's been nearly a year. She and Jack seem happy." But her mother had been wary of a second marriage after the death of Mattie's father and the hardships she had suffered. Mattie hoped this time would be different.

"Well, I'm glad for them," Shirley said.

"Me, too." Mattie made a mental note to return the call. They spoke on the phone at least twice a week, but her mother had moved to San Antonio to be with Jack, and Mattie missed her.

Passing the receptionist's desk, Mattie walked through an open area where busy draftsmen sat at their computers using sophisticated software programs to tackle the work of designing offices, schools, condos and luxury homes.

She caught a wave from Aaron Kreski, a coworker and friend. Thanks to her innovative designs and the overtime she put in, she had recently been promoted to head designer and given an office of her own. She was on her way to becoming a vice president, a step up the ladder in the career she so determinedly pursued.

Pushing open the tall walnut door, she walked over to the matching walnut desk. Polished to a glossy sheen, the desktop was bare, except for a sleek, twenty-inch computer monitor, a calendar, a brown felt desk pad, a black-and-gold pen-and-pencil set, and an old, cherished photo of her parents.

Unconsciously, she reached out to touch the gilded frame. The picture reflected the good, happy years, the times she liked to remember. Then her dad had died in a car accident when she was twelve and everything had changed.

With no life insurance and only a high school education, her mother had been forced to take a job at a local Kmart to support them. Through those difficult times, her mother became convinced that a woman could never truly count on a man, even one who loved her. The only person she could count on was herself.

Mattie had taken those words to heart. She'd worked hard to put herself through UCLA, graduated at the head of her class and continued to live by that philosophy ever since.

She glanced at the files neatly stacked on the credenza behind her desk and the stacks beneath the window, but ignored the itch to pick one of them up and get to work. Instead she sat down at the desk, grabbed the phone and called Sidney Weiss, an attorney who did legal work for the FRC.

"Sid? This is Mattie Baker."

"Hello, Mattie. What can I do for you?"

"Sid, I need your help."

Briefly, she filled the attorney in on the fire at the Towers and the arson charges against Angel Ramirez. Weiss agreed to take Angel's case, assuring Mattie he would advance the money, post bail as soon as it was set and get the boy released.

As she hung up the phone, a trickle of relief slid through her and she tried to think what else she might do.

A sudden thought struck. Reaching into her purse, she pulled out the business card she had been given at the police department.

Raines Construction. Beneath it, *Gabriel Raines, owner.* An address and a couple of phone numbers were printed at the bottom of the card.

A memory stirred of a tall, dark-haired man with a powerful build, long legs and wide, muscular shoulders—if the fit of his faded cambric work shirt and worn blue jeans were any indication. His working man's tan set off brilliant blue eyes above a hard, square jaw softened by a mouth curved faintly in a smile.

Testosterone seemed to seep from his pores and though a man like that was hardly her type, she had to admit he was handsome. And the glint of male interest in those amazing blue eyes might be something she could use to her advantage.

She needed to know who Angel had been out with the night of the fire and if Gabriel Raines had seen the two boys, maybe she could identify the other kid from his description.

Mattie tapped the card a couple of times and set it down on the desk in front of her. Needing to get to work, she retrieved one of the files she was working on, a remodel of a downtown art gallery, and opened the folder.

Later, she vowed, she would get in touch with Gabriel Raines.

EARLY THE FOLLOWING MORNING, Gabe stopped to talk to Sam at a site they were working on down by the Farmer's Market: the redevelopment of a dilapidated apartment building—condemned by the city—that Gabe had purchased last year. He was remodeling the units into attractive, affordable rental housing and he was pleased at the progress being made.

His construction trailer sat in front of the job site, a place for file cabinets, a couple of desks and the part-time secretary who worked for him three days a week. Gabe climbed the metal stairs and opened the door.

"Everything going okay, Becky?" She was forty-one and happily married, with curly blond hair and a weathered complexion from too much time in the sun.

"Just need you to sign some checks, boss."

He ambled over, took the pen from her hand and signed what she needed. "Anything else going on?"

"Mr. Parsons called about the damage to the Tower's lobby. I told him to call you on your cell."

"I talked to him. I'm meeting him this afternoon."

"That's about it, then."

Gabe nodded and Becky turned back to her computer. He left the trailer and drove over to McKinney Court, his biggest undertaking yet—a four-story office building uptown at McKinney near Olive. It was the future headquarters of Wildcat Oil, the small but successful oil exploration company his brother Jackson had once worked for as a geologist. Even with the current economic downturn, oil made money, and there was no lack of funds to complete the building.

He pulled up in front where a huge crane hoisted steel beams into position. The foreman, Jake Turner, a big, beefy man with iron-gray hair, had twenty years experience building multistory structures.

"How's it going, Jake?"

"Better than it should be." Jake lifted his hard hat, mopped his forehead with a handkerchief, then stuffed the cloth into his hip pocket. "Always makes me nervous when things are going too well."

Gabe thought of the destruction at the Towers and hoped that evened things out, at least for a while. "I know what you mean." He toured the site with Jake, made a few suggestions, then fired up his truck and took off for the theater.

As he pushed through the ornate front doors, looking forward to continuing his work on the stage, his cell phone began playing the first few bars of Brooks & Dunn's "Hard Workin' Man." He unclipped the phone from his belt and flipped it open. "Raines."

"Mr. Raines, this is Mattie Baker. We met at the police station."

"I remember." Gabe thought of the woman with the tantalizing auburn hair. She had a damned sexy voice to go with it.

"You mentioned you would be willing to help me with Angel, and I had a couple of questions I was hoping you might be able to answer. I was wondering if you might have time to meet me for a quick cup of coffee."

"Sure, I can do that. Where would you like to meet?"

"Well, I work in the Coffman Building. There's a coffee kiosk in the lobby. Any chance that would be convenient?"

"Not a problem. My condo's just a few blocks away."

"Great. How's four o'clock?"

Gabe checked his watch. He'd be finished with his meeting with Parsons by three. "That'll be fine. I'll see you there."

Mattie thanked him, and Gabe closed the phone. She wanted to see him. He might have found that interesting if he hadn't heard the strictly business note in her voice. Still, he couldn't help a trace of anticipation. Aside from an occasional sleepover with one of his old girlfriends, he hadn't been seeing anyone for the past six months.

His brother had recently married. Jackson was happier than Gabe had ever seen him. After the devastating breakup his little brother, Devlin, had suffered with his fiancée, Amy Matlock, Dev was an even more dedicated bachelor than Gabe.

Which didn't mean he didn't like female companionship. He just didn't really think the pretty little redhead was going to be his type, no matter the physical attraction.

Still, he had promised to help if he could. The Ramirez kid was only seventeen and he remembered the mistakes he had made himself when he was young.

Gabe thought of his four o'clock meeting, thought of the redhead and smiled.

CHAPTER THREE

MATTIE SAT AT a small, round, iron-mesh table in front of the coffee kiosk in the lobby of her high-rise office building. The place was only six blocks from her condo, the reason she had decided to buy it, allowing her to walk to work in the mornings.

Apparently Gabriel Raines lived somewhere in the vicinity, though she had never seen him until their accidental meeting at the police station. She took a sip of her cappuccino, which was hot and foamy, just the way she liked. It was one minute after four. She wondered if Raines would be on some kind of ego trip and make her wait.

She hated the games people played.

A subtle wave of relief slipped through her as she spotted him crossing the lobby, heading for the neon sign above the kiosk. She guessed him to be in his early thirties, maybe three or four years older than her twenty-nine years.

She stood to meet him. "Thank you for coming."

"I said I'd help if I could. Mind if I get myself a cup of coffee before we talk?"

"Not at all. I'm completely addicted myself."

Raines smiled and went to the counter. He had a nice smile, she thought, recalling she had seen it before. She had a feeling women fell all over themselves to get one of those easy smiles, silently grateful he wasn't her type in the least.

Paper cup in hand, he sat down in one of the little white wrought-iron chairs, making it look like it belonged in a doll house. "Now, what can I do for you, Ms. Baker?"

"It's just Mattie, and I'm hoping you can help me figure out who Angel was with the night of the fire."

"Well, I probably won't be much help. Like I told the police, I wasn't paying all that much attention to the spectators. I was more concerned with watching the fire guys put out the blaze."

"But you recognized Angel."

"From a lineup. Yes, I did."

"What did the other boy look like?"

Gabe took the lid off his coffee, blew over the liquid to cool it, then took a sip. She could tell he was doing his best to dredge up a memory of the second boy he had seen.

"Mind if I ask what your connection is to the Ramirez kid?"

She considered how much to say, then decided she had no reason to keep her work a secret. In fact, she was proud of the help she had given families who needed it.

"I do volunteer work at a neighborhood center that helps recovering victims of family violence. Several years ago, Angel's mother showed up at the center. Her husband was abusing her and the children. She didn't want to leave him, but she couldn't take the beatings any longer."

"What happened?"

"Angel and his father got into an argument the next night and Benito beat the hell out of him. Two days later, Angel set fire to an old abandoned building in the neighborhood. He was arrested. Because Rosa, his mother, had come to the center for help, one of the FRC attorneys got involved."

"FRC?"

"Family Recovery Center. Since there were extenuating circumstances—like two black eyes and a broken collarbone—Angel's sentence was reduced. After his release a year later, Angel went into mandatory counseling. His father had moved out by then and I started visiting him and the rest of his family as a volunteer. I began to realize what an unusual boy he is."

Gabe took a sip of his coffee. "In what way?" His hands were as tan as his face. She noticed his nails were clipped short, and there was no dirt underneath.

"Angel is extremely smart. He gets straight As in high school and he wants to go to college. He's always willing to help other kids and because he's the way he is, he has lots of friends. I don't believe he set the fire at the Towers, but I need to find a way to prove it."

Gabe straightened in his chair, making him seem even taller. "I can't say for sure the boys were together, but they were talking and it seemed like they knew each other."

"What did the second boy look like?"

"Hispanic. Around the same age as Angel, but taller and thinner. His hair was long, pulled back in a ponytail at the back of his neck. That's about all I remember."

"That may be enough. There's a kid Angel knows. His name is Enrique Flores. He's got long hair and he wears it pulled back that way. I think they're pretty good friends. I don't know why they would have been downtown that night, but maybe Enrique will tell me."

"Probably ought to tell the police about Flores."

"I'd really like to talk to him first."

Gabe slowly nodded. "I guess that would be all right."

Mattie picked up her paper cup and rose from her chair, giving Gabriel Raines the signal it was time for him to leave. Instead of moving, he just sat there quietly sipping his coffee.

"I'm sorry, but I have to get back to work," she said, hoping he would take the hint.

"So do I...eventually."

"Thank you for your time. I appreciate your coming down here." She fidgeted, anxious now to be away from him. There was something about all that masculinity wrapped in such an attractive package that was putting her on edge.

Gabe slowly rose from his chair. "Where does Enrique live?"

"Somewhere in the Central Oak Cliff district."

"That's a pretty rough neighborhood. When are you planning to go?"

"Tonight. After I get off work."

"Why don't I go with you?"

She eyed him warily. "Why would you want to do that?"

"Because I was in trouble a couple of times myself when I was a kid. If it hadn't been for my older brother, I don't know where I would have wound up. If your friend is innocent, as you believe, and there's a way I can help him, then I'd like to do it."

Mattie shook her head. "I appreciate your offer, but I can take care of this myself."

A slow smile curved his lips, which looked soft at

the same time they looked incredibly male. "I'm sure you can," he said, "but sometimes caution is the better part of valor. If Angel didn't set the fire, maybe Enrique did. If that's the case and you approach him, he might get violent."

Gabe was right. She didn't really know Enrique Flores. And parts of the central Oak Cliff district were extremely rough. Rosa Ramirez lived at the edge of the district, on a slightly quieter street than some of the others.

"The person you need to be thinking of is Angel," Gabe pressed. "The sooner you speak to Enrique, the sooner you get the proof you need that Angel is innocent."

She bit her lip. She was extremely self-reliant. She'd had to be after her father died. On the other hand, it certainly wouldn't hurt to have someone go with her. Particularly if that someone looked as capable at handling himself as Gabriel Raines.

"All right. I've got a couple of things to finish before I leave the office. I'll pick you up at seven."

"What kind of car do you drive?" he asked.

"BMW convertible."

"Nice. Unless you want the wheels stripped off, we'd better take my truck. I'll pick you up at your place at seven. What's the address?"

No way was she giving her address to a man she had barely met. "I'll meet you here at seven. I'll wait for you in front of the building."

"Smart lady. All right, I'll be here then."

Mattie watched him walk away and some of the tension she hadn't realized she was feeling left her shoulders. She hurried to catch the elevator. Twenty minutes on Google and she would know a lot more about Gabriel Raines. Then she would finish her work, go home and change into a pair of jeans and get back here to meet him.

As she walked out of the elevator onto the fifteenth floor, she quickened her pace. She had to hurry. She had a lot to do before seven o'clock.

GABE SPOTTED MATTIE standing on the corner at exactly seven o'clock. He liked that about her, that she didn't seem inclined to play female games. He pulled his pickup into the yellow loading zone in front of the building and reached down to turn off the engine, thinking to go around and help her inside, but Mattie had the door open before he had the chance.

In jeans and a T-shirt, she climbed into the truck and slammed the heavy door. An independent woman, just as he'd guessed.

"Right on time," he said, thinking she looked just as good in jeans as she did in her tailored suit, maybe better. Still, her hair was pulled back in the severe style she had worn before, delivering a very clear message.

I'm not interested in anything other than business.

"When you work for someone else, like I do," she said, "being timely is a necessary habit."

He pulled away from the curb and turned the corner, starting off toward the area where Enrique lived. "You know the kid's address, right?"

"I called the center and they gave me his address. Mrs. Flores came in a couple of times. She was worried about her son."

"Why was that?"

"According to the file, some kid at school was giving him a hard time. She never came back so I guess the problem was resolved."

"What's the best way to get there?"

She gave him the address and the cross street and suggested he head out the 35 freeway. They wove their way down one street after another until they reached the apartment building where Enrique Flores lived. It was old and run-down, some of the windows open, the curtains billowing out in the warm evening breeze.

Gabe parked the truck then went around to the passenger side; but as before, Mattie didn't wait, just opened the door and jumped down. He felt the tug of a smile. He'd always preferred a woman who at least in some way needed a man. This one certainly didn't seem to. On the other hand, even her conservative clothes and severe hairstyle couldn't hide her femininity.

"Apartment twenty-two," she said. "Must be on the second floor."

"Let's go."

She ignored the hand he offered and hurried to keep up with his longer strides. They climbed the iron stairs and Gabe stepped back while Mattie knocked on the door. From the start, she had made it clear she was in control of the situation. He was only there in case of trouble.

The door swung open and a small, thin Hispanic woman stood in the opening.

"Mrs. Flores?"

"*Sí.*"

"I'm Mattie Baker. I'm a volunteer at the Family Recovery Center. This is Gabriel Raines. We'd like to talk to Enrique. Is he home?"

The slight woman eyed Gabe, who was trying to appear as nonthreatening as possible. It must have worked because she stepped back so they could come in. The apartment was cramped, the furniture old and worn, the couch covered by faded fringed throw covers, but the place was tidy and clean.

The woman turned, called down the hall. "Enrique! You have visitors."

Gabe immediately recognized the boy walking toward him as the slender youth he'd seen with Angel. Enrique looked at Gabe with suspicion but didn't seem to recognize him. Mrs. Flores cast them a final glance and disappeared into the kitchen, and Enrique turned his attention to Mattie.

"Hello, Enrique," she said with a smile. "I'm Angel's friend Mattie Baker. I work at the FRC."

"Angel told me about you. He said you helped him and his family."

"That's right. And this is Mr. Raines. You might remember seeing him at the fire last night."

The boy's dark-skinned face lost half its color. "I wasn't… I wasn't downtown last night."

"You were there with Angel, Enrique. Mr. Raines saw the two of you at the Towers watching the fire."

Enrique subtly squared his shoulders and his chin inched up. "I said I was not there."

"Did you know Angel was arrested for setting the fire?" Mattie asked.

The kid's obsidian eyes widened.

"That's right," Gabe said. "He was pulled over because one of his taillights was out. Angel has a record for setting another fire a few years back. The police put two and two together and Angel was picked up and taken in for questioning."

The kid's expression turned fearful. "Angel didn't set the fire. We saw the smoke from a few blocks away. We walked over to see what was happening. That is all we did. We watched the firemen for a while and then we went home."

"It was a school night," Mattie said. "What were the two of you doing downtown?"

Enrique glanced toward the kitchen. "We were just out driving around."

"That's probably true," Gabe said. "The two of you were downtown driving around. But what else were you doing? Why did you go down there in the first place?"

Enrique's gaze darted around the living room as if he searched for a way to escape.

"If you don't tell us the truth," Mattie said gently, "Angel may go back to detention. You're supposed to be his friend. Do you want that to happen?"

The boy shook his head, moving the long black pony-tail at the back of his neck. "No, no, I do not want that."

"Then tell us the truth," Gabe said.

The boy stared down at the holes in his dirty white sneakers. "Tagging. I was tagging a wall. Angel drove me down to finish what I'd started a few weeks ago."

The words and the look on the kid's thin face rang with truth. Angel hadn't wanted to betray his friend, and spray painting the side of a building was illegal.

"Where were you tagging?" Gabe asked.

"A couple of blocks from the Towers. That's how we saw the fire."

Mattie reached over and laid a hand on the boy's narrow shoulders, which were slumped with resignation. He looked up at her touch. "Are you taking me to jail?"

Mattie squeezed his shoulder. "No, Enrique. It was

brave of you to tell the truth. I'll talk to Captain Daily, see what he can do. But they'll probably want to talk to you."

He nodded dully.

"You did the right thing, son," Gabe said.

They left the run-down apartment building, climbed into the truck and drove back downtown.

Gabe flicked a glance at Mattie. "I think this will help your case. I'm not sure it'll be enough."

"I know."

"I want to talk to Angel," Gabe said. "I want to hear what he has to say."

"Sidney Weiss is acting as his attorney. He's arranging bail. You can talk to Angel after he's released—if Weiss says it's okay."

"I think Enrique was telling the truth. But being downtown vandalizing property isn't exactly a terrific alibi. I thought you said Angel was turning over a new leaf."

As the pickup wove through traffic, Mattie sighed. "He's been doing so well. I don't understand it."

"You said he likes to help his friends. Maybe Enrique pressed him and he caved."

"I don't know. Angel is the kind of kid who thinks for himself. He isn't easily influenced by his peers."

Gabe let the subject drop. He was involved in this case to the tune of several thousand dollars, the deductible on his insurance policy. He wanted whoever set the fire to pay for what he'd done. But he wanted to be sure the right person was paying.

"It's early yet. Why don't we stop somewhere and have dinner? You like steak?"

"I'm a vegetarian, mostly. Besides, I've already eaten. Thanks anyway."

A vegetarian. Just his luck. And he didn't believe she'd had supper. She wasn't a very good liar—a point in her favor. She just didn't want to have supper with *him*.

"Maybe some other time," he offered.

Mattie made no reply, which kind of unsettled him. He couldn't remember the last time a woman he was interested in hadn't returned that interest.

They drove in silence the rest of the way downtown.

"Where do you want me to drop you off?"

She cast him a glance. "I live in the Elm Street Lofts. You can drop me off in front."

He grinned. "Why'd you suddenly decide you could trust me?"

"I looked you up on Google. You've been in Dallas for nearly ten years. You're quite a respected figure in the community. Your company is currently working on a number of restoration projects and you've even won awards for contributing to the beautification of the area." She looked up at him and smiled, the first relaxed smile he'd seen. "Besides, you were raised in Wyoming."

He laughed at that. "A good ol' country boy, you figure?"

"Something like that."

"If you'd known me back then, you wouldn't be trusting me to take you home."

She arched an auburn eyebrow. "Why not?"

"I would have driven you to the nearest motel and tried to convince you to let me get a room."

She colored faintly beneath the scattering of freckles on the high bones in her cheeks. "I assume those days are past."

He allowed his gaze to roam over her, taking in the small waist and nicely curved breasts. At the moment, the idea held an amazing appeal. "Mostly," he said.

The soft flush deepened. "This is it," she said abruptly, and he wheeled the truck over to the curb. Mattie opened the door and climbed down to the sidewalk. "Thanks for your help."

"I still want to talk to Angel."

"I haven't forgotten. I'll arrange a meeting once he's released, assuming his attorney approves."

Gabe nodded. He watched her walk away, liking the fit of her jeans over her nicely rounded ass. He found himself hoping he would see her again, even if she was a vegetarian. He had her phone number in the "recent calls" section of his cell phone, he reminded himself. He could phone her anytime he wanted.

He wondered if he'd ever make the call.

CHAPTER FOUR

Too wide awake for sleep, Mattie settled back in the deep, cone-shaped chair in the living room of her loft apartment. Another chair just like it sat at the opposite end of a modern ivory sofa piped in black.

The place was open and airy, with big industrial windows, exposed brick walls and polished concrete floors. There were concrete countertops in the kitchen and baths, while the bedrooms had ebony hardwood floors. Black-framed architectural sketches of European cathedrals decorated the walls.

The simplicity of the apartment suited her. She didn't spend much time at home. Mostly she was working or down at the center. But the two bedrooms and two bathrooms provided just enough room and the modern décor went with her streamlined lifestyle.

She wondered what Gabriel Raines would think of the place, and thought that he would probably disapprove. He'd expect a more feminine décor, maybe some ruffles and frills and a bunch of sentimental clutter. She was nothing like that and never would be.

She heard a familiar meow and turned to see her big orange-striped tomcat, Tigger, padding toward her.

"Hi, baby. Mama's home." As she reached down to stroke his fur, Tigger pushed his head into her palm and began to purr. "All right, I hear you." She rose from the chair. "Come on, let's get you some food." Tigger wound himself between her legs as she walked toward the kitchen to retrieve a pouch of food and refill his bowl of crunchies.

She was a pushover for animals, especially cats, which Gabe would also probably disapprove of. If he had an animal, it would have to be a Rottweiler or a mastiff or something. She almost smiled.

Gabe said he lived just a few blocks away. Now that she'd seen him tonight in a pair of cowboy boots and knew he came from Wyoming, she could imagine him living in a place that sported Frederick Remington sculptures and Western paintings on the walls.

She tried not to think how good he had looked, the black jeans and T-shirt he'd worn, stretching over a powerful set of shoulders and muscular chest, and biceps bulging with muscle. In an article online, she recalled reading that he was a former marine. Clearly he stayed in condition.

She thought of those narrow hips and long legs and a little curl of heat tugged low in her belly. She told herself she liked more sophisticated men, the *GQ* type, guys interested in art and literature, men who enjoyed going to plays and dining in fine restaurants. Gabriel Raines was a man's man, the macho kind she made it a point to stay away from.

Not that she'd had many dates in the past few years.

She was too busy for a relationship. She needed to focus her attention on her job, and what little time was left went to her work at the center.

And somehow with men, the past always seemed to intrude. The two years she'd spent with Mark Holloway had ended in disaster and the memory still haunted her.

They were supposed to get married, or at least that's what she'd thought. She had foolishly believed Mark loved her, but as soon as she found out she was pregnant, Mark disappeared from her life.

Just as her mother had warned, she couldn't count on a man, even one who said he loved her.

Then things went from bad to worse and she miscarried the baby, a tiny part of herself she had already come to love. Her job was all she had to keep her going, the only thing that kept her from total despair.

That and her volunteer work at the center. Aside from manning the hotline, her job was mostly to offer support, to talk to people from needy families who came to the center for help, to listen to their troubles and try to provide resources and help them find solutions. Other people had such terrible problems that even the loss of her unborn child seemed small in comparison.

She was young, she told herself. She could have another baby. But she had never truly recovered from Mark's betrayal and she had never met another man who had interested her enough to put aside her distrust and begin a relationship.

Still, she was a woman, and for the first time in a very long while, Gabriel Raines had made her feel like one. She thought of the way he had looked at her at the end of the evening, his eyes hot and blatantly approving, his lips curving into a slow, sensuous smile. He'd looked like a hungry cat who wanted to eat her alive. He might not be her type, but her body felt the pull of his masculinity even if her mind did not.

Mattie's brain warned her in no uncertain terms to stay away from Gabriel Raines.

AFTER A WORKING WEEKEND, Gabe spent a good part of
Monday tromping through the wreckage that had once
been the nearly completed lobby of the Dallas Towers.
Wearing a pair of high rubber boots, he kicked through
the water-soaked wallboard, burned wood and broken
glass and shoved aside the melted light fixtures that had
fallen from the impressive three-story ceiling.

"Ugly, isn't it?" Sam McBride walked toward him
in his own rubber boots.

"Damned shame, is what it is."

"Heard they charged the kid who set the fire, the one
we saw there that night."

"Kid's only seventeen. And there's a chance he didn't
do it."

"Yeah?"

"Maybe. He was downtown with a buddy that night,
spray painting walls. Claims he saw the fire and went
to check it out."

"Tagging? I hate those little bastards. My dad would
have beat my butt for doing something like that."

Gabe chuckled. Since his own dad had flown the
coop when he was just a kid, he made no further comment, though he didn't like vandals, either.

"I'm supposed to talk to the kid this afternoon." And
since Mattie Baker had set up the meeting and said she
would be there, he was more eager to go than he might
have been.

"Be interesting to see what the kid has to say," Sam
said.

"He's got friends who don't believe he did it. They
say he's a real good boy. For his sake, I hope they're
right."

"What time's the meeting?"

"Two o'clock. A place called the Family Recovery Center."

Sam checked his watch. "That's forty-five minutes from now."

"The address is nearby. Shouldn't take long to get there. Let's finish this inventory, try to see how much equipment we lost."

Sam nodded and settled his hard hat back over his short blond hair and Gabe put his own hard hat back on. They stomped through more water-soaked debris, the fire suppression damage as brutal as the flames themselves.

Half an hour later, Gabe headed for the FRC. When he walked inside, Mattie Baker stood in the waiting room, a big open area lined with brown vinyl chairs and a couple of wooden tables covered with dog-eared magazines.

She was as pretty as he remembered. He felt a sudden urge to unpin all that fiery hair and spread it across his pillow, to strip off her plain gray suit and run his hands over that luscious little body, learn every supple curve.

His groin tightened.

Silently he cursed.

Mattie walked up to him and smiled. "Hello, Gabe."

"Mattie."

"Angel's waiting. Now that Enrique's come forward, he's anxious to talk to you. He wants to tell you himself he didn't do it."

"That sounds good."

Mattie led him down a hall decorated with amateur photos of the city, some of them pretty good.

Gabe enjoyed photography himself, especially when he was out at the ranch in the Hill Country near Kerrville he had purchased a few years back. It was only three hundred acres, but he kept a couple of horses there, and it got him away from the city. One of his other loves was flying, and in his twin Aerostar, it was a fairly short trip. Someday he hoped to live at the ranch full-time, maybe raise some quarter horses. Deep down, he guessed the West would always be in his blood.

He followed Mattie into the conference room and saw Angel seated at a long table next to a gray-haired man in a navy three-piece suit.

"Gabe, this is Sidney Weiss," Mattie said. "Sid, meet Gabriel Raines." The men shook hands. "And this is Angel."

The boy met Gabe's assessing gaze squarely. "I didn't do it, Mr. Raines."

Gabe took a seat across from him. "Maybe you didn't. Your friend, Enrique, said the two of you were downtown tagging walls. Vandalizing other people's property isn't arson but it's still against the law."

The kid never looked away. He had a square face and somewhat blunt features, but he wasn't a bad-looking boy. "We weren't vandalizing. We were beautifying."

Gabe had to smile. "That's what you call it?"

"In this case, I do. I was hoping…maybe you would be willing to take a walk with me and Mattie. I could show you what we were doing that night."

It seemed a fair enough request. And he didn't mind spending more time with Mattie. Watching her with the boy, seeing her concern, made him even more curious about her. On one hand, she seemed purposely remote. On the other, extremely approachable.

"It's just off Commerce, so it isn't that far away," Angel continued.

Gabe flicked a glance at the boy's attorney. "I presume this is all right with you, Mr. Weiss."

"I trust Mattie to look out for Angel's interest," Weiss said.

"Fine, then. I could use a walk, stretch my legs a little. Angel, why don't you lead the way?"

The boy shoved back his chair and they followed him single file down the hall. The waiting room had a couple of people sitting in chairs as they passed, a black teenager with round flat earrings in his ears and an older Hispanic woman.

"We have counselors on hand at certain times of the day," Mattie explained. "We're still a small organization. But we have ten professional, full-time staff members, plus about twenty volunteers. Mostly we deal with families trying to get their lives together after dealing with violence and abuse."

The three of them headed down Commerce and turned onto a smaller street a few blocks later. There was a vacant lot on the north side. Next to it sat an empty three-story concrete building. Angel led them into the lot then stopped halfway across. The boy turned and pointed.

"I brought Enrique here so that he could finish his painting."

For the first time, Gabe noticed the huge mural on the wall. It was a painting of the neighborhood around the building, the scene populated with a variety of interesting and unusual people. Vibrant color leaped from the concrete canvas, snagging the viewer and pulling him inexorably into the scene. The vacant lot was there, but the dirt paths were gone. Instead there were walkways of brilliant red brick lined with pink, yellow, blue and purple flowers.

The painting itself was beautiful, the scene perfectly drawn, each line precise and in exactly the right proportions. But there was something else, something indefinable and strangely compelling that made the mural stunning.

For several long moments no one spoke.

"*Amazing* is too small a word," Gabe finally said. "This is incredible."

Angel smiled. "When we became friends, Enrique told me his dream was to become an artist. He showed me some tagging he had done on some walls in our neighborhood. I thought they were the most beautiful pictures I'd ever seen. I knew no one would see them there, no one who could make his dream come true. I saw the empty wall down here when I came to the center. I wanted to help him so I drove him down at night. He's been working on the mural for nearly two months."

"It's wonderful, Angel," Mattie said.

"We finished the mural that night. We saw the flames and went to see what was happening, but we didn't set the fire, I swear."

Gabe turned to Mattie, his mind still filled with the scope and colors of the painting, the kaleidoscopic effect and emotional pull of the work. "Did you know about this?"

Mattie stared at the painting as if she couldn't drag her gaze away. Finally, she looked at him and shook her head. "I had no idea." She turned to Angel. "Enrique has incredible talent."

"You were right, Angel," Gabe said. "This isn't vandalizing. It's beautifying. Maybe this will give your friend the break he needs." Gabe thought maybe he could do something to help. The city had been looking for some open space to purchase. They needed more parks, more green space, and this lot, done the way Angel's friend had painted it, would be perfect.

"I didn't set the fire," Angel repeated. "I just wanted to help Enrique."

Gabe rested a hand on the boy's stout shoulder. "I believe you, son. Mattie and I will talk to the police, see if there's something we can do to convince them and get them back on the track of finding the real arsonist."

Angel's relieved smile was so full of gratitude that Gabe felt a tightening in his chest.

"Thank you, sir."

Gabe just nodded. When he looked over at Mattie, he caught the glint of tears. *More of a woman than she wanted to admit,* he thought. *Interesting.*

They walked back to the center and Angel went inside to speak to his attorney, leaving Gabe and Mattie on the sidewalk out in front.

"I've got to get back to work," Mattie said.

"Where's your car?" Gabe asked.

"In the lot behind the building."

"So's mine." He started walking beside her, both of them heading toward the lot. "I don't suppose you'd be interested in having dinner tonight? We could talk about the boys. I've got a couple of ideas that might help Enrique. He's an amazingly talented kid."

He could tell she wanted to say no. But Angel meant a lot to her and now it seemed she was concerned about Enrique.

"We'll go anywhere you want," he said, his stomach

quietly rebelling at the thought of a plateful of vegetables for supper.

"All right. I've got to work late, but I could meet you at the Taj about eight."

"The Taj?"

"Indian food. I think you'll find something on the menu you'll enjoy."

He wasn't much on ethnic food. He was more a meat and potatoes kind of guy. "Where is it?"

She gave him the address and he agreed to meet her, not quite certain himself it was a good idea. The lady was a vegetarian, a little too independent to suit him, and probably a raging liberal. Still, politics and palates aside, Mattie attracted him as no lady had in a very long time.

It might prove an interesting evening.

CHAPTER FIVE

MATTIE KICKED HERSELF all the way back to her office.
What in the world was wrong with her? The last person she wanted to spend time with was Gabriel Raines.

As the elevator took her to her floor, she paused.
Why was she so determined to avoid him? Gabe was
obviously intelligent and from what she had read, a successful businessman. He had built his company from
the ground up and become an upstanding member of
the downtown community.

The truth was, she was more than a little attracted
to Gabe Raines and that scared her to death. She hadn't
had sex in more than a year and Gabe was a man whose
every glance made it clear sex was extremely important to him. Though she admired his powerful body,
macho men just weren't her type. At least they never
had been before.

She stepped out of the elevator thinking of Gabe
and her reaction to him, thinking of Angel and grateful
that Gabe had agreed to help him. Now he was trying
to help Enrique. As she passed the reception desk, her
mind was on the dinner she had agreed to share with
him and she jostled into someone. It was Mel Freeman,
one of her coworkers.

"Sorry," she said.

"That's all right, Mattie. I never mind bumping a little female flesh."

Mattie bristled. Mel was a true male chauvinist pig. Six feet tall and fairly good looking, he believed he was God's gift to women, though at forty, his light brown hair had begun to recede and a slight paunch jiggled at his waistline.

Mattie had gone head-to-head with Mel a number of times over the years, starting with the first time he'd asked her out. She had politely refused, telling him she believed in keeping her personal life separate from her work. *Not* telling him she simply wasn't attracted to him. Mel had persisted to the point where she had been forced to be rude. Every once in a while, he still gave it the old college try.

And there was her recent promotion. Mel had been with the company longer than she had. He believed he was the one who deserved the job as head designer and an office with a window.

"Excuse me, Mel. I've got work to do."

"Well, pardon me for getting in your way," he said sarcastically, his smile as phony as the flashy diamond stick pin he wore to company parties.

Mel was the type of guy women sued for sexual harassment, but Mattie believed that if a woman wanted to be equal to a man, she had to stand up for herself, force them to treat her as an equal.

It didn't always work, of course, and there were extreme cases, but aside from being a jerk, Mel seemed harmless enough.

Mattie walked past him into her office and firmly closed the door. She needed to get to back to the art gallery project; she didn't want to fall behind. She loved her job and even obnoxious Mel Freeman wasn't going to spoil it for her.

She had only been working half an hour when a light knock sounded and the door swung open. Aaron Kreski, one of her dearest friends, rolled his wheelchair into her office.

"I hate to interrupt, but I've got a question on the Franklin elementary school project." Aaron was slender, black-haired and wore square, dark-rimmed glasses. At thirty, he was an attractive man in a nerdy sort of way, one of twelve detail draftsmen who worked in the office, the best of them as far as Mattie was concerned. He'd been wheelchair-bound since a car accident in his teens left him paralyzed from the waist down.

Mattie got up from her chair and walked over to where he sat, a rolled-up set of drawings in his lap. He handed her the plans, explained a problem with a covered walkway, and she rolled the drawings open to see exactly what he was talking about.

"You're right. The walkway is a problem. I'll give it some thought and get back to you as soon as I can."

"Great. We still on for dinner Friday night?"

Mattie frowned. "Oh no, I forgot all about it. I planned to work late. I'm getting kind of behind. Could we do it next week?"

Aaron looked disappointed, but he just nodded. "Sure, no big deal."

The door swung open just then. "Aaron, there you are." Emily Bliss, a petite, dark-haired and attractive draftswoman, cast Mattie a guilty glance. "Sorry, Mattie. I just had a quick question for Aaron."

"It's okay. We're finished."

"Talk to ya later," Aaron said.

"I'll have an answer to your problem before the end of the day," Mattie promised.

Aaron rolled out the door and no one offered to help him. Everyone knew Aaron Kreski preferred to take care of himself.

Emily hovered over him, though, her short brown bob swinging forward as she leaned down to ask him a question she probably could have answered herself. Mattie had a strong suspicion Emily had a crush on Aaron, though he didn't seem to notice.

That was too bad. Emily was a great girl and Aaron was a terrific guy. Mattie smiled as she returned to her desk. Her own love life might be the pits but deep down she was still a romantic.

Which made her think of Gabe Raines and inwardly she sighed.

GABE ARRIVED AT the Taj Restaurant a few minutes early, figuring Mattie would probably be right on time. The place was kind of dark, draped with heavy gold velvet curtains and ornate brass latticework along the walls. The maître d' led him to a table in the center of the room and he wondered if Mattie had asked the man to seat them there so they would be surrounded by people.

Gabe just shook his head and pointed to a table in the corner. If he still got the I'm-not-interested vibes again tonight he'd back off and leave her alone. But he could have sworn he'd caught her looking him over a couple of times when she thought he wouldn't see.

He stood as she walked into the restaurant wearing the same drab gray suit she'd had on earlier in the day. Apparently, she'd come straight from work. As she passed the maître d', Gabe saw the subtle shake of the man's dark head and almost smiled.

He pulled out her chair and Mattie took a seat. "Right on time," he said. "But then I figured you would be."

She gave him a single assessing glance as he returned to his chair, made a point of picking up her linen napkin, carefully opening it and draping it across her lap.

"I had some design work to finish before I could leave but it went along without a hitch."

"That's always good."

"I doesn't happen that often."

"Believe me, I know what you mean."

She continued to smooth her napkin. "I hope you're hungry. This place has terrific food."

He scoffed. "If you like eggplant," he grumbled. He was what he was. If she couldn't accept that, there was no use going any further.

Mattie looked up at him and smiled. "I guess you haven't looked at the menu."

"Not yet."

She picked one up and handed it over. "You might like the rack of lamb. It's a specialty of the house."

His eyebrows went up. "Rack of lamb?"

"The curried beef is also very good." Her smile remained in place. "Unless you're opposed to curry."

"I like spicy food. I love Mexican, the hotter the better. I'm pretty much game for anything as long as it has meat."

She laughed at that. He remembered hearing it once before, a kind of throaty, sexy sound that made the blood in his veins head south. Why did he keep seeing her as some sort of sex kitten when the way she dressed, the way she wore her hair, said sex was the lowest item on her list of priorities.

The waiter arrived, a thin, dark-skinned man with a hooked nose and a heavy Indian accent. "Would you care for something to drink?"

"Yes, thank you." Mattie ordered a glass of white wine and Gabe ordered an Indian beer.

"When in Rome and all that," he said.

Mattie smiled, seeming a little more relaxed than she had been when she arrived. "I heard you went to the police department this afternoon."

"How'd you know?"

"Captain Daily called Sid Weiss."

"After talking to Angel and actually seeing his alibi, I'm fairly convinced he didn't do it. If that's the case, I want Daily to find out who did."

"What did the captain say?"

"He said he'd take another look, see if he could find something more than circumstantial evidence, something that might clear Angel's name. Maybe something that'll give them a lead on somebody else."

"Thank you."

"I also spoke to a friend of mine with the Downtown Redevelopment Committee. I asked him to take a look at the mural Enrique painted. I mentioned that the lot next to the painting might be the perfect place to put a park."

Mattie straightened, excitement glinting in her light blue eyes. "Do you really think they might be interested?"

"I think they might. At any rate, it's worth a try."

"Yes, it certainly is. Enrique… The boy has a marvelous talent."

"Yes, he does."

The waiter came and took their orders. Gabe had the lamb and Mattie had curried vegetables and rice.

"So you don't eat meat," he said when the food arrived. "Why is that? Some sort of personal statement or something?"

"Actually, I eat chicken and fish, eggs and cheese. Red meat just doesn't hold much appeal for me."

He cut into his lamb and took a bite. It was delicious. "This is great."

Her lips quirked. "I told you."

He bit into a pita-like bread the waiter called naan and it was great, too. "What else don't you do?"

Her gaze shot to his and soft color washed into her cheeks. She was thinking of sex—he would swear it.

"I don't date much. I'm too busy working."

"No boyfriend? No one you're involved with?"

"No." She didn't ask about his love life, but she did glance down at his ring finger.

"Never been married," he said. "No illegitimate kids that I know of. No girlfriend. Not that you've given me any indication you might be interested."

The color beneath those charming freckles pinkened even more. "That's because I'm not. I'm too busy with my career to have time for a relationship."

"In my book, supper or an occasional movie don't constitute a relationship. In most cases, not even a sleepover counts for that."

She shoved some white rice around on her plate. "I suppose you're right."

"How's your dinner?" he asked, letting her off the hook for the moment.

She looked up at him and smiled. "It's great. I really like to eat here."

"Everything's fantastic." He speared another piece of meat. "So where should we go next time?"

Her eyes widened. She looked like a deer caught in the headlights.

"Just for supper," he said, "not the sleepover. That can wait."

She swallowed, started shaking her head. "I don't think it's a good idea."

"Why not?"

She stared at him, then set her fork down next to her plate. "You want the truth? It's obvious you want to have sex. Sex has never appealed to me that much. I mean, it's okay, but I can take it or leave it. Mostly, I'd rather just leave it. For you, my guess is, sex is like breathing."

He chuckled, appreciating her honesty. Unfortunately, it only stirred his interest. "I won't deny I enjoy it." He wiped his mouth with his napkin, his eyes still on her face. "They must have been real losers."

"Who?"

"The guys you've had sex with."

Mattie straightened, her chin going up. "If it's any of your business, which it isn't, there was nothing wrong with them. It's me, that's all. I'm not a very sexual woman. I'm more interested in my career."

"Seems to me like one isn't mutually exclusive of the other."

Mattie made no reply. It was time to drop the subject before she fell out of the seat she perched on so precariously.

"I have a feeling there's more going on here than

what you're telling me, but as you said, it's really none of my business."

She took a sip of her wine, her hand a little unsteady. She kept her eyes on her plate, yet he could feel something hot and intense in the air between them. He didn't believe she wasn't a sexual woman. Only that she hadn't met a man who could make her feel that way.

"Why don't we talk about Enrique and how we're going to get him noticed by the right people?"

Relief swept through her at the change of subject and he watched her shoulders relax. "You think we could do something like that?"

"I'm involved in a theater project in Deep Ellum. I've gotten to know a lot of people in the arts community. I think I can get a few of them down to the lot, get them to take a look at Enrique's work."

"That would be really terrific. If they like it, I can talk to him, see if he's done anything smaller, some pieces we could show them."

"That's a good idea." They talked amiably through the rest of the meal and he didn't push for more.

Normally, he would drop his pursuit, but there was something about Mattie Baker that had captured his fancy. He was convinced she was more than just drab suits, no-nonsense hair and an aversion to sex.

Gabe was determined to find out what it was.

CHAPTER SIX

MATTIE LET GABE walk her to her car. He hadn't pressed her for another date and she was torn between relief and an odd sense of regret.

She had told him the truth. She simply wasn't a very sexual person. For her, sex had always been more to please her partner than herself. Mark had been a very gentle lover, allowing her to take charge, preferring to let her lead the way. He liked her on top most of the time, liked her to satisfy him. She'd loved him and she wanted to make him happy, but she got little out of the experience herself.

The few times she'd had casual sex had been equally disappointing. She simply wasn't cut out to be a passionate lover. Sex with Gabe would probably be equally disappointing—for him as well as for her.

She said nothing as they walked across the parking lot, nothing as he waited for her to use her electronic key to unlock her car. At the sound of the mechanism releasing, he reached down and pulled open the door.

"Good night, Mattie."

"Good night, Gabe. Thanks for supper and for trying to help Angel and Enrique."

"Supper was my pleasure and we'll see what happens with the boys."

She started to get into the car, but Gabe lightly caught

her shoulders, turning her to face him. Lowering his head, he very softly kissed her.

Mattie had no notion what to expect from such a casual kiss but one thing she didn't expect was the bottom dropping out of her stomach. The softest male lips she had ever encountered settled lightly over hers. They melded, blended, captured. Gabe coaxed and tasted, the kiss completely undemanding, and yet her insides trembled.

She wanted to slide her arms around his neck and lean into him, to part her lips and let those soft male lips ravish her. She wanted him to taste her all over, wanted the kiss to go on and on.

She whimpered when Gabe pulled away.

"Good night, Mattie," he said gruffly, his intense blue eyes holding her a moment more before he turned and started walking away.

Mattie dropped down in the seat of her car. Her hands were shaking so badly she could barely shove the key into the ignition. She didn't enjoy sex. She merely tolerated it. At least that's what she'd always told herself.

She saw Gabe sitting in his pickup, waiting for her to start the car and pull out onto the street. He wasn't the kind of man who left a woman alone in a parking lot at night.

She took a deep breath and managed to compose herself enough to start the engine. Shifting the BMW into gear, she slowly pulled out of the driveway. Gabe followed her to the entrance to her underground parking lot, then headed off down the street.

Recalling the heat she had felt in that simple goodnight kiss and the fierce way she had responded, Mattie closed her eyes, amazingly grateful she had said no to Gabe's dinner invitation.

And terrified she would weaken and call him, tell him she had changed her mind.

HE SHOULDN'T HAVE kissed her. He should have respected her dismissal and let it go at that. Instead, he couldn't resist just a little taste of her.

A little taste, Gabe discovered, wasn't nearly enough.

He sighed as he parked his truck in his designated parking spot in the lot next to his condo and turned off the engine. He could still feel the shape of her mouth under his, recall the scent of spring flowers that clung to her skin. That single little kiss had fired his blood, stirred a hunger he hadn't known in years. It had taken sheer force of will not to drag her into his arms and kiss her until neither of them could think.

He smiled. He could only imagine her outrage. Or maybe she would have clung to him the way she had when he ended the kiss. There'd been fire in her response, not indifference. No matter how hard she denied it, something was there between them, simmering like a pot on the stove, ready to boil over.

As he walked into his condo, Gabe released a breath. He had to know if he was right and Mattie's passion was simply buried. He had to know if the wild attraction he felt for her was returned, as he believed.

Shrugging out of his sport coat and tossing it over a chair, he poured himself a shot of single malt scotch, hoping it would relax him, take the edge of his unsatisfied lust.

He carried the glass over to the comfortable brown leather sofa in front of the stone fireplace and sank down, propping his boots up on the big oak coffee table. The condo was furnished in masculine colors: browns, dark greens and golds. Heavy oak furniture and over-stuffed chairs, a throw rug in those same autumn colors covered the carpet beneath the antique oak coffee table.

There was a modern kitchen with marble counter-tops, twin guest rooms, each with its own bath, and a master bedroom with a big king-size bed. The place had everything he needed. But it was the sprawling Spanish-style ranch house in the Texas hills that felt like home.

Gabe took a sip of his scotch, leaned against the back of the sofa, thought of the kiss he had shared with Mattie Baker and tried not to imagine having her in his bed.

AFTER A RESTLESS NIGHT and waking up with a throbbing headache, Mattie rolled wearily out of bed. Facing a long day at the office and needing to clear her head, she dressed in a pair of navy blue jogging shorts and a blue-and-white tank top. She liked to run early in the mornings, and after her sleepless night, she was desperate for some exercise. Pulling her hair back in a ponytail, she slipped her feet into a pair of running shoes and took off down the stairs.

The sun was up, the morning pleasant as fall moved closer. The breeze felt good on her face as she started along the sidewalk, easing into a steady rhythm. She told herself not to think of the cause of her sleepless night, not to think of Gabriel Raines and her unwanted attraction, tried not to remember his sensual kiss.

Eventually, the warmth of the morning sun began to seep through her and she started to relax. Picking up her pace, she padded along the sidewalk then stumbled at the sound of a deep male voice coming up beside her.

"I didn't know you were a runner," Gabe said, slowing his pace a little to match her shorter strides.

She took a deep breath and flicked him a sideways glance. "I'm not surprised to see that you are, since you obviously stay in shape. I *am* surprised to see you *here.*"

"Coincidence," he said, and she cast him a look that made it clear she didn't believe him.

"Well, sort of. I had you on my mind this morning and I kind of just found myself running in this direction. I didn't think I'd see you, though."

She shrugged. "I like to run. I spend a lot of time indoors. Running gets my blood flowing."

"Mine, too," he said a little gruffly, and she flicked him a sideways glance. Gabe always seemed to be thinking of sex and now that she had met him, she couldn't seem to stop thinking about it, either.

They ran together for a while, the silence stretching out, growing more comfortable than she would have imagined as they jogged along at a steady pace. When her legs began to tire, she started to slow and Gabe slowed, as well. Perspiration made his T-shirt cling to the heavy muscles across his chest and shoulders, and a little shiver of awareness went through her.

She bent over and propped her hands on her knees, fighting to catch her breath. "I've got to get back," she said. "I've got to get to work."

"Yeah, me, too."

Mattie had a feeling he could run twice this far and not be out of breath, but he had a job to do, just as she did.

"Haven't changed your mind about supper, have you?" he asked.

She shook her head and hoped the truth didn't show in her face. She wanted to go out with him. She wanted more of his sexy kisses, wanted to know if they could make her feel the way she had last night.

"Can I ask you a question?"

She eyed him warily. "I guess."

"Are you afraid of all men, or is it just me?"

Mattie straightened. "I'm not afraid of you."

"Oh, yeah? Well, then maybe you're just afraid of yourself."

She started to argue, then wondered if maybe he was right. Because she really wanted to go to dinner with him and she couldn't understand what was holding her back.

"Invitation's still open," he said. "If you say yes, I won't press you to do anything you don't want to do."

Mattie bit back a reply and Gabe shrugged, accepting her unspoken refusal but clearly not happy about it.

"See you around," he said.

Mattie watched him jog away, his body moving with surprising grace for a man of his size and build. For an instant, she fought the urge to call him back.

But she was who she was and that wasn't going to change. Not even for Gabriel Raines.

GABE'S CELL PHONE rang as he got out of his pickup late that morning in front of the Greenwood Apartments, his project near the Farmer's Market.

He pulled the phone out of his pocket and flipped it open. "Raines."

"Gabe, this is Thomas Daily with the arson squad. I thought you'd want to know we dropped the charges against Angel Ramirez. A couple of cans of turpentine were found at the scene. One of my men talked to your foreman. He said they weren't the brand you usually use. In fact they were an oddball brand that isn't sold many places. We traced the cans to a local hardware store. The guy who bought them wasn't Hispanic."

"Have you made an arrest?"

"Unfortunately, the guy paid cash and his description fits about a hundred-thousand white guys. We hoped to get some kind of composite sketch, but the clerk said he wasn't paying that much attention. I'll let you know if we find him."

"Thanks." Gabe hung up, relieved that Angel hadn't set the fire. He knew how happy Mattie would be but resisted the urge to call and relay the news. It was crazy to keep pursuing a woman who didn't want to be pursued. He wasn't some kind of stalker. If she wasn't interested, she wasn't interested.

Oblivious to the pounding of hammers and the buzzing of saws, he walked over to where Sam stood talking to one of the drywallers.

"There's a problem with the job your guys did in apartment twenty-seven," Sam was saying. "You need to get someone in there to do it over."

"Must have been one of the new guys." Jim Pritchard, the drywall contractor, was a burly fellow with a fringe of hair around his bald head. "I'll get it done, Sam. Don't worry."

The tension in Sam's shoulders relaxed. "That's good enough for me, Jim."

Pritchard walked away and Gabe approached Sam. "Looks like we're making good progress," Gabe said.

"Not too many problems. At least no more than the usual bullshit stuff. By the way, Captain Daily called me. He wanted to know about some cans of turpentine the fire department found. I told him it wasn't the kind we use."

Gabe nodded. "He just called. I guess they ran down the guy who bought the stuff. Since it wasn't the Ramirez kid, they decided Angel wasn't the one who set the fire. Daily said they dropped the charges."

"That's good."

"Yeah, except whoever did it is still on the loose."

"Definitely not good. At least the kid's off the hook. You said he was only seventeen?"

Gabe nodded.

"Listen, you haven't been out much, lately. I know a place that's kind of interesting. Got some good-looking ladies who come in on Wednesday nights. How about we grab a couple of beers over there after work?"

He didn't really want to go. He couldn't get his mind off Mattie Baker. But that situation was going nowhere and he might as well face it.

"I've got a meeting with the guys on the redevelopment committee. I won't be finished until after nine. If that isn't too late—"

"That's fine. Place doesn't really get going until about then. Call me when you get out of the meeting and I'll pick you up."

"I'd rather meet you there." Then he'd have time to go home and change, and he could leave the place whenever he wanted. "Where is it?"

"The club is in the bottom floor of the old Hammerfield building. You remember. We bid the remodel job a couple of years back, then the sale fell through. The new owners hired someone else."

"Yeah, I remember. Glad they finally did something with the old place."

Sam slapped him on the shoulder. "So I'll see you there later," Sam said, and both of them headed back to work.

CHAPTER SEVEN

MATTIE STOPPED BY to see Angel and his mother after work. Sid Weiss had called with the news that Captain Daily had found evidence that cleared the boy of suspicion and the charges against him had been dropped.

Rosa and Angel were grateful for all Mattie's help, as well as Gabe's, and seemed thrilled that she and Gabe were hoping to find a way to help Enrique with his work.

Home at last, Mattie fed Tigger and checked his automatic watering bowl, took a nice long shower and began to dress for the evening she had planned. She only had one real vice, which was actually more of a vanity. *Her voice.* She was a very good singer, and when the mood struck, she could really belt out a tune.

In high school, her friends had tried to convince her to consider a career in music, but Mattie wasn't interested. And in truth, she probably wasn't good enough to make it all the way to the top. To her, singing was just for fun. She loved performing once in a while, but she didn't want to be an entertainer full time.

Still, as often as she could on Wednesday nights, she and her best friend, Tracy Spencer, went down to Club Rio to sing karaoke. It wasn't the same as singing with a band, but it felt just as good and it was just as much fun.

Mattie particularly liked disco, everything from the

Bee Gees' *Saturday Night Fever* album to just about any Donna Summer song. She liked Cher, Diana Ross, Tina Turner, pretty much anything hot and fast. It was a sinful addiction, like eating a big, gooey piece of chocolate.

As she stood in front of the mirror, fighting to fasten a dangly rhinestone earring, she heard a familiar rap on the door and hurried into the living room to let her friend in. Tracy was tall and svelte and gorgeous, her straight, blunt-cut blond hair falling around her shoulders, pale bangs covering her forehead.

She gave Mattie a quick hard hug. "See, I'm not even late."

"No, you're not!"

Tracy made a brief perusal of the very short, scoop-necked, sparkly silver dress Mattie wore, so completely at odds with her usual business wardrobe. "You look fantastic!"

She had left her auburn hair unbound and let it dry in natural curls that formed a halo around her face and fluffed out around her shoulders.

She grinned at Tracy, who wore a yellow leather miniskirt and matching halter top, both of them in very high spiked heels. "You look pretty great, yourself."

Tracy grinned back. "We're going to knock 'em dead tonight."

"I hope so. I'm definitely in the mood."

It was the one time Mattie allowed her inner self to surface. When she sang a hot disco song, she wasn't reserved, career-driven Mattie Baker. She was a sexy *femme fatale,* a woman so seductive she left a trail of broken hearts wherever she went.

Fortunately, no one but her closest friends knew her secret passion, only a couple of people at the office she trusted, certainly no one in her business circles. Club Rio was the kind of blue-collar place business people rarely frequented.

Which left her completely free to indulge her secret fantasy self.

"Just let me put in my other earring and grab my purse and we're out of here."

"I'll drive," Tracy offered. "My car's parked in someone else's space downstairs so I need to move it anyway."

Tracy had returned to Dallas a few years after graduating from UCLA. She had a bachelor's degree in liberal arts, but instead of going for her teaching credential as she had once planned, she had chosen a career in real estate. It suited her outgoing personality, and after a couple of years, she'd started making a good deal of money.

The economy might be in a slump, but after the initial drop, Tracy had continued selling houses. She believed the falling market prices and the low interest rates made real estate one of the best investments around, and she made it a point to convince her clients she was right.

Everything about Tracy Spencer spoke of confidence and success, an image Tracy went out of her way to project. It was her way of keeping the awful memories of her childhood at bay. Mattie believed Tracy's outgoing personality masked a deep insecurity that stemmed from the violence she had suffered as a child.

Though Tracy dated a lot, she had never been married, never even had a serious relationship. Since neither of them were particularly good with men, they considered themselves lucky to have each other.

"Okay, come on." Tracy caught Mattie's arm as she

returned to the living room and hauled her toward the door. "Got your purse? Let's rock and roll!"

Mattie laughed, eager for the one night out a week she allowed herself, and headed for the car.

GABE FINISHED HIS meeting and drove home. After a discussion of the pros and cons of various downtown improvement projects, a battle that had dragged on for hours, he deserved a little relaxation. He changed out of his sport coat and slacks into a pair of jeans and a polo shirt. A few minutes later, he was on his way to the Hammerfield building and his rendezvous with Sam, more than ready for an ice-cold beer.

And he was curious to see how the remodel had turned out. He always liked seeing historic places renovated and brought back to life, and the Hammerfield building had been around for a hundred years.

Gabe parked in the lot and made his way to the front of the three-story brick structure that had been refitted and repainted. From what he could tell, the upper floors had been converted into offices. A neon sign above the entrance to the first floor read, Club Rio.

An unusual name, Gabe thought, but as he walked in, he understood why. Karaoke had gotten its start in Brazil. Apparently, the popular amateur singing went on three nights a week at the club. And the menu posted beside the door featured a number of Brazilian dishes including *churrasco,* Brazilian barbecued meat, and cocktails like a *ciparina,* a very strong sugar cane drink. The owner had gone for something out of the ordinary, and from the sound of the noisy crowd inside it was working.

Gabe made a quick perusal of the interior. The walls

were painted with brightly colored parrots and huge banana plants. He smiled his approval and made his way to the bar.

Sam stood in front of the long, sweeping, black granite counter, sipping from a bottle of Lone Star Beer. "You made it."

"You didn't think I would?" Gabe caught the bartender's eye and pointed to Sam's brew, ordering one for himself.

"I wasn't completely sure. You've seemed a little distracted lately."

He thought of the fire, of Angel and Mattie. "Yeah, I guess I have been."

"You talk to Parsons about rebuilding the lobby?"

He nodded, picked up the icy brown bottle the bartender set in front of him. "He wants us to start again yesterday."

Sam chuckled. "Don't they all?"

Gabe took a swallow of his beer. From where they stood, he had a clear view of the stage where the karaoke singers performed. A high-tech projector hidden overhead allowed the amateur entertainers to belt out the words to whatever song was playing at the moment. Currently, a dark-haired guy in skinny black jeans and a T-shirt with a dragon on the front sang the words to an old Beatles tune, an incongruous picture to say the least. Paul McCartney he wasn't.

Still, the crowd appeared to be entertained, giving the singer a hearty round of applause when he finished.

"Fun place," Gabe said.

"You ever try it?"

Gabe grunted. "I've got a voice like a bullfrog."

"Mine's no good, either. Besides, I'd rather listen. Believe it or not, some of the singers are pretty good."

Gabe wasn't sure he believed it. So far, the best of them had only been mediocre. He guessed it didn't matter as long as everyone was having a good time.

He finished his beer and ordered another, sipped this one a little more slowly. A busty brunette got up and sang. She had a moderately pleasant voice but nothing special. He glanced over at Sam, saw that he was watching someone and followed his gaze to a svelte little blonde sitting at a table not far from the stage.

"You like the looks of that, do you?" Gabe teased.

Sam's mouth curved. "Her name's Tracy Spencer. She's in real estate. I've thought about asking her out, but I've got a hunch I'd be getting into something I can't handle."

"How's that?"

"I don't know.... On the surface, she looks like she'd be fun, but I never see her with the same guy twice. I think she's got issues. I'd just as soon steer clear."

Tracy threw her pretty head back and gave out a robust bark of laughter.

"Maybe it would be worth it."

"Maybe."

Gabe returned his attention to the stage as another singer climbed the steps and crossed to the microphone. She was wearing a very short silver dress, the spotlight catching on the sequined bodice, which displayed the tops of a nice pair of breasts. She had a set of legs that wouldn't quit and a figure that made the men in the crowd sit up a little straighter. But it was her hair that snagged his complete attention.

Thick, glossy russet curls that seemed to catch fire

in the spotlight. The music kicked in, a hot disco number. The woman began to sing and conversation slowed, then completely halted. Every eye in the place swiveled toward the stage.

Gabe's attention was as tightly snared as the rest of the crowd and suddenly he felt an eerie sense of recognition.

No way. It couldn't be.

The beat began to swell. The singer moved, began to strut and sway, tossed her head and all that gorgeous red hair. He stared, still unable to believe it.

Hot love, the background music strummed. *Ooooh, hot love.*

The singer smiled and picked up the beat, and Gabe's whole body clenched in arousal. Her voice was crystalline, throaty and sexy. Mattie Baker's voice. It was Mattie who strutted and danced, moved her body in sensuous rhythm to the beat.

The music pounded and so did his blood.

"If you ain't hot, love, you can't have me. I need some hot love, baby, tonight. If you ain't hot, love, you can't have me. Gotta have some hot love. Need to have some lovin' tonight."

Gabe couldn't breathe. This was the Mattie he had imagined, the woman beneath the layers of drab clothing. The woman Mattie had kept hidden until tonight.

He was hard, his erection hot and throbbing. Fate was a hunter, they said, and maybe it was true since the lady who dominated his thoughts was standing on the stage right in front of him. She spun around, giving him a look at her shapely legs and that round little ass he had manhandled in his dreams.

He listened to the music and watched her acting out

a sexual fantasy that had every male in the room panting, and he finally understood.

He'd been right about Mattie. There was more to her than she let people see. A sensual nature that begged to be released.

The music track played on and Mattie kept moving, crossing the stage from one side to the other, holding up the microphone, her hips subtly swaying, the spangles across her breasts jiggling with every drumbeat.

She reached the final chorus and the song played out. Mattie laughed and bowed to a riot of whistles and applause. The disc jockey gave thanks for a fine performance by Club Rio's favorite, Lena Sterling, a name as phony as the straitlaced Mattie she pretended to be.

Gabe wasn't surprised. With Mattie, business came first and she wouldn't want her colleagues to know her secret.

He watched her leave the stage and head toward the stairs leading down to the basement. He assumed the bathrooms were down there. He tossed some greenbacks on the bar, motioned to Sam where he was heading and followed her.

As he reached the bottom, he paused, catching a glimpse of Mattie at the end of the long, dimly lit hallway, disappearing into the ladies' room. He leaned back against the wall to wait, folded his arms over his chest, his gaze riveted to the spot where she had disappeared.

Mattie came out a few minutes later, looking cool and unruffled. He wished he felt the same. Instead he was hot and fiercely aroused. As she made her way down the hall, he stepped out of the shadows in front of her.

"That was some performance, *Lena,*" he said.

Mattie's head shot up. She moistened those glossy pink lips. "Gabe. What...what are you doing here?"

"I didn't know you'd be here, if that's what you're thinking. I came with my foreman, Sam McBride. He seemed to think I might enjoy the entertainment."

For once she didn't back away from him. "Did you?" The words held a note of challenge. He had never seen her more in control.

"I liked everything I saw on that stage. And for the first time since I met you, I think I've got you figured out."

One of those fiery eyebrows went up. "Is that right?"

"Yeah, that's right. Watching you up there gave me the answers to the questions I've been asking myself since the day I met you. I know what you need, Mattie Baker. Believe me, I've got exactly what you need."

And then he caught her face between his hands, lowered his head, and claimed her mouth in a burning kiss.

CHAPTER EIGHT

MATTIE COULDN'T MOVE. The man of her midnight fantasies stood right in front of her. The last person she expected to see tonight was Gabriel Raines.

But as his hands cupped her face, as he lowered his head and those soft lips settled gently over hers, coaxing and at the same time insistent, something hot and ragged broke loose inside her.

"Gabe…" she whispered as he deepened the kiss, and instead of pushing him away, she opened to him, giving in to his subtle demands, tilting her head to allow him better access. Heat rolled through her in long, powerful waves. Desire stirred deep in her belly and dampness slid into her core.

His hands dropped to her waist and he drew her against him. Her palms came to rest on his muscular chest and she felt the power there, the strength, and her heartbeat pounded in her ears.

"Gabe…" she repeated, kissing him back, letting her tongue slide over his, teasing, asking for more. He nibbled and tasted, alternately coaxed and demanded, and desire swelled, began to expand like hot liquid in her stomach.

For an instant, she thought of stopping, ending what would surely wind up a disaster. But the instant she started to pull away, Gabe caught her wrists, lifted and pinned them against the wall above her head.

She tugged a little, testing his determination, felt the implacable strength of his hands. His mouth claimed hers again, a leisurely and thorough exploration that spun her into a world of sensation, and his grip did not lesson. He wanted her and he meant to have her.

Her body relaxed against his. Now that the decision had been taken away from her, she felt free in a way she never had before. Gabe wouldn't let her resist. He was going to take what he wanted.

Give her exactly what she needed.

She moaned into his mouth as he pressed himself more fully against her, let her feel his powerful erection. He was big and hard, promising what she hadn't understood she had been craving.

He was all solid male, nothing like the men she had slept with before, and it made her yearn to know what it would be like to make love with a man like that.

She barely heard the door open beside her, just felt herself being subtly moved into some kind of storage room, then the door closed and the room fell into semi-darkness. A sliver of moonlight poured in through a narrow basement window near the ceiling, just enough to light Gabe's face, enough that she could see the naked hunger in his fierce blue eyes.

"I want you," he said. "I can't remember ever wanting a woman more."

Fresh desire spilled through her. She had to know, had to find out if the wildly sensuous woman she became on stage was really part of her nature, some part that had been dammed up until now. Until Gabriel Raines.

She felt his mouth on her breasts and realized he had unzipped her dress and eased the top down, unfastened the front of her black push-up bra.

"Beautiful," he said, his teeth lightly grazing her nipple, his tongue circling the tip. Her knees felt weak as he took the fullness into his mouth and began to suckle her. His big hands slid up beneath her silver dress and he cupped the bare globes of her bottom, covered only by the tiny red thong panties she wore. Lifting her into the V between his thighs, he let her feel the thick ridge bulging beneath the zipper of his jeans.

"Oh, God…"

His tone gentled. "It's all right, I've got you. I'm not going to hurt you."

She was clinging to him, she realized, practically wrapping herself around him. She should have been embarrassed, should have been mortified at her behavior. Instead, she just wanted more.

She reached toward the bulge in his jeans, tentatively cupped him. He was huge and pulsing. Her fingers itched to pull down his zipper and wrap around his hard length.

Gabe groaned. "Take it easy, sweetheart. I can only stand so much."

"I want you," she said. "I've never felt… I want you so much, Gabe."

His erection leaped beneath her hand. "I want you, too." He dragged in a deep, shuddering breath. "But if I take you like this, in this damnable storage room, tomorrow you'll regret it. You'll never forgive me."

"I don't care. I just… I just need…"

"I know what you need." He eased her skirt down

over her hips and refastened her bra, drew her dress back into place.

"We're leaving." He reached out and took hold of her hand. "Right this minute."

She was shaking with need. She had never been this turned on in her life. "But…where are we going?"

"My place. If we go to yours, you'll turn back into Mattie Baker and it's too soon for that to happen."

He was right. She was already beginning to hesitate, to reconsider her actions. Before she could panic completely, Gabe was tugging her down the corridor, hauling her up the stairs.

"I came with a friend," she said. "She'll worry if I leave without telling her."

"What's her name?"

"Tracy Spencer."

"Stay here." He left her at the top of the stairs, strode across the room to a tall, good-looking man with short blond hair.

In minutes he returned. "Sam knows Tracy. I told him we were leaving. He'll tell her I took you home."

"Maybe I should—"

His hot kiss cut off her words and had her tingling all over. As he tugged her out the front door, she stumbled and Gabe swept her up in his arms.

"All right?"

She just nodded, feeling featherlight and utterly feminine. In seconds they had reached his truck and he had lifted her into the passenger seat. He rounded the pickup and climbed inside, hauled her over next to him on the bench seat and fastened the middle seat belt across her lap.

She must have been in some kind of trance because

she didn't resist when he drove away, heading off toward wherever he lived. It wasn't very far because she was still silent, her heart still thumping madly, when he helped her down from the truck, led her into the elevator in the lobby, and pushed the button for the fourth floor.

"Cold feet yet?" he asked.

When she nodded, he bent down and gave her one of those wet, searing kisses that had gotten her into this in the first place. She felt hot and needy, felt as if her skin was stretched too tight. Inside her bra, her nipples were hard and aching. When the elevator door slid open with a *ding,* Gabe settled a hand at her waist and urged her across the hall. An instant later, she was standing in the middle of his living room.

"You want a drink?"

She needed a dozen straight shots, but there was something she needed more. She moistened her lips. "Would you…would you kiss me again?"

"I plan to kiss you all night, honey, in places you've never been kissed."

A funny little sound seeped from her throat. She didn't protest when he lifted her into his arms, carried her into his bedroom and began to strip off her clothes.

Soon she was naked and lying in the middle of his king-size bed. She watched as he pulled off his cowboy boots and dragged his yellow polo shirt over his head. As he unzipped and slid down his jeans, it occurred to her how exciting it could be to watch a man undress.

A man with a body like Gabe's.

He was solid muscle, his chest wide and lightly sprinkled with curly dark brown hair, his stomach flat and ridged with muscle. His legs were long and muscular and the erection nested between them was immense.

The mattress dipped with his weight as he joined her on the bed, tipped her chin up and captured her lips. Deep, drugging kisses had her melting. Hot, wet kisses had her reaching for him, running her hands over all that hard male flesh.

"Gabe…please…"

"Take it easy, honey." He nipped an earlobe, captured her mouth again. "There isn't any hurry."

She reached up and cupped his cheek, felt the roughness of his late-night beard. "There is for me," she said, worried again that the haze of passion she was drowning in would fade and she would be left unsatisfied as she had always been before.

"Maybe this'll help."

She felt his hand skimming over her breasts, her belly, leaving a trail of fire wherever he touched. Parting her legs, he began to stroke her, lightly at first then more deeply, and hot sensation poured through her.

She groaned. She was so hot and wet. Gabe kissed her slowly, touched her exactly where she ached to be touched, and she arched into his hand. The tension built. She squirmed against him, begging for relief, and his fingers moved more deeply. For an instant, she hovered on the edge.

"Gabe!" she cried out and he caught her cries of passion in his mouth. Waves of pleasure washed over her, sensation so hot and fierce for a moment she couldn't breathe. She was crying when he eased her into his arms.

Gabe smoothed a tear from her cheek. "It's all right, honey, it's probably just been too long."

She shook her head, feeling ridiculous, unable to keep the words from spilling out. "I usually can't…

I mean, making love…it isn't easy for me to reach… you know."

"A climax?" He gave her a wicked grin. "Looked pretty easy to me. Why don't we try it again and see?"

He kissed her before she could answer. Cupping her breasts, he bent his head to taste each one, leisurely suckled and laved, and there she was, hot and trembling and needy all over again.

"It's okay," he said softly as her fingers dug into the muscles across his shoulders. "We'll get there. We've got all the time in the world."

He proceeded to demonstrate that, taking his time, touching and caressing, heightening her arousal almost to the point of pain. When she couldn't stand a moment more, Gabe eased himself inside her until he was completely seated. Keeping his weight on his elbows, he kissed her deeply, kissed her until she was begging him to take her.

Mattie bit back a moan of pure pleasure as Gabe began to move, the heavy thrust and drag of his shaft making her whole body tingle. It was like riding out a storm or being sucked into a whirlpool, like being consumed by flames.

Her stomach muscles contracted and then she was flying, her body clenching as release gripped her again. Mattie moaned his name and clung to him, her body tight around his hard length, but Gabe didn't stop.

Not until she had reached another shattering climax did he allow his own release.

By the time she came back to herself, he lay beside her, one of his powerful arms nestling her close to his side.

"That's what you've been needing all along," he said,

kissing the top of her head. "You're a very passionate woman, Mattie. What you needed was a man."

He meant a real man and yesterday she would have argued. Not tonight. Tonight she was a sexy *femme fatale* and she could handle a virile man like Gabe.

Her insides began to tighten.

Tomorrow she would again be practical Mattie Baker.

And she would have to find a way to deal with Gabriel Raines.

GABE AWOKE LATE the next morning, more relaxed and content than he had felt in weeks. He had turned off his alarm last night, looking forward to sharing coffee and doughnuts with Mattie. He smiled as he reached for her, hard again though they had made love three times during the night. When his hand landed on cold, empty sheets, Gabe rolled onto his side in search of her, but Mattie was nowhere in sight.

Damn.

He had been sleeping so soundly he hadn't felt her move off the mattress, hadn't heard her leave. But the sexy silver dress he had draped over a chair last night was gone and so was Mattie.

Swinging his legs to the side of the bed, Gabe silently cursed. He should have known she would run. Her lusty response to his lovemaking had scared the hell out of her. He almost smiled. She would be even more scared if she knew that as soon as he realized how little experience she had, he had held himself back.

Still, she had run like a scalded cat out the door this morning and maybe even out of his life.

His shoulders tightened. He been lusting after Mat-

tie Baker since the day he'd met her. He hadn't thought
it was more than that until now.

Maybe it was nothing, just that she was one of the
most passionate women he'd ever met and they were
incredibly good together in bed. Maybe it was just that
he wasn't ready to give up the great sex they'd shared.

As he padded naked toward the bathroom, he remembered how upset she had been when she thought
he hadn't used a condom. Funny thing was, once she
realized he had, she seemed almost disappointed. The
lady was definitely hard to read. And yet there was no
question that the mind-blowing sex was beyond anything he'd ever experienced before.

Gabe turned on the shower. As he waited for the
water to get hot, he spotted a note on the granite counter.

Gabe—
Last night was amazing. You showed me the
woman I am inside and I will always be grateful.
But my life is my career. Though we will probably run into each other on occasion, I hope you
will behave like a gentleman and forget about last
night, as I intend to do.
Mattie.

Forget about it? Having her again was all he could
think about. And he was hardly a gentleman. A gentleman wouldn't have undressed her in a storage room. A
gentleman wouldn't have pulled up her skirt and cupped
that round little ass in the palms of his hands.

Gabe clenched his jaw at the memory. He turned
the shower from warm to cold and climbed in, the cold
spray ending his erection. Mattie wanted him out of

her life. Fine, then he would leave her alone. He'd never had a problem with women. He didn't need one who didn't want him.

The icy water poured over him, calming him a little. So what if Mattie only wanted a one-night stand? It was the way things were these days. He should look on the positive side. He'd wanted her. Now he'd had her.

As he ducked his head beneath the cold spray and goose bumps rose on his skin, the thought didn't make him feel any better.

MATTIE WORKED HARD all morning. Her job was never easy, but today she found it nearly impossible to concentrate on the endless tasks ahead of her.

Nearly impossible to keep her mind off Gabriel Raines.

She sighed as she studied the drawing she was modifying on the CAD program on her computer. One of the reasons she had been promoted to head designer was her ability to think outside the box, to come up with ideas that were both inventive and functional. Currently, she was working on a design for a contemporary art gallery over on Olive not far from the Dallas Museum of Art.

The structure sitting on the lot at present was going to be torn down. Mattie had come up with a concept that was architecturally exciting on the outside, which would help bring in business, and also on the inside, where the spaces were large and open, the ceilings dominated by lighting that would show the paintings off to their best advantage.

She couldn't wait to present her preliminary drawings to the customer. She intended to stay late in an effort to finish them tonight.

If she could keep her mind on work and not on the night she had spent in bed with Gabriel Raines.

Mattie felt a tug of heat low in her belly. Last night had been incredible. All these years she had thought of herself as a failure at sex. But Gabe had unlocked the passion buried inside her. Whatever happened, she would always be grateful to him for that.

Unfortunately, her sexuality was a part of her nature she couldn't afford to indulge. She had an important job, a career. If she allowed herself to get involved in a relationship, her future would suffer.

She blew out a breath, moving a loose strand of auburn hair away from her cheek. On the other hand, maybe she was overreacting. Maybe one night of lusty sex was all Gabe wanted. Maybe he had taken her to bed merely to satisfy his curiosity and prove his point.

The men she had dated were sexually wrong for her. What she needed was a virile, masculine, flesh-and-blood male. The kind who made her feel like a woman.

She'd found that man in Gabe, but even if he wanted to see her again, she couldn't let her sexual attraction to him go any further. After one brief night, she was finding it nearly impossible to keep her mind on work, to focus on spatial proportions instead of how it felt to have Gabe Raines on top of her, inside her, driving her to climax.

But there was something more. Something she had almost forgotten in her wild abandon last night. As much as she ached to have a baby, she had never wanted to be a single mother. She'd been careful with Mark, but she had still gotten pregnant. Then Mark had abandoned her and she had lost the child.

For nearly a year afterward she'd been submerged in grief. She couldn't deal with that kind of pain again.

Gabe's handsome image appeared in her mind and a memory arose of his mouth on her breast, his sinfully skillful hands doing things she had only imagined.

A rush of heat poured through her. Dammit, she had to stop thinking about him. The entire event had to be shoved to the back of her mind. With managing her career and her work at the center, her life was full enough.

A relieved sigh escaped when a light knock sounded at the door, interrupting her thoughts. Mattie looked up as Aaron rolled his wheelchair into the office.

"Thought I'd drop by and say hello. You've been holed up in here all day. Anything wrong?"

She felt the slow creep of heat into her cheeks. The only thing wrong was that after her wild night with Gabe, she felt way too good. "Nothing's wrong. I just needed to concentrate, do some catching up."

Aaron eyed her strangely. "You're blushing. And there's something about you that looks…well, different. Did you go to Club Rio last night?"

Aaron and Emily were the only two people in the office who knew about her secret life as Lena Sterling.

"Tracy and I went for a while."

"That's it, isn't it? You met someone. You must have gotten laid."

"Aaron!"

He shoved his glasses up on his nose. "Sorry. None of my business. It's just… I've never seen you blush before."

More color washed into her cheeks. "I'm not blushing."

"If you say so." He wheeled toward her. "You want to get some lunch?"

Mattie shook her head. "Too busy. I'll be working late as it is."

Aaron just nodded. "If you need to talk, you know I'm always willing to listen."

"I know you are." But talking about Gabe Raines was the last thing she wanted. Mattie ignored the quiet closing of her office door and went back to work.

CHAPTER NINE

GABE SLEPT FITFULLY that Friday night. He hadn't dreamed of his days in the Marine Corps for years. He'd been one of the lucky ones, the guys who saw little in the way of action, but his training had been extensive and had given him the skills and confidence he'd needed to deal with the kind of rough-and-tumble guys who worked in the construction business.

The war in Afghanistan hadn't started for a couple of years after he was out of the service, but he'd lost some good buddies there, and occasionally their faces popped up in his dreams. He awakened bathed in sweat, uncertain whether to be thankful he wasn't with them, or to wish he had been.

Gabe sat up, rubbing a hand over his face. He got up and hit the head, wide awake now and thinking how much better the night had been with Mattie in his bed. He was on his way back to bed, hoping he could return to sleep, when his cell phone started ringing.

He picked it up off the nightstand, figuring the news had to be bad for someone to call him at four in the morning.

"Raines."

"Mr. Raines, this is Battalion Fire Chief Alonzo Santori. There's a fire in an office building under construction over on McKinney. Your company name and phone number are on the sign out front."

A knot of dread formed in his stomach. "We're the contractor on the project. The owner is Wildcat Oil."

"We've already called them. It looks like the damage is going to be extensive. We'd appreciate if you could come down here."

"On my way." Gabe closed the phone, the knot going tighter. Two fires in less than two weeks. He'd thought the first was just some nut who happened to pick the Towers. But the odds of a fire on another of his sites being unrelated to the first were slim and none. There was a very good chance he was the target in both cases.

Son of a bitch.

Gabe dressed quickly and headed for McKinney Court, or what was left of it. The building was only half finished, which he hoped meant no one was inside. But until he got there, he couldn't know for sure.

Gabe pressed a little harder on the gas pedal, propelling the pickup through the dark, empty streets. All the way there, his mind kept running over the possibilities of who might want to ruin him.

ORANGE AND RED TONGUES of fire shot more than four stories into the black night sky. Flames roared like Satan's breath out through broken windows and soared up through holes in the half-finished roof. Gabe pulled his pickup over to the curb and turned off the engine. For several long moments, he just sat there, his gaze fixed on the structure engulfed in flames.

Two hook-and-ladder trucks and four other fire units surrounded the building. Hoses stretched from hydrants on the street into the blazing interior. Firemen in full turnout gear hurried efficiently to whatever task they were assigned.

As Gabe climbed out of the pickup, the deep rumble of engines reached his ears, along with the sound of breaking glass and the roar of the flames. Cinders rained down on the pavement and the smell of greasy smoke singed the air.

From the corner of his eyes, something snagged his attention and he looked away from the blaze to a man walking toward him. Gabe recognized the salt-and-pepper hair.

"Thanks for coming down," Captain Daily said.

Gabe glanced back toward the flames. "I guess the first fire wasn't random after all," he said darkly.

"We haven't determined for certain whether or not this was arson. Till we're sure, we can't know if the two fires are connected. Between you and me, however, it's likely they are." Daily pulled a notepad out of his pocket and flipped open the cover. "I need to know, Gabe, if you have any enemies. Anyone who would go to these lengths for some kind of payback?"

Gabe shook his head. "On the way down here, I tried to think of someone I might have pissed off to this extent. I've got to tell you, I haven't got a clue."

"Any woman problems? An irate husband, someone whose wife or girlfriend you're involved with who might not want you in the picture?"

"I haven't been seeing anyone in particular for nearly six months and I don't go for married women." A night with Mattie hardly counted as a relationship. Besides, he hadn't met her till after the fire in the Towers.

"How about business acquaintances? Maybe a competitor, or a subcontractor, someone you had a beef with over a job?"

Gabe thought immediately of Vance Gleason. Gleason Construction was his main competitor for work in the area. The two of them fought over contracts like a couple of Rottweilers but it was strictly business as far as Gabe knew. He couldn't imagine Gleason burning down a building because he lost a contract to Gabe.

"I can tell you're thinking of someone," Daily said. "Who is it?"

"My competition, Vance Gleason, but I don't think he would carry our business rivalry this far."

Daily wrote down the name. "You'd be surprised what people will do. Anyone else?"

Gabe started to shake his head, then remembered a contractor he had fired about a month ago. "Guy named Pete Dare. He was doing the cement work on the Towers. I fired him when I found out he was using a cheaper grade of cement than we had agreed on."

Daily made a note of the name. "Who else can you think of?"

God, if only he knew. "No one offhand. I'll think about it, though, see who else I can come up with."

"Is this project insured?"

Gabe nodded. "American Insurance." He frowned. "If you're thinking I've got something to gain from the fires, you're way off base. I lose money on the deductible, lose some of my equipment, but the real loser is Wildcat Oil. Same with the Towers. Time is money. Until the lobby is finished, the building can't be run efficiently. Here, Wildcat Oil can't move in, which costs them money."

Daily nodded. He made a few more notes. "I gather you didn't have security cameras on this project, either."

"I've never installed them until the work was completed. That's a mistake I won't make again."

Daily made another note and looked up. "I need to talk to the person who called 9-1-1. Sometimes whoever sets the fire has a thing about calling it in. They like to watch the flames build, see the trucks arrive, that kind of thing. Let me know if you think of anything else."

"I will."

Another man walked up as Daily departed, olive-skinned and with a leonine mane of silver hair. "I'm Battalion Chief Alonzo Santori. I take it you're Raines?"

"That's right."

"I saw you talking to Captain Daily."

"He had a few questions for me."

"I've got a few for you, too. To begin with, do you have any other projects in Dallas?"

His chest squeezed. "Actually, I do. Two others in this area."

"Have you considered hiring security?"

Gabe raked a hand through his hair. The buildings were locked up at night. The equipment not being used inside was surrounded by a chain-link fence, the gate locked each evening. He'd been worried about theft. He had never considered anything like this. "Not until now. I'll get on it first thing in the morning." Which was only a few hours away.

"Be a wise move."

Considering what had happened, *crucial* was a better word. "Will you let me know what the investigators find out?"

"We'll keep you abreast of things as much as we can."

"Thank you." He figured Captain Daily had been exceptionally candid because of the favor Gabe had done his father. If the second fire was arson—and he was fairly sure it was—he wanted to know how both fires were started. He wanted to know if it was done by a professional torch or an amateur. From the looks of the flames licking into the sky, whoever set the second blaze had done a very thorough job.

As he watched the firemen gripping their heavy hoses, sweeping the building with dense sprays of water, he unclipped his cell phone and called Sam with the bad news.

"You ready to go to work?" Gabe asked as Sam's sleepy voice came on the line.

"Actually, I'd planned on another hour of sleep. What's up?"

"McKinney Court is turning into ashes as we speak."

"What?"

"I'm there now. The fire has completely destroyed the building. We won't be needing the crew today, at least not here."

Sam sighed into the phone. "I'll take care of it. I'll call the guys and tell them what's going on. Dammit, I can't believe this."

"Yeah, I know what you mean."

Gabe hung up the phone. He stayed until the fire was brought under control, which took well into the morning. By then, the news cameras were rolling. He kept mostly out of their way, checked to see if there was anything else the fire department needed from him, then headed over to the Greenwood Apartments site.

He needed to talk to Becky, tell her what had happened and arrange for around-the-clock security.

He thought of his projects, the theater in Deep Ellum, the Greenwood Apartments, and the warehouse he owned he hadn't started remodeling yet. Unlike the first two fires, he owned those pieces of property himself. They were insured, but he would still lose a bundle of money. And there was always the chance of someone being hurt or even killed.

And he hated the thought of the beautiful old Egyptian being destroyed after all of the years it had managed to survive. To say nothing of the work everyone had done to restore it.

Gabe sighed as he turned off his engine, climbed out of the truck and headed for his office in the construction trailer.

CHAPTER TEN

MATTIE SAT AT her kitchen table, sipping a cup of strong coffee, Tigger winding his way back and forth through her legs. She reached down and lifted the big cat into her lap, stroked his back and felt the soft rumble of a purr.

"Such a pretty kitty," she cooed, nuzzling her nose in his deep yellow fur. "Mama's sweet baby boy." She hoped no one ever heard her talking to him the way she did. They would probably think she was crazy. But she loved animals and Tigger was her dearest companion.

A playful *rap-tap-tap* sounded at the door and Tigger jumped out of her lap. Recognizing Tracy's familiar knock, Mattie pulled her terry-cloth robe a little tighter around her and answered the door.

Tracy breezed past her. In a narrow brown skirt and turquoise silk blouse, her feet in a pair of expensive low-heeled pumps, typical business attire for Tracy, she waved a hand as she walked into the living room.

"I know it's Saturday but I figured you'd be up. I wasn't sure if you'd be home instead of at work, or over at the center."

"It's the weekend, remember?"

"Since when has that mattered?"

Touché, Mattie thought. "I worked late last night. I figured I'd give myself a break, though I *am* going over to the center this afternoon. What's up?"

Tracy sailed toward the kitchen, went over to the coffeemaker and poured herself a cup.

"There's half-and-half in the fridge," Mattie said.

"Great. Thanks."

"So what are you doing here? I thought you had a showing this morning."

"I've always got an appointment. I just thought I'd drop by." As she leaned into the fridge, grabbed the cream and poured it into her cup, she tossed back her straight blond hair. "I haven't talked to you since Club Rio. I saw that hunk you left with. His friend said his name was Gabriel Raines. I'm dying to know what happened. Was he as yummy as he looked?"

Mattie returned to her chair at the kitchen table. Propping her elbows on the top, she cradled her coffee mug in her hands. "I don't suppose I could convince you nothing happened."

Tracy just smiled. "You could try, I guess. If you really don't want to talk about it—"

"I don't."

"So something did happen! I knew it!" Mug in hand, Tracy hurried over to the table and sat down across from her. "Come on, tell me."

"Let's just say it was amazing and leave it at that."

"Oh my God! I can't believe it. You are sooo not into men. I want all the gory details."

Mattie shook her head. "No way. You know me better than that." She took a long sip of coffee and changed the subject. "So what about you? Anything exciting happen to you that night?"

Tracy stared into the creamy liquid in her cup. "Actually, yes and no."

Mattie cocked an eyebrow. "Yes and no? That sounds interesting."

"The friend your hunk sent over to tell me the two of you were leaving? His name is Sam McBride, and he's, well, he's pretty hunky himself."

"Really? So I guess you took him home with you." It was Tracy's *modus operandi*. It wasn't an every night occurrence, but if she liked a guy, she didn't hesitate to have sex with him.

"I invited him over for a drink. I was attracted to him. I figured what the heck?"

"And...?"

"That's the weird part. He turned me down."

Mattie scoffed. "Nobody turns you down, Tracy."

"Sam did. He said he wasn't interested in a one-night stand. He said if I wanted to go out to dinner sometime, he'd like that. He gave me his phone number and told me to give him a call."

"So what did you say?"

"I was royally pissed. I'm not used to guys giving me the brush-off. But after he left... I don't know. I kind of liked that he was different than the other guys I've known. I was thinking...maybe you could ask your friend, Gabe, about him. See if you can find out what he's like."

Mattie shook her head. "I'm not...not seeing Gabe anymore. It was just a one-time thing."

Tracy's lips thinned. "The asshole. I swear they're all alike. It's probably a good thing I didn't go to bed with Sam."

"I'm the one who ended it, Tracy. I left before Gabe woke up."

Tracy's green eyes widened. "I thought you said he was amazing."

"It doesn't matter. I don't have time for a man in my life."

"You mean you're afraid of getting hurt so you'll just stay away from him." Tracy sighed. "I use them and dump them. You're afraid to get involved at all. I guess we both have hang-ups."

It was true. Neither of them knew how to handle a relationship. It was better just to play it safe.

"So are you going to call him?" Mattie asked. "Sam, I mean."

Tracy grinned. "I'll call if you will."

Mattie leaned back in her chair. "No way." But her stomach quivered and she realized calling Gabe was exactly what she wanted to do.

"Well, I guess neither of us will ever know where things might have led," Tracy said a bit morosely.

"I guess we won't."

Tracy finished her coffee and left to meet her client, and Mattie went to shower and get ready for the day ahead. She was dressed in jeans and a sleeveless white blouse when a second knock sounded at the door.

For an instant, she thought it might be Gabe and her pulse kicked up. When she opened the door, Angel stood in the hallway.

"There's been another fire." Worry dug grooves into the teen's wide forehead. "I saw it on the news this morning. I'm afraid, Mattie."

"It's all right, come on in." There were hundreds of fires in Dallas every year. It didn't mean the police would jump to the conclusion that Angel had been involved in this one.

Angel walked wearily into the living room. "I was hoping you would come with me."

"Where? The police department?"

"To see Mr. Raines. It was his building that burned down."

Mattie's pulse quickened. "What? Are you sure?"

Angel nodded. "Some office he was building. It wasn't finished yet. On the news they said it was completely destroyed."

Poor Gabe. Two fires in two weeks. She couldn't help wondering if the second fire could possibly be a coincidence.

"I have to tell him it wasn't me," Angel said.

Mattie gave it some thought. "Maybe that's a good idea." She told herself it wasn't just an excuse to see him. This was about Angel. She didn't really think Gabe would believe the boy had set the second fire, but she had to be sure.

And the more she thought about it, two fires involving Raines Construction likely meant Gabe was the target. The thought worried her more than she would have liked.

"Do you know where the building was?"

"On McKinney. On the news they said it was near Bryan."

Mattie set a hand on Angel's thick shoulder. "If the fire happened last night, there's a good chance Gabe will be down there this morning. Come on, let's go find him."

THE WOODEN FLOOR of the trailer shook a little under Gabe's weight. The walls were bare except for working plans for some of his projects, and his framed contractor's license.

His secretary, Becky Marvin, stared at the computer on her desk at the opposite end.

"I guess you heard about the fire."

She turned and nodded. "I saw it on TV this morning. That's why I came in. I thought you might need me for something."

"I'm glad you're here. It's looking like the two fires are connected and if they are, that means someone may be targeting me specifically. Have you noticed anyone suspicious hanging around here at Greenwood, or have any of the crew been acting strangely over the past few weeks?"

"Sorry, boss, I haven't noticed a thing. At least nothing out of the ordinary. Hank Munro was in here a couple of weeks ago grumbling. Said you were working the black guys harder than the white guys. I told him I was the one who did the scheduling and I don't pay any attention to the color of a man's skin."

"You convince him?"

She shrugged. "It was the truth. Up to him whether he believes it or not."

"Anything else?"

"Benny Jervis was in here bitching. Said you owed him a raise after the job he's been doing, but he's always bitching about something. It's nothing more than the day-to-day crap."

Gabe made a mental note to talk to the two men, see how deep their animosity ran. As far as he was concerned, Becky was probably right and it was nothing more than the usual bullshit. Still, he couldn't afford to leave any stone unturned.

Becky went back to work and Gabe sat down to do some digging, try to figure out which security company to hire. He also intended to install security cameras around each job site. He'd just never been much of a high-tech guy and until now hadn't really seen a need for them, at least until the job was finished.

His cell phone rang. That weird sixth sense he and his brothers seemed to have when one of them was in trouble kicked in and Gabe knew instinctively either Jackson or Devlin was on the line.

He flipped open the phone. The caller ID belonged to his younger brother. "Hey, Dev."

"Haven't heard from you in a while," Dev said. "Thought I'd better call and see if you're still alive and kicking."

After Dev left the rangers, he had started working as a private investigator. The stock market was climbing, and with the money he'd saved over the years, Dev invested like crazy. As Gabe and Jackson had done, Dev had also invested in Wildcat Oil.

The stock took off and Dev made enough to start his own private investigation firm in Phoenix, which later became a chain of security companies with branches in L.A. and San Diego. At thirty-two, Dev was "mostly retired," which meant he still did detective work, but only took the cases that interested him. And was always willing to help his brothers.

"Where are you?" Gabe asked. "I thought you were spending a couple of weeks on your boat in San Diego." Dev owned a forty-foot sailboat he kept in a slip in Mission Bay. Since he lived in Scottsdale, he didn't get there all that often, but with a branch in the area, he used it whenever he was in town.

"The lady I took with me kept getting seasick. Not conducive to playing slap and tickle. We decided to come home and lay out by the pool."

Gabe almost smiled. After Dev's fiancée had broken his heart, he'd become a specialist in fast women and one-night stands. Apparently that hadn't changed.

Gabe took a deep breath. He would have called Dev for advice on who to hire in Dallas for security but he hated to involve his brother in his troubles.

He wasn't willing to lie to him, either.

Better to just get it over with. Besides, he could use the advice. "Listen, I'm glad you called. I need to hire a security company. You know anyone in Dallas worth a damn?"

Dev didn't hesitate. "Atlas will do a good job for you. Trace Rawlins, the owner's son, runs the company now. Trace is an ex-ranger. You having a theft problem?"

"I wish. Looks like I've got an arson problem. Two of my construction sites have gone up in flames in the last two weeks. The second one just last night. It appears I've got an enemy I didn't know I had."

Several long seconds passed. "You need me to come down there, see what I can sniff out?"

Gabe hated to ask his brother for help unless he really had to. "How 'bout you do what you can from your end? Fire department still hasn't confirmed this one's arson, but it's only a matter of time. I'm working on a list, anyone I can think of who might have a hard-on for me. So far, it isn't that long. Maybe you could take a look at it when I'm finished."

"Think back as far as you can. Just because this is happening now, doesn't mean it didn't start a long time ago. You never know what can set off a guy like this."

"Good point, I'll look deeper."

"When you get done, email it to me. I'll make some calls, dig up whatever info I can on the subjects. I'll let you know what I find out."

"Great, I'd appreciate that."

"One more thing…"

"Yeah, what's that?"

"Your condo building. Put a guard there, too. If you pissed someone off enough to burn up two buildings, he might be mad enough to fire one up with you in it."

Gabe felt a chill at the back of his neck. Obvious as it was, he hadn't thought of that. "I'll call Atlas as soon as I get off the phone."

"I'll talk to Trace, give him a heads-up. Call if you need me. And be careful, bro. Fire's a bad way to go." Dev hung up and Gabe flipped his phone closed.

For a minute, he leaned back in his chair and closed his eyes. Things had been good for so long. He hadn't felt this kick in the gut since the days when his mother got drunk and passed out on the worn-out sofa or the torn shag carpet in their living room. The days when Jackson had to use his after-school work money to buy them something to eat.

"You all right?" Becky asked.

"Just peachy," he said. "Thanks for asking."

Becky gave him a worried mother-hen look, which made him sit up straighter. He opened a drawer, pulled out the phone book and began flipping through the Yellow Pages. He was getting ready to dial the number for Atlas Security when the trailer door swung wide and Mattie and Angel stood in the doorway.

"I heard about the fire," Mattie said. "I'm really sorry, Gabe."

He rose from behind his desk. "Yeah, so am I."

"I know you must be busy. Do you have a minute to talk?"

Becky shoved back her chair and stood up. "I've got an errand to run, boss." She cast Mattie an appraising glance and headed for the door. "I'll be back in a few minutes."

Becky brushed past them, giving them some privacy, and clattered down the iron mesh stairs.

"Come on in," Gabe said to Mattie, thinking how good she looked with her hair pulled into a ponytail and freckles standing out on those high cheekbones. Fresh, somehow, and wholesome. And sexy as hell.

His blood stirred. After her note, he hadn't expected to see her again.

All it had taken was a four-alarm fire to get her to come back.

CHAPTER ELEVEN

Mattie stood nervously in the doorway of the trailer. Gabe was bigger and even more powerfully built than she remembered. Heat crept into her face as memories arose of the night she had spent in his bed, and something sensual loosened inside her she recognized as desire.

"We can sit down over here." Gabe pointed to a small round table in the corner with four plastic chairs.

"Angel came by to see me," Mattie explained as she sat down next to the teenage boy. "He saw the fire on TV. We looked for you earlier at the fire scene. Your foreman was there. He gave us this address and said we could find you here." She glanced away from Gabe, wishing she didn't want to reach out and touch him. When she looked back, she noticed Angel's hands were shaking.

Mattie's heart went out to him. She prayed Gabe would say the words the teenager needed to hear.

"So what's this about?" Gabe asked.

Mattie gave a faint nod to Angel and he straightened in his chair.

"I just came to tell you I didn't set the fire."

Gabe pinned him with a stare. "What makes you think I would assume you did?"

"I wasn't home last night. I borrowed my mother's

car and went over to spend the night with Enrique. His mother was visiting her sister in Tyler and I felt sorry for him being home alone."

"What did the two of you do last night?" Gabe asked.

"We went down to the video parlor for a while and then we went back to his house and watched TV. I don't have an alibi except for Enrique and I'm not sure the police will believe either of us a second time."

Angel looked miserable. And scared. Mattie prayed Gabe would believe him, that he would realize Angel hadn't had anything to do with either of the fires.

"The police know you didn't set the fire at the Towers, Angel. They traced the accelerant to someone else. Unless you have some kind of a grudge against me personally, I don't think they'll assume you're the person who set the fire last night."

The tension in Angel's shoulders seeped away. "You have been a friend to me and Enrique. I only wish there was a way I could help you find the man who burned down your buildings."

Gabe's faint smile held a trace of approval. "That's a job for the police. I wish you could help, but I'm afraid there isn't anything you can do."

"Actually, there is," Mattie said, speaking up for the first time. She turned her attention to Angel. "You can keep your eyes and ears open, listen to the gossip on the street. Maybe someone will know something, say something about the fires."

Gabe looked impressed. "That's a good idea. Maybe you'll hear something that might be useful. But don't try to play detective. This guy is obviously dangerous. I don't want you getting hurt."

"Gabe's right," Mattie added. "Just let us know if you hear anything."

The boy smiled, a flash of white in his broad, dark-skinned face. "I will, I promise."

Mattie pushed back her chair, preparing to leave. "Thanks for taking time to listen."

"I'll walk you to your car," Gabe said, and though she could have stopped him, she didn't.

When they reached her BMW, Angel made a point of climbing into the passenger seat and closing the door, giving them a moment of privacy.

Mattie wasn't sure whether or not to be grateful.

"So where are you headed from here?" Gabe asked.

"After I take Angel home, I'm going down to the center for a while."

"Any special reason or just your usual volunteer work?"

"I'm meeting a teenage girl named Lakeisha Brown. Her boyfriend used to beat her. It went on for months before she found the courage to dump him. I'm trying to help her. We sort of bonded, I guess you would say."

One of Gabe's dark eyebrows went up. "Why is that?"

Mattie hesitated only a moment. There was no reason not to tell him. At least some of it. "It's a dependency issue for some young girls. They think they can't live without these guys. I told her about my mother and how she had counted on my dad to take care of the family, but then he died. I told her how important it was for a woman to be independent, to learn not to count on a man. I told her she needed to learn to take care of herself."

"I see."

And from the look in those perceptive blue eyes, Mattie thought that maybe he saw far too much. That maybe he realized the hardship she and her mother had suffered was the reason she refused to get involved with him or any other man. That he represented too much of a threat to her independence.

And of course there was Mark's betrayal. But she didn't tell him that.

"There's a gallery opening in Deep Ellum tonight. The artist is very good, and the owners are among the people I mentioned before." He flicked a glance to where Angel sat in the car. "It might be a chance to set something up for Enrique."

Her shoulders tightened. He was asking for more than a date, and as much as she wanted to help Enrique, she wasn't ready to pursue a physical relationship with Gabe. Not when his lovemaking had such a powerful effect on her.

She started shaking her head. "I don't—"

"I could meet you there," he interjected smoothly. "You'd have your own car. You could leave whenever you wanted."

She bit her lip. She wanted to help Enrique. And she wanted to see Gabe again. Even if it was a dangerous thing to do.

"All right, I'll meet you there. What time?"

"The opening starts at seven-thirty."

"I'll be there at eight."

For an instant, hunger flared in those blue, blue eyes, then it was gone. "Great," he said, "I'll see you tonight." Gabe opened her car door and she remembered the night in the parking lot when he had kissed her. Not today.

Mattie shoved the key in the ignition, torn between relief and disappointment.

THE EVENING TURNED humid but the temperature remained pleasantly in the eighties. By the time Gabe arrived at the Zigman Gallery, the place was humming with people. In a cream-colored sport coat and dark brown slacks, he was dressed pretty much like the rest of the men at the opening, except for his brown ostrich cowboy boots.

The women, in an elegant array of expensive cocktail dresses, sipped from long-stemmed flutes of champagne. Gabe opted for a beer, which the bartender behind the portable bar poured into a chilled beer glass and handed over.

Gabe moved around the room, searching for Sal Zigman or his wife, Barbara. Instead, he ran into Suze Coster, a striking brunette he had met during the remodel of a luxury home in University Park, a woman who still phoned occasionally when she wanted a little intimate company.

"Well, cowboy, I see you're looking as good as ever." Suze's golden-brown eyes ran over him head to foot. "But then when haven't you?"

"Hello, Suze."

She was tall and willowy, with a generous bosom and thick dark brown hair that curled under around her shoulders. She was the daughter of a congressman, spoiled and used to having her way, and extremely inventive in bed.

She ran the tip of her finger over the lapel of his coat. "I didn't realize how much I'd missed you. Why don't

I call you later? Maybe we could get together after the opening."

He only shook his head. "Not tonight, Suze."

"No?" One of her dark eyebrows went up. She followed his gaze over the top of her head and turned to see what had captured his attention. Mattie Baker had just walked into the gallery.

"So...that must be your latest conquest. Or maybe she isn't—at least not yet—and that's what has you intrigued."

"Maybe," he said, but he couldn't pull his eyes away from Mattie, who was wearing an elegant but simple, strapless black cocktail dress, her fiery hair left loose around her shoulders.

There were no wild curls tonight and the dress wasn't terribly short. This wasn't Lena Sterling, and Gabe didn't expect her to give in to her sexual needs the way she had the night he'd taken her to bed.

Still, he was glad to see her. Way too glad, in fact. Which scared the hell out of him.

"Excuse me, Suze. Believe it or not, I have some business I need to take care of."

"Really?" She gave him a catty smile, reached up and patted his cheek. "I can tell by the bulge in your pants the kind of business you have in mind."

Gabe's jaw tightened but he managed to hold on to his temper. Besides, Suze was right. He'd been hard from the moment he'd seen Mattie walk through the door. He blew out a frustrated breath as he realized that even if Suze called and wanted to come over, he wouldn't let her. Gabe silently cursed. The woman he wanted in his bed was standing across the room and no other woman would do.

"Aren't you Matilda Baker? I'm Barbara Zigman. I saw your picture in this morning's paper."

Mattie tore her gaze from Gabe and the stunning brunette hanging on his every word, a woman he seemed to know far too well.

"It's Mattie, actually. Just plain Mattie. The paper got it wrong."

"Well, congratulations, Mattie." She extended a slender hand glittering with diamonds, a petite woman with short black hair spritzed into a spiky style, a pretty face and a very pale complexion.

Mattie shook her hand. "A pleasure meeting you, Barbara." She glanced at her surroundings. "Your gallery is impressive and so is the artist you're featuring."

"Thank you. His name is Michael Ames. His work is being received very well. His future looks extremely promising."

"I'm sure it will be."

"The article said you'd be receiving your award on Tuesday night?"

"That's right."

"What award is that?" Gabe asked as he strolled up to them, his gaze an intimate touch on her face. She suppressed a little tremor of awareness at the feel of him standing so near.

"She's the winner of this year's AIA award for best gallery design," Barbara said. "That's the reason the article caught my eye."

Mattie smiled. "Galleries and museums have sort of become my specialty. Though to tell you the truth, it's been more an accident than anything. One job just sort of morphed into the next." But she was very pleased to be getting the award. After work on Monday, there was going to be a small reception in her honor at the office. And Tuesday night, Aaron was going with her to receive her award.

"I'm sorry I missed the article," Gabe said. "I was a little busy this morning."

"Yes, I saw that on the news," Barbara said, a slight frown creasing her forehead. "I'm so sorry, Gabe. Does the fire department have any idea what might have started the blaze?"

"What or who," Gabe said darkly. "Unfortunately they don't know anything yet."

"They think it might have been arson?" Barbara asked, surprised.

"It's possible."

She shook her head, causing the light to bounce off her spiky black hair. "The way society has been going, it was probably some teenage boys whose parents let them run wild."

Mattie stiffened. "I don't think it's fair to jump to that conclusion."

Barbara's gaze took in her warlike posture and she flashed a repentant smile. "You're right. That wasn't fair at all. Just because my brothers were completely out of control doesn't mean all kids are that way. But whoever did it, I hope they catch them."

Mattie relaxed. She thought she could like a woman as forthright as Barbara Zigman.

"Speaking of teenagers," Gabe said. "There's a boy whose work I think you should see."

One of Barbara's fine black eyebrows went up. "Is that so?"

"Enrique Flores is a friend of Mattie's. He's the reason I asked her to come here tonight. The kid is completely amazing. He's painted an incredible mural three stories high on the side of an abandoned building. I'm hoping you and Sal might be willing to take a look at it sometime."

Barbara shifted her attention to Mattie. "What about you? Are you convinced of the artist's talent, as well?"

"Enrique's paintings are spectacular. I've never seen anything like them. In fact, I stopped by his house this afternoon and picked up a piece of his work. It's in the trunk of my car. I thought if you had any interest, I'd leave it here, let you take a look at it whenever you had a little extra time."

Barbara's dark eyes gleamed. "If you both think it's that good, I'd like to see it right now." She motioned one of her employees forward, a tall, rangy young man with shaggy brown hair.

"David, take Ms. Baker's keys and bring back the painting in the trunk of her car." She looked over at Mattie. "If that's all right with you?"

"That would be terrific," Mattie said, handing David her car keys.

In minutes, the young man returned to the gallery carrying part of an old wooden door. He eased through the boisterous crowd, into the back room where Barbara had set up an easel to view the work.

David struggled to center the heavy wooden panel on the easel.

"Enrique doesn't have money for canvas," Mattie explained. "He paints on whatever he can find."

Barbara made no reply. Her entire attention was focused on the painting. Wild splashes of color—fierce reds, neon yellows, rich deep greens depicted life on the street. But instead of the dismal overtones most artists thought necessary to capture the hardness of urban life, Enrique painted only the beauty.

There was a quiet joy in the faces Enrique painted that made the shabby clothes they wore and the dirt and papers in the gutters seem irrelevant. These were people who saw the positive side of life, people who found hope in the world instead of despair.

"It's stunning," Barbara said a little breathlessly. Spotting her husband through the open back room door, she began to wave at him madly.

"Sal! Sal, come in here a moment!" She turned back to Mattie and Gabe. "I don't want to take anything away from the wonderful artist we're showing, but I am so very glad you brought this to us."

Sal Zigman joined the group in front of the easel. Barbara introduced Mattie to Sal, a small, distinguished-looking man in an expensive Italian suit with the same black hair as his wife. Then Barbara stepped away from the painting so her husband could see.

Sal's eyes widened. For long moments, he just stared. Wordlessly, he turned openmouthed to his wife.

"Exactly!" she said triumphantly.

"Whose work is it?" he asked excitedly. "Is he here? I want to meet him. We need to see what else he's done."

Mattie's eyes stung with tears. "I can arrange for you to meet him. Enrique's only seventeen but he's done a lot of other paintings. I saw some of them at his house. Thank you so much for giving him this chance."

"If the rest of what he's painted is as good as this," Sal said, "the kid is going to be a star."

Gabe grinned. "Wait till you see his mural."

Mattie looked up and her heart squeezed. Gabe was willing to help a boy he barely knew, take time from his own problems—which at the moment were monumental—to help a boy who needed his help very badly.

More and more, she was attracted to Gabe and not just because he was amazing in bed. She was letting herself in for trouble, and yet she couldn't seem to do anything about it.

"Want to take a look around the gallery?" Gabe asked. "Michael Ames is very good."

What she wanted to do was to leave. What she wanted was for Gabe to take her straight to bed. As she stood beside him, she could feel the crackle of sexual energy sparking between them, feel the pulsing of desire. Mattie forced herself to ignore it.

"I'd love to see the gallery," she said, hoping the tremor in her voice wouldn't betray her. "Thank you for inviting me here. And for what you've done for Enrique."

He shrugged as if it were nothing. "The rest is up to him."

Mattie thought of the skinny boy with the incredible talent and a lump formed in her throat. Ignoring the warmth of Gabe's hand at her back, she let him guide her into the gallery. Gabe lifted a glass of champagne off a passing waiter's tray and handed it over and Mattie took a long, calming swallow, enough to relax her but not enough to weaken her resolve.

For tonight, at least, she was going home alone.

The only male in her bed would be Tigger, curled up in a furry ball at her feet.

Mattie looked up at Gabe's handsome profile and her heart lifted dangerously. Worry coursed through her at his magnetic appeal and the power he seemed to hold over her.

Clearly, she was making the right decision.

CHAPTER TWELVE

TUESDAY MORNING, GABE sat at his desk in the construction trailer in front of the Greenwood Apartments. Inside the chain-link fence surrounding the work site, the Atlas night security guard was making a shift change, a new guard taking his place. Other Atlas guards were posted at the Egyptian Theater, at the warehouse Gabe hadn't yet started to remodel, and at the building that housed his condo. He no longer owned Las Posas, where he lived, but he hadn't taken Dev's warning lightly.

His cell phone rang. Gabe dug it out of the pocket of his jeans and flipped it open. "Raines."

"Gabe, this is Thomas Daily. We had the arson dogs on the scene over the weekend. It was definitely arson."

Gabe's stomach tightened. "How does that work, with the dogs, I mean?"

"They're trained to accelerant detection—gasoline, lighter fluid, paint thinner, kerosene—that kind of thing. We know the fire started a little before three in the morning. That's when the 9-1-1 call was made. By then the trailers had done their job and the place went up like kindling."

"Trailers?"

"Starters. Something as simple as a matchbook, or it can be more complicated, like a cell phone detonating some kind of incendiary device."

Tension settled between his shoulders. "Any idea what the starter was in this case?"

"We think it was something fairly simple, but it looks like there was one on each floor."

"Same guy, you think?"

"So far there isn't a pattern. The first job was strictly amateur, a single point of origin. This one had multiple starting points. And the accelerant was gasoline. The job took more thought, more planning. Either it's a different guy or he's learning, studying technique."

Great. A guy who's putting himself through arson school. "You don't think whoever set the fires might have just been picking easy targets? Half-finished construction jobs would light up a lot faster than a completed building. They're easier to get in and out of and there's more flammable material lying around."

"We've considered it. We just don't have enough information to know for sure. Do you have your suspect list ready?"

"I've been working on it. I can fax it over to the number on your card."

"That'll work. We'll keep you posted."

"Thanks, Captain."

Both men hung up and Gabe released a breath. Becky wasn't at work today and he was grateful. He was tired of seeing that worried look on her face. The only woman he really wanted to see was Mattie. But if he called her, she might blow him off the way she had on Saturday night.

Besides, what he really needed to do was talk to some of the people on his list, figure out who might have some animosity toward him, some kind of personal agenda.

Gabe faxed his list to the arson department. Since he had already emailed the list to his brother, he set off to see Hank Munro, one of the men Becky had mentioned. Hank was a big, brawny guy who worked the crane at McKinney Court. Gabe had never had a problem with him—not one he knew about, at any rate. Still, if the man had some grievance against him, Gabe needed to know.

Late that morning, the fire department had given the okay to start removing the debris from the site. The walls were still standing, but they had suffered major structural damage. Everything would have to come down.

Hank was working the crane when Gabe got there. He motioned for the man to turn off the engine, then approached as Hank jumped down from the cab.

"What's up, boss?" Hank was in his forties, with close-cropped curly black hair and a silver earring in one ear.

"I was talking to Becky. She mentioned you might have a problem with the schedule."

Beneath the brim of his hard hat, Hank glanced down as if he were embarrassed. "I was out of line. My wife was getting a lot of crap from one of her coworkers at the office and I let it get to me."

"What was the problem?"

"Seems like her being black and being this guy's boss didn't sit well. I was tired. I let her troubles become mine. Becky set me straight."

"So you got no problems with me or the job?"

Hank shook his head. "Like I said, I was mostly just tired. I drew a couple of extra shifts and missed my kid's dance recital. My daughter was disappointed and I felt guilty. It had nothing to do with you or the job."

Gabe nodded. "All right. I'll let you get back to work."

Hank climbed back in the cab and prepared to crank the big diesel engine.

"Listen, I know this isn't what you signed on for," Gabe said, once more drawing his attention. "We're supposed to be in the building business, not demolition."

"I'm real sorry about the fires," Hank said. "Police got any idea who did it?"

"Not yet." Gabe glanced toward what was left of what was supposed to be McKinney Court. Four stories of smoke-blackened walls and broken windows, twisted metal beams and piles of water-soaked rubble inside. "Keep your eyes open, will you, Hank? If you notice anything out of the ordinary, let me know."

"You bet I will."

Gabe let the crane operator go back to work and headed for the Towers. Benny Jervis, the second man Becky had mentioned, worked on the crew as a general laborer. A rat-like little man with a grating personality, Benny was mostly an outsider with the men. But he was a very hard worker and that won him the crew's grudging respect.

"Hey! Benny!" Gabe waved toward the small man with the dark brown hair and thin, pointed nose. He was busy with a shovel, scraping mud off the walks and digging it away from the side of the building. Benny stopped working, set the shovel aside and began walking toward Gabe.

"Starting to look a lot better," Gabe said as Benny reached him.

"It's a helluva lot harder cleaning up a mess like this than it was to build it in the first place."

"I'm sure it is." Gabe watched the men working to finish clearing the last of the burned debris out of the Towers. "But it looks like you're making good progress."

"Real good. Sam says we should be able to start rebuilding by the end of next week."

"Listen, Benny, I was talking to Becky and she mentioned you seemed a little unhappy with the money you're making."

Benny shrugged his thin shoulders. He was short and wiry, but for a small man, he was strong. "I work hard. I know a couple of the guys on the crew are doing the same job I am and making more money."

Gabe studied him closely. "They were hired after you signed on. Market price goes up. Sometimes that happens."

Benny glanced away.

"I can see where that might piss you off. What I'm wondering is just how upset you really are?"

Benny frowned. "I don't get your meaning."

"Pissed enough to set a couple of fires?"

Benny's narrow face went pale. His small eyes bulged with shock. "You think I set this place on fire just to get a raise?"

Gabe couldn't misread Benny's horrified expression. "To tell you the truth, no I don't. But I have to check out every possibility."

The little man sagged with relief. "I didn't do it, boss. If I did, I'd just have to clean it up."

Gabe felt the pull of a smile. "Good point. Matter of fact, that's the second good point you've made. You're a hard worker, Benny. You deserve to make as much as anyone else. I'll talk to Becky. See what we can do about a pay increase."

Benny Jervis beamed. "Thanks, boss."

"And keep an eye out around here, will you? If you see anyone or anything that looks suspicious, give me a call."

"I'll keep watch," Benny said. "I see anything, I'll call." Heading back to work, he walked over and grabbed his shovel, started digging into the piles of mud.

Mentally, Gabe crossed off two of the names on his list. Which wasn't saying much, since he'd never actually believed the men in his crew had anything to do with the fires.

From the corner of his eye, he spotted Sam walking toward him.

"Hey, what's up?" Sam asked.

"Not much. Daily called. McKinney Court was definitely arson."

"Son of a bitch."

"Yeah."

"They have any idea who might have done it?"

"Not so far. I gave them a list of names—anyone I might have pissed off over the years. I sent the same list to Dev. He's checking it out."

"Your brother's a pro. If anyone can come up with something, he can."

"That's what I'm hoping."

Sam lifted his hard hat and blotted his forehead with the sleeve of his light blue work shirt. "Seen any more of Mattie?"

Gabe shook his head. "Not since she left me in the

parking lot of the Zigman Gallery last Saturday night. How about you?"

"Tracy never called. I guess she wasn't interested in anything more than what I could do for her in bed."

Gabe thought of the night he'd spent in bed with Mattie. "That's a problem I wouldn't mind having."

"It's different with Tracy."

"Yeah, I got that."

Sam looked back at the building. "I'm happy with the progress. I've started ordering what we need to get started again."

"Let's get some security cameras up and working. And I'll get a couple of guards posted. We don't want that SOB getting back inside and lighting the place up again."

"That's for sure."

The men parted company and Gabe headed off to check on his other projects.

In the back of his mind, he thought of calling Mattie, but in the end, he didn't.

WEDNESDAY ARRIVED. THOUGH Tracy did her best to persuade Mattie, she refused to go to Club Rio that night. There was a chance she would run into Gabe and if she did, she was afraid she would wind up in bed with him.

Thursday, Mattie jogged for an hour, then showered and dressed and went into the office. Earlier in the week, at the company reception celebrating her AIA award, she had received congratulations from everyone in the office.

Everyone except Mel Freeman.

She spotted him walking toward her as she was leaving the employee lounge and wished she could turn and go the opposite direction.

"I suppose I should extend my congratulations," Mel said with what was supposed to pass for a smile.

"Not if you don't mean it." She tried to walk past him, but Mel stepped in her way.

"I worked on that gallery design for two months before you got involved."

"Yes, you did. But the client didn't like the design you presented. He wanted something different and that's why Mr. Dewalt turned the assignment over to me."

"You used a lot of the work I did. I deserved to be included in that award."

"I used very little of what you did. And including you was not the way the committee saw it. Now if you'll excuse me…" She started past him, felt the tension in his body as she brushed against his shoulder.

"Just because you're a woman doesn't mean you get preferential treatment."

Mattie gritted her teeth. "I don't get preferential treatment. I do my job and because I'm good at it, I get rewarded. I'm sorry if you can't accept that." Ignoring the dark look on his face, she walked away.

When she reached her office, she closed the door behind her and for a moment she leaned against it. This thing with Mel was getting out of hand. But the fact remained, he was nothing more than a jealous coworker. It happened to people all the time. And she really didn't give a rip what Mel Freeman thought.

Forcing herself to relax and concentrate on what she needed to get done that day, Mattie headed for her desk. She was pulling out her black leather chair when a light knock sounded and Aaron opened the door.

Dressed in khaki slacks and a short-sleeved shirt, he wheeled himself into her office. "Hey, Mattie."

"Hey, Aaron."

He smiled. "If you've got a minute, I'd like your opinion on an idea I've got." He wheeled himself over to the design table and spread out a set of plans.

"This is the school we've been working on. What do you think about moving this wall—" he tapped the plans "—out a couple of feet? The kitchen in the cafeteria could have fourteen more feet of additional counter space with cabinets above and below. It's a small change at this point, but a major benefit to the school."

Mattie checked the engineering. The addition would not change the structural requirements. "This is a great idea, Aaron."

He grinned. "Thanks."

Mattie studied the drawing a little longer, then rolled it up and gave it back to him. "Put in the change. We'll have to get an approval, but I'm sure the client is really going to like it."

As Mattie started back to her desk, Aaron checked his watch. "It's twelve-fifteen. You want to grab some lunch?"

Mattie looked at the gold wristwatch she had bought herself as a reward for her promotion. "I think I'll pass. I've got a couple of things I need to do."

Aaron shoved his glasses up on his nose. "Okay, then, maybe I'll see you later."

Mattie just nodded and returned to her desk. As Aaron rolled out the door, she caught a glimpse of Emily walking toward him. Looping a strand of dark hair behind her ear, she bent down and said something that made him smile. Aaron flicked a last glance toward Mattie's office and left with Emily.

Mattie hoped they were going to lunch. It would be nice to see the two of them together. But so far Aaron hadn't shown the slightest interest in the pretty brunette. Mattie wondered if it would do any good to talk to him.

Reminding herself it was really none of her business, she seated herself behind her desk, reached over and picked up a file and heard the intercom buzz.

The receptionist's voice floated across the desk. "A woman named Rosa Ramirez is on the phone," Shirley said. "She sounds really upset."

"Put her through." Worry kicked up her heart rate. Angel's mother had never called the office. "What is it, Rosa?"

"It's Angel, Mattie. Someone beat him up. He is in the hospital. It's bad, Mattie." She started crying. "They cannot wake him up."

Mattie's heart clenched. "Where is he?"

"He is at Baylor."

"I'll be right there." She hung up the phone with a shaky hand, grabbed her purse and slung it over her shoulder. Her stomach was squeezing. Angel was hurt. From what Rosa said, it sounded serious.

Mattie hurried out of her office, pausing only a moment to tell Shirley where she was going and how to handle her calls.

Silently, she prayed that the boy she'd grown so fond of was going to be all right.

CHAPTER THIRTEEN

THE HUMID HEAT of September spread over the city. The sky was streaked with thin, pale clouds and the air felt dense and heavy. Perspiration settled between Gabe's shoulder blades as he crossed the sidewalk to the glass doors leading into the lobby of Baylor Hospital.

An hour ago, he had gotten a call from Captain Daily.

"I have some news you might be interested in," Daily had said. "Since you spoke to the police on behalf of the Ramirez boy, I thought you might want to know he's in Intensive Care over at Baylor Hospital. Looks like he was assaulted. Someone found him unconscious in an alley and called the police."

Gabe felt a squeezing in his chest. He thought of the boy who was doing his best to climb out of the ghetto he had been born into. He thought of Mattie and knew how upset she must be. "Any idea what happened?"

"Police don't know. So far, he hasn't regained consciousness."

"I appreciate the call, Captain." Gabe hung up and immediately left for the hospital. As far as he could tell and from what Mattie had said, Angel was a really good kid. No gang involvement. Liked by his peers. He couldn't imagine why anyone would want to hurt him.

Gabe reached the heavy glass doors to the hospital and pulled them open, felt the shock of cold as he stepped into the air-conditioned lobby. He crossed to the information desk.

"I'm looking for a patient. His name is Angel Ramirez."

An older, gray-haired woman sat behind the counter. She typed the name into her computer.

"You'll find him in Intensive Care. Unless you're immediate family you can't go in, but there's a waiting room down the hall. Just go through those doors, follow the arrows to the elevator and get off on the third floor."

"Thanks."

Gabe stepped away from the counter and made his way down the hall, passing patients in wheelchairs and a group of nurses in scrubs. The smell of antiseptic hit him with an acrid punch, making his mind spin.

Memories struck. The night when he was ten years old and his mother overdosed on pain pills and wound up in the Wind Canyon Hospital. He remembered how scared he and Dev had been when they went to see her and how Jackson had promised she was going to be all right.

Usually, antiseptic reminded him of his visits to fellow marines he had gone to see in the hospital after their return from Afghanistan. He was out of the service by then but he'd made some damn good friends in the corps. Some of them he'd stayed in touch with over the years, and a couple of guys lived right here in Dallas.

Exhaling a slow, deep breath, Gabe shook off the unpleasant memories, got onto the elevator and pushed Three.

The elevator stopped on the second floor, then opened again on the third and the woman beside him walked out. Gabe followed her until she turned down another corridor and he continued going straight, following the signs directing him to the ICU.

As he approached the nurse's station, an uneasy feeling settled over him, an instinct he'd developed in the marines that warned him when something was wrong. Two fires and now someone he knew had been assaulted and put in the hospital. The warning voice was telling him this wasn't just another coincidence.

A pair of nurses walked past, their soft-soled shoes squeaking on the spotless floors.

"I'd like some information on one of your patients, a boy named Angel Ramirez."

The nurse behind the counter, young, blonde and pretty, looked up at him with concern.

"Are you family?" she asked.

"No, just a friend."

She stared down at the chart on her desk. "Angel has suffered a severe trauma to the head. His skull is fractured in two places. He has yet to regain consciousness. If you want to see his family, they're down the hall in the waiting room."

"Thank you."

Gabe strode off in that direction. When he opened the door and surveyed the cluster of vinyl chairs and people with worried faces, Mattie saw him and shot to her feet.

"Gabe."

He walked over and reached out to her. Instead of moving away as he thought she might, she stepped straight into his arms.

He felt her tremble and tightened his hold.

"How did you hear?" she asked softly.

"Captain Daily called. He told me Angel was assaulted. He thought I'd want to know."

For an instant, she rested her cheek against his shoulder. Then she stepped away. "Thank you for coming. I know Angel would be pleased." She turned to a plump Hispanic woman wearing a flowered housedress. "Rosa, this is Mr. Raines. I'm sure Angel mentioned him. Gabe, this is Angel's mother."

"Mrs. Ramirez," he said. "I'm sorry this has happened to your son."

She nodded, moving several layers of flesh beneath her chin and the shiny black braid hanging down her back. "My son has told me all about you. How you helped him and also Enrique."

"Do you know what happened?" Gabe asked her.

"Only that someone came up and hit him from behind. The police say a baseball bat or something like that. They say…they say his skull is cracked. There is swelling and…" She covered her mouth with a trembling hand and started to cry.

"It's going to be all right," Mattie said, easing the heavyset woman into her arms. "This is a very good hospital."

One of the best, Gabe thought. And by law they would have to help the boy even though he probably had no medical insurance. But as soon as the hospital thought he had recovered enough, he would be gone.

Assuming he *did* recover.

MATTIE SETTLED ROSA back in her chair, filled a small paper cup with water from the cooler and brought it over.

"Thank you, Mattie."

Determined to hide her worry, Mattie forced a smile. When she glanced at Gabe, still trying to get over her surprise at seeing him there, he tipped his head toward the waiting room door, and she nodded.

"How's he doing?" Gabe asked as soon as they were out in the hall.

"He's in critical condition." Her voice wobbled. "They don't know if he's going to make it."

Gabe's breath came out soft and slow. "I'm sorry, Mattie."

"We're all praying and holding positive thoughts."

"Do they have any idea what happened?"

She turned her gaze toward the glass doors leading into the ICU. "The police don't know much. A cook at the A-1 Deli found him lying in the alley behind the kitchen. The doctors don't know how long he was lying there before he was discovered."

"Where did this happen?"

"About a block and a half from the center."

Gabe shook his head. "From everything you've told me and what I've seen, I can't imagine anyone wanting to hurt the boy."

Mattie started trembling. She bit down on her lip to keep her teeth from chattering. Gabe eased her back into his arms.

"Angel's going to be all right," he said softly. "That's what we have to believe."

She told herself to push him away, that she had to be strong for Angel and Rosa, but it felt so good, just this once, to have someone be strong for *her*.

"How long before the doctors know anything?" Gabe asked, his arms still around her.

Mattie released a breath and forced herself to move out of his embrace. "The next twenty-four hours are crucial. After that, it may take weeks, even months before he fully recovers."

There was an unspoken *if* and both of them knew it.

"I'd like to see him. I'm not sure they'll let me in, but I'd like to give it a try."

She took his hand and led him toward the doors, shoved one of them open and led him inside. Better to act first and apologize later than to wait and get stuck with a no.

The white-walled room was lined with rows of beds separated by movable curtains. The linoleum floors were spotlessly clean. She could feel Gabe's tension mounting as they approached where Angel lay beneath a thin white blanket, his head swathed in bandages. A plastic tube came out of his mouth and there were IVs in both of his arms. A monitor beeped and sucked as it measured each breath, and another gauged the beating of his heart.

Gabe stood tensely beside her. "Angel didn't deserve this." The boy's eyes were black and blue, his face so badly swollen she could hardly recognize him as the smiling boy she knew.

A nurse walked up just then, thirtyish and sandy-haired. Her name tag read *Molly*. "I'm sorry, unless you're family, you can't be in here." She looked down at the chart she carried. "Oh, I'm sorry. Mrs. Ramirez told me to expect Angel's sister."

Mattie nodded at the small white lie. "That's right."

The nurse smiled up at Gabe. "And this must be your husband."

A corner of Gabe's mouth lifted, and Mattie managed to force a smile. "Why, yes, it is."

"It's all right, then, but you can only stay a couple of minutes."

"Of course." The nurse walked away and Mattie resisted an urge to look up at Gabe, catch the look of amusement she expected to see on his face.

Instead she looked down at Angel. She wanted to reach for his hand, but she didn't want to do anything that might hurt him. Her heart squeezed at the sight of the limp form lying on the bed, this boy who was Angel but wasn't Angel at all.

They stood there a few minutes more, then Gabe rested a hand at her waist and guided her out of the room. In the hallway, Mattie wiped tears from her cheeks and took a shaky breath.

She thought of Angel, lying there unconscious, hovering between life and death, and wrapped her arms protectively around herself. She couldn't help thinking how much better it felt when the arms had belonged to Gabe.

"Angel is young and strong," he said gently. "And the doctors here are good. They'll do their best for him." He looked over her head and she followed his gaze down the hall to a ponytailed teenager in worn blue jeans, holey sneakers and a T-shirt stained with splashes of bright-colored paint.

Enrique's long, thin legs ate up the distance between them. "Mrs. Ramirez called my mother," he said when he reached them. "Is Angel going to be all right?"

Mattie moistened her lips. "We don't know yet, Enrique. I'm sorry."

The boy stared down at his dirty, frayed shoes.

"It looks like Angel was attacked," Gabe said gently. "Do you have any idea who might have done it?"

Enrique shook his head. A faint sheen glistened in his black eyes. "My mother said it happened down by the center."

"That's right."

"All I know is Angel's been hanging around downtown, asking a lot of questions. He thought someone might have seen somebody near the Towers the night of the fire. Or maybe there had been some rumbling, something about who might have set the blaze."

Mattie's heart started pounding. "You don't…don't think this happened because he was trying to dig up information?"

Enrique shrugged his thin shoulders. He turned to Gabe. "He said we owed you. He said he wanted to help you the way you helped us."

Gabe's jaw hardened and tears flooded Mattie's eyes. "This is my fault," she said. "I'm the one who told him he could help. I got him involved in this. If I hadn't said anything—"

"This isn't your fault," Gabe said firmly. "Whoever attacked Angel is the person responsible."

Mattie swallowed and glanced away. No matter what Gabe said, she was partly to blame.

Enrique's dark eyes followed a nurse rushing through the ICU doors. When he looked back, Mattie could read his fear for his friend.

"So do you think the guy who set the fire was the one who beat up Angel?" he asked, cutting to the heart of the matter.

"I think there's a chance," Gabe said. "He could have just been in the wrong place at the wrong time, but if he's been digging around asking questions, I think there's a very good chance the assault might be related to the fires."

"Oh, God." Mattie turned away. Pulling a tissue from her purse, she dabbed at her eyes. Angel was such a sweet boy. And with his father gone, his family needed him so badly.

She drew in a shaky breath and straightened her spine. "Whoever did this… I'm not letting him get away with it. I'm going to find out who attacked Angel and make sure he pays."

Gabe reached out and gently caught her shoulders. "Listen to me, Mattie. There's a good chance he's the guy who set those fires. The guy is dangerous. I don't want you getting hurt, too."

Mattie made no reply. She was older than Angel, and through the years, she had learned to be cautious. And she had always been smart. She would figure out a way to find the man who had done this to an innocent teenage boy.

"I mean it, Mattie," Gabe said, his hold gentle but firm. "You need to let the police handle this."

Picking up on the tension between them, Enrique nervously cleared his throat. "I'm going to see Mrs. Ramirez," he said, easing past them as they stood there glaring at each other.

Mattie narrowed her gaze at Gabe. "You're telling me to let the police handle it? I'm sure the police will do their best, but they have a thousand cases to work on. Am I supposed to believe that's what you're going to do?"

He straightened to his full height. "I'm a man, not a boy. This guy comes at me, he's going to get a whole lot more than he bargained for."

Mattie's gaze ran over the powerful chest encased in the formfitting T-shirt, the biceps bulging with muscle. Gabe was an ex-marine. He could handle a creep like the one who'd assaulted Angel.

"Fine, then you can help me. I'm finding this guy. You can help me or I'll do it on my own."

"Mattie."

"I mean it, Gabe."

For several long moments, he said nothing. She could read his frustration in the hard set of his jaw. And his certainty that she meant what she said.

"All right, but we do this together. No going off on your own. No knocking on doors without letting me know where you are, no late nights out by yourself."

"Fair enough. When do we start?"

He drilled her with those blue, blue eyes. "How's this afternoon suit you?"

"Perfect." And for the first time since this had happened, she felt a sense of purpose instead of worry and guilt and frustration. "I'll meet you at your construction trailer in an hour."

WITH ALL THE pounding and scraping going on, and the deafening roar of saws, Sam didn't hear the first few rings of his cell phone.

Unclipping the phone from his belt, he walked away from the noise and hustle of the Towers cleanup project, flipped the lid open and pressed the phone against his ear.

"McBride."

"Hi, Sam. This is Tracy Spencer."

Sam felt a warm stirring. "Hello, Tracy. I kind of gave up on hearing from you."

"I've…um…been busy. Is your invitation still open? For dinner, I mean?"

He pressed the phone a little closer to his ear. "It's open."

"So...um...what night would be good for you?"

A smile tugged at the corners of his mouth. It was obvious the lady wasn't used to phoning men up and asking them out on a date.

"I'm busy tonight," he said, though he wasn't doing a damn thing. "How about tomorrow?"

"Tomorrow would be good. What time?"

"How about seven? That'll give us time to get to the restaurant and have a drink before we eat."

"All right. Where do you want to go?"

He ran over his options. A girl like Tracy was probably used to expensive, high-class restaurants. Not this time. "There's a little Italian place down on Lamar. *Bella Sera*. A friend of mine owns it. Have you been there?"

"No, but I'm willing to give it a try."

"Great, I'll pick you up at seven." Tracy said good-bye and Sam hung up the phone. It took him a minute to realize his lips were still curved. Tracy Spencer had called him. She wanted to get to know him. He didn't understand why that seemed so important. Most guys would be happy to take a gorgeous blonde like Tracy straight to bed, even if it was just for a night.

But for weeks, Sam had been watching her at the club. There was something sad and sweet about Tracy, something vulnerable beneath all that bravado. There was something more to her than just sex and goodbye, and he wanted to know what it was.

The bad news was he wouldn't be getting laid tomorrow night. He intended to make that clear right up front. He had a hunch Tracy would act differently if she didn't have to live up to any kind of sexual expectations.

Even if they were her own.

CHAPTER FOURTEEN

A MOIST, HOT, late-afternoon wind had come up outside the trailer, whirling leaves and papers around and whipping the branches on the trees. Gabe was sitting behind his desk in the construction trailer, going over some of the insurance paperwork for the fire at McKinney Court, when his cell phone began to ring.

He recognized the caller ID.

"Hey, Jackson," Gabe said. "Good to hear from you. How's that beautiful new wife of yours?"

Jackson's soft chuckle came over the line. "As sassy as ever."

"I'll bet she is."

Jackson and Sarah Allen, the woman he had recently married, had first met in high school. Jackson had had a serious crush on her, but Sarah had rejected him in front of half the school, humiliating him in the very worst way. It wasn't until she found herself in desperate trouble that she and Jackson had been able to overcome their past and work things out.

"Dev called," Jackson said. "He filled me in on the fires. You should have let me know you were having trouble."

"I figured you'd find out soon enough. Besides, there's nothing you can do."

"Dev's been working on that list you sent him. He

asked me if there was anyone else I could think of who might have it in for you."

"And?"

"You remember that guy you went head-to-head with when the two of you were in the marines at Camp Lejeune?"

"Clayton Sanders?"

"That's him. As I recall, you two went after the same woman. Seems to me, you ended up with her."

"That's right. Rachael Hayward. We dated for a while before I left the corps. What about it? That was a long time ago."

"Maybe not so long to Sanders."

"How's that?"

"After I gave Dev the name, I got to thinking about it. I decided to do a little checking on the internet."

Gabe chuckled. Jackson was a Google whiz. "What did you find out?"

"After you left the service, Sanders re-upped. He went full-bore, Force Recon, and they shipped him off to Afghanistan. When he came back to North Carolina, he and Rachael started dating. A year later they got married."

"How the hell did you find all that out?"

"Newspaper articles here and there. I found their marriage license on the Net. I also found out they got divorced about three months ago."

"So? I still don't get it."

"Here's what makes it interesting. Rachael Sanders's latest address is listed as 5517 Dublin Street, Dallas, Texas. Your old flame is back in town, buddy. I'm thinking maybe Sanders thinks she's there because of you."

Gabe couldn't quite grasp the notion. And yet Rachael had arrived not long before the fires had started. "I haven't talked to Rachael in years."

"Still, it's worth looking into."

"You bet it is." As much as he hated to think Clay Sanders would carry an old grudge to the point of burning down buildings, Clay had always been a hothead. Back in the day, he'd been crazy in love with Rachael. At the time, she had considered him only a friend. Gabe had been the man she wanted and for a while their affair had been hot and heavy. Clay and Gabe had brawled over the lady more than once.

Now she had rejected Clay a second time and recently moved to Dallas. Jackson, as usual, was right. It was worth looking into. "I'll get right on it. Thanks for the heads-up, brother. If you think of anything else—"

"Don't worry, I'll let you know. Take care of yourself, Gabe."

"I'll do my best." Gabe closed the phone. It was probably nothing. Rachael hadn't been part of his life in years. Still, if she'd moved to Dallas and Clay was still as hot-tempered as he used to be...

It was a possibility he couldn't ignore.

"Gabe?"

His head came up at the sound of his name being called from the doorway of the trailer.

"What's going on?" Mattie asked. "You look like you're a thousand miles away."

She stood there outlined by the sun and he felt the same kick in the gut he'd felt at the hospital when she'd let him hold her while she cried on his shoulder. "Sorry, I didn't hear you on the stairs. Come on in."

Dressed in jeans and a sleeveless orange cotton top, she walked into the trailer, her hair windblown as she rarely allowed, a light sheen of perspiration on the scattering of freckles on her cheeks and the swell of her breasts above her scoop-necked top. For an instant, Gabe just sat there soaking up the sight of her.

Mattie walked over to his desk, which was stacked with files and dominated by the computer in front of his chair.

Gabe collected his wits and rose from his chair. "That was my brother, Jackson. I told you a little about him and my younger brother, Devlin, the night we went to dinner."

They'd talked *that* night.

The night they'd spent in bed, he hadn't been thinking about his brothers. He hadn't been thinking of anything but being inside her.

He warned himself not to go in that direction but it was too late. His body stirred and his pulse quickened. He could feel the blood pumping into his groin.

Gabe forced himself to concentrate on the reason Mattie was there.

"Any change in Angel's condition?" he asked as he led her over to the table and both of them sat down.

"He's still the same."

He nodded, wishing the news was better. "Dev called Jackson about the fires and Jackson called me with a lead. Dev's working on the list I gave him, anyone who might have a grudge against me."

"He's a private investigator, right?"

"Mostly retired, so he claims. He also owns a security company."

"And he's investigating the names you gave him?"

"That's right, but to tell you the truth, I can't believe

I've done anything to anyone to warrant this kind of retaliation."

"So what was the lead your brother gave you?"

Gabe's shoulders tightened. He didn't want to discuss his old girlfriend with Mattie. "Just an old buddy from my days in the corps."

"What happened?"

"It's a long story." Gabe rose from his chair. "Why don't I tell you about it on our way over to talk to Pete Dare?"

"Who's he?"

"Concrete guy I fired. I doubt it'll come to much, but I don't want to overlook any possibility."

"You're right. We have to start somewhere. Your enemies are as good a place as any."

Gabe sighed. "I didn't think I had that many, but I'm beginning to wonder if I was wrong."

Gabe held the door while Mattie walked past. He got a whiff of her soft perfume and began to go hard. He forced down his lust and continued down the stairs.

"I thought we might also talk to the cook who found Angel," Mattie said, "see if the guy might have seen him in the area, seen who he was talking to."

"Good idea."

The cab of Gabe's pickup was hot and steamy when he opened the door to help Mattie climb in. He forced himself not to reach for her, bend his head and kiss her. Wondered what she would do if he did. It had been too long since he'd had her. He hadn't stopped wanting her. He didn't think he was going to anytime soon.

"You shouldn't be getting involved in this, Mattie," he said. "This kind of business can be dangerous."

"We're only asking questions."

"That's all Angel was doing," he reminded her.

She looked him straight in the face. "Angel didn't have you there to protect him."

His worry expanded. Then again, at least in this she believed in him. Trusted him. He told himself that after today, Mattie would give up the notion of trying to help him. Her life was busy and complicated, her job all-important.

But part of him wanted this time with her, wanted a chance to see where his fierce attraction might lead.

In the meantime, if the police didn't catch the arsonist who seemed to be targeting him, Gabe intended to find the bastard himself.

MATTIE WALKED NEXT to Gabe as they approached the construction site where Pete Dare was working. A concrete truck with DARE CEMENT on the side churned away in front of the lot, just a few feet from the road.

"How'd you know where to find him?" Mattie asked, though it was clear Gabe knew just about everyone in the construction business.

"I wasn't completely sure Pete would be here, but he does a lot of work for Gleason Construction. I knew they were building a set of apartments over here."

They walked toward the truck, Mattie hurrying to keep up with Gabe's long strides. He slowed when he realized she was almost running.

"Good thing I keep in shape," she said with the hint of a smile.

"Sorry." His gaze found hers, caught and held. There was so much heat in his incredible blue eyes, her stomach contracted. Memories of their lovemaking rushed into her head, the deep saturating kisses, the feel of him inside her.

Mattie jerked her gaze away but it was too late.

"I want you, Mattie." His words came out gruffly. "I haven't stopped thinking about making love to you since the night we spent together."

Mattie just stood there. She wanted that, too. More than anything she could remember. But the powerful desire she felt for Gabe was frightening.

"Give me some time, Gabe. Let me think about it."

"Maybe that's the problem. Maybe you think too much."

Maybe she did. Because her body was aching for him to touch her. If she listened to her needs instead of the alarm screaming through her head, she would welcome him into her bed.

They reached the cement truck and Pete Dare walked toward them. Mattie was grateful for the distraction.

"What are you doing here?" Pete practically snarled. "What do you want, Raines?" Dressed in dirty jeans and a work-stained T-shirt, he was a lean, sandy-haired man in his thirties.

"I want to know where you were the night of the fire at the Dallas Towers."

Pete's eyes widened, erasing the little wrinkles at the corners. "You're kidding me, right? You think I had something to do with the fire?"

"Where were you?"

Pete's jaw tightened. "Home in bed with my wife. I go to work early, remember?"

"How about last Friday when McKinney Court burned down?"

Pete took an unconscious step backward, some of his

bravado fading. "For chrissake, Gabe. I'm the one who screwed up, okay? I should have abided by the contract we made instead of trying to save a little money. You were right. I was wrong. I learned my lesson. I may not like what you did, but I hardly hold you responsible."

He seemed sincere. Mattie thought Gabe believed him.

"You got any idea who might be interested in some kind of payback for something I might have done?"

Pete started shaking his head. "I haven't heard anyone talking. I can't think of anyone who'd do something that drastic."

"The cops may talk to you. If they do, tell them what you just told me."

Pete nodded.

Mattie let Gabe lead her back to the pickup and help her climb inside. She was getting used to his attentiveness. It didn't seem overbearing, just gentlemanly.

Her lips twitched. Remembering Gabe in the back room of Club Rio, pulling up her dress, cupping her bottom and pressing her against his heavy erection, it was hard to consider him a gentleman.

"Whatever you're thinking, it's turning me on."

Mattie blushed.

"Let me make you dinner tonight. Believe it or not, I'm a fairly decent cook."

She wasn't all that surprised. Gabriel Raines seemed to be pretty good at anything he set his mind to.

"I'm planning to spend the evening with Rosa at the hospital."

"How about tomorrow, then? We'll go see Angel first. But sooner or later you have to eat. You might as well let me fix you dinner."

She shook her head. "I promised I'd have dinner with a friend. I can't disappoint him again." She and Aaron planned to catch up. They were going to Taj, Aaron's favorite restaurant.

Gabe was frowning. "You've got a date?" he asked darkly.

"I told you he's just a friend. We work together at the office."

"In that case, we'll make it Saturday."

His hard look dared her to refuse. She knew she should. Her mind was screaming again. "Um…maybe that would work."

His gaze ran over her, swift and hot. "I'll take that as a yes."

Anticipation settled low and warm in her belly. She worked to compose herself. "I know where that deli is, the place where Angel was found. Let's go talk to the cook."

Gabe's mouth curved sensuously, but he just nodded.

THE COOK, ROBBIE CARR, a fat, ruddy-skinned man with a ready smile and kindly eyes, didn't know a darned thing. He'd never seen Angel before he found him in the alley. He had no idea who might have attacked him.

"The cops was already here," Robbie said. "I told them I didn't see nothing. I wish I had."

"Are you sure there isn't something?" Mattie asked, anxious for anything that might help. "Some small detail that maybe you didn't think was important at the time?"

Robbie scratched his head. "Now that you mention it, the kid, Angel, he mighta been here once before. Looked like him, but I can't say for sure. He stopped a couple of guys on the street. Looked like he was askin' them something. Like I said, I ain't real sure."

It wasn't much, but it reinforced their theory that Angel had been asking questions the arsonist didn't want answered. "Thank you, Robbie," Mattie said.

"I hope you find the guy."

Mattie just nodded.

"We need to canvas the neighborhood," Gabe said as they walked away, "see if we can find someone Angel might have talked to." He glanced down at his heavy wristwatch. "Unfortunately, it's too late to start this afternoon."

"You're right. Besides, I need to get back to the hospital, check on Rosa and Angel."

Mattie left Gabe's trailer and drove straight to Baylor Hospital. She planned to stay a couple of hours so that Rosa and the kids could get something to eat. According to the doctors, Angel's condition was stable, at least for the present.

"It's still touch and go," a thin, dark-haired doctor named Burton said. "We'll just have to wait and see."

Mattie nodded, her mouth feeling dry. When Rosa returned, the doctor convinced her and Mattie to go home and get some rest then come back in the morning. It had been a long day. Exhausted and worried, both women eventually agreed.

Tigger was impatiently waiting when she arrived home, meowing and looking up at her as if she had abandoned him.

"Hello, pretty baby." She knelt and scooped him into her arms, stroked his fur as she carried him into the kitchen and set him down in front of his food bowl.

"You finished your crunchies, didn't you? Well, how about a nice can of tuna?"

Tigger meowed.

"Good boy." As soon as the cat had settled in to eat, she went into the bedroom to change into baggy shorts and a T-shirt and kick off her shoes. She was on her way back to the living room to turn on the TV when Tracy arrived at the door.

Breezing through the living room, blond hair flying, she headed straight for the kitchen.

"I brought Chinese. I figured you probably hadn't eaten yet."

Mattie smiled. "Believe it or not, I'd forgotten all about it." But now that she smelled the delicious aromas of chop suey, almond vegetables, rice and fried shrimp, she discovered she was starving.

While Tracy opened the cartons and pulled out a bottle of sake, Mattie set the table in the kitchen. Tracy poured the sake into the smallest glasses she could find, set them next to the plates and both of them sat down and dug in.

"So how's Angel?" Tracy asked, forking in a load of crisply cooked vegetables.

"He's stable at the moment. They'll know more in the morning."

"Poor kid."

"Rosa's beside herself. I'm making arrangements to take vacation time next week so I can be available if she needs me." And keep trying to find the man who assaulted her son. "I've got plenty of days accumulated since I haven't taken any time off since I started working at the firm."

"You're a good friend, Mattie."

Mattie took a sip of sake, enjoyed the interesting nutty taste and the warm relaxing sensation. "So what's the occasion for the unexpected visit?" Picking up a shrimp, she dipped it into some hot mustard sauce.

"The occasion is, I called Sam McBride."

Mattie's head shot up. "You're kidding. What did he say?"

Tracy grinned. "We're going out to dinner tomorrow night."

"Is that so?"

"Yeah. I figured if I took the leap, you should, too. I came by to convince you to call Gabe."

Mattie toyed with her food. "Actually, I saw Gabe today at the hospital. He thinks the attack on Angel had something to do with the fires."

Tracy's eyes widened. "How does he figure that?"

"Apparently Angel had been sniffing around, asking a lot of questions about who might have set them. Gabe thinks someone wanted him to stop."

"Wow, that's scary!"

"I know."

Tracy heaped another spoonful of chop suey onto her plate. "So what else happened? Between you and Gabe, I mean?"

"He asked me to come over for supper on Saturday night."

Tracy's fork paused halfway to her lips. "You said yes, right?"

"Sort of."

Tracy squealed.

"I can still back out," Mattie said. "Maybe I should."

"Don't be ridiculous. The man is a total hunk. No

one needs to get laid more than you do and besides, if it doesn't work out, you can always dump him."

Mattie swallowed the bite she had taken and laughed. "Well, there is that, I guess." But she didn't think it would be that easy to end an affair with Gabe.

She wasn't sure she would want to. "He's trying to figure out who set the fires. After what happened to Angel, I told him I wanted to help him."

Tracy sat back in her chair. "I don't know, Mattie. If Gabe's right and Angel *was* attacked for asking questions, getting involved could be dangerous."

"*I'm* the one who got Angel involved. I have to do this, Tracy. I have to make sure the man who attacked him gets caught."

Tracy sipped her sake. "If the police can't find him, what makes you think you can?"

"The police have dozens of cases to work. I'm taking time off. I'm making this a priority."

Tracy looked uncertain. "I don't know, Mattie."

"Gabe's an ex-marine. I sure I'll be safe enough as long as I'm with him."

A sly smile curved Tracy's lips. "Maybe you're right. You should be safe enough. As long as you and Gabe stick together."

Mattie laughed, not fooled for a moment. Then her laughter slowly faded. For the first time, she realized how much time she would be spending with Gabe.

Suddenly, trying to help seemed like the dumbest idea she'd ever had.

CHAPTER FIFTEEN

GABE HAD TROUBLE SLEEPING. Between erotic dreams of Mattie and nightmares of flames roaring into the sky, he finally gave up at four o'clock, dressed in his gym clothes and headed for the Las Posas fitness center on the second floor of the building.

He worked out for over an hour, lifting weights and moving from machine to machine until he was drenched in sweat. He bench-pressed his usual two-hundred-seventy pounds, his biceps straining as he reached the end of his workout.

Relaxed at last, he grabbed his towel off the hook, draped it over his shoulders and headed back down to his condo. Every other day, he jogged. He liked to stay in shape and he made it a priority. Today, he had hoped that working out would curb a little of his desire for Mattie.

So far that hadn't worked.

With a sigh, Gabe finished his shower, pulled on jeans and a T-shirt and headed for his truck. With Mattie sitting next to him all afternoon, it was going to be a hellish day. Wanting her and knowing he would have to wait was a bad idea of fun.

But tomorrow night he intended to have her and one thing he knew.

Mattie Baker was worth the wait.

AFTER HER FRIDAY morning run, Mattie spent several hours at the office, making arrangements to leave at noon and take the next week off. Besides being able to visit Angel at the hospital, she planned to use the time to find the man who had committed the brutal assault on the boy.

A little after noon, she drove over to the Family Recovery Center. She had no regular hours but they were used to her dropping by to see if there was anything they needed her to do.

"For once, everything is running smoothly," said receptionist Sophie Dominquez, a thirty-year-old Hispanic with a social science degree.

"I may be a little hard to find next week. If you need me, call me on my cell phone."

"All right. But what you're doing for Rosa Ramirez and her son is more than enough."

Mattie just nodded. A memory arose of Angel lying in the ICU, a mass of cuts and bruises, his skin so pale she barely recognized him. She swallowed past the lump in her throat, knowing there was nothing she could do and planning to stop by the hospital later to see him.

From the center, she drove to the Zigman Gallery, another loose end she needed to tie up. Enrique and some of his friends had dropped off a carload of paintings for the owners to look at. Mattie wanted to find out if they liked Enrique's work.

Barbara Zigman, looking elegant yet trendy with her spiky black hair and wearing a short white skirt, black-and-white flowered top, and long strands of heavy black beads, greeted her as she walked into the gallery.

"Mattie! It's good to see you."

"I hope you don't mind my dropping by. I thought

maybe you might have had time to look at some of Enrique's paintings."

"I've been remiss in not calling. Sal and I have just been swamped lately. But we looked at Enrique's work and it's wonderful. We're thrilled you brought him to us."

Mattie smiled with relief. She had hoped this would be the gallery owners' reaction but she couldn't be sure.

"I'll tell him to come by and talk to you," Mattie said.

"I don't suppose he has a cell phone. If he does, I'd like to have his number."

"I…um…don't have it with me." Since he didn't own a phone and his family certainly couldn't afford to buy him one. "I'll tell him you want him to call you." And figure a way to get him the phone he needed.

"So what happens now?" Mattie asked as they strolled through the gallery, Barbara pointing out a new piece of work here and there.

"Once Enrique's signed an exclusivity contract with us, we'll want to have a show." Barbara smiled. "I think it'll be a great success."

Mattie returned the smile. "That's wonderful."

They talked a while longer. Mattie promised to have Enrique come by the gallery and made a mental note to see if Sid Weiss would take a look at the contract before the boy signed it.

Finished with another errand, she used her cell to call Gabe. This afternoon, they were going back to the neighborhood where Angel had been found after the attack. They planned to canvas the area. Both of them were eager to see what they might turn up.

Gabe was working at a property he owned called the Egyptian Theater, she discovered when she phoned. He gave her an address in Deep Ellum and she told him she would meet him there.

"See you soon," Gabe said in his deep, sexy voice as he hung up the phone and Mattie's stomach lifted.

She tried not to think what might happen tomorrow night. She hoped she would be able to keep her mind in control and not listen to the seductive yearnings of her body.

SAM KNOCKED ON Tracy's door at exactly seven o'clock. She didn't keep him waiting, just opened the door and invited him in, smiled at him as he walked into her living room.

Man, she had a kick-ass smile.

"Hi," he said a little lamely.

"Hi, yourself. I'm ready. I just need to grab my purse." She was wearing a denim miniskirt that showed off her long, sexy legs. Her sleeveless white cotton blouse dipped low enough to reveal the shadowy cleavage between a pair of luscious breasts.

For an instant, his resolve weakened. If the lady wanted sex, who was he to object?

Then she returned with her bag and he looked into her pretty face, read her uncertainty, and knew it wasn't going to happen. Not if he wanted to see her again.

Which he did.

They walked outside to his metallic red Dodge Dakota, a smaller pickup than Gabe's big GMC. He'd had it washed and detailed. With the chrome wheels he'd added last year it was a good-looking truck.

Tracy cast him a glance. "I kind of took you for a pickup man."

He grinned. "Work I do, it's pretty much a given."

"Actually, I think it's kind of sexy."

Sam clamped down on a rush of heat as he helped her into the truck and waited for her to fasten her seat belt. "How do you feel about motorcycles?"

Tracy's blond eyebrows went up and she grinned. "I love 'em."

"Good. Next time we'll take my Harley."

Tracy's grin slipped a little as he slammed her door and walked to the driver side of the truck. He could tell she was already thinking there probably wouldn't be a next time.

Sam refused to be daunted. Instead, he drove to the restaurant and parked in the lot, then helped Tracy climb down and led her inside. Bella Sera was full, but he'd called Tony ahead and a table waited for them in a quiet corner in the back room.

The place was hokey Italian. From red-checked tablecloths to little red-glass candleholders flickering in the semidarkness. Bread baskets in a dozen different shapes and sizes hung from the ceiling, and wicker-wrapped Chianti bottles lined the walls.

Tracy surveyed her surroundings as they followed the hostess to the table he had reserved. "So your friend owns this place?"

Sam nodded. "Tony Pierucci. We went to high school together. It was his dad's place before he died. Tony and his brother, Bobby, run it now."

They sat down and opened their menus.

"You like red wine?" Sam asked.

"Definitely. Especially with Italian."

"Good girl." Sam ordered a bottle of Chianti, which a black-haired waiter named Marcus opened and poured into glasses on the table. Sam ordered spaghetti and meatballs. Tracy chose veal parmigiana.

"So were you born in Dallas?" Tracy asked, taking a sip of her wine.

Sam nodded. "Pretty standard stuff. Dad was a plumber. Mom worked in a grocery store. They helped me get through college, but I had to work to make the extra it took to pay the bills. I've got a brother in California who's a stockbroker. I'm doing what I love and so is he." He lifted his wineglass and took a drink. "How about you?"

For an instant, Tracy glanced away. When she looked at him again, there was something disturbing in her eyes. "Let's just say my childhood wasn't the best." She pasted on the flashy, false smile he had seen a hundred times at Club Rio. "But I'm doing great now. That's all that matters."

Realizing the question had upset her, he steered the conversation in another direction. They talked about real estate and he mentioned he was working on the remodel of a house uptown.

"That's how Gabe got started," he said. "I've flipped a couple of houses so far and made some pretty good bucks. Of course, with the market the way it is, I might have to keep the one I'm working on for a while."

"I could try selling it for you."

Sam just shrugged. "I was kind of thinking I might move in, rent the condo I'm living in now."

"My dad was a lawyer. We lived in a fancy house when I was a kid. But it was never a home."

"So your parents didn't get along?"

She got that funny look on her face again. "Let's

talk about something more pleasant. Like how good the food is here."

Sam managed a smile. "It's always been terrific." He went along with her change of subject but it bothered him the way she refused to talk about her past. Whatever made Tracy the person she was today, Sam would bet it had a lot to do with her childhood.

As they finished their meals, Tracy flashed him a bright, sexy smile.

"I like you, Sam McBride," she said. "Why don't we go back to my place and fuck?"

Sam nearly spewed the mouthful of wine he'd just taken. He swallowed, took a steadying breath. "I like you, too, Tracy Spencer. Which is exactly the reason I'm not taking you to bed. At least not tonight."

Her lips turned down in a pout. "What is it with you, Sam? Don't you want to make love to me?"

Beneath the table, Sam reached for her hand, pulling it over into his lap. He was sporting a raging hard-on and had been since he'd seen her in the doorway of her apartment. "What do you think?"

Those pretty green eyes went wide as saucers. Sam let go and she jerked her hand away. "Oh, my God!"

He just smiled. "I told you, I'm not interested in a one-night stand. If you're honest, I think you might want something more than that yourself."

She stared down at the table. "I can't handle relationships, Sam. If I keep it just sex I don't have to worry about messing things up." She stared at him across the table. "And for your information, I don't drag every guy I meet off to bed."

"I'm glad to hear it." He left money for the bill and a tip and rose from his chair, helped Tracy to her feet.

"So why don't I pick you up tomorrow morning? We'll go for a ride on my Harley, catch some lunch along the way."

One of her light eyebrows arched up. "Still no sex?"

"Not yet."

Tracy's features softened. She looked at him differently than she ever had before. "Fine. What time?"

"How's ten-thirty?"

"Okay."

He reached over and caught her hand, started leading her toward the door. "Come on. Time to go home. Whatever you may think, I'm a man and I'm only human."

Tracy's eyes sparkled and she laughed. It was a musical sound and freer than anything he had heard from her before.

Sam glanced at her soft, trusting smile and knew he was doing exactly the right thing.

SATURDAY NIGHT ARRIVED whether Mattie wanted it to or not. Standing in front of the mirror, her stomach churned as she finished applying her mascara, then a light dab of blush. On the concrete countertop beside her, Tigger watched with interest, his ears alert and his golden eyes following her every move.

"I've got a hot date, big boy," she said, reaching out to stroke his soft fur. The words made her stomach churn even more.

Hot date was right. She knew how hot Gabe Raines was, and unless she came to her senses, she was going to get another sample tonight.

Mattie's heart kicked up as she applied lip liner then a light pink shade of lipstick. Yesterday afternoon, after she had left the Zigman Gallery, she had joined Gabe at his pet project, the Egyptian Theater.

"This place means a lot to me," he had said as he gave her his personal tour of the majestic old 1920s theater. "I've been working on it for nearly a year. Everyone in the community has pitched in at one time or another to help bring it back. I don't want anything to happen to it."

"I noticed the security guard."

"There's one on the job twenty-four-seven."

From the theater they returned to the area close to the deli where Angel had been attacked. Going door to door, they showed Angel's photo to everyone they talked to and asked if anyone had noticed him in the neighborhood.

An elderly lady remembered seeing him near the park when she was walking her dog. "I recall he was talking to a couple of young men about his age, but I don't remember anything else about them."

Aside from the cook and the elderly woman, no one remembered seeing Angel. All in all, the afternoon had been a total bust, and Mattie's Friday night date with Aaron hadn't gone much better.

From the moment he wheeled himself over to the table where Mattie sat waiting at Taj, he seemed edgy, even a little hostile.

"I'm surprised you didn't cancel. Seems like lately you've got better things to do than spend time with your friends."

Hurt rolled through her. And guilt. "I've just been busy, that's all. You know how it is, Aaron."

His mouth thinned. "You're seeing that guy you met at Club Rio, aren't you?"

"Not…not the way you mean." The way he meant was sleeping with him, which was exactly what she had done.

"So what's his name?"

She didn't want to tell him. Telling Aaron would be acknowledging that she and Gabe had some sort of relationship, as uncertain as it was. But Aaron was her friend.

"His name is Gabriel Raines." Briefly she explained about the fires and how the assault on Angel might be related to the fact the boy was asking questions, hoping to find information on the arsonist who had started them.

"Gabe and I are working together, trying to find out who set the fires and assaulted the Ramirez boy."

Some of Aaron's anger deflated. "I'm sorry, Mattie. That wasn't fair. I just… I worry about you. I don't want some guy taking advantage."

She almost laughed. "I'm a grown woman, Aaron. I can take care of myself."

But now, as she finished getting dressed for supper tonight at Gabe's, she caught the faint trembling of her hand and flush in her cheeks that had nothing to do with makeup. She wondered if Aaron might not be right.

She was in over her head with Gabriel Raines. Gabe was the kind of man who took charge, made a woman feel safe and protected. He made her feel as if she could let down her guard and trust him when it was exactly the wrong thing to do.

Mattie had learned a long time ago the only person she could trust to take care of her was herself. If she went to bed with Gabe, she would only become more vulnerable, more susceptible to all that muscle and macho appeal.

She couldn't afford to let that happen.

She decided to call him and reached for her cell phone next to Tigger on the counter. His tall swished just then, knocking the phone to the floor. By the time she picked it up, the urge to cancel had passed.

It was only supper, she reasoned. She had promised Gabe he could cook for her. It wouldn't be right to cancel at the last minute.

Mattie took a steadying breath. With a last check in the mirror, she grabbed her purse and headed for the door. She was taking her own car. She could leave whenever she wanted.

She was just afraid that leaving would be the last thing on her mind.

CHAPTER SIXTEEN

THE CONDO SMELLED like garlic and tomatoes. The kitchen was a little bit steamy, the lasagna almost ready. The doorbell rang and Gabe went to welcome his guest, his pulse speeding up at the thought of her arrival.

He stepped back as he opened the door, stood for a moment just staring. In a white flowered sundress with a short narrow skirt, she looked fantastic. But then she always did.

The bad news was she was wearing her beautiful, fiery hair pulled back severely at the nape of her neck, sending him a very clear message. She wasn't there for sex.

Gabe inwardly smiled.

She might not think she was going to spend the night in his bed, but Gabe had no doubt that was exactly where they would end up.

"Welcome to my humble abode."

Her gaze ran over him. "Said the spider to the fly."

Gabe laughed. "Come on in."

Her eyes met his as she walked past him into the condo, a tiny pulse beating at the base of her throat. His body stirred. Gabe bent down and very lightly kissed her, then ended the kiss before she had time to back away.

"What are you drinking? Red? White? Something stronger?"

"A glass of white wine would be perfect."

He led her into the kitchen and reached up for a wineglass, still tasting her on his lips. His groin swelled, pressed against the fly of the black jeans he was wearing with a crisp white shirt. He poured her the wine and carried it over to where she stood in front of the island in the middle of his kitchen.

Mattie took a drink. "Something smells good. What are we having?"

Each other, he wanted to say, but refrained. "Vegetable lasagna. I know you aren't crazy about meat."

"Sounds great." She took another sip of her wine, obviously a little nervous, and glanced at the table, which was set with a white linen cloth, white dishes, wineglasses and a bright yellow spring bouquet he had bought at the market.

"Table looks pretty."

"Thanks." He tossed the last of the freshly washed lettuce into a bowl, diced up a tomato and threw it in. "How was your date last night?"

She glanced up. "I told you it wasn't a date. Aaron is just a friend."

"Must be a pretty good friend to take up your Friday evening."

"We've known each other since I started working at the firm."

"And?"

She shrugged. "And he's very protective. He's worried I'll get in deeper with you than I can handle."

"So you told him about me?"

"I told him we were working together to find the man who is setting your buildings on fire."

"I guess you didn't mention the hot sex we had after we left Club Rio."

Her cheeks turned pink. "That was an anomaly."

"Was it?" He set his wineglass down and moved toward her, took the glass from her hand and set it on the granite countertop. She stiffened as he drew her into his arms, bent his head and kissed her. Then her lips softened under his and for a moment she kissed him back. He could smell her floral perfume, feel the fullness of her breasts pressing into his chest. She tasted like wine and woman, and he breathed her in, wanting her, aching to be inside her.

Mattie pulled away, embarrassed she had given him a glimpse of her desire. "I knew I shouldn't have come," she said, taking several steps back from him.

Gabe reached over and pushed the Off button on the oven, then started forward, stalking her. There was no way they would make it through dinner. Not until this was settled between them.

He dragged her back into his arms and kissed her, more thoroughly this time, urging her to open for him. He felt her hands on his chest, trying to push him away, but her lips clung to his and he could feel the wild pounding of her heart.

"You want this, Mattie." He kissed her again, running his tongue over her lush bottom lip, coaxing, tasting, and felt her tremble. Her body softened, began to yield and her arms slid up around his neck. She was kissing him back, her tongue sliding into his mouth, tangling erotically with his.

His pulse hammered. Need pounded through him, intense and demanding. He kissed her one way and then another, kissed her until both of them were breathing hard and Mattie was squirming against him. Reaching down, he caught the hem of her white flowered skirt and hauled it up around her waist. He cupped that luscious ass and lifted her against his erection, heard her soft moan.

It was déjà vu.

Skimpy thong panties and firm twin globes that perfectly filled his hands.

Mattie shifted, pressing herself more fully against his erection. They weren't in a storage room now and he wanted her just this way. Wrapping her legs around his waist, he shifted her panties aside, found her softness and began to stroke her.

God, she was wet. Mattie whimpered and Gabe groaned. Moments later, he was sheathed in the condom he carried in the back pocket of his jeans and buried deep inside her. Backing her up against the wall, he took her the way he had wanted to that night at the club. Took her and took her and still couldn't get his fill.

Mattie moaned and clung to him, kissing him wildly as he drove himself inside her. Jesus, it was heaven.

He plunged into her, driving deeper, taking her faster, harder. She was so hot and tight. He could feel her pulsing around him, feel the tension in her body, and knew she was ready to come.

"It's all right, baby," he softly encouraged. "Just let yourself go."

With a cry of surrender, she did, clinging to his neck as she moaned his name, her slickness clenching around his shaft, her head back against the wall.

Gabe came in a rush, exploding inside her, his entire body screaming in release. Christ, sex had never felt so damned good.

They rode the crest together then started spiraling back to earth, but Gabe didn't let her go, just carried her into the bedroom, her legs still wrapped around his waist, her head against his shoulder.

The oven was off. The lasagna could wait.

He had something he wanted a whole lot more than food.

MATTIE ROUSED HERSELF from the euphoria she was feeling and slowly opened her eyes. The first thing she realized was that she lay on her side and she no longer wore her flowered sundress or anything at all. She should have been chilled by the air-conditioning but Gabe's warmth wrapped around her spoon-fashion, cocooning her from behind.

She felt a gentle tug as he pulled the last of the pins from her no-longer-neat chignon and set them on the bedside table. He ran his fingers through the heavy auburn curls, setting them free.

"I love your hair," he said, brushing a soft kiss on her shoulder.

Dusk was setting in but there was still enough light in the room to see. Mattie rolled onto her back and looked up at him. The muscles in his arms bulged where he propped himself on an elbow. His chest was wide and heavily muscled, and just looking at all that hard male flesh made her mouth water. Gabe leaned down and very softly kissed her. He didn't push for more and she was amazed to feel faintly disappointed.

She ran a finger along his solid jaw. "You know, I should be mad at you. I said no and you didn't stop. Modern women are supposed to be able to say no to a man and he's supposed to obey her wishes."

"Modern women are supposed to mean what they say." He eased her back onto her side, nuzzled the side of her neck, nibbled her earlobe, and she trembled. She was nestled against his groin and she could feel his erection, as hard and hot as before.

Her breathing quickened. "How do you know I didn't mean it?"

"Part of you did. The part that pulls your hair into a bun and picks men who don't know how to satisfy you. The rest of you wanted me as much as I wanted you."

A big hand skimmed down and cupped a naked breast. His thumb grazed her nipple and it tightened almost painfully.

"I want you, Mattie. Once wasn't nearly enough. I can think of a dozen different ways I'd like to have you."

Her stomach quivered as he eased one of her legs up over his hip and she felt his hardness at the entrance to her passage. His erection slid deeply inside and pleasure washed through her, deep and intense. For a moment, he didn't move, allowing her to adjust to his heavy length, his breath warm against the skin behind her ear. Then his arm slid beneath her waist and he lifted and turned her until she was on her knees. Still inside her, he settled himself against her bottom.

"Let's see if you like it this way." He moved a little, just enough to stir the heat pouring through her.

"Oh, God."

He chuckled, eased himself more deeply inside. "I guess I've got my answer."

Mattie gasped as he began to move, in and out, taking his time, making her so hot she thought she might faint.

Driving deeper, quickening the pace, he carried her

higher and higher. One of his hands found her softness and Mattie cried out at the pleasure. Her body began to tighten, gripping her insides so fiercely she trembled.

Her climax came swift and hard, but Gabe didn't stop, just drove into her until she reached a second, sizzling release. "Dear God," she whispered.

He followed a few seconds later, his muscles taut, a low groan escaping from deep in his throat.

Exhausted, her muscles gave way and both of them tumbled onto the bed then rolled onto their sides. Gabe was breathing hard and so was she. Vaguely she wondered how she could be twenty-nine years old and never have known this kind of pleasure.

Never even realized it actually existed.

As the world slowly righted itself, she heard Gabe's soft curse and realized he was sitting on the side of the bed, removing the condom he was wearing.

"What's the matter?" she asked.

"Bad news, honey. The damn thing broke."

Her insides clenched. Nausea swirled in the pit of her stomach and her head spun, making her feel slightly dizzy. The past rushed in. She was pregnant and frightened. Mark blamed her for what had happened. He was angry. Then he was simply gone.

"Oh, God." Sitting up in bed, she pulled the sheet up over her, suddenly self-conscious.

Gabe skirted the bed, sat down on the mattress beside her and pulled her into his arms. "It's all right. Odds are we'll be fine. It's only happened this once."

She nodded, praying it was true, but there was a lump in her throat and tears sprang into her eyes.

Gabe eased back to look at her. "Even if something

happened, it wouldn't be so bad. I like kids. I wouldn't mind having one."

She swallowed, the tears in her eyes spilling over onto her cheeks.

"What is it?" Gabe asked softly. "Tell me."

Mattie closed her eyes. She wanted to keep silent but the words just began spilling out. "I was pregnant once. It was years ago. I thought…thought he loved me. I thought we were going to get married, but—" Her lips trembled and she glanced away.

"Tell me the rest," Gabe softly urged.

Mattie ran a hand through her tumbled hair, shoving it back from her face. "When Mark found out I was going to have a baby, he ended our relationship. I never saw him again. Five months later, I miscarried. I was devastated. I wanted that baby…so much."

Gabe drew her back into his arms and just held her. "It wouldn't be that way with me. If something happens, Mattie, I won't let you down."

But there was no way to know that for sure and just thinking about what had happened the last time had her drawing away from him, climbing out of the bed in search of her clothes.

Gabe didn't try to stop her. Instead, he pulled on his jeans but didn't bother with his shirt. "Tell you what… I'll turn the oven back on, get the lasagna hot again. You'll feel better after you've had something to eat."

Mattie just nodded. Her throat still ached. She should leave, she knew, but something held her back. She didn't want to be alone with the memories. She needed to push them away as she always did. She couldn't believe she had told Gabe about Mark and the baby. She had never said a word about them to any other man.

The fact that she had shared such an intimate part of herself with Gabe worried her more than anything that had happened between them so far.

CHAPTER SEVENTEEN

LATE SUNDAY MORNING Gabe sat in his condo watching a NASCAR race. He wasn't much of a couch potato, but after last night he had a lot on his mind.

As he sat in a comfortable chair in front of the TV sipping a cup of hot black coffee, he thought of his evening with Mattie, which had mostly gone the way he had planned.

Except that he had meant for her to spend the night, meant for them to wake up together and make love again this morning.

But something had happened between them. Something besides the hot, incredible sex that was even better than he remembered. Mattie had shared an intimate and important part of her past and some fragile element of trust had blossomed between them.

Because of that trust, he hadn't pressed her to stay. Instead, a supper that started off strained had ended up easy and relaxed. They had talked about her parents, her dad's death and how much she and her mother had missed him.

She told him how hard her mother had worked to keep them afloat and the after-school job she had gotten to help pay the bills. She told him about her mom's remarriage and her move to San Antonio and how for the first time in years Margaret Baker seemed happy.

Gabe had talked about his brothers, sharing stories of their early years.

"One night after school Dev and I ran into the school bully, a guy named Jeff Freedman, and a bunch of his friends. Jackson was usually our protector but he was sacking up groceries at the supermarket so we had to take care of ourselves. We were several years younger and it was five against two, but Freedman took the lead. Dev went low, kicking him in the shin. Freedman got off a pretty good punch, but my counterpunch caught him in the jaw and knocked him down."

Gabe grinned. "I was so shocked I just stood there. I guess the rest of his friends thought I was tougher than I actually was because they all took off running. Dev and I had a lot less trouble after that."

Mattie smiled at the image. "I just bet you did."

They cleared the table together and loaded the dishes into the washer, but as the hour grew late, he could feel the tension mounting between them again. When Mattie announced her intention to leave, he didn't try to stop her.

He wanted her to know sex wasn't the only thing he wanted from her.

Which surprised him as much as it did her.

Now, as the morning sun burned through the living room windows, warming his shoulders, Gabe thought about Mattie again. She was an incredibly passionate woman, equal to the demands he made on her. And as he had guessed, in bed she liked a man who took charge. During the day, she worked as hard as a man. She needed someone who took control, took her away from the pressures of her job and allowed her to just be a woman.

The sex was hot and raunchy whenever they were together, and he enjoyed every minute. Funny thing was, he had come to realize he wanted something more. He wanted to make slow, languid love to her for hours on end. He wanted to take his time, savor her luscious little body, pleasure her in a dozen different ways.

His blood stirred and he began to go hard. Damn, he wanted her.

The phone rang.

Gabe released a breath, grateful for the distraction. Switching off the TV, which he wasn't really watching, he plucked his cell phone off the table next to his chair and flipped it open.

He recognized the incoming numbers, then heard his brother's familiar voice.

"Hey, bro," Dev said.

Gabe smiled into the receiver. "I've been hoping to hear from you."

"Took me longer than I thought to come up with anything useful. Like you said, you don't really have that many enemies."

"Unfortunately, all I need is one—if he's willing to burn down buildings to get to me."

"All too true, my friend."

"So what have you got?"

"Couple of things. I've got a buddy down South, a former ranger. Does a little work for me now and then. He checked out Rachael and Clayton Sanders. Jackson was right. Rachael's back in Dallas and her husband isn't happy about it."

"Where is he?"

"That's the thing. No one seems to know. After he left the marines, he and Rachael stayed in Jacksonville.

Her family was there. She didn't want to leave, so Clayton stayed to please her. He got a job working as a car salesman but he hated it. They fought a lot. Rachael finally left him. She filed for divorce and moved to Dallas three months ago. She's been working as a secretary at Infinity Bank."

"No kids?"

"Apparently she didn't want any. It was one of the things they fought about."

"So what happened to Clay?"

"Like I said, no one seems to know. He's not in Jacksonville and nobody knows where he went. He just disappeared."

Not good, Gabe thought. "So you're thinking he might have followed Rachael to Dallas."

"Could be. And if he's there, he might think you had something to do with his wife's decision to leave him."

Gabe shook his head. "It doesn't make sense. I haven't talked to Rachael since I left the Marine Corps. That was ten years ago."

"People have a way of altering their memories of the past. Before she married Sanders, she was in love with you, right?"

"I guess she thought so. I was mostly impressed by how beautiful she was, her great body, and how the guys all panted after her. I think we both knew it wouldn't last."

"Maybe over the years she imagined that if things had been different it might have worked out."

"Rachael was dominated by her parents. She couldn't bear the thought of being apart from them. She was content to stay in Jacksonville and just get by. I had things I wanted to do."

"That the reason the two of you split?"

"Pretty much. I suppose if I'd loved her I would have stayed."

Silence fell over the phone.

"What is it?"

"She stayed because of her parents. Maybe something happened between her and her folks that drove her away. Let me look into it, see what I can find out. I'll get back to you as soon as I know anything."

Gabe hung up, thinking about Rachael. At twenty-one, she'd been unbelievably beautiful, with long, honey-blond hair and golden-brown eyes. And a figure that made men hard just watching her walk by. Gabe and Clay had both been in lust at first sight. But Clay wasn't the man she wanted. At least not as much as she wanted Gabe.

He walked over to the kitchen counter and picked up his keys. He had crews working overtime at the Towers and also at McKinney Court. He had planned to spend the morning with Mattie but she wasn't there. He could check on the work being done then drive over to Rachael's house on Dublin Street, the address Jackson had given him.

He probably shouldn't go. If Clay thought his wife was in Dallas because of Gabe, his visit would only make things worse.

On the other hand, if Sanders was responsible for the fires, Gabe needed to know.

Before he set another one.

MATTIE DROVE OVER to Tracy's late Sunday morning. She always called first, since her friend might well be entertaining one of her male friends. But Tracy was home alone and she didn't sound happy about it.

"Come on in," Tracy said when Mattie arrived, pulling open the door and inviting her inside. "Want a cup of coffee?"

"I'd love one." Mattie followed her over to the coffeemaker in the kitchen and waited while Tracy poured her a cup. She added some of the Coffee-mate Tracy set on the counter then took a sip. "Not bad."

"I just made it. I slept in a little. I'm working today. I've got an open house at one o'clock." Tracy freshened her own cup. "Anything new with Angel?"

"The doctors are optimistic. He's survived the worst of it, but he's still in a coma. They have no idea how long it might be before he wakes up."

"Everyone's pulling for him. That's got to help."

"I hope so."

Tracy studied her a moment. She cocked a sleek blond eyebrow. "So…how did your evening go with Gabe?"

Mattie felt the heat rising to her cheeks. "You first. How was your dinner with Sam?"

Tracy shrugged. "We had fun. Yesterday he took me motorcycle riding. We had a terrific time." She sipped her coffee. "We still haven't had sex."

"You're kidding."

Tracy blew out a breath, moving the blond bangs over her forehead. "I'm not kidding and it's driving me crazy."

Mattie sat down at the kitchen table, cradling her mug in her hand. "So why didn't you invite someone over last night to take his place?"

A tiny line appeared between Tracy's eyebrows. "You must really think I'm terrible."

"You live by your own rules, Tracy. You always have."

Tracy sat down across from her. "It just didn't seem right, you know? Bringing someone else over just because Sam wouldn't compromise his principles. Besides, Sam's the man I want. I'm not interested in sleeping with somebody else."

"This is beginning to really get interesting."

"I know and it's scary."

Mattie thought of the evening she'd spent with Gabe and the secrets she had told him. "I know what you mean."

Tracy leaned forward, mug in hand. "All right, let's hear it."

Mattie sighed. "Gabe's different, Tracy. Great in bed. Totally amazing, in fact. But it isn't just that." She studied the liquid in her cup. "I told him about Mark and the baby."

"You did? What did he say?"

"He said if something happened and he got me pregnant, he wouldn't let me down."

Tracy scoffed. "He's a man. They always let you down."

"I know." Mattie sipped her coffee and tried to convince herself that Gabe was just like the rest of the men she had known. Somehow the notion didn't feel right.

"He's calling me tonight," Mattie said. "We're getting together tomorrow to figure out our next move."

"So you're still playing detective."

"I'm not giving up without doing my best to find this guy."

"Just be careful." Tracy pinned her with a look. "And I don't just mean asking questions about the fires."

She was talking about Gabe, and Mattie's stomach twisted. She set her mug down on the table with a shaky hand. By the time she took another sip, her coffee had gone cold.

GABE PULLED HIS truck up in front of the small wood-framed house on Dublin Street. It was fairly nondescript, single-story, gray with white-painted shutters and a covered porch out in front.

As he reached for the door handle, his cell phone rang. He pulled it out of his pocket and flipped it open.

"It's me," Dev said. "Rachael's parents were killed about six months ago in a car crash. Aside from Clay, she had no reason to stay in Jacksonville."

"How did you get the info so fast?"

"The internet is an amazing thing. But even my buddy hasn't been able to find out why Rachael picked Dallas."

"I'm about to find out. I'm sitting in front of her house right now."

"Be careful, bro."

"Will do."

"Listen, I'll have more for you in a day or two. I'm still checking the rest of the names on your list."

"Thanks." Gabe signed off and closed the phone. Wondering if he'd find Rachael at home, he stepped down from the truck and made his way up the sidewalk, climbed the wooden steps and knocked on the door.

When the door swung open, a vision from his past stood in front of him.

He managed to smile. "Hello, Rachael."

"Gabe! What on earth are you doing here?" She looked like a woman now instead of a girl, with a few fine lines here and there, but she was still beautiful. She wore white shorts and a pink midriff top and her skin was perfectly tanned.

She opened the door a little wider. "It's good to see you. Come on in."

He nearly declined. He didn't want to cause problems for Rachael, and if Clay had really gone off the deep end, there was no telling what he might do.

She took his arm, ending his reluctance, and urged him into the living room. "I'm still unpacking," she explained, tipping her head toward a couple of pictures she hadn't yet hung. "But it's beginning to feel like home."

"It's nice." The house was modestly decorated, but clean and welcoming, with an overstuffed beige sofa and chair and an old wooden rocker set near a fireplace bordered with painted tiles. He sat down on the sofa and Rachael sat down in the chair.

"So how did you know where to find me?" she asked.

"Some…things have been happening. Dev was looking into it for me. He came across your address on the internet."

She started frowning. "Your brother was searching for information about me?"

"Not you, exactly. He was looking for information on Clay. He found out the two of you were getting a divorce and that you had moved to Dallas. He thought it might have some bearing on my…problems."

Her lips tightened. "I should have known this wasn't a social call. You and I didn't exactly part on friendly terms."

She had slashed his tires, he remembered, then cried

and begged him to forgive her. "We were never really friends. Our relationship was too hot for that. I suppose that was part of the problem."

"I was in love. All you wanted was sex."

"I was young. I wasn't ready for anything more."

"And now?"

The question took him by surprise. Maybe Jackson hadn't been that far off the mark. "Now, what I'm interested in is finding Clay. Do you know where he is?"

With a sigh, Rachael leaned back in her chair. "I don't know. Wherever he is, I hope it's a long way from here."

"Why did you move to Dallas, Rachael? Why not somewhere else?"

Her gaze darted away. She toyed with the tie on her midriff top. "I've never been completely on my own. First I lived with my parents, then you and I were together, then I married Clay. When my parents died, I decided to make a fresh start. I knew you moved to Dallas after we broke up. I heard you'd never married. After I left Clay, I thought maybe… I don't know. I guess I thought if something happened, you'd be nearby in case I ever needed anything."

"You came because I was here. Why didn't you ever call?"

"I meant to. I started to call a dozen times, but after all that, I couldn't work up the courage. Still, it was good to know you were here."

And if she had called, he would have helped in any way he could. He had always been the protective sort and she had always been needy. Apparently that hadn't changed.

"Clay knows you're here?"

She nodded. "He came by a couple of times when I first moved in. He tried to get me to come back to him. I told him I wasn't interested."

"Did he threaten you?"

She shook her head. "Not exactly, but he was really upset. I've never seen him in quite such a frenzy."

"If you read the newspapers, then you know that two of my building projects have burned down in the past few weeks."

"I saw the articles. I meant to call you, but…" She shrugged. "I wasn't sure I should."

"Is there any chance Clay could be the one who set the fires?"

Rachael sat up straighter in her chair. "That's why you're here? You think Clay set the fires?"

"Did he?"

"I—I don't think he'd do something like that, but…"

"But what?"

"But he kept asking me why I picked Dallas. I told him I had a lead on a job through a friend—which was true. I'm not sure he believed me."

"Anything else you can tell me?"

She shook her head, shifting her honey-blond hair across her shoulders. "I wish I could help. But that's all I know."

Gabe rose from his chair and Rachael stood up, too. He pulled a business card out of his wallet and handed it over. "If you hear from Clay, give me a call."

She looked down at the card. "If you…um…ever want to get together…"

Gabe just shook his head. "One thing I've learned. It's best to let the past stay in the past." Turning, he walked to the door, pulled it open and stepped out on the porch.

As he strode toward his truck, he thought of the years since he had left the service. Rachael had come to Dallas because of him. There'd been a time he would have been flattered, would have taken her up on her invitation. But he was older now and wiser. And as beautiful and sexy as the lady still was, he just wasn't interested.

Thoughts of Mattie slipped into his head but Gabe ignored them, fixing his attention instead on the problem at hand. Clayton Sanders was the best lead he'd come up with. He would call Captain Daily and fill him in, put the police to work trying to find him. But finding Clay Sanders if he didn't want to be found wouldn't be easy.

He was Force Recon and he was smart.

Smart enough to know how to torch a building.

Smart enough to get away with it.

CHAPTER EIGHTEEN

MONDAY MORNING, MATTIE opened the door and welcomed Gabe into her apartment. She guarded her privacy. Friends from work had been there, of course, but she had never invited any of the few men she had dated into the sanctuary of her home.

Now Gabe was there and it made her nervous. He glanced around the open, high-ceilinged living room with its industrial windows and exposed brick walls, and she found herself holding her breath, waiting for his reaction, certain he would hate the spartan environment.

"Nice," he said, his gaze taking in the cone-shaped chairs at each end of the sofa in front of the glass-and-black-iron coffee table. "Good clean lines, great layout." He looked back at her. "It fits you."

She released the breath she'd been holding, surprisingly relieved. "I'm glad you like it."

"Personally, I prefer a little more clutter, but for you...yeah, it's a good fit."

She wasn't quite sure that was a compliment but she thought that maybe it was. "Coffee?"

"No, thanks, I've had plenty already."

Just then Tigger meandered into the hallway. The cat stopped in front of Gabe, lifted his head and gave him an imperious stare. Mattie hurried over to pick him up, certain Gabe wouldn't want anything to do with him, but he simply reached down and scooped the big orange tom up in his arms.

"Hey, big boy." He ran the tips of his fingers gently back and forth beneath the cat's chin and Tigger raised his head for more. Tigger, who never let anyone pick him up but Mattie, began to purr.

"He's going to get fur on your clothes," Mattie said, trying not to think of those same masculine fingers stroking over her naked body, trying to ignore how sexy he looked in his body-hugging navy blue T-shirt and faded blue jeans.

"What's his name?" Gabe asked.

"Tigger. Sort of an offbeat version of tiger, I guess."

He increased the rhythm and the cat's eyes closed in ecstasy. "Every guy needs a little morning rub, hey buddy?" Gabe's eyes locked with hers. Though neither of them had mentioned what had happened at his condo Saturday night, sexual tension arched between them like lightning in the summer air.

Mattie did her best not to look down at the fly of his jeans and Gabe seemed to be fighting to keep his eyes off her breasts.

But finding an arsonist was more important than a fresh round of sex and both of them knew it—though it would certainly have been more entertaining.

Gabe set the cat on its feet, made a quick perusal of Mattie's white jeans and red-and-white tank top, and cleared his throat.

"My...um...brother, Dev, called. He managed to dig up some info that might help us. I thought we'd do some follow-up today."

For the next few minutes, Gabe explained that the ex-wife of a former marine named Clayton Sanders, once a friend of Gabe's, had recently moved to Dallas. Though their friendship had ended long ago, a good deal of animosity remained, at least on Sanders's side. Devlin Raines thought the fact that Rachael Sanders was in Dallas, combined with her petition for divorce, might have sent Sanders over the edge.

"Clay's the best lead we've got," Gabe said as they stepped out of the elevator and crossed the underground garage to the guest spaces where his truck was parked. "The police are looking for him as a person of interest, but I thought we might prowl around a little ourselves."

Mattie paused next to him at the passenger door and cast him a sideways glance. "There's more to this than you're telling me, isn't there? Otherwise it doesn't make sense. This has something to do with you and the woman, Clay's wife."

Gabe looked away. Mattie could see he didn't want to tell her. He helped her climb into the truck, went around to the driver's side and slid behind the wheel. He turned to face her with a look of resignation.

"Rachael and I were involved years ago when I was still in the marines. Before she and Clay got married."

Mattie felt a sinking in the pit of her stomach. "I think I'm beginning to understand. You're the reason she moved to Dallas, right? Now that she's single again, she wants the two of you to get back together."

Gabe started shaking his head. Fierce blue eyes fixed on her face. "Maybe that's what Rachael was thinking when she came here, but not anymore."

"Why not?"

"Because yesterday I went to see her. I told her as far as I was concerned the past was exactly that. The past."

Mattie studied his expression. She wondered if he

was telling her the truth. It didn't matter, she told herself. She was only using him for sex. All that hot male flesh, all those incredible muscles, were just a way to satisfy her recently awakened sexuality. If he was lying to her, she would end it. As Tracy had said, she could dump him whenever she wished.

"You don't believe me, do you?" His jaw flexed. "You must have known some real losers, honey."

Mattie jerked her gaze away. Mark was the worst, but there had been other men, guys she had begun to trust before she found out they were users and liars just like Mark.

"I'm not lying to you, Mattie." More gentle now, Gabe's voice washed over her. "Until yesterday, I hadn't seen Rachael in nearly ten years. I'm not interested in seeing her again."

She watched his face and a heavy weight eased off her chest. Gabe wasn't lying. She was almost sure. "It really isn't any of my business."

He cocked a dark brown eyebrow. "Or maybe it is."

She tried not to be warmed by the words. She didn't want more from Gabe than she was already getting. Well, maybe a little more of that hot, unbridled sex. Still, she couldn't stop the faintest of smiles.

"Now, can we get going?" he asked. "I know a couple of friends of Clay's from when he was in the service. It was a long time ago, but you never know. If he's here, he might have gone to see them."

"Sounds like a good place to start."

He pinned her with a glare. "I have no idea why I'm letting you come with me—aside from the fact I like being with you and I want to take you back to bed."

She grinned as he reached for the key in the ignition

but his phone started ringing before he had time to start the truck. Gabe pulled his cell out of his jeans pocket.

"Raines."

Mattie could only hear one side of the conversation, but her stomach knotted as Gabe's expression darkened and she began to suspect what the call was about.

"Last night? Jesus, where?" He paused. "I'm not that far away. I'll be there in twenty minutes." Gabe hung up and turned to face her. "That was Captain Daily. There's been another fire. They aren't sure yet if it's the same guy who set the first two, but they think it could be. We need to get over there and find out what's going on."

"Where was it?" Mattie asked.

"Just off the North Stemmons Freeway." Gabe started the truck, backed it out of the guest parking space and drove toward the exit. "A wholesale clothing store, Artie's Men's Wear."

"At least it isn't a project you're involved in."

Gabe cast her a glance. "I worked on that store three years ago, a fairly large remodel."

"Oh, my God," Mattie said.

Gabe set his jaw and kept driving.

FIRE TRUCKS SURROUNDED the smoldering, three-story, metal-roofed building. Hoses snaked out of the back of the vehicles and the asphalt gleamed with puddles of water. Exhausted firemen stored their gear and continued mopping up after they'd put out the blaze that had started last evening.

Gabe and Mattie climbed out of the truck and Gabe rounded the hood to where she stood waiting. Across the parking lot, Captain Daily walked toward them, silver-streaked hair mashed down from the helmet he carried in one hand.

"Thanks for coming," the captain said.

"Thanks for calling." Gabe inclined his head toward the petite, auburn-haired woman beside him. "This is Mattie Baker. She's a friend."

"We met at the station," Mattie said. "I talked to you about a boy named Angel Ramirez."

"I remember."

"What happened here, Captain?" Gabe asked.

"We don't know all the details yet. It's still too hot for the fire dogs to go in, but the arson team's been working. They're taking samples now. They've already reported finding multiple points of origin. The way the accelerant was used was similar to the fire at McKinney Court. That's the reason I called."

Gabe's jaw hardened. "So it was definitely arson."

"It looks that way. But it doesn't look like the blaze was directed at you, the way the other two fires seem to have been."

"Yeah, well, I'm not so sure."

"What do you mean?"

"I know Artie Roser. I did an extensive remodel on this building three years ago."

Daily hissed in a breath. "That certainly throws a different light on the matter."

"Not a good one, either."

"It's worse than that. A body was found in the office at the rear of the building. Mrs. Roser says her husband always worked here Sunday evenings. He did bookkeeping, inventory adjustment, that kind of thing. She hasn't seen him since he left the house after supper last night."

Gabe felt sick to his stomach. "I don't know what to say. Artie was a nice enough guy. Easy to work for."

"His wife's pretty upset. I think she's fairly sure the man we found is her husband."

"Where is she now?"

"She's home with friends. I told her most fire victims don't suffer. They die from the carbon monoxide before the flames ever reach them."

He swallowed. The information didn't make him feel any better. "I didn't know Lucy Roser very well. Artie handled the details of the remodel. I only met her a couple of times."

"Like I said, she seems pretty shook up."

"Any word on Sanders?"

"None so far. The police will be looking for him a whole lot harder now that there's a possible homicide involved."

Gabe just nodded.

"I've got to go," Daily said. "I'll let you know what else we turn up."

Gabe stood there watching him walk away, staring past him at the smoke and debris, the firemen sloshing through puddles, coiling up lengths of hose. He felt Mattie's hand settle gently on his arm.

"This isn't your fault, Gabe. The only person to blame is the man who set the fire."

Gabe shook his head. "It's connected to me. They're all connected to me in some way. That means I did something to someone bad enough to make him want revenge."

"There are nutcases everywhere. He could have picked you randomly because you bumped into him on the sidewalk. Maybe you took the parking space he wanted."

"Maybe. I guess it's possible." He sighed. "I just don't know." He reached for her, gently caught her shoulders. "I want you out of this, Mattie. A man is dead. Angel's in the hospital. If something happened to you—"

"Something happened to Artie Roser and he was nowhere near you. He probably hadn't seen you in years."

"No, but—"

"This man may have already seen us together. Do you really think I'll be safer if I stay away from you? He could set my place on fire just as easily as he set this building on fire. He could assault me the way he did Angel."

Gabe's insides knotted. He raked a hand through his hair. "God, Mattie."

"We're going to keep searching, Gabe. We're going to find this lunatic before he hurts somebody else."

He shook his head. "I don't like it. I don't want you involved."

"I'm already involved and you know it. I've been involved since the day we had coffee in the lobby of my office building. If this man is trying to hurt you, he could go after any person you know."

His gaze found hers. "And especially the woman I'm sleeping with."

Her face turned faintly pink beneath the haze of freckles over the high bones in her cheeks. But she didn't correct the statement.

"We'll do this together and we'll succeed," she said.

Gabe felt a fresh stab of worry. He didn't want her getting hurt, yet he knew she was right. She wasn't safe no matter where she was. Not until the bastard was caught.

"All right, we'll do it together—on one condition."

Her russet eyebrows drew together. "What's that?"

"From now on you spend your nights with me. I want to know you're somewhere I can keep you safe."

She opened her mouth to argue.

"It's that or we stop right now."

Her chin firmed. "I'm not stopping. I owe it to Angel."

"Then I guess from now on, you'll be sleeping with me."

She shot him a glare. "That's blackmail!"

"It's what we both want and you know it. And I'll feel better if I know you're in a place where I can protect you."

Mattie seemed to mull that over. Her gaze measured the width of his chest before her pale blue eyes jerked back to his face. "All right. For a while we'll do it your way."

A corner of his mouth edged up with the first trace of humor he had felt since Thomas Daily's phone call. "We can do it any way you want, sweetheart. In case you haven't figured it out, I'm extremely open-minded."

CHAPTER NINETEEN

"THERE'LL BE QUESTIONS to answer," Gabe said as they walked back to his truck.

Knowing the guilt he suffered, Mattie felt a rush of sympathy. "You're only as far away as your cell phone." She increased her pace. "Come on. We need to find Clayton Sanders and that means calling on your old marine buddies."

He helped her into the pickup. She knew he felt responsible for the death of Artie Roser or whoever it was who had died in the fire. Gabe was the kind of man who shouldered his responsibilities, perhaps more than he should. Mattie realized she had come to admire him.

As the pickup rolled toward the home of Gabe's friend, former marine corporal Bobby Haslim, she thought of the deal they had struck.

She could have said no. She could have simply refused his outrageous demand that she spend her nights in his condo. Besides being oversexed, the man was demanding and wildly protective. She would probably be fine in her own apartment without Gabe hovering over her like her own personal bodyguard.

On the other hand, there was a chance he could be right and the arsonist with Gabe in his sights would aim his weapon at her.

It was the excuse she'd latched on to, though the

truth was far simpler. She wanted Gabe Raines. She had admitted that to herself the night she had left his apartment after supper and realized how much she had wanted to stay. Gabe had awakened sexual yearnings she didn't know she possessed. She was a woman with needs, she now realized, needs only Gabriel Raines seemed able to satisfy.

She intended to have him for as long as their passionate interlude lasted.

And there was the vow she had made. She wanted the vicious man who had attacked Angel Ramirez caught and punished. She intended to do whatever it took to find him.

The truck rounded a corner into a respectable and well-kept neighborhood. Gabe pulled up in front of a set of apartments built around a big, rectangular swimming pool. The splashes and laughter of noisy children and adults filled the air as she and Gabe walked toward the entrance and went in through an ornate wrought-iron gate.

"Bo lives on the second floor," Gabe said. "Number forty-two."

Mattie let him lead her in that direction up a wide set of stairs. Gabe knocked, and a stout, good-looking man in his early thirties pulled open the door. Still wearing a marine buzz cut, he was at least four inches shorter than Gabe but just as powerfully built.

"Gabe! Hey, man, come on in!" Bo stepped back and Gabe rested a hand at Mattie's waist, guiding her into the living room, which was surprisingly neat, considering Gabe had told her Haslim was a bachelor.

"Bo, this is Mattie Baker."

"Nice to meet you, Mattie."

She smiled. "Gabe's told me a little about you. I guess you guys were in the same unit at Camp Lejeune."

"Man, those were the good ol' days." He winked. "Well, maybe not that good as I look back on it. We worked our butts off getting through boot camp, but we made it. We served our country, and as hokey as that might sound, I'm proud of it."

"It doesn't sound hokey at all," Mattie said, meaning it. "I can't imagine where we'd be without guys like you."

Bo seemed pleased. "You two want a beer or something?" He held up the can of Coke he was drinking. "I'm working the night shift this week so I don't have to leave for a while."

"Bo's a chemical engineer," Gabe explained. "Unlike me, after he got out of the corps, he used his G.I. bill to go to college."

Bo grinned, flashing a set of straight white teeth. "Yeah, that way I didn't have to start actually working for four more years."

Mattie laughed, though clearly Haslim was not a shirker. For the first time, it occurred to her that Gabe didn't have a college education. It should have bothered her, considering the high standards she set for any man she might consider dating. But Gabe was smart and successful. He had worked hard and educated himself, and as Mattie thought about it, she admired him even more.

"So what brings you around here?" Bo asked.

"We're looking for Clayton Sanders. We were hoping you might know where he is." Gabe went on to explain about the fires, about Rachael, and that there was a chance Clay might be in Dallas. "I'm not saying he's the guy who set the fires. We just need to talk to him."

"Man, I wish I could help you. Last time I saw Clay was about three months ago. He said he and his wife had split up, but he was sure they'd be getting back together."

"Rachael mentioned Clay's visit," Gabe said.

"That's it. I haven't heard from him since. Dobie might have seen him, though. They used to be pretty tight."

"I figured I'd go by and see him after work." Gabe's mouth faintly curved as he looked at Mattie. "Dwayne 'Doberman' Penser. Dobie for short."

"Interesting name," Mattie said.

"Remember how he got it, Gabe?" Bo turned to Mattie. "A bunch of us were drinking down at Tiny's Bar and Dwayne started chasing after this hot little babe in a miniskirt. She kept telling him to leave her alone, but Dwayne wouldn't give up. Then her boyfriend showed up and grabbed Dwayne by the shirtfront. We all ended up brawling, trying to get him out of there in one piece. Gabe took on about half the guys in the bar. The other half—"

"I don't think Mattie's interested in how Dwayne got his nickname."

Mattie grinned. "Oh, but I am."

"Let's just say the man is tough as nails and so is Gabe."

He cast Bo a warning glance. "On that note, I think it's time for us to go."

Bo walked them to the door. "Man, I wish you luck, but I gotta say, I can't imagine Clay burning down buildings. He could get a little crazy at times, but that's way over the top."

"I hope you're right."

"Nice to meet you, Bo," Mattie said.

"You, too, Mattie." His gaze ran over her and he flicked Gabe a look of approval. "Nice goin', buddy."

Gabe just smiled. His hand returned to the small of her back as he walked her toward the door and she wondered if he could possibly be marking his territory.

Surely not, she thought, a hollow feeling settling in her stomach. Gabe wasn't interested in anything more than she was. Hot sex for as long as it lasted.

"I NEED TO GO to the hospital," Mattie said as they started driving again. "Since we can't talk to Dobie until tonight, maybe you could drop me off at Baylor for a while."

"All right. We'll see how Angel's doing and you can stay for as long as you like. I need to check with Sam McBride and also Jake Turner. He's the foreman on McKinney Court."

Mattie shifted a little in the seat. "I've heard about your friend Sam. He's been seeing my friend Tracy. What's he like?"

"Sam's a great guy. Steady, loyal, hardworking. He's got drive and ambition but they never overpower his sense of responsibility or his principles. I guess you could say, aside from my brothers, Sam's my best friend."

Mattie fiddled with a pleat in her white cotton slacks. "There's nothing…you know, wrong with him? Sexually, I mean."

Gabe laughed. "You mean is he gay or something? Not even close. Sam's interested in your friend. I gather he thinks she's special. Your friend could do a whole lot worse."

Mattie made no reply. Gabe wondered if she thought that because their relationship was mostly sexual it lessened her value somehow.

"Whatever you're thinking, I'm glad you don't have your girlfriend's hang-ups."

Mattie settled back against the seat. "I had plenty of hang-ups before I met you."

He knew she hadn't been aware of her passionate nature, though he had sensed it from the start. Images flashed of her naked and moaning, his erection buried deep inside her, and a rush of heat went straight to his groin.

"Tonight," he said gruffly, "when we get back to my place, we'll see if we can get rid of a few more."

Mattie's eyes widened. She jerked her gaze toward the window, her cheeks flushing prettily. Gabe didn't tell her that as much as he wanted to have her a dozen different and erotic ways, the notion of making slow, sensual love to her was equally appealing.

They went into the hospital together to discover that Angel had been moved to a regular room, but still remained unconscious.

"I wish the news was better," Dr. Burton said. He was a tall skinny man, his fingers long and thin. Gabe liked the concern he read in the man's narrow face. "At least he's stable and all his vital signs are strong."

"I guess that's something," Gabe said. He looked down at the boy who had once been so full of life and energy. His smooth, dark skin was pale, his cheeks sunken in. A blunt-fingered hand lay limply on top of the sheet, scabbed over from his fall to the pavement. Gabe felt a rush of guilt for what Angel had suffered, perhaps because of him.

It was followed by a fierce shot of anger that the bastard hadn't been caught.

"Mattie!" Rosa Ramirez spotted her next to Angel's bed, hurried over and enveloped her in a slightly desperate hug.

"Señor Raines," she said to Gabe as the women ended their embrace. "Thank you for stopping by to see my son."

"We're all holding good thoughts for him," Gabe said.

They talked for a while. Gabe asked about her other two children, which made her smile, then excused himself, leaving the women to sit at Angel's bedside.

As he headed for his truck, he phoned Sam, who had just left Greenwood and was on his way to check on the work being done at the Towers. Gabe fired up the pickup and drove in that direction. He was still a working man with bills to pay and construction deadlines.

But he couldn't get the memory of Angel Ramirez's still figure out of his head.

Or the thought of Artie Roser trapped and dying in the flames.

Tomorrow he would visit Artie's wife. If Artie turned out to be the man who had died in the fire, the least he could do was express his condolences.

Gabe tried to ignore a fresh shot of guilt.

MATTIE WAITED IN front of the hospital as Gabe pulled over to pick her up. She opened the door and climbed inside using the chrome step beneath the door, getting used to the height of the vehicle.

"Everything all right?" Gabe asked.

"Status quo. Rosa is doing better. She's a strong woman."

Gabe just nodded. "I thought we'd go by your house so you could pack some things to take over to my place. It's about time for Dwayne to be getting home from work. We could drive on over from there."

"All right."

Dusk had settled over the horizon by the time they left Mattie's loft and drove to the Oak Lawn area, rolling through streets lined with modest family homes. According to Gabe, Dwayne "Doberman" Penser was married with two small children, a boy and a girl.

A slender, cocoa-skinned woman opened the door.

"Gabe! Come on in!" She was willowy and beautiful, wearing a turban and big gold hoop earrings and looking like a picture from an African travel brochure. "I'm Viola Penser, Dwayne's wife."

"I'm Mattie Baker. It's nice to meet you."

"Dwayne just got home. Why don't you make yourselves comfortable and I'll tell him you're here."

The sound of children's laughter reached them in the living room as Gabe escorted Mattie across the dark brown carpet to a brown plaid sofa. The house was neat, except for a stack of puzzles, a set of dominoes and a coloring book sitting on the walnut coffee table. A small stuffed rabbit peeked out from behind one of the sofa pillows.

Dwayne walked in—a tall, extremely handsome man with short, curly black hair, big brown eyes and a double row of thick black eyelashes any woman would envy. Mattie was developing a new appreciation for marines.

"Hey, man, long time no see."

"Too long." Gabe smiled as he shook his friend's hand and they clapped each other on the back.

Just then, two small faces appeared in the hallway. When they spotted Gabe, they giggled and raced toward him. Something squeezed in Mattie's chest as he knelt and scooped the children into his powerful arms, propping them up, one on each side, against his broad chest.

"Mattie, say hello to Cassie and Jonas."

She walked over and shook each child's small hand. "Hello, Cassie. Hi, Jonas. I'm Mattie. I'm very pleased to meet you."

"Hello," the little boy said shyly.

"How old are you?" Mattie asked. Jonas held up five fingers. "Four," he said.

Mattie laughed. "How about you, Cassie?"

"I'm fwee."

"Good for you, sweetie." Mattie turned to Dwayne and Viola, who had joined them. "They're darling children."

Viola beamed. "Thank you. We think so, too, but then that's what all parents think."

Gabe set the children on their feet and Dwayne shooed them off to play in the bedroom.

"I read about the fires," Dwayne said. "That's a bummer, man."

"There was another fire last night, a building I worked on a couple of years ago. The owner was killed."

"Shit, man."

"I know." Gabe explained that they were tracking down any information that might lead them to the arsonist and mentioned Clay Sanders's name.

"You gotta be shitting me. You think Clay would

burn down your buildings just because Rachael is divorcing his sorry ass?"

"Did you know she moved to Dallas three months ago?"

Dwayne frowned, drawing his black eyebrows together. "She's still here? I thought she went back to Jacksonville with Clay."

"She's here and they're still getting divorced. Have you seen Clay lately?"

Dwayne set his hands on a pair of narrow hips. Like Gabe and Bo, the man was built. "I saw him two weeks ago. He said he just happened to be in town. He must have been here to see Rachael."

"She said she hadn't seen him since she first moved here, three months ago."

"Oh, man." Duane flicked a covert glance at Mattie. "You and Rachael...you aren't still—"

"No. I didn't even know she lived here until all of this started."

Dwayne just nodded.

"Got any idea where I can find him?" Gabe asked.

Dwayne knuckled his bristly black hair. "When he was here we had a drink at a place called the Jolly Roger. It's a bar off the North Tollway. The bartender seemed to know him. If he's still in town, might be a chance you'd find him there." He wrote down the address and handed it to Gabe.

"Thanks, Dobe."

Dwayne drew himself up a little straighter, suddenly looking less like a father and more like the marine he had been. "You want me to go with you?"

Gabe shook his head. "We don't even know if he's still in Dallas."

"You go after Clay, you'd better be careful. You know he went Force Recon?"

"I know."

Mattie looked at the two ex-marines and a shiver ran down her spine. If these powerful men were worried about Sanders, Mattie was terrified.

"I'll be careful," Gabe said.

"Give me a call if you need me."

But the set of Gabe's jaw said he wasn't about to involve anyone else in his troubles. He would face his problems alone, as she suspected he had been doing most of his life.

Suddenly, she was glad she was staying with him tonight. She knew what to do in bed to soothe a man's troubles. Before she'd met Gabe, she'd had no idea there was any other kind of sex.

Tonight, maybe she could give Gabe something in return for the incredible pleasure he'd given her.

CHAPTER TWENTY

IT WAS TUESDAY. They were driving Mattie's silver BMW convertible with the top down. The temperature was in the eighties and the humidity had come down to tolerable. Mattie had suggested it might be nice to combine work with a little pleasure.

Which made Gabe think of making love to her last night.

The sex had been nothing short of fantastic. Mattie had wanted to take the lead, and for a while he had let her. They were naked in his king-size bed when she came up over him, tossed her russet curls over one shoulder and began to kiss her way down his chest.

For whatever reason and his good fortune, she seemed fascinated by his muscular build. Both his brothers had the lean body of an athlete, but Gabe was built like a football player, which, in high school, he had been.

Those muscles she seemed to like so much tightened with the brush of her little pink tongue across his nipple and his pulse kicked into gear.

His hand slipped into the silky hair tickling his navel, cradling her head as she trailed hot kisses over his abdomen, headed downward until she came to his steely erection.

Gabe hissed in a breath.

Her tongue wound around him, licked and tasted. "Jesus, Mattie…"

When she took him into her mouth, he fought not to come. God, she felt so good. He was hard as granite, his hips moving unconsciously as she worked over him. There wasn't a man alive who wouldn't enjoy having a woman as beautiful and sexy as Mattie Baker doing her best to please him.

And yet there was something missing, something that had always been there when they had made love before. She wanted to soothe him, help him forget his troubles for a while, and, Jesus, she did.

But ultimately, he was a man and he liked being in charge and when he took control and rolled her beneath him, when he captured her lips in a searing kiss, Mattie's response went from warm to burning hot. She was breathing hard, whimpering as he suckled her lovely breasts, reached down and began to stroke her.

He tried to slow things down, keep them both in a sensuous haze, but Mattie didn't want to wait and neither did he.

He took her hard and fast, bringing her to a raging climax, then finding his own release. Afterward they fell asleep, Mattie curled in his arms.

This morning they had made love again, the attraction intense and demanding. At least for a little longer his fantasy of slow, sensual lovemaking would have to wait.

Gabe looked over at the woman behind the wheel of the convertible. Mattie was driving, taking control today, which reminded him of last night and he bit back a smile.

"What's the address?" she asked as they wove their

way through an area of expensive homes on huge manicured lots.

"Fifteen-fifteen Jefferson." The address belonged
to Artie Roser. Captain Daily had called this morning to let them know that Artie's body had been identified from his dental plates. The news left an ache in
Gabe's chest.

"There it is." Mattie whipped the BMW to a stop
in front of an impressive brick, mansard-roofed, single-story house that had to be at least five thousand
square feet.

The Rosers hadn't lived in this house when Gabe had
done the building remodel three years ago. Daily had
given him the new address. Now that he saw the house,
Gabe was a little surprised. In his late fifties, Artie
was the kind of guy who had the first dollar he'd ever
earned. Gabe wouldn't have expected him to splurge
on a place like this.

Mattie was already out of the car and waiting for him
on the sidewalk as he closed his door. She untied the
bright red scarf she had worn over her hair to keep it
from blowing in the wind and stuffed it into her purse.
In navy Capri pants, a crisp white blouse and low-heeled
red sandals, she walked beside him toward the double
carved front doors.

Thinking how pretty she looked with her fiery hair
gleaming in the sunshine, Gabe forced his thoughts
away from the night ahead. A night that would include
hot, erotic sex and a soft woman sleeping in his arms.

Gabe sighed. He was in serious trouble and he knew
it. Funny thing was, he refused to do a damned thing
about it.

They reached the house and he rang the doorbell. He

rang the bell several more times but no one answered. On a whim, he crossed the lawn to the side yard and heard laughter coming from the back of the house.

Thinking maybe he could leave a message with whoever was out there, he reached up to unlock the gate while Mattie hurried to catch up with him. They made their way along a path lined with pink flowers to the rear of the house where a huge, kidney-shaped swimming pool dominated the manicured yard.

Beneath a large covered patio, Lucille Roser stretched out on a padded lounge chair sipping a tropical drink, a floppy-brimmed hat covering her shoulder-length red hair. An attractive woman in her early forties, her flowered yellow one-piece swimsuit hid most of the few extra pounds she carried. A few feet away, a good-looking black-haired man several years her junior also sat in a lounger, holding a frosty drink.

The moment Lucy spotted Gabe, she shot to her feet, the pineapple hanging from the side of her glass tumbling onto the cement.

"What are you doing back here?" her companion asked, setting his drink aside and rising from his chair. "Who are you?"

"It's all right, Colin." Lucille picked up a terry-cloth robe and slipped it on over her swimsuit. "We've met somewhere, haven't we? I'm afraid with all that's happened your name seems to have escaped me."

"Gabriel Raines. I did the remodel on your husband's clothing store a few years back."

"Of course. Now I remember."

Strangely, he had the feeling she had known who he was the moment he'd set foot on the patio. "This is my friend Mattie Baker. We came by to express our condolences on the loss of your husband. I didn't mean to intrude." Because he hadn't expected to find Artie's widow entertaining poolside two days after his death. "I just wanted to leave word with someone that I had stopped by."

"I appreciate that," Lucy said. "This is my attorney, Colin Royce." She glanced down at the robe covering her swimsuit. "I hope you don't think I'm being disrespectful…"

"We all grieve in different ways," Mattie said.

"Colin… Mr. Royce and I needed to talk about the estate. I thought it would be better if we were outside in the sunshine rather than sitting inside swamped with memories."

"I understand," Gabe said. "I liked your husband. I just wanted you to know that if there is anything at all you need—"

"I appreciate the offer, Mr. Raines." She turned to Mattie. "A pleasure meeting you, Ms. Baker."

"You as well, Mrs. Roser."

Gabe left the pair on the patio and walked Mattie back to the car.

"Not exactly the grieving widow," she said as she slid behind the steering wheel, dragged the red scarf out of her purse, swept it over her head and tied it beneath her chin.

"Not exactly."

"She knew who you were from the start. I saw it in her eyes when she spotted you."

"I thought so, too."

She fired up the powerful BMW engine, turned and cast him a glance. "You and Mrs. Roser…the two of you were never—"

"God, no."

Mattie looked relieved. "I just thought maybe... You know that old saying about a woman scorned."

"Yeah, I know it. In this case, it doesn't apply." But it did apply to Rachael Sanders. Worry about Clay settled heavily on his chest.

"Where to from here?" Mattie asked.

"No place until tonight. Then I thought I'd stop in at the Jolly Roger, see if Clay might show up."

"Good idea."

He caught her determined expression and firmly shook his head. "Forget it. I'm not taking you with me. If Clay *is* there and he's involved in this mess—"

"If Clay Sanders is the arsonist, you show up looking for him and he spots you, he'll realize you've figured out he's the man setting the fires and he's liable to run. Let me go in, ask a few questions. If he's there, we can call the police. If he isn't, maybe the bartender will know where to find him."

"No way. Besides, if he's been watching me, he might have seen you, too."

"He won't recognize me—I promise. In the meantime, while you're thinking about it and coming to your senses, I need to go to work."

"I thought you took the week off."

"I did, but there are a couple of projects I need to check on. If I stay on top of them, it's going to be a lot easier to play catch-up when I go back to the office. And I want to go by the hospital."

Gabe nodded. "All right. I need to do some work myself. Sam's good, but I don't expect him to handle everything by himself."

"Great. I'll drop you back at your condo so you can get your truck then meet you back there later."

"Deal, but promise me you won't go anywhere else and you'll be careful."

"Bet on it, big guy."

Gabe leaned over and kissed her.

AFTER DROPPING GABE OFF, Mattie stopped by her apartment to feed and check on Tigger and pick up something to wear to the Jolly Roger. She was sure she could find a way to convince Gabe to let her go with him and, dressed as Lena Sterling, Sanders wasn't likely to recognize her even if he had seen her with Gabe. She bent down to give Tigger a final chin rub and the phone began to ring.

Mattie walked over and picked up the receiver. "Hello?"

Nothing.

"Hello? Is anyone there?"

She could hear music in the background and what might have been the sound of someone breathing. A little trickle of fear slipped through her as the person on the end of the line hung up the phone.

The first three or four times it had happened, she hadn't been concerned. The person on the other end never said anything threatening, just seemed to be listening to the sound of her voice.

But lately, with all that had been happening, the calls were beginning to make her nervous. She had done a lot of volunteer work at the center. Some of the kids she came in contact with were pretty rough. Was it one of them? Or did it have something to do with the fires?

After leaving her apartment, she stopped by the Family Recovery Center. She wanted to find out if any of the other volunteers had reported receiving prank calls.

"Not as far as I know," the young black-haired receptionist, Sophie Dominquez, said. "If anybody's been getting calls, they haven't mentioned it. You're thinking it might be someone you met down here?"

"I don't know. It could be random." *Or it could be the guy who's been busy burning down Gabe's buildings.* But she hated to say that to Gabe, who was already ridiculously protective. She didn't want to add to his worries with something so trivial, at least not until she had more to go on than a few hang-up phone calls.

"Thanks, Sophie." Before she headed for the office, Mattie drove to the hospital to check on Angel.

In a room he now shared with another teenage boy, the victim of a motorcycle accident, Angel lay in the exact position he had been in when she had been there to see him before. His eyes were closed, his coloring pale. Monitors attached to his chest beeped his vital signs. As she sat down beside him, Mattie said a silent prayer for his recovery, reached over and took hold of his cool, limp hand.

She talked to him for a while, telling him how much the people at the Zigman gallery liked Enrique's work and that they were planning to have a show for him.

"You have to get well," she said, "so that you can be there that night with your friend."

But Angel made no reply and as she left the boy's side some time later, Mattie's heart felt heavy.

It was midafternoon by the time she reached the Coffman Building and took the elevator up to her office on the fifteenth floor.

"I thought you were on vacation," Shirley Mack said, leaning over to deliver a fistful of messages.

"I am. Sort of." But the minute she pushed through

the doors leading into the drafting area, Aaron and two other draftsmen came hurrying toward her.

"I'm glad you're here." Aaron rolled up beside her. "We ran across another problem on those drawings of the school we've been working on."

One of the newer guys, Matt Davidson, spoke up before she had time to reply. "And I was hoping to talk to you about your gallery project. The mechanical engineer says we need a larger pipe tunnel to accommodate the return air."

"When you get a chance," said the third draftsman, Joey Chin, "I've got a problem with that office building over on Commerce. The client's demanding a conference room that doubles as a media room seating forty. I thought maybe if we put our heads together we might be able to come up with a solution."

Mattie managed not to sigh. "Give me a minute to return some of these phone calls and I'll be right with you."

"Thanks, Mattie," all of them said in unison.

As she continued toward her office, she passed Mel Freeman, whose mouth edged up in a mocking smile. Once inside, she closed the door and let her pent-up sigh escape.

She should have known better than to try to take time off. Too much was happening, too many projects needed her attention. She had a demanding job with endless responsibilities. She needed to be doing what she was paid for, not running off with Gabe in search of an arsonist.

She thought of the decision she had made when she had first started her job at the firm. *Work comes first.* It was her mantra. At the time, she had sworn she wouldn't get involved in any sort of relationship.

Now there was Gabe. The nights she spent with him were amazing. She wished she could say it was just the sex, but she would be lying to herself.

She enjoyed just being with him. She appreciated his intelligence and sense of humor. She wanted to spend time with him.

Way too much.

And there was her promise to Angel. She was the one who had suggested he help Gabe find the arsonist. It was her suggestion that had gotten him assaulted. She had vowed to find the man who had hurt him.

She couldn't let him down.

Mattie rubbed her eyes and tried not to get discouraged. Seated in her leather executive chair, she turned on her computer and set to work. With so much catching up to do, not to mention the help her associates needed, she wouldn't be home until after six. She made a mental note to call Gabe and tell him.

Mattie bit her lip. The phone call was just one more indication that she was getting too involved.

She had to slow things down, put her life back into proper perspective. When the week was over, whether they caught the arsonist or not, she was returning to her own apartment. No more nights with Gabe, only an occasional sleepover, as he called it. Assuming he would still be interested.

A dull ache settled in Mattie's chest.

"Looks like we're making good progress," Gabe said to Sam as they stood in the open, three-story lobby of the Dallas Towers.

"The building inspector was here earlier. Building

passed the electrical inspection. We're getting ready to start on the interior walls."

"That's great."

"I was over at Greenwood earlier," Sam said. "The painters are hard at it. We're about to start putting in cabinets."

"I stopped by on my way over here. Everything looks good." And he had spoken to the Atlas security guard. No one suspicious had been hanging around. No one had been prowling around at night.

"At least we haven't had any slowdowns there," Sam said.

None so far. "We're back down to the foundation on McKinney Court. The bad news is Wildcat Oil is getting nervous. Two of my projects have burned. They're afraid the guy who did it will target their building again as soon as we get it up. And they don't even know about the fire at Artie's."

"What did you say to them?"

"I told them the cops were going to have the bastard in jail long before their building got that far along."

"So what about Artie's? You really figure the fact you remodeled the place three years ago was enough for this nutcase to burn it down?"

"I wouldn't put anything past him. In fact, I'm hiring a night watchman for your place, too."

Sam rifled a hand through his short blond hair. "You can't protect everyone you've ever met, Gabe."

"I suppose not." But he intended to try.

One of the guys in the crew interrupted the conversation. Sam answered a couple of questions then walked with Gabe to his truck.

"So how's it going with Mattie?" Sam asked.

"She's great and I'm in deep trouble. How about you and Tracy?"

"Same here. We've been together every evening, but I still haven't spent the night. It's like she's a different person, Gabe. Free somehow. She trusts me not to take advantage, and I'm determined not to disappoint her. Unfortunately, I have no idea where to go from here."

"To bed, I would say."

"Sounds good to me, but I don't know what will happen once we do. I really like her, Gabe. If I take her to bed, she might treat me like the other guys she's been with. If I don't, sooner or later, I'll lose her for sure."

"Rock and a hard place."

Sam grinned. "You can say that again."

Gabe laughed. "Good luck, buddy."

"You, too."

As Gabe climbed into his pickup and headed for the Egyptian Theater, he heard a faint chiming on his phone. Pulling it out of his pocket, he read the text message rolling across the screen.

Can't you see? It wasn't me. Next time, it will be.

A chill rose at the back of his neck. The arsonist knew his cell phone number. Either that or someone was playing a very unfunny joke.

Christ.

He didn't know if the police could trace a text message, but he sure as hell meant to try. Being careful not to erase the call, he phoned Thomas Daily, then set off for the fire captain's Marilla Street office.

Daily was in when he got there. "Actually, these days we *can* locate the sender," the captain said as he took the phone from Gabe's hand. "We've got the technology. The problem is, if it is the guy who's been setting the fires, he's smart. Too smart to get himself caught by something as simple as this. If it's him and not someone playing a joke, odds are, he used a disposable phone."

Gabe hadn't thought of that but it made perfect sense. "Think the caller could be telling the truth? Is it possible someone else set the fire?"

"Might be. We're looking at a couple of interesting developments. I'm not at liberty just yet to tell you what they are."

Gabe didn't press for more. He considered himself lucky the fire captain had been as up front as he had been, probably wouldn't have been nearly so helpful if it hadn't been for the favor Gabe had done for his father.

"We'll get what we need from this and you can pick it up in an hour or so," the captain said.

"Any word on Sanders?"

"If he's in town, he's staying out of sight."

"Yeah, Clay's good at that. Appreciate your help, Captain."

"Stay safe, my friend."

Gabe just nodded.

He had a hunch the message had come from the arsonist and that the captain was right. A throwaway phone wouldn't lead them anywhere. Which meant his best bet was to find Clay Sanders.

And the place to start looking was the Jolly Roger.

CHAPTER TWENTY-ONE

Mattie decided to return to her apartment and change for the evening before she went back to Gabe's. Once he saw her dressed as a blonde Lena Sterling, he might be easier to convince.

Even though she had called and told him she was on her way, Gabe was pacing the floor by the time she arrived at his condo. Using the key he had given her, she opened the door and stepped into the entry.

Gabe stopped pacing and just stared. "What the hell?"

She did a little pirouette, allowing him to take in the curly blond wig, short white skirt, red top and big white hoop earrings. "I told you Sanders wouldn't recognize me."

Those incredible blue eyes of his darkened for an instant before he strode toward her, hauled her into his arms and very thoroughly kissed her. Her heart was pumping by the time he let her go.

"Why don't we put this bar visit off until a little later?" he said gruffly.

Mattie laughed. "I guess you like me as a blonde."

"I like you as a redhead and even better than that, I like you naked." He drew her close again, let her feel his erection. "See what I mean?"

Mattie grinned and shook her head. "We have something more important to do and you know it. Besides, once we're finished, we'll have the rest of the night to make love."

Gabe groaned. "Lady, you sure know what to say to get what you want."

She spun around once more. "So what do you think? We go to the Jolly Roger. I go in and you watch me through the windows. I'll talk to the bartender, see what I can find out. If we get lucky, maybe Sanders will show up and we can call the police."

"What if the place doesn't have any windows?"

"It does. I drove by on my way over here."

His mouth tightened and he scowled. "Honey, you are pushing your luck."

"You know I'm right. If you go in there asking questions, the bartender will tell Clay you're looking for him. He'll be able to describe you, and Clay will know you're after him. If I go in, he won't have a clue."

A muscle ticked in his cheek. He didn't want her to go. Still, she could see he knew she was right. If they wanted to find Clay, they needed information. In her sexy skirt and low-cut blouse, she had a lot better chance of getting what they needed than Gabe did.

"Time to head 'em up and move 'em out," she said airily as she brushed past him toward the door and managed to get him to smile. "It's from an old Western TV series. *Rawhide.* I had a crush on Clint Eastwood when I was a teen."

His mouth edged up. "So you really do like cowboys."

She glanced down, saw he was wearing his boots. "I really do."

His eyes darkened. "Sure you don't want to stay?"

"I'd love some of what you'd like to give me, cowboy, but I think we'd better go."

Gabe grinned as he urged her toward the door, then his smile slipped away. "I hate this," he grumbled.

"Honestly, the place didn't look that bad. At least from the outside. Besides, if something goes wrong, you can play hero and save me."

Gabe just grunted.

Instead of taking his pickup, which Sanders might have seen, they drove her BMW with the top up and parked at the edge of the lot in a shadowy area out of the reach of the streetlights.

The building itself, a freestanding brick structure, had a covered porch with a red-and-black pirate sign out front. Neon beer signs blazed through windows that lined both sides of the bar, just as she had said. As they moved through the darkness at the edge of the parking lot, the clack and clatter of pool balls from inside the building reached them on the still night air.

"I'll be out here watching you," Gabe said softly. "Anything goes wrong, I'll be there as fast as I can."

Mattie knew he would be. Gabe bent down and pressed a quick, hard kiss on her mouth, then disappeared.

With a deep, calming breath, she moved toward the wide wooden steps leading up to the covered porch. Through the windows in front, she saw several other women sitting at tables or bar stools and relaxed a little. Apparently the place was at least somewhat respectable.

As she pushed through the door, she surveyed the black pirate flags, fake crossed sabers, motorcycle paraphernalia and the skull-and-crossbones on the walls. Three men stood around a pool table off to one side and a couple sat at a small round table sipping beer they poured from a frosty pitcher.

As she had said, it wasn't really a rough joint. It was mostly an after-work crowd in their late twenties and thirties, and it was still early enough that none of them seemed to be drunk.

She walked up to the bar and took a seat on one of the black vinyl stools. The bartender, a few years older than she, dark haired and good looking with an earring in one ear, mopped the bar in front of her.

"What can I get you, darlin'?"

"You wouldn't have a Lone Star back there, would you?"

"Sure do." He set a cold bottle in front of her and popped the cap.

"Thanks." Mattie took a long, refreshing swallow and set the bottle back down on the bar.

"I don't think I've seen you in here before," the bartender said.

"I'm visiting a friend. She lives a few blocks away. She won't be home until later and I was desperate for a beer."

"I get that. What's your name?"

"Lena." She smiled. "What's yours?"

"Tommy. Tommy McClure. I'm the owner."

"Nice to meet you, Tommy." They shook hands across the bar. "You know, my friend Mary has a friend who comes in here. His name is Clay Sanders. You know him?"

"Sure. I know Clay. Nice guy."

A great guy—except when he's burning down buildings. "Has he been in tonight?"

"Not yet, but he'll probably show up. He stops by at

least three or four times a week, usually between eight and nine."

Mattie flicked a glance at the window, wishing she could tell Gabe, but there was no sign of him. *He's a marine,* she reminded herself. *He won't be easy to spot.*

Mattie sipped her beer, taking her time, occasionally watching the door. People came and went. A rougher crowd began to gather. When a couple of disreputable-looking men began making dirty wisecracks and started in her direction, Tommy raised a sawed-off pool cue and shook his head. The men stopped where they were, turned and went back their seats, grumbling but not really mad. Clearly, Tommy's customers had a grudging respect for him.

Mattie glanced at the clock and ordered another Lone Star, sipped it even more slowly. When the clock hit nine-thirty, she set the half-finished bottle down and asked for the check.

Tommy brought it over. "I guess your girlfriend isn't going to show," he said.

"I guess not." She paid the bill with cash and left a hefty tip on the bar. She was just sliding off the stool when the front door opened and a man walked in. In jeans and an olive-drab T-shirt, he was as tall as Gabe but with a leaner, more sinewy build. He would have been handsome if it hadn't been for his slightly crooked nose and uneven eyebrows. Still, he was attractive.

Gabe had shown her a photo of Clay taken ten years ago. But even if she hadn't seen it, she would have known she had just found Clayton Sanders. There was an air of danger about him. He looked like the kind of man who could burn down a building if he wanted.

Mattie picked up her purse, slung the strap over her

shoulder, and started across the wooden floor toward the door. If Gabe was watching, by now he had spotted Clay and called the police. She listened for the sound of sirens, certain she would hear them any minute.

Instead, as she passed Clay's table, his chair moved backward, grating against the floor as he came to his feet.

"Where you goin' in such a hurry, sweetheart?" The words came out a little slurred and she realized he had already had plenty to drink.

"Just heading home." She continued walking but Clay caught her arm and spun her around to face him. His heavy-lidded gaze slid over her, taking in the curly blond hair, short skirt and low-cut top. "I could use a little company. How about I buy you a drink?"

Mattie gently tried to pull free. If he didn't let go in the next few seconds, she had no doubt Gabe would come crashing through the door.

Instead of releasing her, Clay sat down and tugged her into his lap. "Now, isn't that better?"

Mattie's heart was racing. Her eyes shot to the door at the sound of heavy footfalls charging up the wooden stairs. Then Gabe was there, hauling her out of Clay's lap.

"You don't want to mess with her," Gabe warned.

Sanders rose lazily to his feet, not the least bit intimidated by the furious, towering figure leaning over him.

"Well, if it isn't my old buddy Gabe."

Gabe drew Mattie behind him. "What are you doing in Dallas, Clay?"

"Why? Do I need your permission to be here?"

"You do if you're here burning down my buildings."

Sanders's smile turned wolfish. "I heard about that. Nobody deserves it more."

"That right?" Gabe's hands fisted. "How about the boy you beat to a pulp to keep him from asking questions?"

Clay shook his head. "I don't know anything about that."

Mattie ran to the bar. "Call the police, Tommy."

"No way. I don't want any trouble." But he rounded the bar, holding his cutoff pool cue, heading straight for Clay and Gabe.

"You two want to fight? Take it outside."

Gabe's features looked carved in stone. Sanders just smiled. Mattie didn't see the roundhouse punch he threw until it hit Gabe squarely in the jaw. Mattie shrieked and the fight was on. Chairs scraped as patrons stood up and moved back to give the fighters room, then stood watching with a sort of primal glee.

Mattie's gaze flew to the door but no help appeared to be coming. Tommy headed back to the bar, resigned to calling the police. Mattie prayed Gabe had already called them.

Her attention returned to the two big men and for an instant she forgot to breathe. One blow followed another. Gabe was powerful and every punch earned a grunt from Clay. But Clay was quick, and though he struck less often, each blow landed with devastating accuracy and solid force. Gabe threw a body blow that had to have cracked a rib. Clay lowered his head and rammed Gabe in the middle, carrying backward till both of them crashed into the wall.

Blood flew from a shot to Sanders's nose. Clay split

Gabe's lip and blood leaked from the corner of his mouth.

Mattie watched with terrified fascination. She had never seen a real fistfight, certainly not a fight between two powerful men determined to knock each other senseless, or worse. Clay staggered from a heavy blow, then bounced back and got a choke hold around Gabe's neck. For the first time, Mattie realized Gabe could be in mortal danger.

You know he went Force Recon?

Gabe had said that was like being a Navy SEAL or Green Beret. Mattie wasn't waiting a moment longer. Her half-empty beer bottle sat on the bar. Racing toward it, she grabbed the bottle by the neck, ran over to the men and slammed the heavy brown glass down hard on Sanders's head.

The bottle shattered, beer ran down Clay's forehead and he went down like a sack of cement.

Breathing in deep, unsteady breaths, Gabe straightened, propping his hands on his thighs as he worked to bring himself under control. His gaze shot to Mattie, who still held the broken neck of the beer bottle. Her legs were shaking, her hands trembling. Striding toward her, Gabe gently took the bottle neck from her hand, set it aside and eased her into his arms.

"It's all right, honey. The cops are on the way. They know Clay's here. They'll be more than happy to take him into custody."

The wail of sirens reached her through the buzzing in her ears. She took a steadying breath, but couldn't bring her trembling under control.

"You gonna be all right?" Gabe asked.

Mattie nodded. Sanders still lay unconscious. His

nose oozed blood all over his faded olive-drab T-shirt as a half dozen blue-uniformed policemen swarmed into the bar.

"You must be Raines," one of them said.

"I'm Raines. I made the call. He's all yours."

The fair-haired cop just nodded.

Gabe blotted his bloody lip with the edge of his hand and graced Mattie with a crooked half smile. "Looks like you were the one who played hero tonight."

She reached up and touched the purple bruise rising on his cheek. "Are you kidding? You were amazing." She didn't normally condone any sort of fighting, but in this case, she was glad Gabe was such a capable man.

"If he hadn't been drunk, I'd be in a lot worse shape than I am."

Mattie fought to ignore a chill. "At least the police have him in custody. Your buildings will be safe from now on."

Gabe just nodded.

They stayed at the bar long enough to give a statement and pay Tommy for the damages the fight had caused.

"Thanks," the bar owner said, sliding the money into the till and slamming it closed with a ring. "I take it Clay was already in some kind of trouble."

"That's the way it looks."

"Too bad. I liked him."

"There was a time I did, too," Gabe said, and she could read the regret in his face.

"He said he didn't assault Angel," Mattie reminded him.

"That's what he *said*. Doesn't mean it's true."

But if he had done it and Clay proved to be the arsonist, she and Gabe would both be able to finally put the matter to rest.

She left the bar with Gabe's arm around her and they drove back to his condo.

Even battered and bruised, he kept his word about the lovemaking. Mattie told herself it was all right to enjoy the time they had together. Even if she allowed herself to stay through the end of the week, by Monday she would be back in her own apartment.

The thought brought an unexpected stab of regret.

Which meant she was doing exactly the right thing.

CHAPTER TWENTY-TWO

THE SOUNDS OF Wednesday morning traffic rose up from the street below his condo the following morning. Gabe watched Mattie wandering around his apartment, picking up an object here and there, unconsciously straightening the newspapers he'd left on the coffee table.

It seemed so natural for her to be there, not like the few other women who had ever spent the night. He was always eager for them to leave.

Dressed in tan slacks and a pink paisley blouse, Mattie planned to stop at the hospital this morning before heading down to her office. He should have been eager for a little time to himself. Instead, he wished she would stay.

Sipping from her mug of coffee, she disappeared into his study, a room he used as his home office. Carrying his own steaming cup, he followed her inside the room, which was furnished with a big oak desk and swivel chair and landscape photos he had taken out at the ranch, framed in oak and hung on the walls.

Mattie ambled over to the drafting table against the wall and picked up the roll of plans that were lying on top. Setting down her cup, she unrolled the plans and began to examine them. She must have sensed his presence for she looked up and saw him watching her.

"You don't mind, do you? Curiosity is kind of a hazard of the job."

He just smiled. "Be my guest. Those are the old original plans for the warehouse I'm getting ready to rebuild. I only got hold of them a couple of days before all of this started. I haven't had a chance to look at them yet."

Mattie gazed down at the plans, which were tattered, yellowed and greasy. The building was forty years old and needed a complete renovation.

"What are you going to do with it?" she asked.

"I'm not sure yet. I thought maybe shops or galleries on the ground floor, apartments upstairs. At the moment, it's pretty much an eyesore. The neighbors just want me to get started, no matter what I do."

Mattie started thumbing through the drawings and Gabe made his way back into the kitchen to refill his cup. His cell phone sat next to the coffeemaker and Gabe reached over and picked it up, intending to call his brother.

The police had phoned earlier. Clay had professed his innocence, then clammed up tight. Since he didn't have a residence in the area and had been arrested under suspicion of setting three fires that included a possible homicide, he was held without bail.

If Clay was guilty, Gabe had no pity for him.

On the other hand, even after the comments Clay had made in the bar, Gabe had trouble thinking of his one-time friend as an arsonist.

Which was what he told his brother when he punched in Dev's number to let him know that Sanders had been arrested.

"Clay could have done it," Dev said. "The man has

the talent and with his wife in Dallas, he has the motive."

"No doubt it could have been him. Clay's smart and well trained, but…"

"But he's a marine and once was your friend and you can't imagine him burning down your buildings to get back at you."

"That's about it."

"Jackson called. He's worried."

Gabe chuckled. "Jackson's been worried about his two little brothers since he was ten years old."

Dev laughed. "I guess some things don't change."

They said their goodbyes and Gabe hung up the phone and stuffed it into the pocket of his jeans. Mattie wandered out of his study and as she walked past, Gabe leaned down and kissed her.

She reached up and stroked his cheek. "I've got to get going."

"Yeah, me too."

Picking up her purse, she slung the strap over her shoulder. "I'll see you this afternoon." She wiggled her fingers in farewell as she walked out the door. Gabe grabbed his wallet and keys off the kitchen counter, took a last swig from his mug of now cold coffee and followed her into the hall.

Like Mattie, he had work to do.

Twenty minutes later, he arrived at his first stop of the day, the Greenwood Apartments. He had just gotten out of his truck and started toward the rhythmic pounding of hammers when a big white Mercedes S550 rolled up and Carlton Webster climbed out from behind the fancy wood-grain steering wheel.

Tall and silver-haired, at fifty years old Webster was

in prime physical condition. He wore two-thousand-dollar suits, was married to a woman twenty years younger and he could afford her.

"Hello, Gabe."

"Carlton."

Webster lived in one of the expensive high-rise condos near the Farmer's Market. He'd been fiercely opposed to Gabe's notion of rehabbing the then-named Harwood Apartments into affordable housing. Webster adamantly believed they should be converted into expensive condominiums. Webster had even offered to buy Gabe out.

"Haven't seen you around for a while," Gabe said. "What can I do for you?"

"I read about your troubles in the newspaper. Two fires in only a few weeks' time. Must have been quite a setback."

Three fires, Gabe thought. "It's cost us a lot of time, that's for sure."

"And money, I imagine."

"Some."

"You must be a little worried about Greenwood becoming a target."

"I've got security cameras up and guards round the clock."

"Still…it could happen."

"I suppose. Why don't you get to the point, Webster?"

"The point is, I'd like to make you another offer. You're good at your job. The work your company has done on the building so far is above satisfactory. If you were to sell me the apartments, I could have my people take over from here and make the place into the sort of first-class property that would fit into the neighbor-hood."

Gabe hadn't put Webster on his suspect list. He'd had no reason to believe the man would go as far as arson to get what he wanted—not that he would have to do the job himself. Webster could afford to hire a professional. Gabe hadn't considered he would. Now he wondered.

"You want this place that badly?"

"You know how I feel. I've made no secret of it."

There'd been newspaper articles, TV interviews, a neighborhood movement to stop Gabe from getting the permits he needed. But another group just as adamantly wanted the project to succeed.

"The residents who live in the neighborhood have spent a great deal of money on their properties," Webster continued. "They don't want the class of people you'll be renting to living just down the block. It isn't good for property values. The fair thing would be for you to sell."

Gabe just shook his head. He'd worked too hard on the project to give it up now. Aside from that, he didn't believe in Webster's concept. Greenwood wasn't some skid-row development. The apartments wouldn't have marble-floored entries or bidets in the bathrooms, but they were well-designed and were going to be extremely attractive.

"Sorry, Webster. Whatever you might have believed, Greenwood isn't for sale."

Webster's perfectly groomed features tightened. "Whatever you say. But if your firebug strikes again and Greenwood burns to the ground, don't expect my price to be the same."

Gabe's jaw clenched as the man walked away. He

made a mental note to mention the encounter to Thomas Daily. In that same vein, as Webster pulled his flashy Mercedes away from the curb, he clicked open his cell and phoned his brother.

"I've got another name I want you to check on," Gabe said.

"Yeah? You're still thinking Clay might not be your guy?"

"I just want to be sure."

"I hear ya. Fire away."

Gabe told his brother about his encounter with wealthy Carlton Webster and his latest offer to buy the apartments. "Webster figured, since I'd been having so much trouble, I'd be happy to get rid of the place. When I told him I wasn't interested, he wished me the worst. Said after the place burned down, his offer wouldn't be nearly as good."

"Let the cops know. In the meantime, I'll check him out."

"Thanks."

"Listen, I was getting ready to call you anyway. First, about that text message you got…"

"Yeah, what about it?"

"The guy who sent it might be telling the truth. Maybe he didn't set the fire at Artie's Men's Wear."

"Don't stop now, I'm all ears."

"Lucille Roser was the beneficiary of a big fat life insurance policy on the death of her dear departed husband. She's also in line for the insurance proceeds from the destruction of the building. Combined, it adds up to a very hefty sum."

"How hefty?"

"Seven figures. The life insurance policy was for three million. Artie took it out about a year ago."

"You're saying it just might be coincidence that Raines Construction did the remodel?"

"You know how much I believe in coincidence."

"About as much as you believe in unicorns."

Dev laughed. "You gotta figure, if Lucille read the newspapers or even watched the news on TV, she'd know about the fires and that the police have speculated that you, personally, were the target. It makes the arson on her building a lot more believable if the police think it's just another hit on you."

And it would explain Lucy's little celebration two days after her husband's death. "You're figuring she hired a torch, someone who would take care of poor Artie and cover it up with a fire."

"Lots of people out there who make that kind of thing their business. Whoever she hired could have dug up whatever info he could find on how the fires on your buildings were set then tried to make it look like the same doer."

Gabe blew out a breath, praying his brother was right. If Lucy had arranged the fire, Gabe was in no way responsible for Artie's death.

"Captain Daily called this morning," he said. "He was right about the text message coming from a throwaway phone. They didn't come up with a thing."

"Figures."

"Stay on this, will you, Dev?"

"You know I will."

Gabe flipped his phone closed and no more than shoved it into his pocket when his Brooks and Dunn ringtone started and he pulled it out and flipped it open again.

Jackson's voice came over the line. "What's the latest and how are you holding up?"

"I'm fine. They arrested Clay Sanders last night."

"How'd that happen?"

"If you could see the bruises on my face, you'd know."

Jackson chuckled.

"Actually, after we pummeled each other into hamburger, the lady I was with took him down with a beer bottle over the head."

"I take it this wasn't the straitlaced little architect you were seeing."

"Actually, it was. The lady's just full of surprises."

"Interesting. Cops think Clay set the fires?"

"They're pretty much convinced."

"What about the boy? Angel, wasn't it? Did Clay assault the kid?"

"I don't know. If Clay wanted him out of the way, he'd be dead. Of course, he could have just meant to scare the kid into keeping his nose out of things and hurt the boy worse than he intended."

"You still don't sound totally convinced Clay's your man."

"Not completely."

"Then maybe it's a good thing I called. You know that contractor, the guy you butt heads with all the time?"

"Vance Gleason?"

"That's the guy. I did a little checking, no stone unturned and all that. Looks like Gleason's about to go bankrupt. On top of that, his wife's giving him the boot."

"How the hell did you find that out? Never mind. Google, right?"

"Bingo."

"Vance lost the bid on McKinney Court. Also lost out on the Towers. Still, it seems pretty far-fetched to think he'd blame me because he's going broke."

"Just thought you ought to know."

"Thanks. Like you say, no stone unturned."

"Listen, maybe once this is over, Sarah and I can come down and meet your lady. Sounds like my kinda woman."

The kind who would try to protect him against a guy as tough as Clay. Gabe still couldn't quite believe it.

"Maybe that would work." They ended the call and Gabe thought of Mattie. His brother considered them a pair, but Mattie kept her emotions well guarded and he had no real idea what she felt for him, aside from the satisfaction she got from him in bed. Whatever she felt, she was scared to death of becoming too deeply involved.

Damn. What she didn't know and he could hardly tell her was that he was scared spitless himself.

CHAPTER TWENTY-THREE

TRACY NEEDED TO talk to Mattie. She had tried calling her cell phone but the call had gone straight to voice mail. Figuring she was probably at the office, Tracy tried that number next, found her friend there and managed to convince her to take a break and meet her at the coffee kiosk in the Coffman Building lobby.

"I thought you took the week off," Tracy said as she carried two paper cups over to the small wire-mesh table, a cappuccino for Mattie and a mocha special Egyptian blend for herself.

"I did. I'm just working for a couple of hours. I've got some problems I need to take care of."

"Right." She handed the cappuccino to Mattie and settled herself in one of the chairs. "Listen, it's Wednesday. I was thinking maybe we'd go down to Club Rio tonight. We haven't been there in nearly three weeks."

"Sorry, I can't." Mattie took a cautious sip of the scalding drink. "Gabe and I are going out to dinner. I'm taking him to Asian Fusion. I think he'll like it. He's discovering he likes a wider range of tastes than he thought."

Tracy sipped her coffee. "Sounds like the two of you are getting pretty serious."

Mattie shrugged. "Not really. I'm only staying with

him until my vacation time is up. That's the end of the week."

Tracy took another sip. "Well, I think I'm going anyway."

"Sam won't mind?"

"We aren't a couple, you know. So far our relationship is strictly platonic."

"That's too bad."

"In a way, I guess. In another way it's been nice. He's really a sweet guy. I'm glad I had a chance to get to know him."

"That sounds like past tense."

Tracy looked away. "Maybe. I guess I'll see what happens tonight."

Mattie reached over and caught her hand. "Whatever you do, be sure you're making the right decision. If Sam is really special, you might not want to lose him."

Tracy ignored the heaviness in her chest. She wasn't cut out for a serious relationship and that seemed to be where she was headed with Sam.

She remembered the terrible fights her parents had had, the beatings she and her mother had suffered. She didn't need a man. She didn't want one.

Not even Sam.

"I've got to get back to work." Mattie stood up. "Thanks for the cappuccino. You know it's my favorite." She held up the cup, which she planned to take back with her.

"You're welcome. Your treat next time."

"Be careful tonight."

"I'm always careful." But Tracy was less sure what she really wanted to do than she had ever been before.

She thought of Sam's sweet laugh, the wicked glint

in his warm brown eyes when he looked at her. Sam made her wonder if maybe she was wrong, if there really could be such a thing as happily ever after.

Tracy shook her head. Who was she kidding? Sam was no different from any other man she had known.

Returning to her office, she made some client calls, dropped some loan applications off at the mortgage company, showed a house and finally went home.

Eventually it was time to dress for the evening and she chose one of her sexiest outfits, a flashy hot-pink leather miniskirt and matching vest that closed with only three buttons up the front and required no bra.

Club Rio was packed by the time she pushed through the doors, filled with the sounds of laughter and the clinking of glasses. The karaoke singer on stage finished a slow Sinatra song and drew an unenthusiastic round of applause. Tracy searched for a friendly face, spotted a girl she knew—another real estate agent who was sitting at a table full of men.

"Hey, Tracy!" Heather waved her over. "I'm glad you're here. I can use a little help." She grinned and tipped her head toward the table full of admirers.

Tracy laughed as one of them jumped up and pulled out a chair. As she sat down, her gaze unconsciously went to the bar in search of Sam, but he wasn't there. She didn't expect the tug of disappointment. She was out on the town tonight and she was ready to party.

"Bring the lady a Cosmo," one of the guys at the table said. "Make it a double." He was handsome and well-built, the kind of man she might have taken home. Tonight the thought was strangely unappealing.

The evening progressed. Tracy drank a couple of double Cosmos but her mood didn't improve. One of the guys told a dirty joke and she forced herself to laugh. Then her eyes strayed toward the bar for the tenth time that night and there he was.

Her breath caught.

Sam leaned against the bar, his gaze fixed on her face. An empty beer bottle sat in front of him, which meant he had been there a while. Been there and just stood watching.

He raised the bottle he was drinking from in a silent salute, finished it off, set it back down on the bar and started for the door.

Tracy felt sick to her stomach.

Her hand trembled as she pushed back her chair. Her legs were shaking so badly, she could barely get them to move. Once she did, the door seemed miles away.

"Hey, Tracy," the handsome guy Nick called out. "Where you goin'?"

Tracy didn't bother to answer, just kept moving toward the door.

In the parking lot, she spotted Sam's flashy red pickup. He hadn't reached it yet, but he was walking with purpose and she knew if she didn't stop him, she would never see him again.

"Sam! Sam, wait!" She hurried faster, stumbled and almost fell. "Sam, please, wait!"

Her eyes filled. She had to reach him before it was too late. "Sam, please." She couldn't see him anymore through the haze of her tears. She didn't realize he had spotted her, stopped and turned, until she slammed into him.

"Sam…"

He gripped her shoulders. "What do you want, Tracy? You've got half a dozen men in there willing to take you home."

The tears in her eyes spilled over, began to roll down her cheeks. "I don't want them."

"What *do* you want, then?" He pushed her up against the door of his truck. "You want me to fuck you right here? Because I'm sure as hell ready."

She had never seen him so angry. She should have been frightened. She didn't understand why she was not. "I don't…don't want it like that. Not with you."

"No? I think you do."

She swallowed past the lump in her throat and shook her head, her straight blond hair sliding around her cheeks. "No, I… I don't know… I just… I don't want you to go, Sam."

Some of his anger faded. Very gently he eased her into his arms. "I think I know what you want." He reached down and took hold of her hand. "Come on, we're leaving."

She clung to his arm, dashed the tears from her cheeks. "Where are we going?"

"My house."

She didn't fight him, just let him help her into his truck, snap her seat belt across her lap and close the door. She leaned back against the seat as he drove out of the parking lot.

She had no idea what would happen when they reached his place. But the sense of relief she was feeling told her going after him had been the right decision.

She had never been to Sam's apartment and as she walked in she discovered it was tidy and nicely decorated in dark, masculine colors. She didn't have much time to look around since he led her straight to the bedroom, turned her into his arms, and very thoroughly kissed her.

She was breathless when he stopped. Tracy slid her arms around his neck. "What if this ruins everything?"

"If it does, there was nothing there worth keeping anyway."

She knew he was right, yet the comfortable feeling she'd always had when she was with him began to fade. It was time for her to perform. She reached for the buttons on his shirt and started unfastening them, but Sam eased her hand away.

"We'll get to that eventually, just not yet."

She looked up at him, a little nervous, and also intrigued. More so as he slowly began to undress her, kissing each part of her body as he removed each piece of her clothing. Every time she reached for him, Sam shook his head and simply kissed her. She was on fire by the time he had her naked, lifted her into his arms and carried her over to the bed.

"You have the softest, most kissable lips," he said as he captured her bottom lip between his teeth then sank his tongue into her mouth. He kissed her long and deep, kissed her as if he could go on just that way all night. She felt warm all over, her body liquid and pliant, so distracted by his attentions she didn't even notice when he left her to remove his own clothes.

As he walked back to the bed, she surveyed his tall figure, his solid chest, wide and lightly furred with golden hair, his body so lean each muscle stood out and she could watch them flex and bunch as he moved.

He was hard, she saw. Bigger than she would have imagined and fiercely aroused, his erection riding high against his flat belly. Still, when he came up over her and started kissing her again, she didn't feel rushed, didn't feel as if she had a performance to give.

"This is what you wanted, Tracy." He kissed the line of her jaw, bent and softly kissed each of her breasts. "You wanted me to make love to you and that is exactly what I'm going to do."

"Sam…" The tears returned to her eyes. She reached up and touched his dear, beloved face. "I think… I think I'm falling in love with you."

Sam traced his thumb over her tear-damp cheek. "Then my plan is actually working."

Tracy breathed a sigh into his mouth as he very softly kissed her. She was falling in love with Sam. She had said so and he wasn't even scared.

"I'm not going to hurt you, Tracy. Whatever happens, I'd never do that."

"Oh, Sam…" For the first time in her life, she felt as if everything was going to be all right, that at last her life had settled onto its proper course.

Winding her arms around Sam's neck, she welcomed him into her body with a joy she had never felt with any other man.

CHAPTER TWENTY-FOUR

THE KITCHEN WAS fragrant with the smell of rich, dark French roast coffee. Gabe had made breakfast this morning. Mattie declined the bacon and eggs he wanted to cook for both of them, inwardly wincing at the thought of all that cholesterol.

But she was thrilled with the nicely halved bagels, cream cheese and raspberry jelly he set on the kitchen table. Gabe put two pieces on her plate and she slathered one of them with cream cheese and jelly and dug in.

"I know Debbie Gleason," she said as she took a sip of the dark, steaming brew in her mug. "I did some design work for her husband and she and I kind of hit it off."

Gabe had told her he planned to visit the contractor's wife today, see what she might be willing to tell him about her husband. "If you want to find out what's going on with Vance, maybe I can help."

"They're getting a divorce. That's what Jackson said. And Vance has filed bankruptcy."

"That's too bad. It's got to be hard on Debbie." She smoothed her knife blade over a gob of raspberry jelly and took a bite.

"I thought he was a pretty good husband," Gabe said, "and fairly savvy in business. I guess you never know."

"You're thinking that if Clay turns out to be innocent, maybe the arsonist is Vance. You figure the stress he's been under might have gotten to him and he shifted the blame for his failures onto you."

"I guess it could happen. The police are convinced it's Clay, but I think it's worth checking out."

"All right." She popped the last jelly-coated bite of bagel into her mouth and took a final sip of her coffee. "Let me grab a quick shower and we'll go see what we can find out."

A wicked blue glint came into his eyes. "Sounds like a good idea to me."

Mattie grinned when he joined her in the shower, not the least surprised. By the time they got out, the water had turned cold and she was shivering.

It was worth it.

Vance Gleason lived in a two-story brick home in Highland Park. Or at least he had until his wife kicked him out.

According to Gabe, Debbie Gleason and her two young children still lived there. Gabe had called ahead and asked if he and Mattie might stop by for a few minutes. Debbie had agreed. Mattie spotted the pretty brick house with the white shutters and vast expanse of well-cared-for lawn and wondered, with the divorce and bankruptcy, how long Debbie and her kids would be able to stay.

Pulling the Beemer over to the curb, Gabe turned off the engine and they both got out of the car. They made their way up the flower-lined walk and Gabe knocked on the front door.

The door opened and a small, dark-haired woman

with her hair pulled back in a ponytail stood in the entry. "Hey, Mattie, good to see you."

"You too, Debbie."

"Hi, Gabe. You're right on time. I admit I'm a little intrigued that you wanted to see me."

"I hope this isn't too big an imposition," Gabe said as Debbie invited them inside.

"Not at all. The kids are in school and as everyone in town seems to know, Vance isn't here, since we're getting a divorce."

"I heard," Mattie said. "I'm really sorry, Debbie. The two of you always seemed so happy."

"I thought we were." She led them down the hall into the great room at the back of the house. Beneath high-beamed ceilings, children's toys filled a box in the corner and an assortment of kid's books were stacked on the coffee table in front of an overstuffed sofa and chairs. "Unfortunately, Vance figured he'd be a lot happier with that little blond piece of ass he hired as his secretary."

Mattie made a face and Debbie laughed.

"You guys want something to drink? Some iced tea or something?"

"Thanks, but we won't be staying that long," Gabe said.

"So what can I do for you?"

"I know you've been going through a lot lately," Mattie began, "but maybe you read about the fires that were set on two of Gabe's projects?"

"I saw it on the news. I'm sorry, Gabe, that's just terrible."

"How long has it been since Vance moved out of the house?" he asked.

"He's been gone almost a month. I've been too mad at him to miss him."

"After he left, did he seem… Well, how was his mental state? Did he seem depressed? Was he angry about what was happening to him?"

"He was glad at first. He got to be with his little hussy. I think now he's starting to regret what he's done."

"What about the bankruptcy?" Mattie asked. "How did that affect him?"

"He blamed himself. He said he should have been paying closer attention to business."

Gabe exchanged a look with Mattie. If Gleason blamed himself, he wouldn't have any reason to be going after his chief competitor.

Debbie was eyeing him darkly. "You don't think Vance had anything to do with those fires, do you?"

"Truthfully? No. I think the man who set them is currently in jail. But I didn't want to overlook any possibility."

"Vance is an asshole, but he isn't crazy. And he doesn't want any more trouble than he's got already."

Gabe nodded.

"We just wanted to get your take on things," Mattie said. "Sometimes people react to stress in different ways."

"Like I said, Vance is a little screwed up right now, but he isn't crazy."

"We don't want to take up any more of your time," Gabe said. "We appreciate your talking to us."

"Hey, with Vance gone, I don't have much else to do."

"I hope things work out the way you want," Mattie said.

"They might. I don't know. I think Vance is really sorry. And he's still my husband."

Mattie leaned over and hugged her. "Good luck."

They left the house and made their way back out to the car.

"Well, we've done all we can," Gabe said as he slid behind the wheel. "While you were getting dressed this morning, I called Thomas Daily and told him about my chat with Carlton Webster. I don't think he was particularly interested. The police have their suspect. Apparently Clay hasn't got an alibi for the nights of either fire. Says he was in his motel room asleep. Unless something else happens, he's going to stay in jail."

"I'm sorry it turned out to be your friend."

"I'd really like to talk to him, see what he has to say, but he refuses to see me." He stuck the key in the ignition and cranked the engine.

"At least he's not still out there roaming the streets."

"Yeah, there is that."

"Maybe this is finally over."

Gabe pulled away from the curb. "Maybe. Speaking of which, your vacation is almost over and you'll be going back to work. What do you say we fly up to the ranch this afternoon and spend the night? If something new turns up, we can be back in a couple of hours."

"You own a ranch?"

He shrugged his shoulders. "It's only three hundred acres but it's the place I feel most at home." He reached down and caught her hand, brought it to his lips. "I'd really like you to see it."

A little curl of heat tugged low in her belly. Her mind replayed all the conversations she'd had with herself about not getting more involved with Gabe.

"Come on. It's only one night and we deserve it."

Dammit, she wanted to go.

"All right," she heard herself say. "I'd love to see your ranch."

GABE TOOK MATTIE back to his condo to pack an overnight bag, making sure she threw in a pair of jeans and sneakers. She could change out of the floaty little flowered sundress and sandals she had worn to Debbie's once they got to the ranch.

On the way to the airport they stopped by the hospital, but there was no change in Angel's condition. Gabe waited while Mattie sat with the boy for a while, talking to him as if he were awake and encouraging him to get well. Then they left for the private airstrip south of Dallas where he kept his twin Aerostar, one of his favorite possessions.

"You know what they say about the difference between men and boys," Mattie said as Gabe tossed her bag aboard, helped her into the cockpit and settled her in the copilot's seat.

"The only difference is the size of their toys?" he teased with a wicked grin.

Mattie laughed. "No, it's the *cost* of their toys, you rogue."

Gabe just laughed. Walking beside the red stripe down the side of the plane, he made his final inspection, then climbed aboard and settled himself in the pilot's seat. A few minutes later, they were rolling down the tarmac.

"How often do you get to fly?" Mattie asked as they left the ground and began to skim over the patchwork pattern of farms and ranches below, lots of green and the occasional gleam of water.

"Not often enough. I head up to my brother's place in Wyoming a couple of times a year and get to the Hill Country as often as I can, but I'm usually busy working."

"I know what you mean," Mattie said, leaning back in the butter-soft-cream leather seat.

"Sometimes I wonder if it's worth it." The plane carried five passengers comfortably, though he had never hauled that many people at one time.

"I've never given it much thought," Mattie said. "I work to support myself, to have the things I want and put enough away to take care of myself when I get older."

"Sometimes I think maybe I should take the time to enjoy a little more of the here and now."

"Give up your business, you mean?"

"I wouldn't do that. I was thinking more about taking time to have a family, raise a couple of kids." He watched her from the corner of his eye. "You wanted a baby once. You're still young enough to make that happen."

Mattie turned her gaze out the window. "I haven't thought about it lately."

"Maybe it's time you did."

She made no reply, and the hum of the engines filled the cabin.

Gabe didn't say more. He was afraid she would feel boxed in, afraid she would stop seeing him if he pressed her for a more serious relationship.

But he had started to think that he wanted just that, had begun to think of Mattie as his woman, the one he wanted by his side over the years. He couldn't get her out of his mind, couldn't seem to stop wanting her.

And he was coming to believe that wasn't going to end.

After less than two hours in the air, the plane landed at a small strip south of Kerrville and taxied to the condo hangar he'd bought to store it in whenever he came to the ranch. He kept an old Jeep at the airstrip, and they drove along the curvy Hill Country roads till he reached the turnoff for Rolling Acres, the name that had been burned into the weathered sign on the property when he'd bought it.

"The land around here is beautiful," Mattie said as they drove down the narrow, bumpy road to the house. "I don't get out in the country often enough."

"Neither do I, but I sure enjoy it while I'm here."

He pulled up in front of his white, Spanish-style ranch house with its red-tiled roof, and turned off the engine. He helped Mattie down from the Jeep, then carried her overnight bag inside.

She paused in the entry that opened into the tile-floored living room.

"Oh, Gabe. This is exactly how I pictured the house you would live in. Western paintings on the walls, bright-colored serapes over the furniture, wildlife bronzes on the tables. I can see now what you meant—this is really your home."

He didn't try to hide the pleasure he felt at her words. "I'd be here full-time if I could figure out how to make a living." He had put away money enough to retire when he was ready, but he was still building his nest egg and the truth was he liked what he was doing. He wasn't ready to quit.

Mattie ran her hands over the back of the brown leather sofa, gently picked up and admired the hand-painted Indian pottery jar on the roughhewn table next to an overstuffed chair upholstered in a colorful Indian print.

Gabe watched those slender fingers carefully glide over each piece of artwork, thought how good it would feel to have them skimming over his body, and his groin tightened.

The housekeeper had filled the fridge, freshened the sheets and towels and, at his instruction, left for the next two days. Pedro Vasquez, who took care of the horses while Gabe was away, wouldn't return until late tomorrow evening.

Seeing Mattie there in his house, looking so pretty and feminine and exactly as if she belonged there, sent a wave of desire sliding through him. His blood began to pulse, pool thick and heavy in his loins. He was hard when he turned her into his arms and settled his mouth over hers, felt the softness of her lips under his. Mattie made a little mewling sound in her throat and slid her tongue into his mouth. Her nipples tightened into firm little buds against his chest and her hands slid up around his neck.

Lust kicked in. Big-time.

"I want you," he said between hot, wet kisses. "Right here, right now."

Mattie trembled. Her gaze shot to the open windows. "I want you, too, but maybe we should—"

"Not a soul around," he promised, and kissed her again, his tongue mating with hers as he deepened the kiss. He felt her hesitation. This kind of desire was new to her, but Mattie liked sex and so did he, and he knew her now, knew that she liked it when he took charge, took away the decision.

Turning her around, he drew her fiery hair aside and kissed the nape of her neck as he bent her over the low back of the sofa. He slid up the skirt of her flowered dress, pulled aside her tiny pink thong panties and began to stroke her.

Mattie moaned.

"You like this, don't you, honey."

"Gabe..." She whimpered, arching her back to give him better access.

"Part your legs for me, sweetheart."

She did as he commanded, giving him a little more room. Unzipping his jeans, he freed himself, rolled on the condom he slipped out of his pocket, positioned himself and took her with a single deep thrust.

Mattie made a funny little sound in her throat and Gabe fought for control.

"God, you feel so good," he said. "I can't seem to get enough of you."

Mattie trembled as he gripped her hips and began to move, easing himself out, then driving deeply again. She felt hot and snug as he increased the rhythm, felt the heat and need building inside him. A few deep thrusts and she started to come, crying his name and trembling as her body clenched around him.

Gabe didn't stop. Not until she came again.

An instant later, he exploded in a powerful release.

MATTIE TURNED INTO Gabe's arms and just held on to him. Lord, she felt like a wanton. Clearly Lena Sterling wasn't entirely a fantasy person. She buried her face in his solid chest, embarrassed to look at him, and felt his fingers beneath her chin. He gently brushed a light kiss over her lips, adjusted her skirt and zipped up his jeans, then reached down and picked up her bag.

"Come on, honey." He took her hand and started leading her down the hall as if what they had just done in the living room wasn't the least bit out of the norm. Apparently it wasn't for men like Gabe. She thought of the pleasure he had given her. Maybe it was all right with her, too.

She forced her mind to the present, noticed the framed photographs lining the hallway, a picture of a giant oak tree, its branches drooping toward the earth. A field of tall, billowing grasses. A winding dirt lane that seemed to have no end, and an old wooden barn.

She paused to get a better look. "These photos are wonderful. I noticed some similar pictures in your study. Where did you get them?"

"I took them. It's kind of a hobby of mine."

She was only a little surprised. For such a masculine man, Gabe had a fine sense of design. "They're beautiful, Gabe."

"Thanks."

He was a talented man, she was discovering—in more ways than just as a lover. It was one more thing she hadn't expected when she had first met him.

Gabe led her farther down the hall till they reached the master bedroom. "I'll give you some time to freshen up, then I'll show you the rest of the ranch."

She needed a moment. Her heart was still hammering from their mindless bout of sex and her body still felt slightly boneless. After a few minutes in his big, Spanish-tiled bathroom, Mattie emerged in jeans, sneakers and a short-sleeved white cotton blouse. Gabe gave her a quick perusal and his crystal-blue eyes gleamed with approval. They made a tour of the house, which continued in the Spanish motif, then he led her outside.

"You have horses?" she asked, catching sight of a beautiful palomino and a big, stout bay.

"Just a couple. That's Sundance and Warrior. I always wanted a horse when I was a kid but we were too poor. Someday I'd like to raise quarter horses. Might happen. You never know."

"You told me once you never knew your father. What was your mother like?"

His mouth tightened. "She was a drunk and a pill popper. When we were little, her boyfriends used to knock us around. As soon as Jackson got old enough, that came to a screeching end."

"You said your brother was a champion boxer."

"That's right. He boxed in the Olympics. Didn't win, but he made a damned good showing."

"And Devlin is an ex-ranger. I guess tough guys run in the family."

He shrugged those powerful shoulders. "It was kind of a matter of survival."

Mattie paused at the wooden fence that surrounded the pasture where the horses were kept. "Families like yours…that's the reason I got involved in the Family Recovery Center. When I was young, I had a friend whose father used to beat her and her mother. She begged me not to tell anyone and I didn't. I always regretted that decision."

"You said you were young. It wasn't your fault, and getting involved might have made things worse."

"That's what my friend said."

Gabe's blue eyes searched her face. "That friend wouldn't be Tracy Spencer, would it?"

Mattie glanced away.

"Still keeping your promise, I see."

"She still isn't entirely past it."

"You didn't help Tracy, so now you do whatever you can to keep that from happening to other kids."

"That's right. Though mostly the center deals with families who aren't being abused anymore, just trying to recover from what's happened to them."

She thought of Angel, who'd survived his father's abuse only to wind up beaten and in a coma, and her chest went tight.

"I can see where your mind is going. We'll call the hospital a little later and check on him, but Angel's going to be all right."

She nodded, though neither of them could know for sure.

"In the meantime, we're here in the wide-open spaces. Let's enjoy it."

He was right. Taking a few hours to enjoy themselves wasn't a reason to feel guilty. Mattie smiled up at him. "Can we ride the horses?"

"I can't think of anything I'd rather do." He laughed. "Well, maybe I can, but for now let's do the other kind of riding."

Mattie blushed and hoped he didn't see.

CHAPTER TWENTY-FIVE

GABE GRILLED A steak for himself and a couple of pieces of chicken for Mattie. The rest of their supper, a crisp green salad, au gratin potatoes and garlic French bread, had already been prepared and were waiting for them in the fridge.

The meal was delicious. Though Mattie was a little bit saddle-sore from riding Sundance over the winding trails through the lush Hill Country, it had been worth it. After supper, they took what was left of the bottle of cabernet they had shared and sat out on the patio, snuggled together on a comfortable outdoor sofa.

"Think you could ever live in a place like this?" Gabe asked as she settled against his shoulder. "Or would it be too quiet for you?"

A little tremor of unease trickled through her. This was the second time Gabe had mentioned something that hinted at a deeper relationship.

"I don't know... I was raised in the Dallas suburbs. At least until my dad died. Then Mom and I moved into an apartment closer to town." She surveyed the lush foliage, the horses frolicking in the field. "I'm sure it's a great place to raise kids."

"Yeah, that's what I was thinking."

Mattie looked up at him, a knot beginning to form

in her stomach. "You aren't thinking about me in that scenario, are you, Gabe?"

He shrugged. "I think you'd make a great mother."

"And wife?"

Those beautiful blue eyes fixed on her face. "You're intelligent and caring. You're an amazing lover. Those are the kinds of things a man looks for in a wife."

Mattie straightened away from him. "Making love with someone is a lot different than being married. I'm not ready for something that serious, Gabe. You know that. My career comes first. It always has."

He glanced away. "Yeah, that's what you said. I guess being here… I don't know…it makes me wonder about my priorities."

Uncomfortable with the direction of the conversation, Mattie stood up from the sofa. The pink-and-gold sky over the horizon had faded to a soft, shadowy darkness, the quiet broken only by the sound of the cicadas and the occasional whicker of the horses.

"It's getting late," she said. "Why don't we go to bed?" She knew it would distract him. Never one to turn down sex, Gabe stood up and scooped her up in his arms.

"Why don't we? I've got this fantasy of making slow, incredibly erotic love to you."

Mattie smiled, relaxing as they returned to a safer subject. "Is that right?"

"Yeah. How about I show you?"

But once they got in bed, things heated up the way they always did. Mattie didn't want to go slow and in the end, neither did Gabe.

"One of these days…" he grumbled as he wrapped a thick arm around her and curled her against his side.

Mattie just smiled.

But slowly her smile began to fade. Gabe had hinted at a future together. Little by little, she was coming to trust him. She was letting down her guard, beginning to rely on him as she had vowed she never would another man.

She thought of Mark and the baby and how he had abandoned her. She thought of her mother and the miserable years they had suffered after her father had died.

She valued her independence, valued her career more than anything else in the world.

More, even, than the man she could so easily fall in love with.

Mattie's chest tightened. She couldn't do it, couldn't risk falling in love.

It wasn't until Gabe began to kiss her, till after he made love to her again, that she was able to fall asleep.

BROOKS AND DUNN were singing. Lost in slumber, for an instant, Gabe was enjoying the performance. Then he realized it was his cell phone and his eyes popped open. His heart was slamming as he grabbed the phone off the nightstand, swung his legs to the side of the bed and flipped open his cell.

"Raines."

The clock read 2:00 a.m.

"Gabe, it's Thomas Daily. There's been another fire."

His fingers bit into the plastic. "Where?"

"The Egyptian Theater."

His stomach sank. He felt Mattie come up behind him, press her cheek against his shoulder. "I had a guard watching the place. How'd the bastard get in?"

"Hit the guard over the head. The attack was similar

to the one on the Ramirez kid. It supports the theory it's the same guy. The good news is, someone coming out of a bar down the street witnessed the assault. He ran back inside and called the police. They got there just as the fire was getting started. The damage is minimal."

Some of the tightness eased from Gabe's chest. "How's the guard doing?"

"They took him to the hospital and got him checked out. He's got a lump on his head, but he's okay."

"He get a look at the perp?"

"No, but the witness did. Said he was average height, lean, dressed completely in black and wearing a hood over his head. He used a baseball bat to take out the guard. Must have disabled the security camera before the attack, smashed it while the guard was making his rounds behind the building."

Gabe blew out a long, frustrated breath. "Pretty clear Sanders isn't our man."

"He'll be processed and released."

"Listen, I'm out of town. I was planning to head back to Dallas tomorrow. I can be there tonight if you need me."

"Tomorrow's fine. Call me when you get here."

Gabe ended the call and hung up the phone. Mattie reached down for the T-shirt he'd tossed at the foot of the bed and pulled it on, scooted over beside him.

"Another fire?"

"Egyptian Theater."

"Oh, Gabe, no."

"Daily says the damage isn't that bad."

"Thank God. I know how much you love that place."

"He assaulted the night watchman. Same M.O. as Angel."

Mattie sighed. "I guess your friend Sanders is innocent after all."

"Apparently. Daily's taking care of his release."

He felt her hand on his arm, lightly rubbing up and down to ease some of his worry. "You never believed he was guilty."

"No, but part of me wanted him to be. Now we're right back where we started."

"Oh, Gabe."

He raked a hand through his sleep-mussed hair. "There was a witness to the assault on the guard. He said the guy was average height, lean and dressed completely in black."

"Not much to go on."

"Not much." He stared off into the darkness. "Who the hell is it?" he said to no one in particular.

When Mattie leaned toward him, Gabe drew her into his arms. Sensing how much he needed her, she didn't resist when he eased her back down on the bed and began to make love to her again.

Mattie didn't want more from him than sex.

He was good at that.

For the first time in his life, it wasn't enough.

INSTEAD OF SLEEPING late as they had planned, Mattie followed Gabe out of bed at six o'clock the next morning. They ate a quick breakfast of scrambled eggs and toast, which she cooked while Gabe went outside to tend the horses.

She was still having trouble getting used to the quiet, just the wind sighing through the trees and the rustle of the leaves on the branches. Maybe the quiet gave her too much time to think.

She didn't want that. Not when most of her thoughts centered around Gabe.

Still, it was lovely in the country.

As soon as they'd finished eating and put the dishes into the dishwasher, they headed for the small airstrip south of Kerrville. They were back in Dallas before ten o'clock, and at Gabe's condo less than an hour later.

Which was why it was such a surprise to find someone waiting when they got there.

The intruder had the same six-foot-two-inch frame, Mattie saw as he rose casually from an overstuffed chair, the same crystal-blue eyes and nearly black hair. He was leaner, but just as solidly built, his shoulders wide, his hips narrow inside a pair of designer jeans, and the biceps exposed by his short-sleeved, yellow oxford cloth shirt were impressive.

Mattie knew in a heartbeat she was about to meet Gabe's brother.

"Devlin! Damn, I can't believe you're here." Gabe strode toward him. The younger Raines met him halfway across the room and they shared a brotherly hug.

"How'd you get in?" Gabe asked. "Never mind, I don't want to know."

Dev chuckled. "I thought it was time I came. I heard what happened at the theater. I'm glad the damage wasn't too bad."

"It only happened last night. How the hell did you find out?"

"The guard works for Atlas. Trace Rawlins called and told me. Figured I'd want to know."

Gabe turned. "Dev, this is Mattie Baker. I've told you a little about her."

Dev grinned, carving dimples into his gorgeous

cheeks. This was definitely the pretty boy of the Raines family and yet there wasn't a thing about him that didn't ooze masculinity.

"I hear you've got a great swing," Dev said to her. "I'll bet Clay Sanders still has a headache. Nice to meet you, Mattie."

"I didn't tell him," Gabe said with a lift of his eyebrows. "I swear."

"Jackson mentioned it. He thought I'd appreciate the story as much as he did."

Mattie just smiled. "It seemed like a good idea at the time."

Dev laughed.

Leaving her overnight bag in the entry, she walked with the men into the kitchen.

Gabe headed over to the sink and began making a pot of coffee. "I'm glad you came, little brother. I'm running out of airspeed and altitude here."

Dev sat down at the round oak kitchen table. "That's because we're missing something. We've overlooked something important and now we've got to find it."

The coffeemaker gurgled to a halt. Mattie reached up for coffee mugs, filled three of them, put Coffeemate in hers, and carried all of them over to the table. She took a seat across from the men.

"Missing something," Gabe repeated. "We must be."

"We need to start thinking outside the box," Dev said, turning the cup around so it fit his left hand. "Which buildings has the arsonist hit so far?"

"The Towers, McKinney Court and now the Egyptian."

"And maybe Artie's Men's Wear," Mattie added, "though it doesn't really fit the pattern since Gabe's no longer involved, and the arsonist—or someone pretending to be—claims he didn't set it."

Dev flashed her a wide, approving smile. "That's exactly right. Which reminds me—I guess you haven't seen the morning paper?"

"Not yet," Gabe said.

Dev got up and retrieved it from beside the over-stuffed chair where he had been sitting.

"Section B. I guess it wasn't headline material but it should be pretty important to you."

Gabe took the paper, leafed through it until he found section B and started to read. He let out a soft whistle.

"What is it?" Mattie asked.

"Looks like we were right about the grieving widow. Says here Lucille Roser has been arrested in connection with the fire at the building she and her husband owned, the home of Artie's Men's Wear. She is also being charged in connection to the murder of her husband, Arthur Roser."

Gabe folded the paper in half so that he could read the rest. "Man, that's a relief. At least I'm not responsible for poor Artie's death."

"You never were, bro."

Gabe made no reply, just continued perusing the rest of the article. "It says arson investigators discovered valuables usually kept at the store had been removed before the fire, as well as certain records."

"Idiots." Dev sat back down at the table. "They hire a torch but they can't resist taking out the stuff they don't want to see burned."

Gabe read the last of the article aloud. "'The police have indicated more arrests may be made in the future.'"

"I bet her attorney's involved," Mattie said. "She and Colin looked pretty chummy."

"And there was a lot of money involved." Gabe returned his attention to his brother. "So now we know the guy we're after was telling the truth in his text message. The fires he's set are strictly targeted at me. Where does that leave us?"

"Good question," Dev said. "He's hit three of your projects so far. Let's look at what else you're involved in."

"That would be the Greenwood Apartments and the warehouse I own down on Cadiz Street."

"Tell me about the warehouse. You haven't started work on it yet, right?"

"Not yet. I'd hoped to start before now, but with the way things have been going…"

"Was there any opposition to your purchase? Anyone competing with you to buy it?"

Gabe shook his head. "Sellers couldn't give the place away. That's the reason I bought it. The price was too good to pass up."

"What about your plans for it?" Mattie asked, beginning to follow Dev's thinking. "Anything controversial? Anything someone might want to stop you from doing?"

"Are you kidding? The place is an eyesore. The neighbors have been pushing me to get started."

"So there shouldn't be a reason for anyone to give you any trouble about it," Mattie said.

"Not that I can think of."

"Which leaves us with Greenwood," Dev said. "If I remember right, that place has caused you nothing but trouble since the day you bought it."

"I was expecting it. The city had condemned the

place. The building wasn't anywhere near up to code. It took me forever to get through the permit stage."

"And you fought with this guy, Webster, right? He wanted the apartments remodeled into something more high-end."

"That's right."

"So far Webster looks clean," Dev said.

"Oh, my God." Mattie's mind suddenly raced backward. "I remember reading about the condemnation proceedings at the time. The tenants were very upset about losing their homes. There were over thirty units in the building and—"

"Forty," Gabe corrected.

"And all those people had to move out, find another place to live, probably pay higher rent. What if that's it? What if someone was forced to move out and he's blaming you for his bad luck?"

"Doesn't make sense," Gabe said. "All those evictions happened before I bought the place. It was empty by the time I closed the deal. If someone was mad about being evicted, why wait until now?"

"Mattie could be right," Dev said. "This is the only place we haven't looked. Forty tenants, some of them with families. The city cost them their homes, but whoever this is doesn't see it that way. He can't blame the city. City hall's too big to fight. He has to blame someone and he's decided it's you."

"We can't be sure that's it," Gabe argued. "Why would the guy wait until now?"

"Maybe there was a trigger," Dev said, "something that set him off."

"I don't know...."

"Then give me somewhere else to go. Give me another name."

Gabe rocked back in his chair, released a slow breath. "Forty units. All the people who lived there have moved, started their lives all over again. Even if you're right, how the hell do we find them?"

"Good question," Dev said.

"We need a list of the people who were evicted," Mattie added. "The names of the tenants who lived in each unit at the time. That's where we start."

Gabe straightened, ready to move forward now that they had decided on a course of action. "I know my way around city hall. I'll see what I can find out."

Mattie reached over and caught his arm. "I know my way around there, too. Your brother's here. There are probably things you need to discuss. I'll see if I can get the list and bring it back to you."

She could read his gratitude in his eyes. He had just started to believe this might be over. Last night's fire had ended that belief. Now he had to start all over again.

"Thanks, that'd be great. I've got to talk to Captain Daily. And I need to take a look at the damage down at the Egyptian and check on my crews."

Mattie stood up from her chair. "Can we talk for a minute?" She tipped her head toward the living room.

Gabe's brow furrowed, but he stood up as well. "Sure."

She led him over to where her travel bag still sat in the entry. She hadn't meant to do this now, but with Dev there, it seemed a good time.

"I'm going home, Gabe, back to my apartment. I don't want to leave Tigger alone any longer and there are things I need to do."

"You could bring Tigger here. I like cats."

"I suppose I could, but—"

"The arsonist is still out there, Mattie. You might not be safe."

"He's not after me, he's after you. I think that's become fairly clear. Your brother is here and you need the room, and I was planning to leave in a day or two anyway."

His jaw tensed stubbornly. "My brother can sleep in one of the guest rooms. You won't even know he's here."

"This isn't about your brother. This thing between us…it's moving way too fast. I need to slow down. You know I never meant for this to go so far."

"We're getting to know each other, that's all. How can that be bad?"

"I need some space, Gabe. I want to be back in my own home." It took an instant to recognize the lie. She wanted to be right where she was. She wanted to stay with Gabe, sleep in his bed, make love with him.

Her heart squeezed. She had to leave.

Now.

Before it was too late.

"I'll get the rest of my things when I come back with the list of names."

"I'll carry your bag down to the car."

"It's got wheels. I'll be fine." She could tell he wanted to go with her. He was the most protective man she'd ever met. His jaw clenched as he held open the door.

Forcing herself not to look at him, Mattie grabbed the handle of her bag and rolled it past him out the door.

CHAPTER TWENTY-SIX

"I LIKE YOUR GIRLFRIEND," Dev said as Gabe returned to the table and sat down across from him. "She's smart and loyal, willing to help any way she can."

"And beautiful and sexy."

"That, too."

"Unfortunately, she's not my girlfriend. And she doesn't want to be."

Dev's dark eyebrows went up. "Could have fooled me. Looked to me like she cares about you a helluva lot."

"You think so?"

"That'd be my guess."

"Then you'd be wrong. All Mattie Baker wants from me is what I can give her in bed. Which I'm sure you'd see as a plus. Great sex and no strings."

"What's good for me isn't necessarily good for you."

Gabe made no reply. After Dev's breakup with his fiancée, who had left him high and dry just a few days before the wedding, Dev had become a different man. He no longer trusted women. Though he would never admit it, Dev was afraid to get involved again, afraid of getting hurt as badly as he had been before.

Instead, he settled for hot sex and a line of women that seemed to have no end. There was a time Gabe hadn't been interested in a lot more than that himself.

He thought of Mattie, knew how much he would miss her in his bed tonight, and wished there was some way he could change things.

"I've got a couple of ideas how we might get information on those tenants," Dev said.

Gabe didn't bother to ask him how. His brother had an endless supply of people willing to dig up information. "You really think this is the right track?"

"It's the only track we've got, bro."

"Yeah, I guess you're right." Needing to call Captain Daily, he dragged his cell phone out of his pocket. "How long will you be able to stay?"

"Long enough to get the information we need and see what I can track down here."

"Mattie's going back to her own apartment. Might as well make yourself comfortable in one of the guest rooms."

"Already have," Dev said.

"After I talk to Daily, I want to take a look at the damage at the Egyptian."

"Good idea. I'll go with you."

Gabe didn't argue. He needed his brother's help.

The way things were going, he needed all the help he could get.

A STRONG SUN beat down as Mattie reached the visitors' parking area at Gabe's condo, grateful he hadn't insisted on coming with her. As she had said, she needed some space, needed to put some distance between them. Still, her heart was aching and tears burned behind her eyes.

Better to deal with it now, she told herself, before her feelings got any deeper.

A horn honked. Pacific Street was crowded with traffic. An old woman with a cane ambled slowly down the sidewalk. A female jogger passed by and continued on her way. Mattie had almost reached her car when an odd feeling came over her. Slowing her pace, she glanced back over her shoulder, searching for someone, scanning the shrubs and trees along the sidewalk. Nothing. No one was there.

She shook off the sensation. All this talk about arson was making her paranoid.

Still, until the man was caught, it didn't hurt to be cautious.

Mattie took a last look around, saw nothing out of the ordinary and continued on to her car.

STAYING OUT OF sight behind a tall box hedge, Jacob watched the woman, Mattie Baker, cross the parking lot of the Las Posas Condominiums. Pressing her remote key, she unlocked the door to her shiny silver BMW and slid into the leather seat behind the wheel.

He knew who she was. He had seen her picture in the newspaper for winning some kind of architecture award. She was pretty, so he had remembered her face.

Then he had seen her with *him*.

The nerves in his hands twitched, making his fingers jerk. He'd been watching Gabriel Raines for weeks, charting his movements, discovering information about his friends, the people who worked for him. The women he fucked.

Raines had only met Mattie a few weeks ago but he was the kind of man women wanted—handsome and well-built, money enough to impress them. The kind who had no trouble seducing a woman into his bed.

The engine of the BMW roared to life and Jacob

watched the woman drive away from Raines's apartment. He had seen them together, seen him kissing her. Raines cared about the woman. It would be interesting to know just how much.

But from the checking he had done, his opponent had a history of brief affairs. He rarely got involved with a woman for any length of time and probably wouldn't this time.

If the woman was merely a passing fancy, Jacob had no reason to hurt her.

But if she truly mattered, she might be the means he needed to reach the end he had in mind.

He would have to bide his time, wait and see.

In the meantime, he was beginning to enjoy the path he had chosen. Setting the fires, developing the skills he needed, was more exciting than he had ever dreamed.

Soon he would use his newly acquired skills again.

In the meantime, he would watch his quarry and wait.

As the BMW disappeared from sight, Jacob strolled off down the sidewalk. And he smiled.

As an architect, Mattie knew a lot of people in city hall. She started her search with a longtime friend in the permit department who directed her to a colleague who worked with building-code violations and condemnation proceedings. His name was Richard Lopez and he had been with the city for years.

"Sure, I remember that place." Richard was a competent, attractive Hispanic man with silver beginning to thread through his black hair. "It was called the Harwood Apartments back then. The setting was nice. Lots of trees and shrubs around, but the building itself was in terrible condition. We tried to work with the owner, but he didn't really have the money to fix things right, so the repairs he made were minimal. Finally, a water leak got so bad it cracked the foundation. The building started to settle, then became dangerously unstable. We condemned the structure for safety reasons."

"I'm going to be honest with you, Richard. We think one of the tenants who got evicted might be the guy running around Dallas setting fire to Gabriel Raines's construction projects. I'm sure you've heard about that."

He nodded. "I know Gabe Raines. He's done a lot for downtown redevelopment."

"I'm trying to help him. You're probably going to get a visit from the arson squad asking for the same information on the tenants. But I'd like to take a look at it, too, see if something stands out that might be important."

"It's public record. I don't have a problem with you looking at it. But all the tenants are gone. We don't have forwarding addresses."

"I figured you probably wouldn't. At least we'll have the names. It's a place to start."

Mattie left with a copy of the list that included each person who was on the lease at the time and a copy of the notices of eviction. There was no way to tell who else might have lived in the apartments: children, relatives, friends.

They needed to interview as many of the people on the list as they could find. Hopefully, the police would be involved in the same activity. But even if her theory proved correct, it was going to be nearly impossible to figure out who the arsonist was.

Mattie left city hall and returned to Gabe's condo.

When no one answered the door, she used the key he had given her to let herself in, then walked into the kitchen and left the list on the round oak table.

Her hand trembled as she set the house key down next to the list. The gesture seemed so final, a severing of the bond the two of them had been building.

An unexpected lump rose in her throat. It was ridiculous. She had known from the start she couldn't get involved with Gabe. She shouldn't have let things go as far as they had. If she'd been more cautious, she wouldn't be experiencing this sick feeling in the pit of her stomach.

She took a steadying breath. She would continue to help him. At the very least, she and Gabe were friends. And she had made a promise to Angel. She wouldn't give up until the man who had attacked him was caught.

She returned to Gabe's bedroom and packed the last of the things she'd brought into the suitcase stored in the bottom of his closet. As she started to walk back out, she paused.

His king-size bed was neatly made, covered with a handmade quilt Gabe had said was a gift from a friend, a woman named Livvy Jones, the housekeeper at his brother's Wyoming ranch. A half-read Elmer Kelton Western novel lay on the nightstand next to his pillow. She took a breath and caught the scent of his cologne and the clean smell of soap and man.

She thought of the pleasure Gabe had shown her since they had met, thought of how empty her life had been before she had met him, how empty it was going to be again, and something squeezed inside her chest.

Her time here with Gabe had been wonderful. She had enjoyed being with him far more than she ever would have guessed. But it was time to leave, to go back to the life she'd lived before.

Mattie steeled herself against the stab of loneliness welling inside her and the ache that throbbed in her heart.

MAKING HER WAY along the now-familiar corridors to Angel's semiprivate room, Mattie caught sight of Dr. Burton outside the door. After a quick update on the boy's condition, which hadn't really changed, she spent an hour sitting with him, then took Rosa and the kids down to the cafeteria to get something to eat.

"The doctors say he is improving," the robust, black-haired woman said. "He is getting back some of his strength."

"Yes, that's what Dr. Burton told me. It's wonderful news, Rosa."

"*Sí,* it is very good news." But there was still no certainty that Angel would ever wake up.

Anger slipped through her. What kind of man would brutally assault an innocent teenage boy?

The same kind who had assaulted the night watchman at the Egyptian, the kind who had to be found and arrested.

From the hospital, Mattie went back to her loft apartment. With Gabe's condo so close by, she had been checking on Tigger at least once a day, but she knew he was lonely. He came racing toward her the minute she opened the door, meowing loudly and begging for her to pick him up.

"My big, beautiful kitty," she said, lifting him into her arms, hearing the heavy rumble of his purr. "I've missed you, too."

As she stroked his soft fur, the phone started ringing. For an instant, Mattie wondered if it was going to be another hang-up call, but when she lifted the receiver, it was her mother.

"Mom!" It felt good to hear the sound of her voice. Her mom was a small, auburn-haired woman, a little overweight, with the same freckles across her nose and cheeks as Mattie. Cuddling Tigger in her lap, Mattie sat down on a stool at the counter. "I've been meaning to call you. Things have just been so crazy lately. How are you doing? How's Jack?"

Instead of an answer, her mother burst into tears. Worry tightened a knot in Mattie's stomach.

"What is it, Mom? What's happened?"

Her mother sniffed, worked to compose herself. "I shouldn't have done that. It's really nothing so terrible. It's just…well, Jack lost his job."

"Oh, no."

A sigh whispered thought the phone. "With the economy the way it is, I guess we should have expected it."

"I can help, Mom. You know I make a very good living."

"I didn't call for money. I plan to go back to work."

"But you don't have any skills. What would you do?"

"They're looking for help at Walmart. Jack's gonna get something temporary until he can get a position with another dealer."

Mattie's heart ached. Jack sold cars. He'd earned a good living when he and her mother had met. But dealerships were closing all over the country.

"We'll make out okay," her mother said. "I just needed to vent."

Mattie almost smiled. "Yeah, sometimes we all need

to vent. But please let me help. I'll send the checks to you personally. Jack will never have to know."

"I don't think I should."

"You took care of me, Mom. After Dad died, you took care of both of us." And now, just when it looked like someone was going to take care of her mother, Margaret Baker Kendall was once more forced to look after herself. "Mom…?"

"All right, but just send a little. I would rather have you putting your money in the bank. You never know when you might need it."

That was the truth. But Mattie had always been a good saver, a lesson learned from the hardships she and her mother had faced after her father had died.

"I feel better just talking to you," her mother said.

"Me, too."

"I've got to run. I can hear Jack calling."

"Okay. I'll call you in a couple of days."

Mattie heard the soft click on the opposite end of the line, set the receiver back in its cradle and made a mental note to start sending checks once a week to her mom. It was the least she could do.

And it reminded her again why she couldn't afford to get more deeply involved with Gabe. She couldn't afford to do anything that might interfere with her career. She didn't want to end up like her mother, always pinching pennies, always on the edge, never knowing where the next dollar would come from.

The phone rang again. Still thinking of her mom, Mattie picked up the receiver. "Hello."

Soft music played in the background but no one said a word.

"Is anyone there?"

No answer.

Uneasiness crept down her spine. "This isn't funny. Call again and I'm changing my number." Mattie slammed down the phone, hoping the sharp noise rang in the caller's ears.

It isn't the arsonist, she told herself. It's just some kook.

But the calls were making her more and more nervous and she decided to tell Gabe about them.

A familiar *rap-tap-tap* sounded at the door, Tracy's special knock. Mattie walked over and peeked through the keyhole just to be sure, opened the door and stepped back to let her in.

"God, I'm glad to see you," Mattie said. "I'm so glad you came by."

"It seems like it's been ages."

"In a way, it has been." Mattie closed the door and they hugged, walked arm-in-arm into the kitchen. "You want a Coke or something? I could make us some iced tea."

"That sounds great." In low-heeled pumps and an apricot suit, Tracy was dressed for work.

Mattie put a kettle of water on to boil, filled Tigger's bowl with crunchies and the two of them sat down at the kitchen table.

"How's Angel?" was the first thing Tracy asked.

"The doctor says he's improving. They still can't say when he'll wake up." Or if he ever would. "How's Sam? You're still seeing him, right?"

A dreamy smile brightened Tracy's face. "I'm crazy about him, Mattie. I think I'm in love with him."

"Wow. I never thought I'd hear those words from you."

"Sam's the best man I've ever known. I don't have to impress him. I don't have to pretend to be something I'm not. Sam likes me just the way I am."

"And you don't miss all the attention from other men? You're content to just be with Sam?"

"If you want to know the truth, it's a relief. Sam's the only man I want. The only man I need. I never thought I'd feel this way about someone. I never thought I could trust a man this way, but I do."

Mattie felt a pang of envy. Tracy was working through her problems. She was allowing herself to fall in love. But Mattie couldn't imagine ever allowing herself to become that vulnerable.

She managed to smile. "That's really wonderful, Tracy." And it was. No one deserved to be happy more than her very best friend. Though she wasn't completely convinced things would work out for Tracy and Sam, Mattie truly hoped they would.

The kettle whistled. She went over and turned it off, poured the steaming water over a couple of tea bags in the bottom of a pitcher and left it to steep.

"Have you told Sam about…your family?"

Tracy's gaze moved out the window. "I don't see why I should. It happened a long time ago. Mom and Dad are divorced. I don't see my dad at all, and I rarely see my mom."

"The past is important, Tracy. It makes us the people we are today."

"I don't think it's necessary. I don't like talking about it and I don't want Sam looking at me differently than he does right now."

"I know the way you feel, but—"

"So how are things going with Gabe?"

Mattie swallowed. Just thinking of Gabe brought the unexpected sting of tears. She hadn't realized how much her decision to end their affair was going to hurt.

"We're slowing things down. I'm moving back in here. We'll still see each other, just not that often."

"And Gabe's okay with that?"

"He wasn't happy about it."

"You really seemed to like him. Are you sure this is what you want?"

She looked down and her eyes filled. "I'm not sure of anything right now. I just know I can't risk everything for Gabe or any other man. I did it before and look what happened. If I married Gabe and it didn't work out, I couldn't handle it. I'd rather just not take the risk."

Tracy's eyes widened. "Gabe asked you to marry him?"

"No, but…" She wiped away the tears with the tip of her finger. "He mentioned it."

Tracy studied her so closely Mattie shifted in her seat. "So I guess you told him you weren't interested."

Mattie nodded, her chest clamping down, making it hard to breathe.

Tracy got up, walked around to her chair and hugged her. "I'm scared, too," she admitted. "But I'm more scared of how I would feel if I lost Sam."

But Mattie was more afraid of coming to trust Gabe the way she had Mark Holloway.

And the pain she would suffer if he broke that trust.

CHAPTER TWENTY-SEVEN

ON THE TERRACE four stories below Gabe's condo, a slight breeze ruffled the canvas umbrellas around the swimming pool. The air was clear and warm, the humidity lessening as September roared toward October.

Gabe checked his watch. Mattie was due any minute. She was coming over to help him and Dev plan their next move. Gabe still didn't like getting her involved in so dangerous a situation, but she was determined.

And he really wanted to see her.

Last night had been hell, sleeping alone, wishing Mattie was there in his bed. He could kick himself for getting in so deep, but now that he was, he couldn't figure a way to extricate himself.

And he didn't really want to.

As he opened his front door and she walked in, a familiar rush of pleasure stirred inside him, followed by a jolt of desire. Bending his head, he lightly kissed her, felt her mouth soften under his an instant before she pulled away.

Gabe sighed, wishing this wasn't the same place they had been before.

"I've got the list over there on the table," he said, trying to sound nonchalant. "Why don't we sit down and take a look?"

She glanced around the living room. "Where's your brother?"

"He had a couple of things to do. He should be back any minute."

They sat down in the kitchen when what he wanted to do was carry her into his bedroom and start stripping off her clothes. Start kissing her and caressing those lovely breasts. She looked pretty and sexy and he wanted her the way he always did.

Inwardly he groaned, glad she couldn't see what was happening to him beneath the table.

"How much damage was done to the Egyptian?" Mattie asked, slinging the strap of her purse over the back of a kitchen chair.

"The fire started in the back room. The man who witnessed the assault called 9-1-1, so the fire department got there in a hurry. The flames never reached the main part of the building."

"That's great, Gabe."

"The bad news is Captain Daily says the arsonist is getting better every time. After he clobbered the night watchman, he took the key and used it to get in. He disabled the smoke alarms then broke out a couple of windows and knocked some holes in the ceiling. The place would have gone up like tinder if the fire department hadn't gotten there so fast."

"Maybe Daily put the local departments on notice, since this is the third fire on one of your projects."

"Could be. Unfortunately, as soon as my insurance company found out, they cancelled my policy. I've had my secretary trying desperately to find another company to handle it, but so far nobody's biting. Not after all the stuff that's been in the media."

"Then we'll just have to stop the guy before he burns up something else." She looked down at the sheets of paper she had left for him yesterday afternoon. "Have you had a chance to look at the names on the list?"

"I've gone over them twice. None of the names stand out."

"Look at them again. Maybe there's someone you missed, something that will jump out at you this time."

Gabe picked up the list and studied the names again, but none of the forty entries seemed the least bit familiar. Men's names, women's names. He had no idea who might have had a family, or a roommate, or just a relative or friend living with them—someone who might be pissed enough to set his buildings on fire.

One thing he knew. If he hadn't bought the place, sooner or later it would have been torn down. Because of the location near the Farmer's Market and the beautiful old trees and shrubs on the lot, he had taken a chance and after some major repairs, been able to start remodeling the place into attractive apartments.

He set the sheets of paper back down on the table. "Sorry. Nothing."

"When you talked to Captain Daily, did you tell him about the evictions?"

"I took him a copy of the list. He said he was short on manpower but he'd try to have some of his people look into it."

A light knock sounded. Gabe heard the rustle of the key he had given his brother since he didn't want his locks jimmied again, and Dev walked in.

"Hey, you two, how's it going?" Dev shoved the key into the pocket of his perfectly creased blue jeans. His expensive burgundy polo shirt was equally pristine.

Hard to believe he had once lived in poverty on the wrong side of the tracks in Wind Canyon, Wyoming.

"Things aren't going so great," Gabe confessed. "I've been going over the list. So far those names don't mean a damned thing."

"I didn't really figure they would." Dev walked toward them with an easy gait that reminded him of Jackson. "Would have been nice, though, if one of them had pushed a button." For the first time Gabe noticed the dog-eared manila file tucked under his brother's arm.

Dev set the file down on the table in front of him. "Fortunately, I managed to come up with something."

Gabe sat up straighter in his chair. "Oh, yeah? What'd you find?"

"I told you I had an idea I wanted to try. It was a long shot, but it paid off. I talked to the landlord, the former owner—" he glanced down at the folder, read the name he had written on the front "—Harley Jones, right?"

"That's him."

"He was an old guy, the type whose house is full of yellowed magazines, old newspapers and crap. The kind who never throws anything away."

"And?"

"And he had a file on the Greenwood Apartments—Harwood—before you changed the name. It took him a while to find it, but the guy's folder contained every rental application he had taken in the years previous to the condemnation." Dev held up the file, which was ragged on the edges and stained. "And guess what's on each application?"

"I'd hate to venture a guess," Gabe said darkly.

"Social security numbers, bro. All we've got to do is sort the old from the new, match the apps with the people on the eviction list, and we can find them. Track them down like dogs."

Mattie cast him a glance.

Dev grinned. "Bloodhounds."

She laughed, a soft, sweet sound, and the heat rushed back into his groin. "You never cease to amaze me," he said to his brother, trying to ignore his untimely desire.

"Of course a few of the numbers may be false, or the person might have died or whatever, but it's a helluva lot more than we had. And guess what else?"

Mattie brightened. "You've got a friend who works at the social security office?"

"Not exactly. I do, however, have a buddy who's a computer whiz. He can tap into—" He paused, sliced Gabe a sideways glance. "At any rate, Chaz can be a big help to us."

Gabe chuckled softly.

"I think I like your brother," Mattie said. "He's amazingly inventive."

Gabe's mouth curved into a wicked half smile. "I guess it runs in the family."

Mattie's cheeks colored as she followed his thoughts. Whatever happened between them, clearly the sexual attraction remained.

Not that it seemed to matter.

As the evening progressed, darkness fell outside the kitchen windows. Gabe ordered pizza and while they ate a half pepperoni, half Alonzo's garden special, they talked about their plans. As soon as Dev's friend Chaz came up with a list of current addresses for as many of the people on the list as he could find, they would start tracking them down.

Mattie helped Gabe clear the table, tossing the used paper plates into the trash.

"I need to get going," she said as soon as they had finished. "Let me know when you get that list. I'll be happy to run down some of the names."

"Not a chance," Gabe said, sliding the empty pizza box into the garbage container. "You're not going to make house calls unless I go with you."

"We can cover more ground if we're all out knocking on doors."

"Too dangerous. I'm not taking any chances. Besides," he added because he needed a reason for her to come with him, "maybe with the two of us working together, one of us will pick up something the other missed."

Mattie hesitated.

"You want to find the guy who assaulted Angel, here's your chance."

Mattie sighed. "All right. As soon as you're ready, give me a call."

"We might have something as soon as tomorrow," Dev put in, casting his brother a glance, knowing him well enough to know exactly his intentions.

"That would be great. I start back to work on Monday. After that, I won't have nearly as much time."

"I'll call and let you know," Gabe said as he guided her toward the door. "It's dark outside. I'll walk you out to your car."

For once she didn't argue.

She wasn't going to invite him home with her, Gabe could tell. And yet she wanted him. He wasn't wrong about that. Maybe it wouldn't take all that much to convince her.

On the other hand, Mattie had made her feelings clear from the start. He had pursued her against her wishes, seduced her into his bed. Whatever his feelings for her, he didn't want a woman who didn't want him.

The notion began to strengthen, settle deep in his bones. In the weeks since the fires had started, he had been forced to examine his life. With an arsonist breathing down his neck, anything could happen. The danger he faced had made him realize what he truly wanted.

A wife and family sat at the top of his list, which began with a relationship based on trust and love. If he couldn't have that with Mattie, he needed to get over her and get on with his life.

There had to be someone out there, someone who would care about him as much as he cared about her.

Gabe wished the notion made him feel better.

MATTIE LET GABE walk her to her car. Her heart felt heavy at the thought of going back to her empty condo and yet she knew it was for the best. Gabe waited while she dug through her purse for her keys, then bent his head and lightly kissed her, but the heat that was usually there was missing.

There was something remote in his manner, something that hadn't been there before. Something that told her he had finally begun to pull away.

Her heart squeezed. She had known it would happen. The more she pulled back, so would he. The thought of losing him made her stomach feel queasy. Moisture blurred her vision. She knew she was going to lose him. Gabe wanted more and she simply couldn't give it to him.

"I'll call as soon as we hear from Chaz," he said, but

he wasn't looking at her, not the way he usually did. Instead, his gaze moved off toward something across the parking lot.

Her glance followed his and she realized he was staring at his big white four-door pickup. Mattie caught the slight flicker of red and orange inside the cab the instant before Gabe started running.

The flames grew, suddenly blossomed. Mattie's heart lurched, lodged tight in her throat. She dropped her keys as she frantically dug through her purse and pulled out her cell phone. She flipped it open and dialed 9-1-1.

Gabe had almost reached the truck when the vehicle exploded, rocking the ground beneath her feet, knocking both of them down. Sizzling pieces of metal sliced through the air, huge chunks of rubber crashed into cars, and shards of broken glass whirred by just inches away from her face.

"Gabe!" She saw him roll, taking shelter behind the tire of a shiny red Cadillac parked a few cars away.

Hands shaking, she came to her knees on the pavement still holding on to her phone. She heard the emergency dispatcher's voice and tried to stay calm as she answered the woman's questions.

"Yes, yes, that's right… There's been…been an explosion. A car was…blown up. It's engulfed in flames." She gave them the address of the Las Posas condominiums, then rushed over to where Gabe now stood staring at the blazing destruction of what had once been his truck.

"The fire department's on the way," she said shakily. "Oh, Gabe, are you all right?"

Instead of answering, he pulled her into his arms. She felt the tremor that ran through his big hard body.

He took a deep breath, released it slowly. "I'm okay. What about you?" He held her away to get a look at her, surveyed the torn knees of her khaki pants, the cuts and scrapes on her hands and the dirt on her turquoise blouse.

She shoved back her hair with a trembling hand. "Kind of shaky, but okay."

Gabe's face was cut and bleeding, his shirt hanging in tatters, part of it completely gone, exposing the six-pack ridges across his flat belly. There was a burn on his arm where a piece of hot metal had struck, and broken glass had sliced a neat line down his cheek.

Mattie's stomach rolled. With an unsteady hand, she pulled a Kleenex out of her purse and pressed it against the blood oozing down his cheek. "Dear God, if you had…if you'd been any closer, you would have been killed."

He reached up and wiped something off her forehead and bright crimson stained his fingers. "Dammit, you're bleeding."

She couldn't feel any pain so she didn't think it was too serious. "I don't think it's too bad." She pulled another tissue out of her purse. Gabe took it from her hand and pressed it against her forehead. They stood there that way, each of them worried about the other. Mattie's throat swelled. Her heart was hammering, beating with fear for Gabe.

Footsteps pounded on the pavement. She looked up to see Dev racing across the parking lot.

"Son of a bitch!" He looked over at the flaming truck. "Are you two all right?"

"More or less," Gabe said darkly. The bleeding had stopped on her forehead. Mattie dabbed at the cut on

Gabe's cheek a few more times before the caught her hand. "I'm okay," he said, though his burned arm had to be hurting like the devil.

"I heard the explosion," Dev said. "What the hell happened?"

Gabe explained about the flames he had spotted inside the truck and that he'd been running toward the vehicle when it blew up.

"Shit, you're lucky you weren't killed."

Gabe shook his head. "I don't think that's what he wanted."

Mattie's gaze snapped to his. "What do you mean?"

"I think he was watching. I think he rigged the truck so he could set it off whenever he wanted."

She jerked her gaze around, frantically searched the parking lot and realized Dev was doing the same.

"I didn't see anyone," Gabe said. "I think he left a few seconds after the truck exploded."

"Oh, God."

Gabe eased her back into his arms and she didn't resist.

"If he'd wanted me dead," he said, "he could have done it. He's playing this out. He likes the control."

"That's right," Dev agreed. "He wants to show you how powerful he is."

Mattie buried her face in Gabe's shoulder. As hard as she had tried to tell herself she would get over him, that she could live without him, seeing how close he had come to dying, how close she had come to losing him forever, tied her insides into a knot.

As if he read her thoughts, his arms tightened around her. Then he let her go.

"You're out of this, honey. I know you want to help, but I'm not going to let you risk your life. Not anymore."

The distant shriek of fire engines cut off the argument they were about to have. Mattie trembled as Gabe's cell phone started to chime.

Reaching into his pocket, he pulled out the phone and flipped it open, read the text message running across the screen.

Did you like the pretty flames? Don't worry, you'll get to see more.

Gabe cursed.

A crowd gathered to watch the firemen put out what was left of the blazing vehicle. Mattie wondered if the man who had started the fire was among them. As the firemen sprayed water and foam onto the flaming truck, Mattie spotted Captain Daily walking toward them.

"Tell me what happened," Daily said without preamble and she and Gabe relayed the entire story again.

"Whoever this is, he's smart," Daily said. "And he is determined."

Tomorrow, the captain said, the police were going to start working on the names on the eviction list. Dev told him about finding the applications that contained the socials and promised to get a copy over to him in the morning.

Gabe held up his phone, displaying the text message. "The bastard sent this."

Daily read the message. "He's escalating. Getting more and more personal. We can run a trace, but I think the result will be the same as before. He won't make it that easy."

Daily gave orders for Gabe to have the medic take a look at his face and arm, which he ignored. It was another hour before they were finished.

"I don't want you home alone tonight," Gabe said to Mattie. "You could stay here, but I'm not sure you'd be safe here either. Is there someone you can call?"

She wanted to stay with him so badly she ached. "I can...can stay with Tracy tonight."

"Sam's there."

"Oh. I'm sure I'll be all right at home."

"Isn't there someone else?"

"I suppose I could phone a friend at the office. Emily Bliss. I don't think she'd mind."

Mattie phoned and Emily immediately invited her over.

"You remember where I live?" Emily said, worry clear in her voice.

"I remember. Thanks, Em. I'll be there in twenty minutes." Mattie closed the phone. She wanted to stay with Gabe. Every time she closed her eyes, she saw the truck bursting into flames, then the deadly explosion. He had come so close to dying. It was all she could do not to reach out and touch him, reassure herself that he was okay.

But Gabe wanted her to leave, which made her wonder if she had already pushed him too far away.

She swallowed, managed to look up at him. "Emily lives uptown. It won't take long for me to get there."

"I'll follow you over in Dev's rental car."

"That's not a good idea," Dev said. "The guy might be watching you. If he is, you don't want to lead him to Mattie. I'll make sure she gets there safely."

Gabe nodded but his jaw looked tight. "I want this over," he said.

Mattie's heart went out to him. And as she looked into his worried, handsome face, it struck her. Gabe wasn't like any other man she had ever known. He was stronger, more protective, more caring.

And God help her, she was wildly, desperately in love with him. Her throat tightened. As much as she wanted to deny it, as much as she wished it weren't so, the truth was suddenly plain.

She was deeply and irrevocably in love with Gabriel Raines.

CHAPTER TWENTY-EIGHT

A COCKROACH CRAWLED across the floor and disappeared beneath the sagging brown sofa. The lingering smell of the fish he'd cooked for supper hung in the air.

Seated at a rickety card table next to the hot plate in what served as a kitchen, Jacob stared down at the photos he'd spread across the top of the table.

Vera Mercedes Mueller was once a beautiful woman. Tall and blonde, with lips the color of cherries. She had even posed for a few cosmetic ads when she was a girl.

Jacob carefully rearranged the pictures and the magazine ads she had cut out and saved, and he had carefully stored away. Old black-and-white photos from when she and Jacob's father were first married. Pictures taken with her sister, Betty, after Jacob's father had died.

He'd only been two at the time. Vera had raised him, loved him. She had been an older woman when he was born, a *wonderful accident* she had called him. Jacob, she had often said, was her whole world.

Some of the photos he had taken himself in her later years. She hadn't aged well. The stress of raising what people called a *special child* had been too great. She had tried so hard, worked two jobs to pay for his education as a gifted student. Ignored her prescriptions, even gone without groceries so that she could save more to send him to college.

Jacob had worshipped her, as close to a saint as any person he had ever known. He'd tried not to disappoint her, but he knew in some ways he had. He had never fit in with the other kids at school, never made friends. Never really wanted to.

His mother was all he needed.

All he truly cared about.

She took care of him, praised him, told him he was better than the other kids, smarter, more clever. That he would be more successful.

But he hadn't been. Instead, he'd dropped out of city college in his second year and started smoking pot. When he couldn't find work, his mother gave him money from the jar on the kitchen counter where she kept it. She had always been there when he needed her and now she was gone.

Jacob didn't do drugs anymore. He had stopped smoking pot years ago and didn't smoke cigarettes or drink. He had gotten a job in a music store two years ago and begun to make something of himself. His mother had been so pleased.

He thought of the apartment she had lived in, a place she truly loved. Then the eviction notice had come and she had been utterly distraught. He remembered the assisted-living home she'd been confined to after her stroke.

It never would have happened if she had been able to stay in the place she loved, where she could feed the birds outside her window and take care of her tiny garden.

It was all *his* fault. Gabriel Raines. If *he* hadn't used his influence to trick the city into condemning the building, his mother would still be in her home.

If *he* hadn't been so greedy, if *he* hadn't been more concerned with himself than the people who lived in the apartments, his mother would still be alive.

But three months ago, she had died, and now Jacob was alone.

His hand spasmed and his fingers jerked, knocking one of the photos off the table.

Jacob reached down and picked it up, set it carefully back in its place. He studied the picture he had taken of his mother, her hair turned to silver and wrinkles on her face. She looked old, but her soft smile was meant just for him.

Vera understood him as no one else ever had.

As no one else ever would.

He took out his personal cell phone, not one of the cheap disposables he had purchased with the money from his mother's social security checks that still kept coming in. Jacob had been forging the signatures and cashing them without a hitch.

He smiled as he flipped open the phone, pushed the button and began to replay the video he had taken tonight in the parking lot: the big man running across the pavement, the truck exploding at precisely the instant Jacob commanded, the blazing wreckage that was all that remained.

He closed the phone.

One way or another, Gabriel Raines was going to pay for what he had done to his mother.

For what he had done to both of them.

In the bedroom of her apartment, Tracy lay in bed next to Sam. He was not quite dozing.

She felt Sam's finger lightly tracing a circle around

her breast, trailing lower, moving over her rib cage. As he got close to the scar across the left side of her abdomen, her body began to tense. Sam drew his finger along the pale line of the scar, which barely showed anymore, and she rolled away from him onto her side, pretending not to notice.

He came up over her, his chest against her back and pressed a soft kiss on the side of her neck. "Tell me about it, baby."

Tracy ignored him, praying he would let it go.

"I know you don't want to. I know it must have been bad, but I care about you, Tracy. Your past is always there between us. I need you to tell me what happened."

She didn't want to tell him. She never said anything to anyone. Only Mattie knew the truth. They had both been ten years old when it happened, best friends even then. Tracy's dad was a lawyer and Mattie's dad had a good job with one of the oil companies, so the families lived in a nice neighborhood just a couple of houses away from each other.

Tears burned Tracy's eyes. She didn't want to tell Sam what her life had been like back then, but she knew his feelings for her ran deep and so did hers for him, so maybe he had a right to know.

Sam eased her back down on the bed. "You can trust me with whatever it is, baby. Tell me what happened."

She swallowed past the lump in her throat. "I don't like to think about it. And I don't want you to look at me with pity."

"The only way I'll ever look at you, Tracy, is with love. I love you, baby. I haven't told you. I didn't want to scare you, but I do."

"Oh, Sam." She slid her arms around his neck and he held her close against him. He felt so solid, so strong.

"Tell me," he softly coaxed.

She dragged in a shaky breath and relaxed on the bed. "My father…drank. Sometimes he was a good father, but once he started drinking…he…he couldn't stop. He just kept going until he was falling-down drunk. He got mean when he drank and he…he beat us. My mom and me."

Sam took her hand and kissed her palm, silently encouraging her to continue.

"It happened a lot. Mattie tried to get me to tell the teachers at school, but I made her swear she would never tell a soul. I was embarrassed. And I was afraid of what he would do to Mama and me."

Sam leaned down, gently pressed his mouth against the scar, and something loosened inside her. "Go on."

"He was drunk that night. He slapped Mama so hard she fell and hit her head. She was lying there and her eyes were closed and I was so scared." Tracy's eyes filled with tears. "Oh, Sam, I don't want to remember."

He gentled her with a tender kiss. "You don't have to if you don't want to. It's just… I think if you got it out, if you said it right out, you might be able to get past it."

She stared up at him through the wetness spiking her lashes. He was so handsome. And there was that look on his face, the love for her he didn't try to hide.

"I started screaming. 'You killed Mama! You killed Mama!' Then I hit him. I punched him in the stomach as hard as I could, but it only made him madder. He said he hadn't killed her. He said he'd show me what happened when I tried to interfere." She started crying and Sam pulled her into his arms.

"That's enough," he said. "You don't have to say another word."

"It was the buckle on his b-belt that made the scar."

Sam's eyes briefly closed and his hold subtly tightened. "Oh, baby."

She felt the tremors running through his lean, hard body. "It's all right," he whispered. "No one's ever going to hurt you again. I swear it on my life."

Tracy clung to him. "I love you, Sam."

"Marry me, Tracy."

She had never imagined she would get married. She was too afraid she'd wind up with a man like her dad. But this was Sam and he was nothing at all like Marty Spencer.

She smiled at him through her tears. "Oh, yes. I'll marry you, Sam."

In the moonlight coming through the window, his eyes glistened for an instant before he kissed her.

"Soon," he said. "We're getting married very soon."

Tracy didn't argue, just looked up at Sam and gave him a wobbly smile. For the first time in as long as she could remember, she felt completely at peace.

DEV'S FRIEND CHAZ came through for them. It was highly illegal to break into a federal data bank, but Chaz liked the money, and he loved his work.

Thirty-two of the forty names on the eviction list had been matched to the social security numbers on the tenants' rental applications. Through the data bank, Chaz had found addresses for twenty-nine of them. The rest of the numbers were either for people who had died, phony or the numbers had somehow gotten reversed or were otherwise useless. It wasn't a hundred percent, but it was more information than they'd had before.

"The police are going to get on it," Gabe said to Dev that Sunday morning. "They'll have to run the socials on the apps themselves, but that way it'll be legal. The addresses they come up with will be the same as the ones we've already got. Daily says this is the best lead they have and they're going to be pushing hard."

Dev nodded. "That's good news. Maybe they'll come up with something."

In the meantime, Gabe planned to call on some of the evicted tenants himself. Chaz had done a little extra research and found six former tenants with criminal records. Three still lived in the Dallas area. Gabe had circled the names, intending to call on them first.

His brother's cell phone rang. Dev answered and Gabe heard Jackson's name.

"I know you want to come down," Dev said into the phone, "but it would be better if you didn't. We aren't sure how far this guy is willing to go and even if you were here, there's nothing you could do."

Dev filled Jackson in on the investigation so far and that the cops would soon be on the trail of the former tenants of the Greenwood Apartments.

"You've got a family to think of now, big brother. And like I said, there's nothing you can do that we aren't doing already."

Dev chuckled. "Swearing at me isn't going to change anything. Take care of your wife and daughter." Dev hung up the phone. "He called me a few choice names but I think I've convinced him not to come—at least for the moment."

"I don't want to put anyone else in danger. Matter

of fact, I'm thinking maybe it's time you went back to Phoenix."

Dev cast him a sideways glance. "Good idea, I'll be on the next plane."

Ignoring Dev's sarcasm and knowing it was useless to argue, Gabe went back to sorting through the names, trying to come up with the most likely suspects.

There wasn't much to go on.

Someone knocked. Absently, his hand went to the bandage covering the burn on his arm as he went to the door. He felt a tug in his chest as Mattie walked into the condo.

"You're not supposed to be here," he said.

Since she had made her feelings clear, he was doing his best to forget her. Seeing her only made that harder to do. "I told you I don't want you getting hurt."

"I was just out jogging and—"

"You were supposed to be staying with your friend."

"I did, but I went back home this morning." She was wearing shorts and a tank top, her arms and legs faintly gleaming with perspiration. It made him think of hot, sweaty sex, and heat pooled low in his groin.

"I had to go home, Gabe," she was saying. "I've got to get ready to go back to work. My job is important to me."

"No job is worth your life."

"No, but we have no idea where this guy might strike next. Even the police have no idea."

Gabe blew out a long, disgruntled breath. "I suppose you're right. All we can do is be careful."

"That's the reason I came by. There's something I need to tell you."

"Yeah, what is it?"

"I've been getting phone calls, Gabe. Hang-ups. I thought you ought to know."

His jaw tightened. "And you just decided to tell me? *Christ.* When did they start?"

"A couple of weeks ago. I thought maybe some kook had seen my photo in the newspaper and somehow got my phone number."

Gabe caught her shoulders. "Dammit, you should have told me as soon as it started."

"You had enough on your mind without adding more. Besides, I didn't think it was anything to worry about."

"So what changed your mind?"

"I guess watching your truck blow up last night and you nearly getting killed. I thought the calls might be important. I figured you ought to know." She looked down at the bandage around his arm. "How's the burn?"

"It's healing. In a day or two I'll be fine."

Dev appeared just then. "Do these phone calls come at any certain time or on any specific day?"

"There haven't been that many, and so far they seem to be totally random. But I've been gone a lot, so maybe he calls and I'm not there."

"So he doesn't call on your cell."

"No."

"You're sure it's a man," Gabe said, "not a kid or a woman."

"I have no idea. All I hear is the sound of music playing in the background. He listens for a while, then hangs up."

"What kind of music?" Gabe asked.

"Nothing specific. Just soft jazz of some kind."

"That doesn't sound like a kid," Dev said.

"If he calls again, I want to know," Gabe told her.

Mattie just nodded. "Can we…ummm…talk for a minute?"

"Don't mind me," Dev said. "I need to get a copy of those names and socials down to the department. They'll have to do some digging to get the addresses, but they have access, and I can't risk them finding out about Chaz."

"Don't forget you're taking me to the car rental place this afternoon," Gabe called after him.

"I know you need transportation. I'll be back in a couple of hours." The door shut behind him.

"What is it?" Gabe asked, wishing Mattie hadn't come. Wishing he wasn't so damned glad to see her.

"We were talking about my safety. Well, this morning, I…um…started thinking. If the arsonist is the guy who's been calling me, maybe I should…um…maybe I'd be safer here with you."

Gabe frowned. "Two days ago that was the last thing you wanted."

"I know, I just…"

"Which is it, Mattie? You want to be with me, you don't want to be with me. I can't handle this back and forth." He frowned as he thought about the night they'd made love and the condom had broken. "You aren't pregnant, are you?"

Her cheeks colored prettily, making those appealing little freckles stand out. "No!"

Gabe sighed, surprised he wasn't more relieved.

And yet what he'd told her was true. He was tired of playing games. Until she knew what she wanted, he was no longer willing to continue as they had been.

"I've done some thinking, too," he said. "Maybe you

were right. Maybe we ought to slow things down, take some time to sort things out."

Mattie glanced away. Several heartbeats passed before she looked back at him with a forced smile. "Yes, of course. You're right. We both need a little time. It was just the explosion last night, I guess. You always make me feel safe and—"

She gasped as he caught her shoulders and hauled her into his arms. Bending his head he kissed her. He made her feel *safe?* Dammit, he needed to be certain she was. He wanted her to stay more than he wanted to breathe, but he didn't want to get in any deeper than he was already.

Mattie's soft lips parted and his tongue slid inside, tasted, mated with hers. Her fingers tangled in his white T-shirt, slid underneath, moved over his chest, and the blood pumped through his veins. The kiss grew hotter, wetter, deeper. Her arms went around his neck and his resolve weakened. Completely dissolved. He wanted Mattie Baker and he no longer cared what game she played. All he wanted was to be inside her.

Scooping her into his arms, he carried her into the bedroom and settled her on his bed. Dev wouldn't be back for hours. Plenty of time for what he had in mind.

If sex was all Mattie wanted, he was about to give her the kind of hot, raunchy sex she wouldn't easily forget.

CHAPTER TWENTY-NINE

MATTIE TREMBLED AS Gabe kissed her. She hadn't been able to sleep last night on Emily's couch. She kept thinking of Gabe, thinking of how he had started to pull away from her, and how she knew deep down she was losing him.

She had tried to convince herself not to come here this morning, but she'd simply had to see him. She was in love with him. She knew that now without the slightest doubt. She needed more time with him, enough time to figure things out.

Gabe deepened the kiss, the hot demanding glide of his tongue into her mouth telling her what he wanted. He pulled her tank top over her head, dragged her jogging shorts down over her hips. Her panties went next, then he settled her naked body in his bed.

Mattie watched as he stripped off his jeans and T-shirt and joined her, claimed her mouth again in a hot, soul-burning kiss. He cupped her breast, molding and caressing; he bent his head and his teeth grazed her nipple. The heavy bands of muscle across his chest contracted as he worked over her, laving each peak, turning them into stiff little buds, making her stomach quiver. Hot wet kisses trailed over her rib cage, continued down until his tongue circled her navel.

Mattie swallowed at the erotic sensations. "I—I need a shower," she whispered, but Gabe just laughed.

"Honey, I like you just the way you are. Besides, you'll only get sweaty again."

"But—" She bit back a cry as his head dipped and hot kisses burned across her abdomen and lower still. Gabe spread her thighs and settled himself between them, his fingers tracing a fiery path through the crisp auburn curls at the juncture of her legs.

Her heart was pounding. Heat seemed to burn through her blood. Gabe parted her sex and his mouth settled there, making her quiver and moan. Feeling the sweep of his tongue on her most sensitive spot, Mattie forgot to breathe.

She sucked in a ragged gasp and twisted her fingers in his thick, dark hair, meaning to pull his head away. But the sensations were so hot, so sweet, she found herself holding him in place, instead.

"Oh…oh, my God."

Gabe suckled and tasted, used his hands to heighten the sensations, and Mattie's whole body trembled. Her skin felt hot and damp, stretched too tightly over her bones. Heat flared in the pit of her stomach. She arched upward as pleasure washed through her, spread out through her limbs. Higher and higher, she climbed, the sensations unlike anything she had known before.

For an instant, she hung suspended. There was only the feel of Gabe's silky hair beneath her hands and the sweet, burning pleasure. Then heat and need swamped her and she tumbled over the edge.

She was floating toward the surface, her body limp and sated, when she realized Gabe hadn't stopped and her body began to respond again. Fresh sensation hit her, thick and intense, and a second powerful climax rippled through her.

She didn't remember Gabe moving above her, only stirred to life when she felt his heavy erection sliding deeply inside.

"We're good together, Mattie. I was hoping you'd see that." And then that big powerful body started to move.

Deep thrusts carried her higher. Long, slow strokes filled her with pleasure. Faster, deeper, harder. She was there again, flying free, letting him take her to the place she had been before. Mattie cried out Gabe's name as he came, his powerful muscles straining with the intensity of his release.

Mattie clung to his muscular neck, unwilling to let him go, wishing she had the courage to tell him the truth. She was wildly in love with him. The phone calls had only been an excuse to see him. She wanted to be with him so badly. And yet she was afraid.

Gabe kissed her softly, deeply, then lifted himself away and settled himself beside her. A finger traced the outline of her lips.

"You all right?"

She swallowed past the lump in her throat. "I've never... I didn't realize how good that would feel."

"Yeah? Well, there's more where that came from." He flashed her a cocky grin that had her smiling through the tears she hoped he wouldn't see.

Then his grin slid away. "I don't want you to stay here, Mattie. Sooner or later, he's going to come after me. I don't want you anywhere near me when that happens."

"But what about the phone calls...?"

Wearily he shook his head. "I don't know. I don't

like it, I can tell you. I'll talk to Daily, see if there's a way the police can run a trace."

"If it's him, he could be watching me."

A muscle jerked in his cheek. She could see the wheels spinning in his head. "I'll call Sam. Since he's practically moved in with Tracy, I'll ask if you can stay at his place."

She didn't want that. She wanted to stay with Gabe. After the explosion last night and how close he had come to dying, she needed to be with him. She knew the risk she was taking in loving Gabe, but it no longer seemed to matter, not the way it had before.

"Tracy's never let a man stay at her house," she said. "At least not for more than a night."

"That right?"

"She says Sam's special."

"He's crazy about her."

Mattie said no more. She had no idea what the future held for Tracy and Sam.

Or what would happen between her and Gabe.

At the moment, finding the arsonist before he killed Gabe or somebody else was all that mattered.

IN THE END, Mattie refused to stay at Sam's, though he firmly insisted. Gabe tried to bully her, of course, until she convinced him that since Sam was his best friend, there was no way to know whether his place would be any safer than anywhere else.

"Fine, if you refuse to stay with Sam, you might as well stay with me. At least if something happens, I'll be here to look out for you."

Since that was exactly the reason she had come to

his house in the first place, she shrugged as if it were the only logical solution.

"The police have put a car in the area," he said, still clearly worried. "That's something, I guess. And I've got a guard on duty twenty-four-seven." Which hadn't prevented the fire at the Egyptian or the truck bomb last night, but the Atlas guards were now on high alert.

The owner of Atlas Security, a friend of Dev's named Trace Rawlins, had driven down from his main branch office in Houston to meet with his men and make sure they understood the danger of the situation. Make sure they kept a close watch for the man setting fire to Gabe's property.

Both Gabe and Dev were hopeful that if the arsonist tried again—which they were certain he would—this time the guard would spot him.

Mattie spent the night with Gabe, who made several rounds outside the building to talk to the guard and check for any sign of trouble. He carried a deadly looking pistol, she noticed, stuffed into the back of his jeans.

On Monday, she returned to work, her pseudo-vacation over. Shirley handed her a stack of messages and she headed for her office. She caught sight of Emily and gave her a little wave.

The night Gabe's truck had exploded and Mattie had stayed with her friend, Emily had confessed that she and Aaron had been seeing each other.

"It's strictly against company policy," Emily had said as she had carried sheets, a blanket and pillow over to the sofa. "But Aaron was sure you wouldn't tell."

Mattie smiled, thrilled at the news. "They couldn't pry it out of me with a crowbar."

Emily laughed.

"I'm really happy for both of you."

A soft smile curved Emily's lips as she set to work on the makeshift sofa bed. "I've had a crush on Aaron for years. I kept hoping he would ask me out, but he was too obsessed with you."

"Me!"

"I think he was pretty much in love with you."

"You've got to be kidding. We've always just been friends."

Emily smoothed the sheet into place. "Maybe that's how you saw it, but not Aaron. I was always a little jealous of you, even when it was obvious you didn't return his feelings. Then you started dating someone you really seemed to care about and something changed."

"What?"

"I think Aaron knew how you felt about Gabe even before you knew it yourself. He was angry. That's what he told me. Then he realized he wanted a woman who felt that same way about him, and he could finally see you never would."

Mattie stuffed the pillow into a crisp white cotton case. "So he asked you out?"

Emily nodded. "For the first time, Aaron seemed to see me as a woman, not just a coworker. He asked me to dinner and we had a terrific time. We've been seeing each other ever since."

"That's terrific, Em." Mattie leaned over and hugged her. "I'm so happy for you. You've always seemed perfect for each other. For years, I hoped the two of you would get together."

They had talked late into the night, their friendship deepening after Mattie had confessed her feelings for

Gabe. It was amazing how much clearer things seemed once she had said the words out loud.

She was thinking of Gabe as she made her way toward her office that morning, messages in hand.

"Hey, Mattie, how's it hangin'?" Mel Freeman intercepted her before she got there. His mouth curved into a lascivious smile. "Things must be going well with that new boyfriend of yours. Word is you've finally been getting laid."

Anger boiled to the surface, making her cheeks burn. Mattie tamped it down. "What I do outside the office is none of your business." She tried to walk past him, but he caught her arm.

"I was just being friendly. Isn't that the way coworkers are supposed to act?"

"We aren't *friends,* Mel. We never have been. Now, if you'll let go of me, I have work to do."

Freeman's lips curled, but he let her go.

Refusing to let Mel ruin her morning, she carried the messages into her office, sat down at her desk and started returning calls. With so much catching up to do, she decided to skip lunch and work straight through the day.

After a couple of hours, her back began to hurt and she shifted in her chair, trying to get comfortable. Her muscles were sore from landing so hard on the pavement during the explosion Saturday night, and her head had begun to pound. She rubbed her temples and leaned back in her chair, thinking what she needed was a fresh cup of coffee.

For a moment, she closed her eyes and let the office music playing in the background begin to soothe her. She was usually so busy she didn't notice it, but something began to niggle at the back of her mind. She sat up a little straighter, tuned into the sound. Soft jazz. It reminded her of something…and suddenly she knew.

It was the same kind of music she had heard during the hang-up phone calls.

Her attention sharpened as she concentrated on the song. Kenny G. played faintly, not loud enough to interfere with work. She recognized the tune. She had heard it, she realized, the day she had received that last hang-up phone call.

Mattie shot up from her chair. The office music was on a loop, the songs repeating over and over. The calls had come from the office! The more she thought about it, the more sure she was.

And there was only one person who would be perverse enough to do that kind of thing.

Marching to the door, she pulled it open and stormed out into the main work area toward Mel Freeman's desk, which sat in an alcove in front of a window.

"I need to talk to you, Mel."

He glanced up at her, while the rest of the employees continued to work. He rose languidly from his chair. "I'm busy. What is it?"

"I want to know if you've been calling my house. If you've been calling me and hanging up. I want to know if you're the jerk who's been making the crank calls I've been getting."

Mel's eyebrows came together. "I don't know what you're talking about. If you've been getting calls, it's probably from that guy you've been boffing."

"It was you, wasn't it? I recognized the music playing in the background. You're the one who's been calling. I'm going to Mr. Dewalt. I'm telling him—"

"It wasn't him, Mattie."

Mattie whirled toward the familiar voice. Aaron's face was ashen.

"Can we…" He cleared his throat. "Can we go into your office?"

Mattie glanced from Aaron to Mel and back. "Of course."

Mel just grunted and walked away.

The look in his face said it all. Grabbing the handles on his wheelchair, she took charge whether he liked it or not, rolled him to the door of her office, waited till he turned the knob, then pushed him inside.

She walked around to face him, crossing her arms over her chest. "Are you going to tell me you know who's been harassing me?"

Aaron hung his head, a lock of dark hair falling over his forehead. He looked up at her and behind the rim of his glasses, his eyes looked bleak.

"I was me, Mattie. I called to see if Gabe was at your apartment. I was jealous. I felt like I had to know."

"Oh, Aaron."

He swallowed. "It took me a while, but eventually I started to get my head on straight. At first I was hurt, thinking about you and Gabe and how much you seemed to care about him, jealous that you were attracted to him but not to me. But then I thought about what I was doing and how insane it was. I realized I was turning into someone who wasn't remotely me."

Tears stung Mattie's eyes.

"I decided right then that things had to change. I asked Emily to go out with me. We started dating and it was great. With the fires and all, I knew you had to be worried those calls I made might somehow be connected. That last call… I wanted to tell you it was me, that you weren't in any danger, but you were so angry, I just…well, I chickened out. I'm really sorry, Mattie."

Tears welled. "You're a dear friend, Aaron. We could have talked things out."

"I'm so embarrassed. I was an idiot! Emily…well, she's the best thing that's ever happened to me and I nearly blew it. Can you ever forgive me?"

Mattie bent down and hugged him. "Of course I can." She wiped the tears from her cheeks. "I really hope things work out with you and Em."

"I hope it works out with you and Gabe," he said, and she thought that he was sincere.

Mattie had no idea what would happen with her and Gabe. She needed a little more time, needed to decide if she dared to risk losing the feeling of security she had worked so hard to build, risk giving Gabe her heart.

Aaron left her office and Mattie returned to work, thinking about the phone calls, her mind going round in circles. If she told Gabe the truth, that the calls had nothing to do with the arsonist, Gabe would want her to go back to her apartment or somewhere else he thought she would be safe. Mattie wasn't ready to leave.

Thanks to her uncertainty, Gabe had started pulling away, and if she left now, she might lose him completely. She released a long, uneasy breath. It wasn't fair to let Gabe continue to worry.

On the other hand, she wanted to stay with him, see where things went. She was in love with him and she believed he still cared for her.

She would keep Aaron's secret for as long as she dared.

CHAPTER THIRTY

GABE PULLED UP in front of the Greenwood Apartments, turned off the engine and climbed out of his rented Dodge Durango. Though the apartments and the rest of his current projects were now uninsured, his truck had still been covered at the time it was destroyed. As soon as he got a chance, he would go down and find a replacement. In the meantime, the big SUV would have to do.

Gabe sighed. He hoped to hell they found the arsonist before the bastard did any more damage, or financially he was going to be in a world of hurt.

He spotted Sam talking to one of the crew. The remodel was coming along very well. From the start, he'd been careful to do as little as possible to disturb the landscape, the trees and shrubs that surrounded the units. The setting and location near the Farmer's Market had been the reason he had bought the dilapidated building in the first place.

He had added a pool, which was just about finished, and cement walkways winding through the big old oaks were about to be poured.

"Hey, Gabe!" Sam had spotted him and was walking toward him. A worried frown appeared on his forehead as he assessed the gash on Gabe's cheek. "You okay?"

Sam knew about the explosion. Gabe had called him

first thing Sunday morning. "Aside from this burn on my arm, a couple of cuts and bruises, I'm fine."

Sam looked down at the white gauze wrapped around Gabe's forearm. "Any word on the guy who did it?"

"None I know of. I'll be talking to Daily today." He checked his wristwatch. "Matter of fact, he's meeting me here. Maybe he'll have something new to report."

Sam shifted his weight from one foot to the other. "Listen… I know how much you've got on your mind right now, but I wanted you to be the first to know." His lips slowly curved. "Tracy and I are getting married. And I want you to be my best man."

Shock kept him silent. It took him several seconds for the words to actually sink in. "You're getting married?"

Sam grinned. "I'm biting the bullet. Going down for the count. Giving up my bachelor ways. And I can hardly wait."

Gabe's lips twitched. "If that's the way you feel, I'd be honored to be your best man. But I have to say, I'm a little surprised. You two haven't known each other very long."

"I think I knew she was the one almost from the start. I love her, Gabe. And Tracy loves me. I know this is right for both of us."

Gabe's chest felt oddly tight. Knowing Sam wouldn't make such an important decision without a great deal of thought, he smiled, truly happy for his friend. "Congratulations."

He couldn't help thinking of Mattie and wishing things were different, wishing there wasn't so much left unsettled between them.

Hell, he didn't really have any idea what Mattie felt

for him. She loved what he could do for her in bed. But that was hardly the same.

And he refused to let his own feeling go any deeper. Not until he knew what was going on.

Gabe slapped his best friend on the back. "I wish you and Tracy all the happiness in the world."

"Thanks."

"When's the wedding?"

"I'm not sure." He flicked a glance at Gabe's rented SUV. "Not till after we catch the bastard who's setting these goddamned fires."

Gabe released a breath. He looked over at the men carrying heavy boxes of tile into the apartment building, thought of how much he had invested that was no longer insured. "I hope it's soon."

Sam's gaze assessed him. "Everything okay with you and Mattie?"

Gabe just shook his head. "I don't have a clue."

Sam chuckled. "Hard to know what a woman's thinking."

Gabe grunted. "That's for sure."

Sam stared past his shoulder toward a car pulling up to the curb. "Looks like Captain Daily's here."

The sound of the running engine turned silent. "I'll let you know what he has to say." Gabe went to meet Daily as he climbed out of his red Suburban.

Daily's gaze took in the bandage on Gabe's arm and the gash on his cheek. "Could have been worse."

"A lot worse," Gabe said.

"I wish I had more to report. The photos we took of the crowd around the parking lot didn't turn up anyone out of place or anyone with any priors. No one we talked to remembered seeing anyone near your truck.

The security cameras caught the image of a man dressed completely in black, but they didn't get a clear shot of his face."

"You think he avoided the cameras on purpose?"

"I'm sure he did."

"What about the bomb?"

"It was a fairly simple device. Made of ammonium nitrate. Used a blasting cap to detonate, set off by a cell phone he modified for his purpose. Usually it's a paging signal that sets off the bomb."

"So he was watching, just like I thought. He saw me running toward the truck, timed it so I wouldn't quite get there and then blew it up."

"Looks like it."

"He wasn't ready to kill me."

"No, but that could change at any time."

Gabe's jaw hardened. "I don't suppose the bomb was that hard to make. Information's all over the internet."

"And there are books on the subject. If you want to blow something up and you're smart enough not to kill yourself in the process, it can certainly be done."

"Anything else?"

"The police have located the current addresses for most of the evicted tenants of Harwood. They've got uniforms out on the street, knocking on doors. There's always a chance they'll come up with something."

"I sure as hell hope so." And he meant to make a few calls of his own, starting with the three men in Dallas who had criminal records.

The other three were spread over the southern half of Texas. Dev had used his connections to discover that one who fit the general description of the arsonist had flown into Dallas three days ago. He'd gone back to

Austin on a late flight Sunday night. Dev had decided to pay him a visit.

"There's one more thing," Gabe said.

"What's that?" Daily asked.

"Mattie Baker's been getting hang-up phone calls at her condo. She's worried it might be the arsonist."

"She have caller ID?"

"She says the number comes up blocked."

"Does she have any reason to believe it's our guy and not just some kook who likes the sound of her voice?"

He shook his head. "Caller doesn't say anything and the calls seem to be random."

"Doesn't sound like something our guy would do. He isn't the sort to do something random. He doesn't make a move that isn't completely calculated. But if you give me her phone number, I can get a list from the phone company of the calls that have come into that number. We can track the hang-up caller from there."

"That'd be great." Gabe gave him Mattie's home number, which Daily copied down in his notebook.

He closed the cover and stuck the notepad back in his pocket. "I'll let you know once I get the information." Daily turned and started back to his car.

Gabe watched him go. He was tired of waiting. Tired of being targeted by a madman. Dammit, he had worked too hard all his life to let some bastard ruin him. Maybe even kill him or someone close to him.

Gabe was determined to find him.

Before it was too late.

MATTIE STOPPED BY her house after work to pick up some clothes and a few other items she needed. And she was picking up Tigger, dropping him off at Cats on Broadway, a place that boarded felines. He didn't much like going there, but if the arsonist started a fire in her building or at Gabe's while they were at work, there was no way Tigger could escape.

She scratched his chin, set him back on his feet and headed down to the underground parking garage to put her stuff in the car, planning to come back upstairs and get him. As she set her clothes in the trunk and closed the lid, she spotted Tracy's Lexus pulling into a visitor's space.

Mattie walked over to the Lexus. "Come on up. I was just moving a few things over to Gabe's. I'm taking Tigger to Cats on Broadway for a while."

"That's a good idea. This arson thing is really getting serious." Mattie had phoned Tracy and told her about the bomb that had destroyed Gabe's truck. "It was awful, Tracy. Gabe was nearly killed."

"Oh, Mattie." Tracy looked up at the small scabs on Mattie's forehead. "You're okay, though, right? Both of you are okay?"

"We're okay."

"So you're moving back in with Gabe?"

"This time it's more my idea than his. I'm hoping this will give me a chance to figure things out."

They stepped into the elevator and Mattie pushed the button. When she looked over at Tracy, her friend seemed to be practically glowing.

They walked into the living room and Mattie closed the door. "All right, so what's going on?"

Tracy grinned. "I'm getting married!"

Mattie just stared. Of all the things she might have guessed, this wasn't one of them. "You're kidding me, right?"

"It's true. Sam and I are getting married. I love him, Mattie, and he loves me. He asked me and I said yes."

"But you said you'd never get married. There was no way in the world you could ever trust a man that much."

"That was before I met Sam," she said with a dreamy smile.

"Are you sure, Tracy? You haven't really known each other that long."

Tracy just smiled. "I don't have a doubt in the world. In fact, I've never been so sure about anything in my life."

Mattie walked over and sat down in one of the cone-shaped chairs, her legs no longer steady. "You're just engaged. This isn't happening right away."

Tracy came up and stuck out her hand, waving a beautiful diamond ring in front of her nose. It was ornate, understated and lovely, nothing like Tracy might have picked for herself.

"It was Sam's mother's ring. He wasn't sure I'd like it, but I love it. It means something, you know. Sam loved his mother. She's gone and now he's giving the ring to me."

Mattie stared up at her. "Something about you is changing. You're different than you used to be."

Tracy seemed pleased. "It's Sam. He's made me see myself in a different way. He believes in me. He makes me believe in myself."

Mattie smiled. "I think I'm really gonna like this new you."

Moisture glistened in Tracy's eyes. "I like her, myself, so I hope you do, too."

Mattie stood up and hugged her. They remained

that way for several seconds, two lifelong friends who wanted only the best for each other.

"You didn't answer my question," Mattie finally said, easing away. "When is this wedding going to happen?"

"Soon, I hope. Sam's worried about Gabe. He wants to wait until they catch the arsonist."

"He's a good friend."

"The best."

"Just like you," Mattie said, her own eyes glistening.

Tracy smiled. "So what about you and Gabe? Are you going to marry him?"

Mattie sighed. "I don't know if he's interested in marrying me anymore. I'm not sure how he feels."

"But you love him, right?"

A week ago, she would have denied it. Instead, she nodded, pushed the words past the lump in her throat. "I love him."

"Then everything is going to work out."

Mattie said nothing.

"It will," Tracy said determinedly.

But there was no way to know.

MATTIE FINISHED COLLECTING her things while Tracy talked excitedly about the wedding she and Sam were planning.

"I want to keep it small. Just a few close friends. But elegant, you know? I think we should—"

Mattie's cell phone began to ring, stopping Tracy mid-sentence. Mattie grabbed her purse, dug out the phone and flipped it open. "Hello?"

"Mattie? It's Rosa." The woman started crying. "Something has happened to Angel."

Her stomach clenched. Mattie forced herself to stay

calm. "Rosa, take a deep breath, slow down and tell me what's going on." She looked over at Tracy, who worriedly bit her lip.

"I do not know exactly. His head…something happened inside. They took him to surgery. He is in there now." She started crying again, so hard Mattie couldn't understand the rest of what she was saying.

"Just hang on. I'll be there as quickly as I can." She closed the phone and turned to Tracy. "It's Angel. Something happened and they took him to surgery."

"Oh, God."

"I need to get down there. I don't want to leave Tigger here any longer. Not with that firebug running around. Do you think you could take him over to where he's supposed to be boarded?"

"Sure, I can do that. But why don't I just take him home with me? I love Tigger. He's a real sweetie."

"What about Sam?"

"Are you kidding? The man is a cream puff when it comes to animals."

"Tracy, thank you, that would really be great. I know Tigger would far rather go home with you than board with strangers. You'll need his bowl and watering dish. And I just changed his litter box."

"Great."

Together they carried the big tom and all his gear down to the garage and loaded them into Tracy's car. Mattie steeled herself against Tigger's meowing, which ended when Tracy settled him in her lap and started stroking his head.

"It's all right, sweetheart," Tracy said. "Mama will come for you as soon as it's safe."

Mattie grinned.

"Call me," Tracy said as she started the engine. "As soon as you know anything."

"I will."

"I'll say a prayer for Angel," Tracy called after her, and Mattie thought again how much her friend had changed.

"Thanks."

On her way out of the parking garage, she phoned Gabe and told him that Angel had been taken to surgery and that she was on her way to the hospital.

All the way there, she prayed that her friend would have a chance to become the man he was meant to be.

CHAPTER THIRTY-ONE

GABE'S LONG STRIDES carried him down the wide, lino-leum-floored hallway toward the waiting area in the surgical wing. Mattie had called half an hour ago to tell him what little she knew. He had forgone the visits he had been planning to make on former tenants of Greenwood with prison records, and driven directly to the hospital instead.

He found Mattie sitting with Rosa and her two younger children, both of whom sat quietly, their faces pale and grim.

Mattie stood up the moment she saw him. He started toward her, opened his arms and she walked straight into them. God, he had never known a woman who felt so right in his arms.

"Come on," he said softly. "Let's go out in the hall and you can fill me in."

She nodded. He could tell she was fighting not to cry. They pushed through the waiting room door and stepped out into the corridor. Several nurses hurried past, pushing a cart loaded with equipment toward a room at the far end of the hall.

"Tell me what happened."

Her lips trembled. She took a shaky breath and slowly released it. "A blood clot formed in Angel's brain. The doctors called it a hematoma. Apparently, after the kind of trauma he suffered, sometimes it happens. Blood solidifies between the skull and the outer layer of the brain. It causes the pressure to build. They took him to surgery to remove the blood mass and reduce the pressure."

She glanced away and when she looked back, he caught the sheen of tears.

"They make a hole in the skull," she continued, wiping at a tear that slipped onto her cheek. "That's how they remove the clot."

"The surgery's over, right?" Gabe asked gently.

She nodded. "Angel's in the recovery room."

"Did they give you any prognosis? Tell you whether or not the operation was a success?"

She shook her head. "I don't think they really know. We're...we're staying with him tonight. The doctors want us to remain hopeful. But the priest...the priest is coming, just in case." She started to cry and Gabe eased her back into his arms.

"It's all right, honey. Just hang on. We'll get through this together."

"It isn't fair," Mattie whispered against his shoulder. "He's just a boy. He was only trying to help us."

Gabe felt the words like a punch in the stomach. Angel had been out on the street asking questions, trying to help him find the arsonist. Now the boy hovered on the edge of death. Mattie was right. It wasn't fair.

But then, when had life ever been fair?

She pressed a wadded-up Kleenex beneath her nose. "Rosa wants to go over to the church across the street before Father Michaels arrives. I'm going with her."

Gabe just nodded. He rarely went to church, but he

believed in God and he didn't mind saying a prayer on occasion. Tonight seemed exactly the right time.

"I know where it is. I'll walk over with you."

She swallowed and nodded. When they returned to the waiting room to collect Rosa, another woman sat with her, a cousin named Lupe, Rosa said as she introduced him. A younger Hispanic woman in her mid-thirties with black hair cut short around her head, Lupe waited with the children while Gabe escorted the women over to St. Mary's church.

It was small but beautifully kept. A lone woman dressed in black sat in the very last row, her head covered by a black lace shawl. Candles flickered on the altar, casting shadows on the stained-glass windows behind the cross on the wall. A Bible sat open on a white satin cloth.

Rosa genuflected, crossed herself and sat down in one of the pews. Mattie sat down, looked a little surprised when Gabe sat down next to her.

He reached over and squeezed her hand and some of the tension in her shoulders eased. Gabe sat there in the silence, his chest feeling heavy. Angel deserved to live. Gabe prayed the boy would get the chance he deserved. As the minutes passed, he could hear the faint click of rosary beads as Rosa repeated the prayers. Mattie's lips silently moved and Gabe said his own simple prayer.

Then it was time to go.

The priest was coming to perform the last rites, just in case. Gabe's throat tightened as he led the women out of the church and back to the hospital. When they reached the waiting area in the surgical wing, cousin Lupe sat alone.

"My husband came and I sent the children home with him."

Rosa's lips trembled. "Thank you. And please thank Alberto for me."

Lupe's dark eyes looked sad. "The children…they didn't want to go. They wanted to stay with their brother. They said that when he wakes up, we must be sure to tell him they love him."

Rosa made a pitiful sound in her throat and Mattie reached down and caught her hand.

"Father Michaels came while you were at church," Lupe said. "He has already gone in to Angel."

Rosa's knees buckled. Gabe caught the heavyset woman and helped her into a chair.

"My boy," she said on an anguished cry. "God, please help my beautiful boy."

Tears collected in Mattie's eyes as she sat down next to Rosa. Watching her, Gabe's chest constricted. Seeing her with Angel's mother, knowing how deeply she cared, moved him as nothing had before.

Rosa and her cousin repeated the rosary over and over while Mattie wiped away tears. Time slid past. The priest came out, an imposing man with iron-gray hair. He spoke quietly to Rosa then left the waiting room. Rosa sobbed softly.

"You don't have to stay here, Gabe," Mattie said as the hours slid past. "There's nothing you can do."

"I'm staying," he said flatly. Mattie caught the hard set of his jaw and didn't argue.

Midnight came. Two o'clock. Rosa fell asleep against her cousin's shoulder. Mattie had moved next to Gabe and held on to his hand.

Four o'clock came. He must have fallen asleep, his

head tilted back against the wall behind his chair. When he opened his eyes, the first gray light of dawn filled the room. His back ached and there was a kink in his neck. Mattie slept against his shoulder. She opened her eyes as if she felt him watching her, and the people in the room began to stir.

The door swung open and Dr. Burton walked in. His narrow face reflected the exhaustion that all of them felt.

"He's been moved to Intensive Care. If one of you would like to sit with him for a while, you can go on in. Just don't stay too long."

Rosa came wearily to her feet. They all moved down to the floor that housed the intensive care unit of the hospital, a place they had been before. Rosa sat with her son for a while, then returned to the waiting area.

At nine o'clock that morning, Angel's friend Enrique shoved through the waiting room door, looking as worried and haggard as everyone else.

He spoke to Rosa. "How is he? My mother got a call from Alberto. He told her what happened. He said they took Angel to surgery. He said Padre Michaels had come."

Rosa started crying.

"He made it through surgery," Gabe said gently. "What will happen now is uncertain."

Enrique's dark eyes filled with tears. "He has to get well." He looked over at Mattie, whose eyes also glistened. "Mr. Zigman from the gallery called. He said one of the artists cancelled and an opening came up. My show is set for this weekend. If it wasn't for Angel, it wouldn't be happening. He has to get well so he can be there." The tears in his eyes spilled onto his cheeks.

Turning away, he walked out of the waiting room, his long black ponytail bobbing against his narrow shoulders.

Gabe followed him into the hall, where the teenage boy stood silently weeping. He settled a hand on Enrique's shoulder.

"There's still a chance he'll make it," he said gruffly, pushing the words past the lump in his throat. "Sometimes miracles happen."

Enrique sniffed and turned away, embarrassed that Gabe had seen him crying.

"It's all right. That's exactly the way all of us are feeling right now."

The waiting room door swung open and Mattie joined them in the hall. She didn't say a word, just put her arms around Enrique and held him tight. Both of them cried.

Enrique finally let her go. "I want to see him," he said. "I want to tell him about the show."

Only immediate family members were allowed in patient rooms, but no one stopped the boy when he walked through the doors and went over to his best friend's bed.

Through the double glass doors, Gabe could see Enrique talking to Angel, though he couldn't hear what he was saying. Next to Gabe, Mattie stood with her head on his shoulder and he suddenly felt her tense.

"Oh, my God!" She straightened away from him, started racing for the door. She shoved it aside and rushed into the room, Gabe right behind her.

"Gabe, look! His eyes are open! Angel's awake!"

Out of nowhere, doctors and nurses rushed in, surrounding the bed and ordering everyone out. Hearing the commotion, Rosa and Lupe ran toward them.

"What has happened?" Rosa's face paled in fear. "Angel…he hasn't—"

"He opened his eyes, Rosa!" Mattie gripped the woman's arm to steady her. "Enrique was talking to him and he just…he opened his eyes." Tears rolled down her cheeks. "Dr. Burton… Dr. Burton is with him now."

Rosa started praying. Huddled outside the door, no one made a move to leave.

When the doctor finally came out, he was smiling. "He's conscious. He seems to understand who he is and why he's in here. There could still be complications, of course, but if everything continues to go well, I think he's going to make it."

Gabe felt a sweep of relief so powerful he had to fight to keep himself steady. Fresh tears rolled down Mattie's cheeks and Gabe's own eyes burned. Angel was going to make it.

"Thank God" was all he said.

He didn't remember much after that, just the grateful tears, the laughter and the hugs.

He was exhausted and so was Mattie, who didn't protest when he told her he was taking her home.

Angel was alive. Some of the guilt he'd been feeling slipped away.

Still, the madman who had nearly killed the boy remained at large. The danger hadn't lessened. None of them would be safe until the arsonist was stopped.

CHAPTER THIRTY-TWO

MATTIE TOOK A RARE sick day and didn't go in to work. After their exhausting night at the hospital, she and Gabe went back to his condo, crawled naked into bed, and fell soundly asleep, too tired even to make love.

At least until later. Dev's call awakened them. He was staying in Austin, doing a little background research on the man he was investigating, a former tenant of Greenwood with a criminal record and a timeline that made him viable as a suspect. So far he had found nothing to link him to the fires.

"By the way," Gabe said as he emerged from the shower, looking like a big, dark, satisfied cat, "I talked to Captain Daily about those calls you were getting." A towel rode low on his hips. The bandage was gone from his arm, but a nasty red welt still marred his skin. "He says he can get the number of the guy who's been calling. He says it won't be a problem."

Mattie felt the blood draining out of her face. She should have known Gabe wouldn't let the matter drop, and now he had involved the arson squad!

He walked over and caught her shoulders. "What is it? You've gone pale as a ghost. What's wrong?"

"Oh, Gabe. I'm sorry... I... I...meant to tell you. I found out who was making the calls."

"What?"

"I should have said something, I know. I didn't realize you would get Captain Daily involved."

"You didn't think I'd want to follow up, find out if you were really in danger?"

She glanced away. She'd wanted to stay at his apartment. She'd wanted to sleep in his bed. It was only a little lie, a lie of omission. "I'm sorry. I just forgot."

Gabe eyed her darkly. "When did you find out?"

"Um…yesterday morning."

His frown deepened. "You're staying here because both of us were worried about those calls. If you found out who was making them, letting me know should have been your first priority."

She tried to look repentant. "You're right, I should have called and told you."

His jaw hard, he tipped his head back and studied her down the length of his nose. Then a gleam entered those crystal blue eyes. "Maybe there's another reason you didn't tell me. A far more interesting reason."

The heat rushed into her face and she glanced away. "It must have been all the excitement with Angel."

"Try again. You're a terrible liar, Mattie."

She opened her mouth, closed it again and simply lifted her chin.

Instead of the tirade she expected, his mouth curved up at the corners. "You wanted to stay. That's it, isn't it? That's why you didn't tell me. You wanted to stay here with me."

She straightened, thought about denying it. She hated to give him the upper hand. But she hated lying to him even more. "Fine. All right, I wanted to stay. I needed time to think things over, figure things out."

His mouth swooped down over hers in a fiercely possessive yet tender kiss. Mattie made a soft little sound in her throat and relaxed against him, kissed him back.

"You could have just told me the truth," Gabe said as he nibbled the side of her neck.

"Would you have let me stay?"

"Probably not, but you could have admitted you wanted to."

"I could still be in danger," she said, planting soft little kisses on the corners of his mouth.

"Yeah, I suppose you could be."

"So I'm staying, right?"

He drew away, took a steadying breath. "You'd probably be safer at home."

"Or maybe not."

He was frowning again. "Or maybe not."

"So I'm staying. At least for a while."

"Yeah." He bent his head and softly kissed her lips. "Who was it, by the way? If it's one of Lena Sterling's secret admirers, I am going to kick his ass."

Mattie laughed. "He's a friend. He's been working through some problems. He's okay now. In fact, he's great. He's dating someone he really likes."

"It's that guy from your office. Aaron. The one you had dinner with? I knew he was going to be a problem. He called because he was jealous you're sleeping with me."

He was far too perceptive to suit her, and yet his intelligence was one of the things that made him so attractive. "Aaron got a little mixed up, is all. He admitted to making the calls. He said he was sorry."

"I'd still like to kick his ass."

"He's in a wheelchair, Gabe."

"Oh."

Mattie almost smiled. Instead, she went up on her toes and kissed him very softly on the mouth. A little yelp slipped from her throat as his towel fell away and she felt his heavy erection pressing against her. Gabe scooped her up in his arms and carried her back to bed.

It was another hour before he called Captain Daily.

FRIDAY NIGHT ARRIVED, the date of Enrique's opening at the Zigman Gallery. In the days after the truck explosion, Gabe had been extremely cautious, taking extra care whenever either of them left the house, staying in touch during the day, checking and verifying their arrival times wherever they went. It was beginning to drive Mattie crazy, and yet she understood.

Until they caught the madman stalking Gabe, everyone he knew was in danger.

And so she was looking forward to tonight. For the occasion of Enrique's first gallery opening, Mattie had chosen one of her favorite black dresses, low-backed, with a narrow, black fabric belt, a string of pearls and matching earrings, and very high black heels.

Dev had returned from Austin two days ago, with the news that the former Greenwood tenant's alibi had checked out. He wasn't the guy they were after. The police were still checking other names on the tenant list, but so far nothing useful had been discovered.

Gabe walked out of the bedroom, looking gorgeous in a dark blue pinstripe suit, a crisp white shirt and a red-flecked blue tie. Mattie let her gaze wander over him. The man looked good in everything—even better in nothing at all.

He said something and she noticed the cell phone he held against his ear.

"Dev's friend Chaz came up with something," he said to the person on the other end of the line. "He's checking it out. I'll let you know if it goes anywhere." Gabe glanced over at her and rolled his eyes. "I know you want to come down here, but I'm asking you not to. Give us another week, okay?"

It was Jackson, she realized. Gabe's brother was champing at the bit—as Gabe would have said—to come out and catch the arsonist. If he didn't have a wife and daughter he adored and a ranch to run, there would have been no keeping him away.

Gabe closed the phone. "That was Jackson."

"So I gathered."

"He'll be here on Monday. I tried to tell him there's nothing he can do that we aren't already doing, but—"

"But he loves you and he's worried."

"Yeah." His gaze ran over her, that brilliant blue that never failed to make her stomach lift. "You look gorgeous."

"Thanks, so do you."

His mouth edged up. "I'd prefer incredibly handsome."

"Too weak a word for how beautiful you are."

He grunted but he was smiling. "I guess we're ready."

Though Angel was still in the hospital and unable to attend, Gabe had promised to drive the boy over to see Enrique's work, which would remain in the gallery till the end of the month, as soon as he was released from the hospital and strong enough to make the visit.

The party didn't start until eight, so she and Gabe were going to catch a quick bite at a little place she knew called Stone Cellars before they headed over to the show.

"I'll just get my purse." She walked into the bedroom, which had begun to feel far too comfortable even though she had to share a closet with Gabe. Picking up her black silk bag, she returned to the living room.

Gabe was back on the phone. "What did you say your name was? Ryan Franklin," he repeated. "Hold on a minute, Ryan." Walking over to the desk, he picked up a clipboard, flicked through a couple of pages, checked something and set the board back down. "All right. I'll be there in twenty minutes."

Gabe hung up the phone. "That was the security guard at the warehouse. There's a broken water line. I guess the pipe is flooding pretty good. I need to stop by on our way to dinner and turn off the main valve."

"The warehouse? What about the arsonist? How do you know this isn't some kind of trick to get you over there?"

"I checked the security roster. Atlas provided a list with each guard's name and their corresponding shift. Ryan Franklin is on from four to ten. That's who called on the phone."

She still didn't like it. The arsonist hadn't given up and both of them knew it. He was just waiting for the right time to strike. "Couldn't you just call a plumber?"

"I'd still have to go. The guard doesn't have a key to the equipment room. That's where the main valve is."

"So I guess you've got no choice."

"It won't take long. Maybe you should stay here and I'll come back and get you when I'm finished."

"No way. We don't want to be late, and besides, I'm really getting hungry."

"Me, too."

"You're always hungry."

He flashed a wicked grin. "Yeah, but not necessarily for food."

Mattie laughed.

"I'll be right back," Gabe said.

She watched him walk into the bedroom and when he came out, he was holding the pistol he'd been keeping in a drawer in his nightstand.

"Glock 9 mil. I'm not expecting trouble, but it never hurts to be prepared."

Mattie didn't argue.

"We'll have to take the SUV," Gabe said as he tucked the gun into the back of his waistband and let his suit jacket fall over it. "My tools are in there."

She eyed his perfectly tailored suit and the black lizard boots he was wearing, and her eyebrows went up. "That's kind of an expensive outfit for a plumbing job."

He chuckled. "With any luck, all I'll have to do is turn a knob. Then we're out of there."

She took his arm and let him lead her to the door. "You think Dev will show up at the opening?"

"He said he would. First he wanted to run down something Chaz turned him onto."

"Did he say what it was?"

"Something about social security checks. He said he'd fill us in when he saw us tonight."

Us. Until lately, she wasn't used to hearing the word. The way Gabe said it made it sound as if they were really a couple. The kind of people who grew old together, the kind it was hard to tell where one of them started and the other one ended.

She was staying with Gabe, practically living with him. Instead of feeling trapped or frightened, instead of worrying about what would happen if she let down her guard and allowed herself to love him, she felt as if she were exactly where she should be.

Of course she wasn't sure Gabe felt the same. He had mentioned marriage that one time, but only in general conversation and he'd never brought up the subject again. And he had certainly never said the word *love*.

It was early evening, the sun beginning to weaken into soft yellow rays, when Gabe's rented SUV turned onto Cadiz Street and pulled up in front of an oversize lot where a dilapidated three-story building with a rusty metal roof sat badly in need of repair. The core of the wood-framed structure looked solid, but several crude additions had been built on over the years.

Large paned windows provided light to the interior, though a number of the panes were broken and the rest too dirty to see through. A security guard wearing a black uniform and an Atlas cap stood near the front of the building, a holstered weapon on his heavy belt, along with a flashlight and a ring of keys.

Mattie caught the reflection of evening sunlight on the badge pinned to the pocket of his shirt. The Atlas Security Company truck was parked at the side of the warehouse.

"Everything looks okay," Gabe said. "Wait for me here. This shouldn't take long."

She watched as he walked to the back of the SUV, opened the rear door and dragged out his heavy leather tool belt. "I probably won't need this, but you never know."

Tool belt swinging from his hand, he strode toward the guard, who waited on the walkway leading to the steps up to the front door. Reaching behind him, Gabe checked his pistol then let his coat slide back down over it, concealing it once more from view.

It occurred to her that the guard fit what little description they had of the arsonist: white male, average height, lean build, but there were a lot of lean white males in Dallas. The men spoke briefly, then walked together up the wide, wooden front steps and disappeared inside the warehouse.

THERE WAS SOMETHING about Ryan Franklin. Nothing Gabe could put a finger on, but the skin at the back of his neck had begun to tingle the way it used to when he was in the marines.

As they crossed the rough planks of the raised warehouse floor, he could hear the rush of water coming from underneath where the pipes were located. If the water ran unchecked too long, it could damage the foundation.

The main part of the warehouse was big and open, but the rear had been chopped into storage rooms and offices, all strung together by long, narrow halls.

A small amount of sunlight made its way through the dirty windows, but the corridors remained shadowy and dim. Franklin flicked on his flashlight and pointed it toward the floor. Following the beam, they reached the cement stairs leading to the equipment room, partly below ground, and started down, the guard walking beside him. From the corner of his eye, Gabe noticed the slightly sunken eyes, the hollows in Franklin's cheeks and the tingling started again.

Careful not to let the man get behind him, he reached into the pocket of his slacks and pulled out a set of keys.

They jangled as he stuck one into the lock on the heavy steel door, then turned the knob and shoved it open.

A row of windows up near the top of the walls allowed weak rays of sunlight into the room. The weight of the gun at his back felt comforting as Gabe stepped inside and set the tool belt down on the rough cement floor.

"Is that the valve over there?" the guard asked, making a jerky motion with his hand as he aimed the flashlight, the circle of yellow landing on a metal knob.

"That's it."

Gabe took a single step before the piercing shock hit him, an electrical jolt that sizzled through his body and rolled out through his limbs, stole his breath and took him to his knees. The second jolt left him flat on his back on the floor, his eyes wide-open and staring, completely unable to move.

"Welcome to my world, Gabriel Raines." The guard grinned, and in the faint light his sunken eyes appeared nearly black. He looked like a demon straight from hell and as he zapped Gabe with another million volts of stun gun power, he was.

The blast scrambled the electrical signals from his brain and turned his muscles to mush. The recovery period, Gabe remembered from his training, could take as long as ten minutes.

"Just so you know," the man said with a maniacal gleam in his jet-black eyes, "my name is Jacob Mueller, not Ryan Franklin. My mother was Vera Mercedes Mueller."

Still frozen, Gabe watched as the man knelt beside him, pulled the cell phone out of Gabe's pocket and slammed it into the wall, sending pieces of black plastic flying through the air. Mueller used a roll of duct tape to bind Gabe's ankles, then his wrists. The man's hand jerked as he picked Gabe's pistol up from the floor next to his paralyzed body.

"You wouldn't remember my mother," Mueller continued. "You never even knew her. But I remember everything about her. Her beauty, her kindness, the joy she felt when she was working in her tiny flower garden, how much she loved me." His fingers jumped as if the nerves were somehow out of order as he toyed with the weapon.

His mouth curved into a vicious, oddly twisted smile. "It was your greed that killed her. Your lust for money. Now I'm going to kill you."

Gabe tried to speak, tried to shake his head, explain he had nothing to do with the evictions, but he couldn't move. Not a hand, not a finger, not a single, solitary muscle.

"I hate to cover your mouth. I'm going to be right outside while the place is burning. I'd love to hear you screaming. But alas, some do-gooder might try to save you." He rolled a piece of duct tape over Gabe's mouth.

"No one will hear you now. Not even your lady friend. I didn't know you were bringing her. But now that I know she'll be watching, tortured to know you're roasting in the flames, it makes all this so much better."

Gabe's stomached lurched. Or at least it felt as if it did. He would have swallowed the bile in his throat if he could have. He had underestimated his opponent and now there was every chance he was going to die in this warehouse, burned alive for something he didn't do.

And what about Mattie? What did the bastard have in mind for her? He forced the thought away, knowing if he let himself go in that direction, he would lose what little self-control he had left.

The stun gun jabbed into his thigh, and he felt the frying jolt of pain through every muscle, joint and tendon. The blood rushed through his veins and his heart thundered as if it would explode through his chest. When his mind cleared enough to think, he wondered if the device had been modified to enhance the pain, make the paralysis last even longer.

"I'm sorry to leave in such haste," Mueller said with that cruel, twisted smile, "but I have a few things left to do." He walked over and turned off the valve, ending the flow of water running in the crawl space beneath the raised warehouse floor.

When he returned, Gabe felt another lightning jolt, the burning, wrenching pain sear through him.

"Oh, I am so going to enjoy this."

And then he was gone.

Mueller didn't close the door. He wanted the smoke and flames to reach the room. There were piles of rubbish everywhere, and Gabe caught the smell of diesel fuel, the accelerant Mueller had used to start the fire that would engulf him in a grotesque, hideous death.

Even knowing it would do no good with the cement walls around him and the thickness of the heavy timbers in the floor above, if he could have, Gabe would have screamed.

CHAPTER THIRTY-THREE

MATTIE NEVER WAS much good at waiting. And the old warehouse intrigued her. As she sat there staring at the basic shape of the structure, at the timbers holding up the roof and what appeared to be solid construction, she began to consider the possibilities of what Gabe might do with the place.

Leaving her evening bag on the seat, she climbed out of the SUV and started around the perimeter of the building, just to see what she might come up with. There was a sidewalk of sorts. Though grass grew up through the cracks, it was better than walking in the dirt with her high heels.

She rounded the corner and surveyed the side of the structure. Gabe should definitely tear down the poorly constructed additions, she thought, and continued toward the back of the building, wishing the light wasn't fading so quickly.

Considering the building's age, she was surprised at how well constructed the main portion was, but then Gabe was good at what he did and he wouldn't have bought the place if it hadn't been worth saving.

She walked a little farther along the path, turned the corner and something caught her eye. A man's shoe, black and shiny, protruded from beneath an overgrown shrub. Wariness trickled down her spine. She drew closer, saw that the shoe wasn't empty, saw that there were two of them, and they held a pair of black-stockinged feet whose ankles were wrapped in duct tape.

Mattie bit back a scream. She knew even before she shoved aside the shrubbery and saw that the man's shirt was missing, along with his belt, gun, and badge, this was the guard and that Gabe was inside with the arsonist.

The man, shorter than average, early thirties with buzz-cut brown hair, started squirming, trying to get free. Mattie jerked the tape off his mouth.

"Call the police! I'm the security guard. There's a man inside setting fire to the building. He's trying to kill someone!"

Mattie trembled. "I'll call them!" She turned and started running. "I'll be back!" She stumbled, shed her high heels and kept running, snagging her black, thigh-high nylons on the rocks and twigs on the walkway. Heading back to retrieve the cell phone in her purse, she rounded the corner just as a curl of smoke escaped from beneath the eaves of the roof.

Her heart jerked. The building was already beginning to burn. Dear God, Gabe was inside with a madman! She glanced toward the SUV, which seemed miles away, trying to decide what to do. She wanted to rush inside, find Gabe and warn him, but she had no idea where the arsonist might be and without help, all of them might wind up dead.

With a renewed burst of energy, she raced toward the car and pulled open the door, but when she looked inside, her purse was no longer where she had left it on the seat.

Fear tore through her. The arsonist had been inside

the SUV. He had taken her cell phone. She looked back at the building, saw the thickening smoke and the first orange blossom of flame. Dear God, what had he done to Gabe?

She no longer had a choice. Running toward the warehouse, she climbed the wooden steps and opened the door, rushing inside through the smoke.

She knew Gabe was headed for the equipment room. Earlier, she had heard water running under the floor, then it had been turned off. She knew the main valve was located in the room at the far left corner of the building that also held the furnace. She'd seen it when she'd examined the old, original plans that day in his study.

The fire was beginning to burn at a terrifying rate of acceleration. Staying low and away from the piles of burning rubbish that were fueling the flames and the fire climbing the walls, she raced across the wide-planked floor toward the back of the warehouse. There were rooms there that hadn't been on the plans, small storage areas and makeshift offices. A long corridor, lit only by the last of the faint dusk light streaming through a window, stretched in front of her.

She took a deep breath, coughed several times and forced herself to think of the drawings. In the eye of her mind, she saw the set of stairs that led to a room below the main floor in the far southwest corner.

Praying the arsonist had fled, but afraid he might be lurking in the shadows, she ran down the hallway, her heart thundering madly. She hissed in a breath as splinters jabbed into her feet, coughed as more smoke filled her lungs and continued on. Her heart was hammering by the time she neared the cement stairs and paused to search for some kind of weapon.

What had happened to Gabe's pistol? Why hadn't he used it to defend himself? Spotting a three-foot length of pipe, she picked it up and hurried toward the stairs. Smoke was everywhere now, stinging her eyes, making her struggle to breathe. Some of the storerooms were burning. The flames had bloomed into a full-fledged fire and yet she wasn't sure how long it would take for someone outside to notice.

The smoke grew thicker, heavier, curling along the floor, rising along the walls. The noise of the fire began to build, a dull roar punctuated by the snap and crackle of burning wood. Mattie bent double, trying to stay low, trying to suck air into her lungs.

The stairs were exactly where the plans had indicated. Gripping the pipe, she made her way to the bottom step, surprised to find the heavy metal door standing open. Flames had already begun to chew through the ceiling of the equipment room. A sob caught in her throat as she spotted Gabe on his back, his ankles bound with duct tape, his wrists bound in front of him. He was struggling to free himself, every muscle straining.

His face went pale as she ran toward him, knelt and ripped the tape off his mouth.

"Mattie! For God's sake, it's him—get out while you still can!"

"I'm not leaving. I'm getting you out of here." Reaching down, she began to loosen the tape around his wrists.

"My tool belt! Over by the door!"

But when she turned, the man wearing the black Atlas shirt stood in the opening, his stolen badge gleaming.

"Sorry, change of plans," he said, a twisted smile curving his lips. Madness flashed in his eyes the instant before he slammed the heavy metal door. Mattie bit back a cry and rushed forward as more metal clanged and grated, the sound of something being wedged against the door to hold it in place. She pushed with all her strength, but the door wouldn't open.

"Get my tool belt!" Gabe repeated, trying to be heard above the crackle of the flames. The sound was growing louder, the ominous pop and snap, a noise like the rush of wind. Soon the flames would burn through the floor over their heads, ignite the walls and the piles of fuel-soaked rags and stacks of old newspapers piled in the corners.

Her insides trembled. Ignoring the fear, she grabbed Gabe's tool belt and ran back to where he lay. Pulling out a box cutter, she sliced through the duct tape binding his wrists.

"Stun gun," Gabe explained, jerking free. Taking the sharp blade from her hands, he started sawing the tape around his ankles, his movements were slower and less coordinated than they usually were.

"I could hear the water running," he said. "I didn't think he was our man, but my sixth sense was shouting and I always listen. I was ready for him to make some kind of move. Stun gun never crossed my mind."

Finally, the tape broke free and Gabe came to his feet. He shoved the box cutter into his pocket and hauled her into his arms.

"Mattie." He held on to her, turned her face up and

gave her a quick, hard kiss. "Dammit, you shouldn't have come in here."

She moistened her trembling lips. "I found the guard. So far he's okay. I went back to call 9-1-1 but the arsonist stole my purse. I had to find you. There wasn't time to wait."

He kissed her one last time, let her help him peel off his navy blue suit coat and toss it away. He tried the door, shoving his shoulder hard against it, then turned and began to study his surroundings. The burning ceiling lit the room enough to see even as the light outside faded away.

"We've got to find a way out of here."

Mattie nodded. Her chest felt tight. It was getting harder and harder to breathe, but so far the smoke was rising, not billowing down toward the floor. But when she looked up, the flames overhead were bigger, brighter tongues of fire beginning to leach down into the walls of the equipment room. As soon as they reached the piles of debris on the floor, the place would become an inferno.

"The windows are way too small," she said. They were long and narrow, impossible for either of them to climb through. As it got hotter, the glass would explode and shower glowing shards into the room below.

"Even if we could fit, that's where Mueller will be waiting. He wants to be close by, somewhere he can hear us screaming."

"Oh, God."

"We're going to disappoint him."

She swallowed, worked to breathe, prayed Gabe was right.

"This room is in the southwest corner of the building," he said. "It's partly belowground. The walls are covered with wallboard and behind them it's solid cement."

Mattie shuddered. Smoke curled down into the room. Every breath was a labor. She fought not to cough, forced herself not to think of the flames scorching through the ceiling overhead and focused instead on the floor plans.

"But the cement only goes to ground level," she said. She had taken a good look at the room, wondering if Gabe might be able to expand it to hold more modern equipment.

"That's right. The rest of the wall is wood-framed up to the floor above. We break through up there and climb out into the crawl space." Gabe grabbed her face between his hands, planted a last hard kiss on her mouth. "And that's how we're getting out of here."

A hole appeared above their heads and flames shot down the wall behind the stairway. Gabe coughed roughly as he bent and pulled out the claw hammer hanging from his tool belt, dragged out the small, powerful LED flashlight next to it and shoved it into his hip pocket. Climbing up onto the furnace, he started lashing at a portion of the wall about four feet down from the ceiling. Chunks of wallboard flew, exposing two-by-four construction. Mattie climbed up beside him and began helping him peel the wallboard away.

It was becoming harder and harder to breathe, but they kept working, chipping away at the wallboard until a large enough portion of the framing was exposed. Gabe used the hammer to knock one of the 2x4s loose at the top, giving him enough room to maneuver his big body through, and slipped into the four-foot crawl space. Crouching in the four-foot area below the heavy oak floor, he stuck the hammer into the black lizard belt that matched his boots and he held out his hand.

"Come, on, honey. Let's get out of here."

Mattie took his hand and climbed in beside him. It was easier to breath down here, the air moist and the smoke spiraling upward away from the heavy wooden floor that protected them from the flames. Behind Gabe, the fire had chewed through the wood, the orange glow outlining his broad-shouldered frame and making it possible for them to see in what otherwise would have been total darkness. Mattie let him guide her away from the room, her feet sinking into the muddy earth caused by the broken water line.

The crawl space was high enough for her to stand partway up. Bent nearly double, both of them staying low where the air was still fresh, Gabe took her hand and they started making their way toward the front of the warehouse.

"He'll be in back of the building, enjoying his moment of triumph."

Mattie shivered, dragged in a breath. "He's insane."

"His name's Jacob Mueller. He thinks I'm responsible for killing his mother. She was one of the tenants who got evicted when Harwood was condemned."

"So we were right."

Gabe coughed, dragged in a lungful of air. "Looks like it."

They moved forward, mud squishing through her torn black nylons, the fire creeping ominously closer. Mattie glanced up at the sound of breaking glass as some of the windows on the first floor exploded, but the thick wooden floor remained a barrier to the flames.

"Keep going," Gabe commanded, taking her hand and tugging her forward. Something heavy crashed down and a hole opened up in the floor above them not that far away. "Don't look back, just keep moving."

They dropped to their knees, trying to find fresh air. Mattie tried to drag in several labored breaths between coughing fits, then continued forward.

Another loud noise sounded as timbers collapsed on the upper level. "Oh, God. I hope someone's called the fire department. The guard is still tied up out there."

"Probably used a stun gun on him, too." Gabe coughed. "Guard didn't stand a chance."

They trudged through the muddy earth, the water in places well past Mattie's ankles, both of them bent over, moving one direction, then changing course to dodge the flames eating through the floor overhead.

Finally in the distance, the sound of sirens cut through the evening air, loud enough to be heard even over the snap and roar of the flames.

Fighting through the muddy crawl space, Mattie searched the darkness, grateful Gabe seemed to know exactly which way to go. "How…how are we going to get out?"

"There's an access to this area on all four sides of the building." He coughed a couple of times, caught a breath. "Guy who designed it was pretty conscientious about maintenance needs."

She remembered that now. Still… "What…what if the access is locked?"

He held up his hammer, and in the glow of the distant flames, she thought that he grinned. He paused, turned to face her, his expression serious once more.

"You risked your life to get me out of that room. I'll get you out of here, honey. I promise you."

And she trusted that he would. She trusted Gabriel Raines with every ounce of her soul. She was surprised she hadn't realized it sooner.

They reached the access. It was locked from the outside just as she had feared, and when an explosion hit, shaking the entire building and crumbling another portion of the floor, fear curled in her stomach.

She gasped for breath, felt Gabe's hand reach for hers, steadying her. "Easy. We're almost there."

"But it's locked from the other side!"

She watched the heavy claw hammer come down, wood chips flew, then the hammer turned and chipped away several big chunks. Gabe struck again and she realized the door was made of nothing more than plywood.

He swung and chipped until she could see through to the latch holding it closed, watched it tumble uselessly to the ground on the opposite side, then he pushed open the door.

He eased halfway out to take a look around. "All clear. Let's go."

He took her hand and hauled her out behind him. They crawled into the darkness, far enough away to be safe, both of them coughing, dragging fresh air into their smoke-filled lungs. Fire trucks were pulling up at the curb in front of the warehouse as Gabe came to his feet, hauled her to hers and they raced away from the blazing inferno.

"What about the guard?" Mattie asked hoarsely, lungs burning, her bare feet leaving traces of blood on the walkway. Her gaze flashed toward the big wooden structure almost completely engulfed in flames.

"Looks like the fire guys have him."

Mattie followed Gabe's line of sight to a man in black pants and a plain white T-shirt standing next to one of the firemen. His face was pale, his hair disheveled, his T-shirt hanging out of his pants. "Yes, that's him."

Gabe let go of her hand and tipped his head toward a familiar man walking rapidly toward them. "Talk to Daily. Tell him what happened." He dragged in a lungful of cleansing night air. "I've got something to do."

Mattie caught his arm. "Where are you going?"

"You know where I'm going. This has to end, Mattie."

"But you can't go after him alone! You don't even have a gun!"

"I had my gun before and it didn't do me any good. I don't need a gun to take this guy down. I just need to outthink him for a change." He leaned over and kissed her hard, turned and darted away.

"Gabe!" Mattie started coughing as one of the firemen ran up with an oxygen tank and placed the plastic cone over her mouth and nose.

Her eyes found Gabe, but he was already disappearing into the darkness.

And Mattie was terrified she would never see him again.

JACOB STOOD IN the shadows of a thick-trunked tree just a little ways away from the warehouse. When the fire trucks arrived, he'd retreated from the spot he had chosen, the place close enough to hear the screams.

He'd really wanted that. After the woman had arrived to join his little party, he couldn't wait for the screams. Here, he was either too far away or the smoke had reached them first.

He hoped not. He wanted Raines to suffer. And the woman? Well, she was just a little bonus.

His fingers twitched as he held up his cell and pushed the video button, took a few seconds of footage, pictures of the flames leaping high into the air, the whirling tongues of orange and yellow, the firefly sparks rising into the darkness.

If he let his imagination run, he could almost smell the greasy odor of burning human flesh, of singed hair and skin.

He was smiling as he drew a little farther back, putting a bit more distance between himself and the scene. He didn't want to get caught. Not yet. He was having too much fun.

His smile widened. His mother always said his smile made him special, like everything else about him. Tonight he was getting revenge for Vera Mueller. From now on, what he did would be for himself.

He looked up just then and caught a glimpse of someone moving silently among the shadows near the bushes at the edge of the property. Someone searching, looking for footprints, looking for *him*.

It was past time for him to leave. Tucking the cell phone into his pocket, he eased farther back into the shadows, turned and started walking away. He lived just a few blocks from the warehouse, not that far from the apartment he had shared with his mother. He hadn't burned Harwood down yet, still a lot of sentimental attachment there. But sooner or later the time would come.

Jacob slipped farther into the darkness, wishing he

could stay till the fire was out and the bodies were discovered, but headed back home instead. He liked being downtown and close to everything, liked that he didn't need to drive his mother's ancient Oldsmobile very often. Tonight he enjoyed walking home in the smoky night air.

The pleasant thought lasted only a moment, only until he spotted the big man walking toward him. The muddy black cowboy boots, the dirty white shirt with the sleeves rolled up, the muscular forearms, the long legs eating up the distance between them.

Gabriel Raines.

Fury poured through him. He was still alive! Jacob's hands fisted, shaking almost uncontrollably. He took a deep breath. So the game wasn't over yet.

He took a steadying breath. Perhaps it was better this way. More time to savor his triumph.

Jacob started running.

CHAPTER THIRTY-FOUR

MOVING QUIETLY THROUGH the shadows, Gabe kept his quarry in sight. He had spotted Jacob Mueller in back of the warehouse in his black clothes, minus the guard's badge and heavy leather belt. Odds were Mueller had kept both and could use them as weapons.

The arsonist stood in the darkness behind a tall hedge at the perimeter of the lot. Gabe closed the distance between them but didn't want to alert the man to his presence. He knew the moment he was spotted, still too far away to catch him, and watched Mueller turn and run.

Gabe didn't stop. Somewhere behind him, he could hear the sound of sirens, knew the cops would soon reach the warehouse. He knew Mattie would have warned Daily and that backup would soon be on the way.

But Jacob Mueller had a good head start and he seemed to know the neighborhood. If Gabe waited for the police, there was every chance Mueller would escape.

It wasn't going to happen. The bastard wasn't getting away again. Gabe increased his speed, his long legs pounding the earth. He kept in shape. He could run like this for hours if he had to.

He didn't believe Mueller was actually trying to

get away. Mueller wanted him to follow. Tonight Gabe had escaped the man's death trap in the burning warehouse. Now the arsonist had a chance for a final showdown. Which meant he had some secondary plan for this kind of scenario. A plan to get rid of whoever was fool enough to fall into another of his traps.

Not this time, Gabe thought as he followed Mueller around another corner, watched him disappear through the wooden side gate of a single family home, cross an empty backyard and come out in an alley. *This time I'm the predator and you're the prey.*

Mueller ran down the alley and rounded a corner onto another street half a block away. Gabe followed. An old white stucco duplex lay ahead, the exterior cracked and dirty in the pale yellow glow of a porch light. Mueller headed for the entry into the building, pulled open a black, wrought-iron gate and ran down a lane that separated the two units.

Wishing like hell he had his phone, Gabe cautiously followed. He wasn't sure this was Mueller's final destination, but he didn't dare stop long enough to knock on doors and ask to use someone's phone or the bastard would get away.

Gabe couldn't let that happen. Mueller wouldn't stop setting fires and the next time, Gabe might not be as lucky as he had been tonight.

Mattie might not be as lucky.

A chill ran down his spine.

He could have lost her tonight. Both of them could have been killed. He would never forget how brave she had been, how she had risked herself to save him.

It could have ended for them in that warehouse. His

close brush with death had shown him again how precious time was and reminded him not to waste it.

He had never told Mattie he loved her. It was past time he did. If she felt the same, he was going to ask her to marry him. And pray like hell she would accept.

Gabe reached the entry, flattened himself against the wall beside the wrought-iron gate. The sound of a child's voice in the hallway talking to the arsonist made him stop short.

"Hi, Mr. Mueller."

"Hello, Billy." Mueller paused, seemed to be considering his options. "Where's your mother?"

"She went next door."

"Then why don't you come in and have one of those big peanut butter cookies you like? I bought some fresh ones just this morning."

At the sound of small, shuffling feet, Gabe silently cursed. Pushing away from the wall, he peered around the corner into the hallway lit by a single bare bulb. Mueller was backing away with the boy carefully positioned in front of him.

Gabe pulled open the gate and stepped into plain sight. "Let the boy go, Mueller. This is between you and me."

Mueller ignored him. Drawing the little boy backward, he disappeared into a shadowy alcove that marked the entrance to unit number one. Gabe heard the sound of a key in the lock, the creak of the door being opened, then quietly closing again.

The guy made bombs. Gabe's military training kicked in. He pulled the small, high-powered LED flashlight out of his back pocket and cautiously made his way toward the doorway, searching the floor and walls for a trip wire or some kind of pressure plate, something Mueller would have left for unwanted company.

Nothing.

Not until he reached the alcove.

Then there it was—IED, an Improvised Explosive Device. A fine strand of wire was strung across the doorway near his feet. It was held in place by a simple clothespin with the tip wrapped in foil. Pulling the wire would trigger the homemade device camouflaged by the potted plant just inside the alcove.

Mueller must have set it on his way into the apartment.

Gabe pulled the box cutter out of his pocket, grateful he had brought along his makeshift defense arsenal, crouched down and carefully cut the wire.

Something moved in the darkness a few feet away. "What the hell…" a familiar voice said.

Gabe came to his feet at the sound of his brother's deep voice, relief washing over him. Dev opened his mouth but Gabe put a finger to his lips, cutting off the question.

Taking in Gabe's soot-covered shirt, torn slacks and mud-covered boots, Dev realized in an instant they were dealing with the arsonist.

"He's inside," Gabe said softly. "Got a hostage. A little boy."

"Shit. You armed?"

Gabe shook his head. "Not anymore."

Dev pulled up the leg of his jeans and drew his .38 backup revolver out of his ankle holster. He handed it to Gabe, who checked the load and stuck it in the waistband of his pants.

Dev stepped far enough away from the door that he couldn't be heard and punched in 9-1-1 on his cell phone, quietly relayed the situation, then pocketed the phone. Flipping back the tail of his light-colored sport coat, he pulled out the 9 mm Browning he carried in his shoulder holster.

A look passed between them.

"I.E.D.s?" Dev asked.

Gabe nodded, tried the doorknob, slowly turned it. It wasn't locked and he didn't feel any pressure, nothing that told him the door was rigged.

"I'm going round back," Dev whispered. "Keep him busy till I can get in position to take the shot."

Dev had been a marksman with the rangers. Gabe had never seen a better shooter.

Gabe eased open the door but didn't step inside.

Gun clasped in both hands, Dev disappeared into the darkness.

The apartment was dimly lit. A light burned in the hall and another in a room at the opposite end. Using the flashlight to scan the floor, Gabe spotted a second wire just inside the doorway. Crouching down, he shined the flashlight beam on the explosive device, saw the way the pin was inserted and carefully cut the wire.

He took in his surroundings: a living room with a makeshift kitchen, bathroom down the hall leading to what he assumed was the bedroom. The couch was old, the cushions sagging, the dingy brown fabric torn. A pillow rested at one end and a wrinkled sheet draped over it, as if Mueller had been sleeping there. The place was cluttered with stacks of old newspapers and rags. Mueller's collection of fuel to be used for future fires.

Gabe's jaw clenched. He eased farther into the room,

checking every step of the way for more explosive de-
vices. But Mueller had the boy and handling the child
took valuable time. Gabe heard muffled sounds coming
from the bedroom and made his way toward his quarry.

Silently, he moved down the hall, checking for trip
wires or pressure pads. Mueller had taken Gabe's pistol.
Probably had the guard's, as well. But shooting Gabe
wasn't what the arsonist wanted.

Flames drove his demons. Fire was his god.

Gabe heard the muffled sounds again. The boy struggling, then fell silent. He inched farther along the passage until he could see into the bedroom.

The bed had been removed, replaced with a pair of
sawhorses with a piece of plywood on top. Mueller's
worktable. Fertilizer, a coil of wire, a can of gasoline,
one of motor oil. A length of steel pipe. Blasting caps.
All it took to make a bomb. Or three.

Gabe's eyes locked with Mueller's. "Let the boy go,"
he said with deadly calm.

Mueller held the child. He was no more than five
years old with blond curly hair, his mouth duct-taped,
wrists bound in front of him. Big brown terrified eyes
stared at Gabe. Mueller's arm wrapped around the little boy's neck.

"It's me you want, not the boy."

Mueller flashed his odd, twisted smile. "That's right.
But one has to expect a certain amount of collateral
damage."

Gabe didn't recognize the revolver Mueller pressed
against the boy's head, the guard's mostly likely.
Smaller, easier to handle than his Glock semiautomatic.

"Doesn't have to be that way. Just let him go."

"Actually, I've decided on another change of plans."

For the first time, Gabe noticed the door behind Mueller. The man had planned an escape route. It wasn't surprising. Mueller had been prepared from the start.

Gabe flicked a glance toward the window, saw faint movement outside. Not wanting to give away his brother's position, he kept his eyes fixed on Mueller's face—thin, dark eyebrows, a blade of a nose and those odd, twisted lips.

"You're an amazingly flexible guy," Gabe said.

"That's right. And I've decided to take young Billy with me." Mueller turned the knob behind him, cracked open the door. "His mother's a whore. Stays out till all hours of the night. She ignores Billy most of the time."

Gabe figured his brother was ready to take the shot, but with Mueller's pistol against the little boy's head, the timing had to be perfect.

"The woman is nothing like your mother, right Jacob? Not like Vera."

His lips thinned. "I told you, Billy's mother is a whore. My mother was a saint." He shifted, his anger building. "And you killed her."

"I didn't kill her. I had nothing to do with her death. People get old, Jacob. Sooner or later, they die."

"You're a liar! You killed her with your greed and now I'm going to kill you!" Turning the pistol away from the boy, Mueller swung it toward Gabe.

Everything happened at once. Gabe dove for cover beneath the table at the same instant Mueller and Dev both fired. Glass shattered as Gabe rolled to his feet on the opposite side of the table, Dev's revolver in hand, a hot sensation burning across his ribs.

Dev's bullet creased Mueller's skull, spinning him around, but the kill-shot missed deadly penetration by a millimeter, leaving Mueller alive but off balance. He lost his hold on the boy as he toppled to the floor and something clicked as he landed. Gabe recognized the sound of a pressure plate being activated, a bomb about to explode.

"No!" Mueller cried out, his black eyes wide with terror. "No!"

Gabe charged toward the boy, grabbed him and slammed through the back door. He dove for the ground, shielding the child with his body as the I.E.D. exploded and the bedroom turned into a ball of flame.

MATTIE SCREAMED AS the explosion at the back of the duplex shook the ground. A ball of flame climbed above the roof of the apartment building, orange and red tendrils spiraling into the black night sky. Jumping out of Captain Daily's Suburban, she started to run. A uniformed police officer caught her as she raced across the front lawn toward the rear of the building.

"Sorry, ma'am. You can't go back there."

"But Gabe's in there!"

Daily reached her, turned her to face him. "You said you'd stay in the car if I let you come with me."

When the dispatcher's call had come and Daily had told her Gabe and Dev had found the arsonist, she had begged him to take her to the scene. When he refused, she told him she was going anyway—if she had to run every step of the way.

She shoved her soot-covered hair back from her face with a shaky hand. "Please…can you at least find out if he's all right?"

Daily pointed toward the small, ragged group round-ing the side of the apartment building. "Looks to me like he's on his way over to tell you himself."

Relief hit her so hard her legs wobbled. Mattie covered her mouth to hold back a sob. Gabe's face was covered with soot, his dark hair hanging over his forehead, his shirt and navy blue dress pants torn and muddy. To her, he had never looked better.

Mattie ran toward him, her heart in her throat. Gabe walked next to Dev, who was also covered with dirt and soot and holding a little blond boy propped against his shoulder.

The EMTs ran up and took the boy, carried him over to the ambulance to check him for injuries.

Mattie kept running. "Gabe!" When she reached him, she hurled herself against his chest and heard his swift intake of breath.

She backed away. "Oh, my God, are you hurt? What happened? H-how bad is it?"

"Bullet just grazed him," Dev said. "He'll be all right."

"Bullet?" Her voice went up on an edge of hysteria. "You've been shot?"

"Mueller wasn't trying to kill me," Gabe said. "He just wanted me to stay in the bedroom long enough for him to blow it up."

"Oh, my God!"

Gabe eased her back into his arms. "You were incredible tonight. I was so proud of you. I love you, Mattie."

"Oh, Gabe, I love you, too." Tears burned as her arms went around his neck. "I was so frightened. I was afraid I'd never see you again."

He grinned. "Well, I'm still here." He caught her chin and kissed her. "I love you, honey. Will you marry me?"

The tears spilled onto her cheeks. She swallowed, her throat so tight it was hard to speak. "I'd be honored to marry you, Gabe."

It was a huge risk. Marriage meant giving up her security, trusting her life to someone else, trusting Gabe not to hurt her. Marriage went against everything she had taught herself to believe, and yet there seemed no other possible answer.

"No hesitation?" he asked. "No doubts?"

She shook her head. "Not that I can think of at the moment."

Gabe laughed. "I'm crazy about you, honey. I want to spend my life with you. I want to have kids with you."

She smiled up at him through her tears. "That sounds perfect."

Gabe leaned down and kissed her.

And passed out cold at her feet.

"NOTHING TO WORRY ABOUT," Dev said as Mattie hurried to catch up with the EMTs rolling Gabe along on the stretcher. "Slight concussion. Loss of blood. He'll be fine in a day or two."

She looked over at the ex-ranger. To him this whole thing was no big deal.

"Thank God you showed up when you did," she said. "How did you know where to find him?"

"Chaz came across a former Harwood tenant named Vera Mueller. She was supposed to be dead but the funny thing was, she was still cashing her social security checks. I followed the lead, found out Vera had a stroke right after she got the notice of eviction and was put in a rest home. According to the people at Shady Lane, Mrs. Mueller died a little over three months ago. A couple of months later, the fires started."

"Her death must have been the trigger," Mattie said.

"Apparently her son was always spouting off about how his mother would still be alive if it weren't for the greedy bastards who condemned the building where the two of them lived."

"So you tracked Mueller here?"

"The rest home gave me his address."

Gabe stirred on the stretcher, reached out and took hold of Mattie's hand. "You okay?"

She nodded, teared up. "You saved that little boy."

He shrugged those powerful shoulders that seemed willing to take on the weight of the world. "I like kids."

Her lips trembled. "I know you do. We're going to have a houseful."

"That's going to take a lot of work. What do you say we get started as soon as I get home?"

Mattie brushed away the wetness on her cheeks. She tried for a playful, sexy smile but she was still worried about him and it didn't work. "Sounds perfect to me."

Dev rested a hand on Gabe's shoulder. "You'll be happy to know Billy's mom had just left their apartment. She was over at the neighbor's, borrowing a cube of butter. Apparently, she works nights as a waitress. The neighbors told the police she's a very good mom."

Gabe seemed relieved. "Glad to hear it." His beautiful blue eyes shifted to Mattie's face. "Just so you know…we missed Enrique's opening, but I'd already stopped by the gallery and picked out one of his paintings."

She squeezed his hand, leaned down and softly kissed him. "You're the most amazing man."

There wasn't time for his reply as the EMTs loaded him into the ambulance and Dev helped Mattie climb in beside him.

She had told him she would marry him. She should have been overwhelmed. Should have been scared to death.

Instead, an odd sort of calm had settled over her. They were alive. The threat was gone and they were going to build a future together.

For the first time in a long time, she felt as if her life was exactly as it should be.

EPILOGUE

One year later

THE MUSIC THUNDERED against the brick walls of Club Rio. It was Wednesday night and the place was packed. Up on stage, the long-haired singer, his belly gyrating more than his hips, seemed to think he was the king of rock and roll.

Mattie smiled. Tonight was her birthday. Gabe had done his best to make it special for her. They had been celebrating all evening, beginning with a poolside barbecue that had extended into the evening when everyone decided to finish their party at the club.

Besides her handsome husband—she loved thinking of him that way—Sam and Tracy were there, also happily married. They were moving into Sam's newly remodeled house. Mattie was planning to give them a kitten as a housewarming gift.

Aaron Kreski was with them, there with Emily Bliss. After the fire and explosion that had put Gabe in the hospital, Aaron had gone to him with a personal apology for his frightening phone calls. Gabe had restrained himself and politely accepted.

Mattie's mother and her husband, Jack Kendall, were in town for the birthday party, snuggled up at the table like a pair of lovebirds. Jack had found a job just weeks after his dealership had closed and he claimed he was working for the best employer he'd ever had.

"It wouldn't have mattered if he'd had to take a job as a dog catcher," Mattie's mother had said. "I love him no matter how little money he makes."

Which was kind of an epiphany to Mattie, who thought that perhaps she had been seeing things the wrong way ever since her father died.

"I don't think there's really such a thing as security," she'd once told Gabe. "Things happen. Earthquakes. Fires that destroy our homes and everything we've worked for all our lives. Investments fail and we lose our savings. We just have to do the best we can."

"The important thing is to live our lives to the fullest," he said, "and be as happy as we possibly can."

And they were. Incredibly so.

Just weeks after the fire, Gabe had come to her with another proposal, since she had already accepted his first.

"This is just an idea," he'd said. "I'm not pressing you or anything. Your job is important to you. I know that, but…"

"But what?"

"But I was thinking maybe we could form our own company. You could do the design work. I could do the construction. We could work for ourselves but also for our clients. We could start with the warehouse. I've still got to get caught up on my other projects, so you'd have plenty of time to do the plans. Like I said, I'm not pressing you. Just think about it, okay?"

Mattie looked up at him. "Could we build our own apartment on the second floor?"

Gabe just grinned. "You're the architect."

Mattie had thought it over for all of ten minutes before she had agreed. It had never occurred to her that she and Gabe could build a business together. That the success they achieved could belong to both of them.

She looked around the table at her very dearest friends. Sam and Tracy had eyes only for each other. Mattie believed that together they had found exactly what each of them needed to feel complete.

At the end of the table sat the evening's special guests. Gabe's brother Jackson, a slightly taller, more chiseled version of Gabe, with warm brown eyes and the lean-muscled build of a cowboy, which being a rancher, he was. A beautiful brunette—his wife, Sarah—sat beside him, Jackson's arm draped protectively over the back of her chair. Only Dev was missing, off on some new adventure.

Jackson and his family were staying in Mattie's loft apartment during their long-overdue visit, since she and Gabe lived in his condo until their new, larger apartment was completed. Little Holly Raines, Jackson's adopted daughter, was already tucked into bed, Rosa Ramirez babysitting until they got home from the club. Mattie figured the child couldn't be in better hands.

Angel had made a full recovery. He had graduated high school in June and had just started downtown at El Centro Community College. He and Enrique were still best friends. The young painter's show had been a tremendous success. The artwork Gabe had purchased, a brilliantly colored painting of the projected park, now complete, with the mural on one wall, hung in the dining room of the condo. It had already more than doubled in value.

Whenever she was needed, Mattie still volunteered at the Family Recovery Center, but her life was fuller now and she and Gabe often spent weekends in the Hill Country at his Rolling Acres ranch.

Life was ridiculously good.

And tonight, once she told Gabe her secret, it was going to be even better.

He stood up just then, grabbed her hand and hauled her to her feet. "All right, honey. Time to sing for your supper."

"What?" Mattie shook her head. "No way. I'm a married woman now. I don't need to get up on stage."

"I think you do." He turned to the others. "What do you guys think? Do we want Mattie to sing?"

They all clapped and cheered.

"Give us a song, Lena," Aaron teased.

Emily grinned. "I don't know. It's her birthday. Maybe she's getting too old to belt one out like she used to."

"Come on, Mattie," Tracy coaxed. "It'll be just like old times."

Mattie groaned.

"Tell you what," Gabe said. "I'll go first."

Her eyebrows went up. "I thought you couldn't sing."

"Can't carry a tune in a bucket. Which means once I'm finished you'll have no excuse."

Mattie laughed. "All right, you win. Let's go." They walked over to the DJ, each picked out a song and Gabe walked up on stage. He looked so sexy up there and watching the women drooling over him like a juicy piece of meat, she wasn't sure this was such a good idea.

Then the music began. A Ray Charles song was the last thing she would have expected Gabe to choose. The orchestra music swelled. His gaze fixed on her face.

"I…can't…stop…loving you… It's useless to say."

He sounded like a bloodhound howling at the moon and everyone at the table cracked up. Everyone but Mattie, whose eyes filled with tears.

Gabe kept singing and everyone kept laughing, but the beautiful lyrics were meant just for her and her throat closed up.

She knew why he wanted her to get up and sing. He knew how much she had always loved doing it and he never wanted her to feel as if she had given up anything when she had married him.

The truth was, Gabe had given her the part of herself that she had always been missing.

Gabe's song came to an end—thank God. As he came down the stairs to where she waited, she cupped her hand against his cheek, went up on her toes and kissed him. "Thank you."

Gabe kissed her back. "Your turn," he said a little gruffly. "Knock 'em dead, honey."

Mattie made her way up onstage and the music started. She had chosen the song she had sung the night Gabe had seduced her in the hall. The night her life had truly changed.

She picked up the microphone, tossed back her curly auburn hair and began to sing. She was wearing the short white skirt and turquoise midriff top she'd had on at the barbecue, but she had changed into a pair of strappy, high-heeled sandals before coming to the club. Tapping her foot to the music, she waited for the intro, then fixed her attention on the man she loved.

Swaying to the beat, she let the mood sweep her up, let herself feel the rhythm of the fast disco song.

The crowd went wild.

And from the scorching look in Gabe's blue eyes,

hot love was exactly what she would be getting when they got home.

The second chorus was nearly drowned out by wolf whistles, catcalls and cheers. She found her old confidence and began to really enjoy herself, strutting back and forth across the stage, tossing her hair and generally having fun.

When the song came to an end, applause erupted. Mattie bowed and blew a kiss, then left the stage. At the bottom of the stairs, Gabe stood waiting. Instead of leading her back to their table, he caught her hand and tugged her toward the stairway leading down to the basement. Halfway along the hall, he opened the door to one of the storage rooms, dragged her inside and closed the door.

Moonlight poured in through the high basement windows, lighting the solid line of his jaw and the indentation in his chin. When his eyes found hers, she could read his desire, his hunger. Her mouth went dry as he backed her up against the wall.

"Gabe…"

Claiming her lips in a scorching kiss, he shoved up her skirt and cupped her bottom in his big hands. Hot, wet kisses followed. Deep, burning kisses that took away her breath.

"I'd have you right here if our friends weren't up there waiting," he said as he nibbled the side of her neck.

Mattie slid her hands into his silky dark hair. "Then I think…think it's time for us to go home."

Gabe chuckled and kissed her. "Nice slow lovemaking tonight?"

Mattie laughed. "You know the answer to that."

His eyes gleamed. She liked it hot and hard.

He kissed her deeply one last time. "You know how much I love you?"

She combed back his hair. "You've made me so happy, Gabe." She went up on her toes and kissed him full on the lips. "And by the way, I love my birthday present." The pretty little sorrel filly he had given her last weekend at the ranch. "She's beautiful."

"I'm glad you like her."

Mattie's heart trembled with love for him. "I've got a present for you, too."

He eased back to look at her. "You do?"

Taking his hand, she rested it against her stomach, still flat but soon round with their child. "He's right in here. Or maybe he's a she."

Gabe's breathing halted. "Tell me this isn't a joke."

"No joke."

"You're serious? You're pregnant?"

She nodded, grinned. "In about eight months, you're going to be a daddy."

Gabe let out a shout that rang in her ears, captured her face in his hands and kissed her long and deep. "You're the best thing that's ever happened to me, honey."

"I love you, Gabriel Raines." She let him take her hand and guide her toward the door leading out into the hall. "One of these days we're going to finish what you keep starting in here."

Gabe laughed and kissed her. "That's a promise."

* * * * *

AUTHOR'S NOTE

I HOPE YOU enjoyed Mattie and Gabe in *Against the Fire,* the second book in my Raines Brothers trilogy.

Devlin's story is next. The handsomest of the Raines brothers, with Gabe's same dark hair and blue eyes, Dev is also the wildest and most determined to remain a bachelor.

Even tall, sexy Lark Delaney with her wild, cherry-cola hair and passion for life isn't going to tempt him. But Lark has come to him for help, and since she is the friend of a man who once saved his life, Dev has no choice but to agree.

Lark has promised to find her sister's little girl, a child given up for adoption when her sister was only sixteen. It seems an easy enough task to Dev. But when they discover murder is involved and the little girl is missing, the job takes on a whole new set of terrifying problems.

On top of that, Dev is beginning to fall hard for Lark, and that is the last thing he wants to do.

I hope you'll look for *Against the Law,* the last book in the trilogy.

All best wishes and happy reading.

Kat

OUTLAW LAWMAN

Delores Fossen

CHAPTER ONE

MARSHAL HARLAN MCKINNEY heard a soft clicking sound.

He waited, heard a second one and eased back the covers on his bed. In one smooth motion he snatched up his Glock from the nightstand and got to his feet.

Just as someone opened the back door of his house.

Harlan listened, hoping it was one of his foster brothers who sometimes crashed at his place. But no such luck. Since all of his brothers were federal marshals, they wouldn't have risked sneaking in at 2:00 a.m., knowing that he was armed and a light sleeper.

He heard the door being closed. Then footsteps. They were barely audible on the tiled floor of the kitchen, but the person seemed to be making a beeline for the hall that led to his bedroom and home office.

There was no time for him to pull on his jeans or boots. It was bad enough that he had an intruder, but now he'd have to bring down this person while he was wearing only boxers.

Harlan ducked behind his bedroom doorjamb and kept watch. There were no lights on in the house, but there was enough moonlight seeping through the windows that he could see the shadow that appeared on the wall.

Just a few feet away.

He didn't move. Didn't make a sound. He wanted to see if the person was armed, but he couldn't tell.

"Put your hands in the air," Harlan growled, his voice shooting through the silence.

The intruder gasped and turned as if to bolt. Harlan wasn't going to let that happen. He darn well intended to find out who was brassy or stupid enough to break into a lawman's house in the dead of night. He lunged toward the person, slamming him back against the wall.

Except it wasn't a *him*.

It didn't take long for Harlan to figure that out, because his chest landed against her breasts.

"It's me," the woman said, her breathing heavy.

Harlan instantly recognized that voice, and he reached behind him and slapped on the hall light.

Caitlyn Barnes.

It had been a few years since he'd seen her, but there was no mistaking that face.

Or that body.

Harlan had firsthand knowledge of her breasts— bare, at that—pressing against him. And while that was a pretty good memory made years ago, there weren't too many recent good memories when it came to the woman herself.

He stepped back, met her wide blue eyes. He caught just a glimpse of panic in them before she lifted her chin defiantly. He knew she was trying to look a whole lot more confident than she was. That's because he was six-three, a good eight inches taller than she was, and he outsized her by at least eighty pounds. He was a big guy, and no one had ever accused him of looking too friendly.

Plus, there was the part about him having a Glock aimed at her pretty little head.

"Most visitors just knock, even the uninvited ones," he snarled, easing the Glock back to his side. However, Harlan didn't ease up on the glare.

She made a sarcastic sound of agreement, huffed and put her left palm on his chest to push him back. "I didn't think you'd be here."

Well, that wasn't much of an explanation for breaking and entering or for driving all the way out to his family's ranch. The place wasn't exactly on the beaten path and was a good fifteen miles from the town of Maverick Springs, where he worked. Much too far out of the way for a friendly spur-of-the-moment visit, and Harlan let her know that with the hard look he gave her.

Caitlyn stared back, and then her gaze drifted lower. To his chest. Then lower. To his boxers. Since it wasn't anything she hadn't seen before, and because he was still waiting on that explanation, Harlan didn't budge.

But he felt that old kick of desire.

Hard not to feel it, since they'd been lovers. Well, onetime lovers anyway when they were teenagers. But once was enough. Stuff like that created bonds that weren't worth a thimbleful of spit.

Unless...

The heat was still there. Much to Harlan's disgust, it was. Probably because Caitlyn and he had spent way too much of their teens driving each other hot and crazy. He didn't intend to let it cloud his head.

For Pete's sake, the woman had broken into his home.

Just as he would have done to any other criminal caught in the act, he took her by the arm, turned her and put her face-first against the wall. Another gasp, and she tried to fight him off, but he grabbed the Colt she had tucked in the back waist of her jeans.

So not only had this blast from his past broken into his house, she'd come armed.

Harlan turned her back around and dangled her gun in front of her. "Last I heard you were a reporter," he said.

"Still am." She managed to hold her glare a moment longer before she lost the staring match and glanced away. "I came because I needed answers."

Again, no explanation for the gun or her presence, but Harlan made a circling motion with the Colt so she'd continue.

Her blue eyes snapped back to his. "Do you want me dead?"

Now, that wasn't a question he'd expected. "No," Harlan answered, and he stretched out the word a bit. "Is there a reason I'd want you dead?"

"You might think there is."

Another puzzling answer, and Harlan was getting tired of them. He wasn't a patient man, even on good days, and this didn't qualify as good in any way, fashion or form.

"A Texas Ranger came to visit me," Caitlyn said.

His heart slammed against his chest, and things became a lot clearer. "About Kirby?"

But it wasn't really a question. The Rangers were indeed investigating the sixteen-year-old murder of Jonah Webb, the SOB headmaster of the pigsty of an orphanage where Harlan and his five foster brothers had been raised.

Caitlyn, too.

Several months ago the Rangers had identified the

headmaster's killer, Webb's own wife. Webb had been physically abusive, and she'd killed him during one of his beatings. But there'd been an accomplice. Neither Harlan nor any of his foster brothers had been ruled out as suspects, but the Rangers no doubt had their foster father, Kirby Granger, at the top of their list. Kirby had motive, too.

Six of them.

Because that was how many kids he'd saved from the orphanage—Harlan and the five other boys who'd become his brothers. But Kirby hadn't saved them until after Webb had been murdered.

"What'd you say to this Ranger?" Harlan asked. And it better not have been anything incriminating.

"I told him there was nothing to tell." Caitlyn paused, pushed her choppy blond hair from her face. "But he didn't believe me. He thought I was covering for one of you—even though I told him I haven't seen you or any of your foster family since we left the Rocky Creek facility after it was shut down."

That part was true. Caitlyn had been sent to another children's home, and Harlan and his foster brothers had left with Kirby. Harlan had written her, for a while anyway, and then they'd lost touch.

Until now.

Of course, he wasn't ignorant of what had happened to her. Nope. Caitlyn had become a high-profile investigative journalist. Heck, he'd even seen her on TV a couple of times while reporting stories. But then she'd practically disappeared. Why, he didn't know, and he hadn't given it much thought. Until now.

"I don't want you dead," Harlan clarified. "But I also don't want you saying anything that might get Kirby arrested. He's sick. Going through cancer treatments. And I won't have you or anyone else making his life harder than it already is. Got that?"

She nodded. "And that's why I thought you might want me out of the picture, to make sure I wouldn't implicate Kirby in Webb's murder."

Harlan didn't roll his eyes, but it was close. He tapped the top of his boxers. "Normally I wear a badge there, and I took an oath to uphold the law—"

"An oath you'd break in a heartbeat to protect Kirby," Caitlyn interrupted.

Harlan shook his head. "I can't argue with that. But murder? Really?"

"There's no love lost between us," she reminded him.

Yeah, thanks to her renegade brand of journalism that had trashed the marshals and others in law enforcement. Heck, a couple of times she'd revealed names on investigations that had come under fire, including Harlan himself. So she was right—no love lost. Still, something about this didn't make sense.

"If you thought I was out to kill you, then why come to my house?" he demanded.

"As I said, because I didn't think you'd be here." She cursed under her breath. "I wanted to search the place, to see if there was any evidence."

"Sheez. Evidence of what?"

"That you hired someone to come after me."

Harlan tried to hold on to his temper, but this was a very frustrating and confusing conversation. "Start from the beginning," he insisted.

Her gaze dropped to his boxers again. "Get dressed. Your file is in my car."

He didn't budge. "My *file?*"

"Yes, with a sworn statement from a criminal informant that you paid him to scare me, 'or worse.'"

Now it was Harlan's turn to curse, and he didn't keep it under his breath. "I've hired no one. And I want to see this file."

Another glance at his boxers. "Then I suggest you put on your jeans, because I'm parked at the end of the road."

Of course. A good quarter of a mile away. Harlan didn't mind the walk, but his mood was getting more ornery with each passing second.

Why the heck would Caitlyn think of him as a killer?

Harlan turned to go into his bedroom but decided he wasn't going to take any chances where she was concerned. He latched on to her wrist, pulled her into the bedroom with him and shut the door.

"How'd you know I lived here?" He put both her gun and his on the dresser while he pulled on his jeans.

"Research." She glanced around. Not much to see, though. A bed, dresser and nightstand. The entire house was the same—a no-frills man cave, exactly the way Harlan liked it.

"The place used to belong to Kirby's father," she remarked, probably to let him know that she had indeed done her research. "And the main ranch house where Kirby and the others live is about a mile that way." Caitlyn tipped her head in the opposite direction from where she'd said her car was parked.

"My brother Dallas doesn't live there," he disagreed, just to show her that her research sucked. And it did. Because there was no way she had any real proof that he'd hired someone to kill her.

She nodded and didn't look away when he zipped his

jeans. "Because Dallas married Joelle, and they built a house on the property."

Joelle, a woman who'd once been Caitlyn's friend at Rocky Creek Children's Facility. He doubted his sister-in-law knew anything about this little visit, but he would ask her first chance he got.

Harlan put on his boots and a shirt and stuffed her Colt into the back waist of his jeans. "Why'd you think I wouldn't be here?" he asked, heading for the door.

"The P.I. that I hired said you were transporting a prisoner to Dallas."

He had been, but had finished early. The transport of a prisoner wasn't usually classified info, unless it was a high-risk, high-profile case. In this case, it wasn't. Still, it wouldn't have been common knowledge, and along with all the other things he wanted to know, Harlan would need to address that.

"What's the name of this P.I.?" He opened the front door and held it for her so that she'd be in front of him.

"I'd rather not say."

"I'd rather you did say," Harlan insisted. "In fact, I've got grounds to arrest you for breaking and entering. Don't add failure to cooperate to those charges."

Caitlyn whirled around and would have tumbled down the flagstone steps if Harlan hadn't caught her. "You're not going to arrest me."

"Who says? Give me the name of that P.I."

"Mazy Hinton." Her teeth were clenched so tightly that he was surprised she was able to speak. She tore herself from his grip and stomped through the yard toward the road.

Harlan didn't recognize the name, but within an hour or two, he'd know everything there was to know about this P.I., who was either incompetent, stupid or an out-and-out liar. None of those possibilities sat well with him.

He glanced up the road, spotted her car right where she said it would be, and he cursed both it and the August heat. There was a breeze, but it was muggy and still hot despite the late hour.

"What exactly did you think you'd find in my house?" he pressed.

She shook her head. "I wasn't sure. An email, maybe. Or a paper trail to prove you hired someone. I wanted something in your own handwriting or from your personal computer."

Something she wouldn't find, because he hadn't done anything to set this crazy visit into motion. "I guess it didn't occur to you that if I was really a rogue marshal you should go to the cops?"

"Wasn't sure I could trust them." Ahead of him her steps slowed, and she wiped her forehead with the back of her hand. "I wasn't sure I could trust anyone. Like I said, someone's trying to scare me…or something."

"Considering your job, is that much of a surprise? You've riled a boatload of people, including me."

She turned, and in the moonlight he got a glimpse of her expression. Not the fake bravery she'd tried to sport in the hall. Not the emotions from their past. But something else. Something Harlan couldn't quite put his finger on.

"Some people do hate me," she said, as if choosing her words carefully. "But this isn't about that. The threatening notes had, well, personal details in them."

"Personal?" Harlan caught up with her, and even

though they were still yards from her car, he stopped her. He whirled her back around to face him.

Not the brightest idea he'd ever had.

That whirl put them too darn close, and the breeze hit just right so that her scent washed over him. Through him, actually. Yeah, not a bright idea.

"Personal," Caitlyn verified. She took a deep breath. "The notes were typed, and they warned if I said anything about the investigation into Jonah Webb's murder, I'd be sorry. Your name was on them."

It didn't take Harlan long to figure out what this might be. "So? Anyone could have typed them."

"No. Not anyone." She didn't say anything for several moments. "Remember when we were together that night at Rocky Creek?"

Even though they'd had a lot of nights at that hellhole, Harlan figured he knew which one she meant.

"Jonah Webb went missing that night," she continued. "And we heard they were closing the place, that we'd all be split up and sent to other facilities. Well, except for Kirby Granger's *boys*. Kirby was getting all of you and some of the others out of there."

"He couldn't get you out," Harlan reminded her. "He couldn't locate your next of kin to get permission to request guardianship of you."

She gave that a dismissive nod and started walking again. "And that night we met down in the laundry room."

Their usual meeting place, where they'd talked, and kissed, for hours. They'd been barely sixteen then, but the making out had started a month earlier. It had escalated that night, and they'd had sex.

With a surprise ending.

Caitlyn had had one of the worst reputations at Rocky Creek, but Harlan had found out unexpectedly that she'd been a virgin.

"Remember what you said to me?" Caitlyn asked. *"Afterward,"* she clarified.

Yeah, he did. After sixteen years, he still did.

It had been Caitlyn's first time. Not his, though. He'd gotten lucky a few other times with girls who'd found him attractive. Sometimes he regretted that and had regretted even more that Caitlyn had given him something special—her virginity.

You'll always be my first, Caitlyn, he'd said to her. And in his crazy sixteen-year-old mind, that meant something, even though he'd omitted the critical word— *love.*

That was probably for the best, considering how things had turned out between them.

Caitlyn got to the car and threw open the passenger door. "Did you ever tell anyone else what you said to me that night?"

Harlan didn't have to think about that answer. "No. It's not the sort of thing a teenage boy chats about with his friends."

Caitlyn made a sound of agreement, fished her keys from the front pocket of her jeans and unlocked the glove compartment. She pulled out a manila folder and used her phone as a flashlight on the pages.

Harlan thumbed through the pages and saw that the first three were all typewritten and were just a few lines long.

Each had his name typed at the bottom.

But it was the threats that caught his attention.

Talk to the Rangers about Kirby and you'll be sorry,
the first one read.

The second escalated. *Talk to the Rangers, and you'll
die.*

He flipped the page, and he felt the knot tighten in
his stomach.

Don't make me kill you had been typed in bold letters. And beneath it, *You'll always be my first, Caitlyn.*

"Hell." And that was all Harlan could manage to
say for several seconds. "Believe me, I didn't send you
these. If I'd wanted to warn you to keep quiet, I would
have said it to your face."

She studied him, as if trying to decide if he was telling the truth, and then huffed. "There's more. Look at
the next page."

He looked at the next page, but saw only a list of
names and contact information.

"I'm sure you recognize them," Caitlyn said.

Harlan did. There were three names, including Caitlyn's. The two others were girls who'd lived in her dorm
at the Rocky Creek Children's Facility.

Sherry Summers and Tiffany Brock.

"The three of us lived in the room nearest Jonah
Webb's family quarters," Caitlyn supplied. "We were
all questioned at length when Webb disappeared."

Harlan shook his head. "You think one of them sent
you the threatening notes?"

"No. Tiffany's dead, killed in a car accident about
two weeks ago near San Antonio." Caitlyn drew in a
breath, blew it out slowly. "Her fiancé said before she
died, she was getting threatening letters, warning her
to stay quiet about the Webb investigation. Maybe the

threats came from you. Maybe from one of your foster brothers or Kirby."

"Not a chance," Harlan jumped to answer. "Did those have my typed name on them, too?"

"No," she repeated. "And until I talked to her fiancé, he had no idea who might have sent them."

"How kind of you to fill in the blanks for him. I just wish you'd filled them in with a little truth and not some stupid speculation." He glanced at the other names. "What about Sherry?"

Another deep breath. "She's missing—for nearly three weeks now. I'm the only one left on the list, and earlier tonight I found this on my car windshield." Caitlyn turned to the next page.

It was two typewritten lines. Just a handful of words, but they caused Harlan's heart to slam against his chest.

Hell, what was going on?

Time's up, Caitlyn. Tomorrow you die.

CHAPTER TWO

TIME'S UP, CAITLYN. Tomorrow you die.

Caitlyn had read the latest threat so many times that she didn't need to look at it again. It was branded into her memory now, but Harlan kept his attention fixed on it for several long moments.

"I got that before midnight, which means tomorrow is already here," she added, though he no doubt had figured that out. Now what Caitlyn had to figure out was if Harlan had anything to do with it.

Judging from his reaction, the answer was no. But there was still the likelihood that someone very close to him was responsible.

He cursed and scanned the area as an experienced marshal would do to make sure they were safe. A moment later Harlan held up the note for her.

"You didn't report this to the local cops?" he demanded.

Caitlyn huffed. "If I couldn't trust you, how could I trust them?"

He cursed again. "Hell's bells, Caitlyn. According to you, a woman's dead. Another's missing, and the whack job behind all of this has clearly got you in his crosshairs." Harlan added a few more words of profanity. "How the devil could you think I'd do this to you?"

"Partly because of our last phone conversation." She

gave him a moment to recall the call in question, but judging from his instant smirk he remembered it readily.

"You'd trashed the Marshals Service and me in one of your so-called pieces of journalism," he said. "And I told you what you could do with your *story*."

Exactly.

Caitlyn had only reported the facts of the case in question, but they had clashed with Harlan's version of events. Yet a dangerous criminal managed to escape while in custody of federal marshals, and that was what had happened.

Too bad it'd been on Harlan's watch.

She'd felt duty bound to report it and equally duty bound to do a follow-up piece when Harlan had been cleared of any wrongdoing. However, the follow-up hadn't soothed Harlan much.

"That phone conversation wasn't a threat," he insisted. "I was riled because you didn't wait for the whole truth before you got on TV and blabbed about it."

"It wasn't just that conversation." Caitlyn tapped the pages to remind him of something else, and in doing so her hand brushed against his. The jolt was instant.

She silently cursed it.

How could she possibly still be attracted to Harlan?

She wasn't a starry-eyed teenager anymore. She was thirty-two. Yet her hormones were zinging with just a simple touch. She blamed that on his hot cowboy looks. That black hair. Those gray eyes. Oh, and those jeans. No one should look that good in such basic clothing.

Well, it ended now. She couldn't be one of those women attracted to dangerous men.

Or potentially dangerous anyway.

Her obsession with bad boys was over, even if once she'd been proud of her own bad-girl reputation.

"It wasn't just that conversation," Caitlyn repeated after she cleared her throat. "There's the part about what you said to me that night in the laundry room at Rocky Creek. We're the only two people who knew about that." She paused. "Weren't we?"

"I thought we were." He groaned. "But obviously not. Unless you told someone."

"No." And she couldn't answer it quickly enough. "Before you ask, I didn't keep a diary. I said nothing about it in a down-memory-lane blog post. Didn't mention it in a drunken stupor either."

But yes, Caitlyn had gone through all those possibilities before she'd decided it was Harlan.

Or someone Harlan knew well.

"Maybe one of your foster brothers overheard us?" she suggested.

"And wrote the threats sixteen years later?" he finished for her, after he glared at her. "Not a chance."

"Harlan, none of you is a bloomin' Boy Scout. Kirby and all of you have reputations for bending justice now and then."

"Never justice, just the law. Something you know all about." He stared at her, practically daring her to disagree. She couldn't, especially since she'd just broken into his house.

Caitlyn did know the difference between the law and justice, but at the moment she would settle for just knowing the truth.

"How about Kirby, then?" Caitlyn tried for a slightly different angle. "Maybe he wrote the threats to keep me from talking to the Rangers?"

"No way. He's too sick. And besides, he'd rather implicate himself than me or the others."

Yes, that was exactly what she'd thought. Kirby wouldn't sell out any of them. And if Harlan had wanted to threaten her, he wouldn't have used typed notes with his name at the bottom. Still, she'd had to rule him out because of that one intimate line added to the threat.

Harlan looked at the third threat again. "The wording is exact, so it means someone overheard us. And watched us."

Caitlyn had already considered that possibility, but hearing it confirmed made her a little queasy.

Mercy.

She'd been butt naked. Harlan, too. And someone had perhaps not only watched them have sex, they'd also remembered verbatim what Harlan had said to her.

Now it was her turn to curse. "This would have been a lot easier if you'd written the notes."

He gave her a look, as if she'd sprouted a third eyeball or something.

"Easier because I'd know who was behind this," she clarified.

"Maybe, but it's obvious that someone's trying to set me up. Someone who would have been at Rocky Creek that night." Harlan looked around again. That quick, edgy sweep of the road and the pasture on both sides. "Come on. If this nut job is planning to try to kill you today, you shouldn't be out in the open like this."

That reminder unnerved her even further. She felt as if she was walking barefoot on razor blades. But she wasn't stupid, and she had taken precautions.

"That's why I brought the gun. And besides, no one followed me," she insisted.

"No one that you saw," Harlan growled. He tucked the folder under his arm, shut her car door and took her by the shoulder again.

Caitlyn wanted to argue with that. Heck, at this point she wanted to argue with anything and anybody. She was exhausted, scared, and she'd been forced to come to the last man on earth who wanted to see her.

"Let's go back to my house so I can check some things on the computer," he added, and he got her moving in that direction. "Other than the threatening notes, has anything else happened?"

"A while back. But that had nothing to do with this."

He smirked at her again. "You got more than one person threatening you?"

"Lots of people threaten me." Caitlyn returned the smirk. "I don't exactly make a lot of friends in my job."

"That's not hard to believe," Harlan mumbled. "Anyone specific?"

She lifted her shoulder. "I had a stalker named Jay Farris. He'd leave me marriage proposals stuffed into bouquets of roses. When I turned him down, the roses became bunches of dead rats and death threats."

That required a deep breath. Caitlyn still had nightmares about him. Always would.

"The rats escalated to an attempt to strangle me one night after he'd seen me on a date with another man," she explained, not easily. Nothing was easy when it came to talking about Farris. "He wanted to kill me to prove how much he loved me."

"A real charmer, huh?" But there seemed to be more anger than sarcasm in his voice. "What happened to him?"

"He was diagnosed as a paranoid schizophrenic and

placed in a mental institution. Haven't heard from him in nearly a year."

But what she left out was that Farris still had mentally haunted her all these months later. Haunted her to the point that she'd moved five times and had rarely gone into the office. She'd done most of her work from home.

"You're sure you haven't heard from Farris?" Harlan asked. "He could have sent you those notes."

Caitlyn shook her head. "No way would he have known what you said to me that night. He's seven years younger than we are, and that would have made him only nine when we were together. There weren't any kids that young in Rocky Creek."

Besides, she would have recognized an all-grown-up Farris if he'd been a fellow Rocky Creek resident. Those hard times had created bonds. Not necessarily good ones. But Caitlyn had no trouble remembering each face.

Including those of the dead and missing women.

They'd been her friends. One, Tiffany, had been her bunk mate. They'd shared every secret but one—Caitlyn hadn't told Tiff about losing her virginity to Harlan. No time for that, since both Tiff and she had been removed from Rocky Creek the following day and sent to different facilities. Caitlyn to Austin and Tiffany to San Antonio.

"Maybe Farris wasn't at Rocky Creek," Harlan said a moment later. "But he could have found out from the person who did see and hear us."

True. And despite the balmy night, that sent a chill through her.

Judas priest.

Farris had money from his family's hugely successful computer software business and could have hired someone to do his dirty work.

But why would Farris tell her not to talk to the Rangers?

He wouldn't.

Farris had no connection to what had gone on at Rocky Creek and Jonah Webb. At least, she was reasonably sure of that, but Caitlyn made a mental note to do more checking.

"How did you find out about Tiffany's car accident and that Sherry was missing?" Harlan did another of those glances around, and it made her consider running to his house. Thankfully, it wasn't far away, and she could see the light he'd left on in the hall.

"Tiff's fiancé called to let me know about her death. He asked me to get in touch with anyone from Rocky Creek who might want to know. I haven't stayed in touch with anyone, but I tried to track down Sherry. She runs an investment firm in Houston, and her business partner, Curtis Newell, said she left without giving him any notice."

"Maybe Sherry doesn't want to be found." Harlan shrugged. "Could be she just needs some downtime."

Caitlyn had already considered that and more. "None of her friends knows where she is. *None*. That's suspicious to me, and there doesn't appear to be any crisis going on in her life that would make her disappear. Also, she didn't actually tell anyone in person that she was leaving."

Harlan made a *hmm* sound to indicate he was thinking about that. "I'll call around, see what I can find. It could turn out to be nothing." He led her through the yard and to the porch. "Still, it's suspicious, especially when you consider everything else."

Harlan opened the front door, but then stopped and turned to face her. "For the record, if anything like this happens again, don't assume I'm out to kill you. And don't break into my house—*ever*."

The last word had hardly left his mouth when Caitlyn saw alarm go through Harlan's eyes. She shook her head, not understanding, but she didn't have time to ask what had put the alarm there.

Harlan dropped the folder, letting it slip from his arm and onto the floor, and in the same motion he spun away from her. Toward the living room.

But it was too late.

Caitlyn saw the movement behind them. Someone in the shadows. And that someone pointed a gun directly at Harlan.

But it wasn't a gun.

It was a Taser.

One hit from it, and Harlan let out a choked groan. She watched in horror as he dropped to the floor.

Caitlyn heard the scream bubble up in her throat, and she turned to grab Harlan's gun.

God. This couldn't be happening. Not again. Here she was fighting for her life, and worse. Harlan was in grave danger, too.

She didn't get a chance to grab the gun. No chance to do anything. She made it only a few steps before she felt the jolt from the Taser. It crackled through her entire body.

Just like that, she had no control. No chance to scream or get away.

Nothing.

Caitlyn couldn't even turn to see her attacker's face. But she heard the voice. It was like something from a cartoon. There was no humor in it, though, only fear that spread like ice through her veins when he whispered a warning.

"Time's up, Caitlyn."

CHAPTER THREE

HARLAN WINCED AT the dull throbbing ache in his head. But when he opened his eyes, the glare of sunlight turned the ache into a jolt of pain that nearly knocked the breath right out of him.

No time to adjust to the light and pain, though. He had to fight back.

He had to save Caitlyn and himself.

That reminder gave him a much-needed spike of adrenaline, and he shot to a sitting position and reached for his gun.

It wasn't there.

He blinked, focusing, and glanced around for his Glock. No shoulder holster. No Glock. In fact, the only thing he was wearing was his boxers.

Hell.

What was going on?

He dragged in a few quick breaths, hoping to clear his head. It helped. The last thing he remembered was being in the doorway of his house and someone shooting him with one of those long-range projectile Tasers. Well, he wasn't in his house now.

But he didn't know where he was.

It was a motel room from the looks of it, and he was on the bed. Not alone, though. That gave him another jolt of adrenaline, and his body went into fight mode until he realized the person beside him was Caitlyn.

She was wearing only her bra and panties. Skimpy ones at that.

And she wasn't moving.

Harlan nearly shouted out her name, but then realized it wouldn't be a smart thing to do. That was because he noticed something else—his left wrist was handcuffed to her right. He certainly didn't remember that about the attack, but he was guessing Caitlyn hadn't been the one to do this.

That meant they were not alone.

"Caitlyn?" he whispered.

No response. He put his left hand to her throat and felt her pulse. Steady and strong. That was good. But other than being alive, there wasn't much else good about this.

He tried again to wake Caitlyn while he looked around to assess their *situation.* It was a bare-bones kind of room. Bed, dresser, two nightstands and a TV. No phone, though. The adjoining bathroom door was wide-open, and while he couldn't see anyone, that didn't mean someone wasn't in the shower. Or the closet.

The someone who'd cuffed them.

But in the main part of the room there were no signs of anyone but Caitlyn and him. Heck, he didn't even see their clothes. Whatever had happened, they were clearly being held captive, and that meant they needed to get out of there. Or at least find some way to defend themselves.

Harlan gave Caitlyn's arm a hard shake, and this time he got a response. A groggy moan.

"Wake up," Harlan insisted. "We have to leave now."

Easier said than done. Because of the cuffs and the tornado going on in his head, he couldn't just bolt from the bed, but he hauled Caitlyn to a sitting position, anchoring her in place so she wouldn't topple back over. Her eyes finally eased open, and as he'd done, she looked around.

"Where are we?" she mumbled at the same moment that Harlan asked, "Any idea how we got here?"

Caitlyn groaned when she looked first at what she was wearing. Or rather what she wasn't wearing—clothes. And then at the cuffs.

"What happened after I got hit with the Taser?" he asked. Harlan got to his feet, looped his arm around her waist and helped her stand.

"I don't know." She tried to put her hand against her forehead. Probably because like him, she was in pain. But the handcuffs sent Harlan's arm brushing across her breasts.

"Sorry," she mumbled. Caitlyn blew out another breath. "I saw you get hit with the Taser, and I tried to get your gun. My gun," she corrected. "You'd put it in the back waist of your jeans."

Yeah. He remembered that part. The part about falling flat on the hardwood floor, too—emphasis on the *hard*. But that was where his memories stopped. Obviously Caitlyn had been attacked second, and that meant she might recall more than he did.

"You remember anything after he got you with the Taser?" he asked.

"No." She glanced around the room again. "I certainly don't remember being brought here. Or having my clothes taken off. Did you do that?"

He shook his head and was reasonably sure he would

have remembered undressing Caitlyn. Or someone else undressing her in front of him. And that could mean only one thing.

"After the Taser hit, someone must have drugged us," Harlan explained. It was the only thing that made sense, and yet it didn't make sense at all.

"God," Caitlyn mumbled. She jerked her uncuffed hand to her mouth and pressed her fingers there for several seconds.

Harlan didn't like that *God* one bit. "What do you remember?"

She looked at him, blinked, and along with the grogginess, he could see fear in her eyes. "The person was using one of those voice scramblers, and he said something to me." She gulped in some air. "'Time's up, Caitlyn.'"

Tears watered her eyes, and he saw the muscles in her body tense. She was terrified. With reason.

"It's okay," Harlan tried to assure her. But it was a lie. Everything was far from *okay,* and it wouldn't get even marginally better until they were in a safe place. "You're still alive, so he obviously didn't carry through on his threat."

But why not?

It was a sickening thought, but their attacker had had plenty of time and opportunity to kill them both.

With his arm still looped around her, Harlan grabbed the lamp from the nightstand, the only semi-weapon in the room, and went to the window. He stayed to the side, keeping Caitlyn behind him, and eased back the curtain.

Yeah, they were definitely in a motel, and not a high-end one either. The window and front door faced a parking lot where there were several vehicles. However, he didn't see his truck or Caitlyn's car.

"Ever heard of the Starlight Inn?" he asked, noting the large sign at the end of the parking lot.

"No." She pressed her body against him when she peered over his shoulder. "It doesn't look familiar."

Not to him either, and they sure weren't in Maverick Springs. Harlan had lived there for sixteen years since he'd left Rocky Creek, and he knew every nook and cranny of the town.

So where were they, and who'd brought them here?

"I need to check the bathroom." With Caitlyn in tow, he started in that direction. Where their captor could be hiding.

Of course, there was no reason for the person to hide, since he was calling the shots here. But Harlan hoped he was there so he could bash the moron to bits for doing whatever the hell he'd done to them.

That gave Harlan a moment's pause.

What exactly had he done to them?

He glanced at Caitlyn again, specifically at her body, running his gaze from her face to her breasts to her belly, where he spotted a tiny black ink tattoo with letters.

And then below.

There didn't appear to be anything obvious, like love bites or bruises, but they were wearing just underwear and had woken up in a bed.

"Did we…?" she asked, clearly picking up on the reason he was gawking at her body.

"No." And that, too, could be a whopper of a lie, especially if someone had given them a drug that had caused memory loss. But Harlan wasn't going to worry about that now, particularly since they had more immediate problems.

With the lamp ready as a club, he went in ahead of Caitlyn. The shower curtain was closed. Of course. No chance that any of this would be easy. Harlan readied himself and used his foot to shove back the vinyl curtain. It slithered open, the metal rings jangling on the overhead bar and sounding far more sinister than it would have under normal circumstances.

Empty.

Well, it was empty except for their clothes and shoes, which had been neatly folded and placed in the tub.

Harlan tossed the lamp aside and rifled through the garments, looking for either his or Caitlyn's gun. They weren't there. Neither were their phones or a key for the cuffs.

"What's going on?" Caitlyn asked. She grabbed her jeans and started to put them on. Not easily because of the blasted handcuffs.

Harlan put on his jeans, too. Best not to go after their captor while he was practically butt naked. "I'm not sure. But judging from what this dirt-for-brains said to you about time being up, it's all part of the threats. That could mean we're back to someone who doesn't want you talking to the Rangers or your stalker, Farris. He could have hired someone to do this, or maybe he's out of the institution."

That sort of stuff happened all the time. Inmates were released and no one bothered to tell the victims.

"No," she said while she put on her shoes. "If Farris were out, he would have just killed me. He wouldn't have drugged us and brought us here."

She was obviously basing that conclusion on his previous attack, when he'd tried to strangle her. Something that turned Harlan's stomach. But Farris could have taken a new direction in his criminal activity, so Harlan wasn't going to rule him out. No. Just the opposite.

Farris—or the person he'd hired—was at the top of his list.

Harlan tugged on his boots and looped his shirt over his arm, since there was no way he could put it on. Caitlyn, however, ripped the right side and sleeve of her top so she could cover herself. Probably for the best. Her bra and what was beneath it were just plain distracting.

Too many memories.

Harlan headed back to the front door, but he took a moment to rifle through the nightstand drawer to find something—anything—he could use to pick the lock on the handcuffs. But there wasn't a stray paper clip. That meant going outside without being able to give Farris, or whoever had done this, a full fight.

There was a local telephone directory in the bottom drawer. Not thick or big enough. While it wouldn't stop a bullet, he grabbed it and rolled it so that it formed a nightstick of sorts. Hardly his weapon of choice when they didn't know what they were up against, but maybe he could avoid a showdown until he was in a better position to kick somebody's butt for doing this to Caitlyn and him.

"Stay behind me," Harlan warned Caitlyn, and he eased open the door and looked outside.

It was early morning, maybe seven or so, and there was no one in the parking lot, but a car did go by on the street in front of the motel. It didn't stop, and Harlan didn't call out to the driver.

That was because he had a bad feeling they were being watched.

After all, why would someone go to all the trouble of using a Taser on them, drugging them and bringing them to this place only to let them easily escape?

Harlan kept close to the building and headed for the office sign at the front. Right by the road. Once inside he could call his brothers, who were no doubt wondering where the heck he was. It was a workday, and he should have already been at the marshals' office in Maverick Springs.

He and Caitlyn were still a good twenty yards from the office when a dark blue truck turned into the parking lot. But it didn't just turn. The tires squealed as the driver whipped into the lot, and Harlan automatically pulled Caitlyn to the ground in front of one of the parked cars, an older-model red four-door sedan.

The truck slowed once it was in the lot, and the driver inched around, pausing in front of each door. Maybe checking the numbers? Maybe looking for any sign of them.

Or witnesses.

That was a strong possibility, since there appeared to be other guests staying at the motel. The driver finally came to a stop in the parking spot directly in front of the room they'd just escaped from.

Harlan stayed low, pulling Caitlyn as far behind him as he could manage. He watched. And held his breath. He didn't want to fight like this. Not where Caitlyn could be in the line of fire and also in his way. He wouldn't be able to fight while handcuffed to her.

It didn't take long, just a few seconds, before the truck door flew open and the driver stepped out. A man wearing dark clothes. He kept his back to Harlan, so he couldn't see his face, and he didn't recognize the man's gait. However, he thought he might recognize the gun he held next to his right leg. It looked exactly like Harlan's standard-issue Glock.

Harlan tried to take in as many details of the man as he could, including the number of his license plate and the way he practically kicked down the door of the motel room. Whoever this guy was, he was riled to the core, and that meant there'd be no showdown between Harlan and him. Not at this moment anyway, but once he had Caitlyn someplace safe, he was coming after this dirt wipe.

"You know that guy?" Harlan asked her.

"Hard to tell." Her breath was racing, hitting against his bare shoulder and back, and every muscle in her arm was iron hard. "But it could be Farris. We need to find out if he's out of the institution."

He would. And maybe Caitlyn would be able to confirm if it was or wasn't Farris when she got a look at his face. The trick was to let Caitlyn get that look without the guy seeing her. Harlan didn't want the man using that Glock on them.

From inside the room, Harlan heard a loud crash, as if someone had bashed something against the wall. Harlan waited with his breath held, and within seconds the man burst out of the room.

Caitlyn groaned softly, and Harlan knew why.

They couldn't see his face to determine if it was her stalker because the guy was wearing a ski mask. He jumped back into the truck and sped away. He was already a few yards past the vehicle where they were hiding when the driver of the truck slammed on his brakes.

"What's he doing?" Caitlyn asked, her voice a hoarse whisper.

Harlan didn't answer. Didn't want to make a sound, but he eased himself lower to the ground so he could watch from beneath the car.

His heart slammed against his ribs when he heard the truck door open again. And Harlan saw black combat boots when the guy stepped out. The man didn't move for what seemed to be an eternity, and it gave Harlan too much time to think of all the things that could go wrong.

"Get back in the truck," Harlan said to himself, hoping the guy would do just that.

But he didn't.

He took a step. Then another.

Oh, hell.

The armed man was walking straight toward them.

CHAPTER FOUR

IT TOOK EVERY bit of Caitlyn's self-control—and Harlan's bruising grip on her arm—to stay in her place. Her instincts were screaming for her to bolt. To get far away from the ski-masked man who was just a few yards away and closing in fast. But running would only get her shot.

Harlan, too.

Because she hadn't missed that the man coming toward them was also armed. And angry. Everything about his body language told her he was working on a short fuse and a hot temper, and it was too much to hope that all that fury was aimed at someone other than Harlan and her.

But why?

Soon she wanted to know the answer to that, but unfortunately they might be killed before they learned why this man was after them.

Even though she tried not to make a sound, that was just about impossible with her heart and breath galloping out of control. Unlike Harlan. He was focused only on the man's movement, and he didn't show any sign of the fear Caitlyn was feeling.

She glanced around them, looking for anything she could use as a weapon. The only things within reach were a couple of small rocks, so Caitlyn scooped them up and waited. God, she wished they had a phone so she could at least call the cops.

The man stopped, and Caitlyn pulled in her breath. Held it. Waiting and praying that he would just turn around, go back to his truck and drive away.

That didn't happen.

Because her attention was nailed to him, she saw the shift of his weight to the front of his feet, and he slowly bent his knees. Lowering himself. Stooping down. And there was only one reason for him to do that.

So he could look beneath the cars.

Caitlyn tried to hold out hope that he wouldn't see them. Or that someone would see him and send him running. After all, a man in a ski mask was bound to look suspicious.

Harlan turned his head slightly to the side. "Get ready to move," he mouthed.

That caused panic to shoot through her again. Move where? There were only two places for them to go—right or left—and either way the man would see them.

Even though she'd braced herself for the man to fire, it was still a hard jolt when the blast came. In the same second, Harlan used their handcuffed connection to jerk her to the side. Away from the bullet that slammed into the ground.

The sound was deafening, and it seemed to echo through the parking lot. No way the guests would miss that, and it would certainly prompt someone to call the cops.

She hoped.

Still, it wouldn't help them now.

The sound she didn't hear was a car alarm. Caitlyn had hoped there'd be one and that the blaring noise would send the man running back to his truck. It didn't. No alarm, just the man coming for them.

Harlan didn't stay put. He shoved her behind him as far as he could. Which wasn't far. And he dragged them to the side of the vehicle.

Even over the roar in her ears, Caitlyn had no trouble hearing the man's footsteps. Definitely not light. More like stomps. Of course, she already knew he was in a rage, so it was no surprise that he was coming at them like a madman.

But why was he trying to kill them now when he'd had plenty of time to do it while they'd been unconscious inside the motel room?

Caitlyn didn't have time to consider an answer because there was another shot. This one tore through the hood of the car and came so close to them that she could swear she felt the heat and movement of the bullet.

Shoving her along, Harlan hurried to the back of the car, and he dragged her behind the beat-up old station wagon next to them. She caught just a glimpse of the shooter before another bullet came their way. This one tore off a chunk of the car's bumper.

Still no car alarm.

Harlan kept them moving. Away from the shooter and toward the motel check-in. That didn't deter the man. She could still hear his stomps, but she also heard something else.

Shouts.

Someone was yelling out to call 9-1-1, but the shots kept away anyone who might otherwise want to help. She prayed no one inside the rooms would get hurt.

Harlan pulled her to the far side of the station wagon. Still three vehicles away from the motel office. Way too far to make a run for it, and besides, if the clerk was smart, he would have already locked the door.

"Hell," she heard Harlan mumble.

And she soon realized why. The shooter wasn't just stomping now. He'd broken into a run.

Heading right for them.

Harlan levered himself up and hurled the rolled-up phone book at the guy. From the sound it made, it smacked him somewhere on the body, but she didn't see exactly where. That was because Harlan got them moving again—this time to a small car that put them one step closer to the office.

Another shot.

Then another.

The bullets tore right through the small car and slammed into the truck parked next to it. The sound was instant. A shrill blast from the truck's security alarm. But the noise did something else that Caitlyn hadn't counted on.

It drowned out their attacker's footsteps.

She had no idea where he was, but that lasted only a few seconds. She soon saw his exact location.

The man barreled around the back of the small car, and before he even came to a stop, he was already taking aim. Harlan was moving, too. Trying to get them out of the line of fire.

Caitlyn scrambled as Harlan dragged her along, but she turned and tossed the handful of rocks right at the guy.

Pay dirt.

The rocks distracted him, and his shot was off. The bullet slammed into the ground, sending a spray of sharp chunks of concrete at them. Even with the debris, Harlan managed to get them to cover behind the next vehicle.

Their attacker made a feral sound. A sort of outraged growl, but he didn't speak.

He fired another shot, but this one didn't come anywhere near close to them. Good. Maybe he was no longer in control.

Over the shrill car alarm Caitlyn heard another sound. A welcome one. Sirens. And they already sounded close.

Harlan pulled her farther down to the concrete, and for a moment she thought he'd done that because he'd gotten a glimpse of the shooter, but he peered under the vehicle.

"He's getting away."

Because of the clamor of sirens and noise, Caitlyn didn't actually hear Harlan's words, but she saw them form on his mouth. The relief was instant, but it was quickly replaced by another feeling. Major concern. If the shooter managed to escape, they might never know who he was or why he'd launched this attack.

Harlan made a quick peek over the hood of the car, and he cursed. She soon figured out why. The truck zipped past them, flying across the parking lot.

That got Harlan and her to their feet, and she prayed the cops were there, in place and ready to stop this guy.

But they weren't.

The truck bolted out of the parking lot and onto the street that fronted the motel.

Still cursing, Harlan got them moving again toward the motel office. "Keep your hands up so everyone can see them," he warned her.

Mercy. Caitlyn hadn't considered that someone might

think they'd fired those shots, but in the chaos of a situation, anything could happen. They lifted their hands just as two police cruisers braked to a stop. Not in the parking lot but on the very street where the gunman had just escaped.

With their guns drawn, the cops barreled out and used their cruisers for cover. They aimed their weapons at Harlan and her.

"I'm Marshal Harlan McKinney," he shouted over the alarm. "You need to go after the driver of a blue truck." And he rattled off the license plate.

The cops didn't move, and she couldn't blame them. Harlan and she were handcuffed together, disheveled and probably didn't look like victims of a kidnapping, even if that was exactly what they were.

Now Caitlyn cursed. It would take precious minutes, maybe longer, for the cops to sort all of this out, and the shooter could be long gone by then.

The door to the motel office opened just a fraction, and a lanky man poked his head out a few inches. "The guy that drove out of here fired shots at them," he confirmed.

But that still didn't get the cops moving. The four officers said something to each other. Something she couldn't catch because of the alarms, but Harlan started lowering himself to his knees. Caitlyn did the same, and soon she found herself facedown on the concrete.

Finally the cops came out from cover and made their way toward them. Also, the alarm stopped so she could actually hear what they were saying.

"Marshal McKinney?" one of the uniforms called out.

"Yeah," Harlan verified. "There's probably a missing persons report on me."

"There is," the cop verified. He looked at his phone and then at Harlan, probably comparing a photo to his face.

She hadn't even considered that Harlan's brothers would be looking for him and would have alerted the authorities, but Caitlyn was thankful they had.

"No missing report on you," the cop said to her. "But you look familiar. Are you that reporter?"

She settled for mumbling a yes, since she and the cops were rarely in the same corner. This was one exception, though. She was thankful beyond words to have been rescued.

The cop reached down and helped them back to their feet, but Harlan didn't stay put. He immediately started toward the cruisers.

"We need to go in pursuit now," Harlan insisted, and it sounded like an order. "And get us out of these damn cuffs."

The cop didn't argue, and as they approached the other officers, she heard one of them phoning in the shooter's license plate. Maybe they'd get lucky and catch him, but Caitlyn's heart dropped when she saw they were on an access road. The ramp to the interstate was literally just yards away.

One look at Harlan, and she saw the frustration and anger in his eyes, too.

"What happened to you two?" the lanky officer asked them. His name tag identified him as Sergeant Eric Tinsley.

Harlan threw open the side door of the cruiser and jumped in, pulling her practically into his lap, since there wasn't much room in the passenger seat.

"I can't let you do this," Tinsley said.

Harlan met the cop's gaze. "This guy kidnapped us and tried to kill us. He's not getting away."

And while Harlan's tone left no room for doubt about that, they both knew the shooter was doing just that—getting away.

"When the motel clerk called 9-1-1, he gave a description of the vehicle," Tinsley said. "Law enforcement will be on the lookout for it."

"That's not enough," Harlan insisted. "I need to find this guy."

Tinsley looked around as if figuring out what to do, but then he tipped his head to the backseat of the cruiser. "Get in and buckle up so my partner can ride with us. Can't do this without backup, and you're not exactly in any position to assist."

Harlan made an even more frustrated sound of agreement and got her moving into the backseat. There was a metal mesh divider between the front and back. Clearly for prisoner transport, but she didn't care about that. Caitlyn only wanted to go after the shooter.

Thankfully, that didn't take long.

Tinsley's partner tossed Harlan a key that he took from the glove compartment, and he jumped in. "It's a universal key," he explained as they sped away from the motel.

Harlan didn't waste any time unlocking the cuffs, and Caitlyn's hand dropped like a stone. The muscles in her hand and arm were knotted. Her head was still pounding, too, but those were minor things. At the moment no one was shooting at them, and maybe they could get a lot of answers as to why this had happened, if they could just catch up with that blue truck.

A truck she didn't see.

Tinsley drove up the ramp and onto the interstate, and while there were a few other trucks on the road, the blue one was nowhere in sight.

Mercy.

They had to find him.

"Who's this shooter?" Tinsley asked.

Harlan didn't have time to answer because Tinsley's phone rang. A few moments later he hung up and shook his head. "You're sure that was the right license plate for the blue truck?"

"Positive." Harlan didn't look at the man when he answered. He was literally on the edge of the seat, checking out the traffic while he shoved his arm through the sleeve of his shirt.

"Then it's bogus," Tinsley informed them.

She didn't know who groaned louder—Harlan or her. Now there was no way to know who owned the vehicle unless they found it, and with each passing mile, her hopes were getting lower and lower in that department.

"He's not working alone," Harlan said, glancing first at her and then briefly meeting Tinsley's gaze in the rearview mirror. "Someone hit us with a Taser, drugged us and put us in that motel room."

"You saw more than one person?" Tinsley asked.

"No, but if the shooter had been the one to put us there, he wouldn't have had to look for the room."

Caitlyn thought back to those terrifying moments before the shooting. The man hadn't gone directly to the room, and he'd spent some time inside looking around. He probably wouldn't have had to do that if he'd known all along they were there.

That tightened the knot in her stomach.

God, how many were in on this?

"One man probably couldn't have carried me," Harlan muttered, as if he knew exactly what she was thinking.

Yeah. Harlan was a big guy, and that meant there had probably been at least two who'd carried them from his house and to the motel. Caitlyn didn't want to think of what else those men had done, but she was positive she hadn't been raped. That was something, at least. A *big* something.

"This has to be connected to Rocky Creek," she said to Harlan. All those threats couldn't be coincidence.

But then she had to shake her head.

Time's up, Caitlyn. Tomorrow you die. That had been the last threat she'd received, and it hadn't happened. The guy with the Taser hadn't killed her, though he would have had ample opportunity to do just that. Plus, it would have been a heck of a lot easier than drugging them and dragging them to that motel.

Almost as if they'd been bait.

Or something.

"What's the date?" she asked.

The officers seemed surprised, but Tinsley checked his watch. "The fourteenth."

"It's still *tomorrow*," Harlan verified. "And I'm pretty sure the shooter was supposed to make that threat come true."

Yes. And he nearly had. She'd lost count of how many shots he'd fired, but any one of them could have hit Harlan and her.

"He wasn't an expert shot," Harlan continued. "And it was personal."

Caitlyn couldn't argue with either of those points. "That leads us back to Farris."

She was about to ask for a phone so she could make some calls to find out if Farris was indeed still in the institution, but she stopped when she spotted the truck just ahead. Not speeding away. Not even on the interstate.

But rather at a standstill in the emergency lane.

"That's it," Harlan told the officers.

Tinsley turned on the lights and siren, called for backup and eased to a stop behind the truck. Caitlyn tried to look inside the vehicle, but Harlan didn't give her a chance. He caught the back of her neck and pushed her down on the seat.

"Stay put," Harlan insisted.

Tinsley looked back at Harlan as if he might tell him the same thing, but he didn't stop Harlan from getting out with him and his partner. Both cops drew their weapons, and they stayed behind the cover of their doors while they kept their attention fastened on the truck.

Caitlyn lifted her head just a little so she could look, too, but the back window on the truck had a heavy tint, and she couldn't see inside the truck cab.

Tinsley called out for the driver to exit the vehicle. No response, though. Ditto for his second attempt.

The seconds dragged by, and even though Caitlyn tried to keep her heartbeat and breathing steady, she failed big-time. She'd known she was in danger before she even went to Harlan's place, but she hadn't considered that she could be bringing the danger to him.

He could be killed.

Right here, if the gunman started shooting.

Even though there was bad blood between them, the last thing she wanted was him to be hurt. Or involved in this. But then she rethought that, too.

Harlan was involved.

One of the threats had even mentioned what he'd said to her that night they'd had sex. So maybe the person behind all of this had written that knowing it would make her suspect Harlan. Knowing that she would go running to him.

If so, this was all her fault.

Her breath stalled again when the cops began to inch toward the truck door, and Harlan stayed right with them despite the fact that he wasn't armed. Each step they took put her heart higher in her throat, but she could only sit there, watch and pray that this was all about to end. If they had the shooter, then they would know who was behind this.

And why.

Tinsley approached the driver's side. His partner, the other. But Harlan moved even closer to Tinsley when the officer peered into the window. He said something to Harlan. Something she couldn't hear, but Caitlyn didn't need to hear the words to see the frustration in Tinsley's body language.

It was Harlan who threw open the driver's door, and again she didn't need to hear what he said to know he was cursing a blue streak. That was the last straw.

Nothing could have held Caitlyn back at that point.

She bolted from the cruiser to see what had caused the profanity and frustration. And she soon saw.

The truck was empty.

She looked back to the interstate, hoping she'd catch a glimpse of the shooter—maybe on foot, maybe driving away in another vehicle. It was possible he was doing just that, but if so, he was nowhere in sight.

"He left something," Harlan said.

Caitlyn followed his gaze and soon saw what had captured Harlan's attention. A folded piece of paper was on the steering wheel.

"I want it processed for prints." But Harlan didn't touch it. No doubt because he didn't want to disturb any evidence that the shooter might have left, not just on the paper but in the truck itself.

"Something's written on it," Tinsley pointed out.

"Yeah." Harlan shook his head, repeated it. "It's a message," he said, looking at Caitlyn. "For you."

CHAPTER FIVE

HARLAN CURSED THE bad phone reception at the Maverick Springs Hospital, and everything else he could think of.

There was a lot on that particular list.

He could make out only half of what his brother Slade Becker was saying, but even so, Harlan wasn't hearing anything good.

His other brother Declan had brought Harlan his phone from the house because it had all his contact numbers, but what he needed was to hear some good news.

According to Slade, there was no sign of the shooter and no security cameras at the motel in Cross Creek where he and Caitlyn had been taken, cuffed and left for a killer to finish them off. If the crappy news had ended there, it might not have been so bad.

But it didn't.

Sergeant Tinsley had added to the growing heap of *bad* by telling Harlan that there didn't appear to be any prints or traces in either the truck or on the note the SOB had left with Caitlyn's name scrawled on the folded sheet of paper. A note with just a handful of words.

This isn't over. You're a dead woman.

Harlan wanted to disagree with that threat, but he couldn't. As long as the shooter and his accomplice were out there, this was far from over for Caitlyn. And as for the dead part—well, that's what he had to stop from happening.

"What about any info on Jay Farris?" Harlan asked his brother.

"Still trying. He was transferred to a private facility about a month ago—" And the rest was static gibberish, but Harlan thought Slade said something about the facility not giving them access to records without a court order. "You've got to call the Ranger back, Harlan."

Now, that part came through loud and clear.

Figures.

It was the one thing in this conversation that he didn't want relayed, because the Ranger in question was none other than Griffin Morris, who'd been assigned to investigate Jonah Webb's murder. If Harlan had thought for one second that Morris had any info about this incident, he'd be on the phone to him, but no. Morris wanted to question Harlan as a possible suspect—accessory to Webb's murder.

Harlan didn't have time for that.

The door to the examining room opened finally, and Harlan told Slade that he would call him back. Right now he needed to make sure Caitlyn was all right, and judging from the glimpse that Harlan got of her face from over the doctor's shoulder, she wasn't. She was shades too pale and looked ready to collapse.

Dr. Cheryl Landry stopped in the doorway and met Harlan's gaze. "She'll be okay. Your turn now. Want to go into the examining room next door so I can give you a checkup?"

"It can wait." Yet something else he didn't have time for—and besides, he'd already done the important part.

He'd had the lab draw a blood sample to see if they could identify what had been used to drug him.

The doctor frowned, but she didn't look surprised. Probably because she'd been stitching up Harlan and his brothers for the better part of a decade. She knew cooperation wasn't their strong suit.

"At least get some rest," the doctor grumbled. "And that goes for both of you. I'll call as soon as I have the lab results from the tox screens." She walked away, still mumbling and scribbling something on a chart.

Caitlyn didn't get up from the examining table. Practically limp, she sat there wearing green scrubs that were identical to Harlan's. One of the first things on his to-do list was to get them a change of clothes, since theirs had been bagged for processing. He doubted there'd be any usable trace evidence on them, but their luck might change.

He sure as heck hoped so anyway.

Harlan walked closer, easing the door shut behind him so he could ask her a question that he wasn't sure how to ask. He played with the words in his head, but Caitlyn beat him to it.

"I wasn't sexually assaulted," she volunteered. "No signs of recent sex, consensual or otherwise."

Harlan was relieved but not surprised. Well, not surprised except for the recent-sex part. With Caitlyn's looks, he figured she must have a current lover, but maybe Farris had destroyed that part of her life, too.

Thankfully, he'd seen no indications on her body of a violent attack, and he'd gotten an up-close-and-personal look at it, since she'd been wearing only panties and a bra in bed. Besides, if they'd had sex he would have remembered.

Even drugs wouldn't have blocked that out.

Hell, bad blood and sixteen years hadn't been able to make him forget having sex with her.

"I'm guessing there are no breaks in the investigation," she mumbled, pushing her hair away from her face.

Harlan shook his head and caught her arm when she practically stumbled off the table. "There's some red tape involved in getting more info about Farris at the private facility where he was transferred. Did you know he'd been moved?"

"No." She gave a weary sigh and looked up at him with those equally weary blue eyes. "I went in the wrong direction on this. All those threats seemed to point to you."

And he wasn't too happy that she'd jumped to believe the worst about him. But then he mentally shrugged. She'd probably thought the worst because in their last conversation they'd been at each other's throats.

He'd blasted her six ways to Sunday over that article she'd written about him.

"We can go back to my place and wait," he insisted. "You need to get some rest and something to eat. And we can make a few calls to try to speed up all the wheels that are turning right now."

He'd also have to put some time in at the office, but the adrenaline crash was getting to him, too.

"Is my car still at your house?" she asked.

"Yeah." It was one of the things he'd managed to hear Slade confirm. Her car was there, and there'd been no damage to the place. "But you're not driving anywhere. It's not safe, Caitlyn."

He braced himself for a big argument. Caitlyn was

even more pigheaded than he was, but it had to be a sign of exhaustion when she only shrugged. "I just want to catch this bastard."

Harlan was right there with her. Literally. She took a step but then stumbled again. And this time she fell into his arms. Except it was more than a fall. She was so weak, she didn't hit him with a thud. She melted against him.

Not good.

Because their arms went around each other. Their bodies met. And she looked up at him. At the same moment he looked down at her.

Everything seemed to freeze.

In fact, lots of weird things happened. The memories came. Not those of the attack—something that should have been occupying his thoughts—but other memories. Those that involved kisses.

And more than kisses.

The corner of her mouth lifted, and that half smile seemed as wobbly as the rest of her. She gave his arm a pat, grazing his chest in the process. The rest of her did a little grazing, too. But she didn't move away.

Neither did Harlan.

Oh, man. He didn't need this now. Not ever. The memories were bad enough, but now his asinine body was starting to act as if it was about to get lucky.

It wasn't.

And Harlan repeated that to himself.

"Even hate can't cool *that* down," Caitlyn mumbled. With that shocker of a remark, she brushed her mouth over his, opened the door and headed out.

Harlan was right behind her, but it took him a moment to get his tongue untangled over that blasted half kiss. Man, something that wussy shouldn't have packed such a wallop.

"I don't hate you," he clarified, choosing to deal with the easier part of that shocker. He didn't intend to touch the other with a ten-foot pole. "I hated what you did. I don't like it when people screw around with my badge and career."

"That article was my career," she countered. "If I hadn't written it, someone else would have."

That was probably true, but this wasn't a reasoning kind of thing here. Her article had painted him and the Marshals Service in a bad light, and he'd caught a boat-load of flak over it. Flak he'd aimed right back at her when he'd called her.

"I'm not a jerk," she added, "but sometimes I have to make decisions I don't want to make." Caitlyn stopped and looked out when they reached the door.

Just as Harlan did. He didn't see anyone ready to gun them down, but his brother Declan was waiting, leaning against his truck, which was parked next to one of the standard-issue cars that Harlan had used to drive them from headquarters to the hospital.

"Declan," Caitlyn said, and she hurried to him and pulled him into her arms for a hug.

Harlan wasn't jealous of his little brother, but it was a little unnerving to see Caitlyn nestled there as if it were the most natural place on earth for her to be.

Declan smiled and lifted a strand of her hair. "Last time I saw you, it was pink, and you had a nose ring."

She returned the smile. "Last time I saw you, you weren't taller than me."

Declan put his mouth to her ear, whispered something. When he was done, Caitlyn did the same and then they finally pulled away from each other.

"Best not to stand out here in the open like this," Harlan grumbled.

He frowned, first because they were out in the open with a gunman loose and then because he was—hell's bells—jealous.

Yeah, he was.

He didn't want to be, but wanting the feelings to go away didn't make it happen. He forced himself to remember that blasted article she'd written. And the fact that Caitlyn had thought he was a would-be killer.

That gave him the attitude adjustment he needed.

Harlan took her by the arm and pulled her toward the car. "Slade told me there was a problem getting info on Farris," he said to Declan.

"There was. The facility wouldn't confirm or deny they had a patient by that name. The court order was taking too long, so Dallas threatened to close them down for harboring a fugitive."

"Good." Harlan wished he'd been the one to do the threatening even if a threat like that was little more than a bluff. For Pete's sake, this was an attempted-murder investigation, and in his book that should trump privacy issues of someone who shouldn't have been granted privacy in the first place.

"Farris is out, isn't he?" Caitlyn asked.

Harlan looked at his brother and wondered how she'd come to that conclusion. He didn't see anything in Declan's expression to indicate that particular piece of bad news.

But then Declan nodded. "He only spent a few days

at the private facility before he was released to his personal shrink."

Caitlyn didn't make a sound, but she dropped onto the seat. "How did he get out?"

"Not sure yet. The court order should tell us that, but in the meantime, we have his name and his picture that we got from old articles on the internet."

Old articles probably connected to the time he'd attacked Caitlyn. Harlan was looking forward to putting this guy right back where he belonged. It took a special piece of slime to try to kill a woman.

"Every law enforcement agency in the state will be looking for Farris," Declan added.

Yeah, but according to Caitlyn, Farris was rich. That meant he had resources and could already be out of the country or at least hidden away. Well, if he didn't still want to kill them, that was. If he did, then Farris wouldn't go far. He'd continue to stalk Caitlyn.

"It might not be Farris," Declan reminded them. "That's why we need to take a harder look at all of this."

Harlan couldn't agree more. "I'll be by the office later, and I can expand the search."

"Not until tomorrow," his brother corrected. "Saul's orders. He put you on quarters for twenty-four hours and doesn't want to see you before then. Made it official and everything with some paperwork."

Great. Just great. Saul Warner, his boss, was forcing him to get some rest. Rest that Harlan needed badly. But he'd much rather be working the case, and the best place to do that was at the office.

Harlan hit the accelerator much harder than he'd planned and ended up peeling out of the parking lot.

"Is the anger for me, Farris or the fact you can't go to work today?" she asked.

Harlan didn't even try to lie. "All three."

She made a sound to indicate she wasn't surprised. "Don't worry." Caitlyn reached over and took the phone that was sticking out of his front pocket. "I'll make arrangements to stay elsewhere."

He snatched the phone back from her and headed for the ranch. "Elsewhere?"

"Yes. As in with a friend or something."

"Sheez. Are you trying to get yourself and your *friend* killed? That last threat wasn't a joke, Caitlyn. This whack job isn't backing down."

The color drained from her face again, and she swallowed hard. Okay. So he hadn't meant to yell at her, but he also had to make it clear that the danger wasn't over just because they were no longer cuffed together and half-naked in a motel room.

"We have ranch hands who can set up security," he went on. "They can keep an eye out for this guy." And he could do a better job of securing his own house. He didn't have a burglar alarm, but he could lock all the windows and doors and keep watch.

"If I stay with you, I'll put you in danger, too," she said, her voice catching.

"I'm already in danger. The threats were meant to send you to me. The guy was waiting in my house with a Taser." Not exactly a pleasant thought that someone had gotten the jump on him and that it could have cost them both their lives.

"Besides," Harlan added, "I'm a marshal, and until we work out what's going on, you're not leaving my sight."

Her left eyebrow swung up. "Really?" she said with a massive amount of skepticism. "You want to *protect* me?"

There it was again. That irritating nails-on-a-chalk-board effect, since she was questioning his intentions as a lawman.

"I *will* protect you," he insisted. Wanting to do it was an entirely different matter. "And so will my brothers."

Declan included. Not a surprise, but that encounter in the parking lot still was.

"What'd you whisper to Declan?" And why he was wasting time on this, he didn't know. Oh, wait. Yeah, he did. Caitlyn was making him crazy, and not in a good way.

"Old joke." A smile bent her mouth just a little. But she didn't share either the reason for that smile or the joke itself.

Cursing again, he was about to shove his phone back into his pocket when it buzzed, and it wasn't one of his brothers' names on the screen. However, it was some-one he recognized.

"Ranger Griffin Morris," Harlan snarled, and he let the call go to voice mail, where the Ranger would no doubt leave a message, adding to the others he'd al-ready left.

"Morris," Caitlyn repeated. "The guy investigating Webb's murder. He's interviewed you?"

"Several times." And then it occurred to Harlan that the Ranger had almost certainly interviewed Caitlyn, too.

"Yes, I've talked to him," she confirmed. "He thinks one of us helped Sarah Webb kill her husband."

Harlan waited for more, but she didn't add anything. "What'd you tell him?" he came out and asked.

"The truth." She didn't hesitate either. "That I hated Webb just like the rest of you did, but I didn't help put a knife in him."

"Morris believed you and your alibi?"

Now there was some hesitation. "I think so. Again, I told him the truth—that I was with you. Why?"

"Because he sure as hell doesn't seem to believe me. I guess he figures I was big enough to help Sarah haul a dead body down a flight of stairs."

"You were. *Are*," she corrected. Caitlyn paused, then huffed. "And I guess because of my history, I'm not exactly reliable in the eyes of the law."

Probably not. Even though her juvie records were supposed to have been sealed, the Rangers had likely discovered that Caitlyn had spent some time in reform school, and she'd been in more than a fight or two both before and during her stay at Rocky Creek Children's Facility, where Webb had been murdered.

"My bad-girl past is coming back to haunt us," she mumbled. "I'm sorry about that."

Despite the mumble, he heard the sincerity, and he didn't want her apologizing for her past. Especially when part of that past was a facade.

"You weren't a bad girl," he reminded her. "You just wanted everyone to think you were." Harlan tossed her a look, daring her to argue with that fact.

After all, she'd been a virgin when they'd had sex.

"You'll always be my first," Caitlyn said under her breath.

Normally that wouldn't have caused a chill to snake down his spine, but it did now because it was the exact wording in one of the threats. He'd given it plenty of thought, but he wasn't any closer to figuring out who had written those threats. However, Caitlyn was right about one thing—whoever it was either knew them or knew someone who'd been spying on them that night at Rocky Creek.

That was just one of the puzzling things about their situation.

"Why me, Caitlyn? Why give yourself to me?" Harlan hadn't actually meant to say that aloud, but it just popped out of his mouth. It figured. He'd been saying and doing a lot of dumb things since Caitlyn had broken into his house the night before.

She lifted her shoulder as if the answer were obvious. "I really liked you and knew you wouldn't just use me." She glanced at him. "And for the record, I know it wasn't your first time, but the *you'll always be my first* was a nice touch. Made it feel special."

She made *nice touch* seemed like a ploy or lip service. It hadn't been. He'd blurted it out much as he'd just done his question. And even though it grated on him to have her believe he'd used that as some line, this time Harlan kept his mouth shut.

Sometimes the memories should just stay buried. Especially since they had so many other things to work out.

He took the turn toward Blue Creek Ranch, and he tried to remember all the things he had to do. Calls he had to make. Security arrangements. Updates on all the moving wheels of this investigation. The list was growing by leaps and bounds, but he needed to add something important.

Find Sherry Summers.

The missing former Rocky Creek resident might have answers about what was happening to them now. Of course, Sherry might not be alive. The killer might have already gotten to her.

In addition to Sherry, Harlan also needed to go through the list of suspects who could have helped Sarah Webb kill her SOB of a husband.

The Rangers had Caitlyn and him on that list.

But there had to be someone else, someone who'd actually done the crime.

"Who's your best guess for Sarah's accomplice?" he asked Caitlyn.

"Rudy Simmons," she answered right off the bat.

Yeah, the caretaker was on Harlan's suspect list, too. But so far, there'd been no evidence pointing to the man. Plus, Webb and Rudy had actually been friends. Maybe Webb's only friend.

"Kirby," Caitlyn mumbled.

He hated to hear her mention his foster father's name in the context of a murder, but Kirby could have indeed done it, especially after the beatings that Webb had given Harlan and his foster brothers. Kirby knew about the abuse, had been working hard to try to stop it, but maybe his foster father had reached a boiling point.

"Rocky Creek was supposed to be closing," Caitlyn continued, "but there were rumors that Webb had found a way to keep it open. If Kirby thought he couldn't get any of you out…"

She didn't finish. Thank God. Because that was indeed a huge motive, one that made his stomach tighten and churn.

"I'm worried about Declan's alibi," Harlan confessed. Or rather his lack of an alibi. Declan should have been in the infirmary that night, since Webb had given him a hell of a beating earlier that day. But no one had seen Declan there, and so far his foster brother wasn't volunteering any information in that department. Of course, Harlan hadn't pushed too hard either, because if Declan did confess, then Harlan would be duty bound to do something about it.

Declan knew that, too.

"There are plenty of other suspects," Caitlyn went on.

It sounded as if she were dismissing Declan as the accomplice. Maybe because of that warm and fuzzy hug. But Harlan couldn't argue with her. Declan had been barely thirteen at the time and small to boot, and there was a long list of people who would have gladly helped Sarah squash a monster.

Including her own son, Billy Webb.

"Neither the Rangers nor any of us has had any luck finding Billy. What about you?" Harlan asked.

"None. I know he tried to commit suicide, so God knows what Webb did to him to mess up his head. I'm sure the routine beatings didn't help. Webb gave many of us enough physical and psychological scars to ruin us for life."

And Billy and Declan weren't the only ones on the receiving end of those beatings. Webb had come after most of them—including Sarah and even Caitlyn.

She made a *hmm* sound. "He had a wicked punch," Caitlyn mumbled, rubbing her jaw. "He was the first man who ever hit me, and I swore he'd be the last."

That tightness in his gut moved to his chest, and it didn't matter that all of this had gone down sixteen-plus years ago. It still stung to know what Caitlyn had gone through.

What they all had.

He hated that this attack had brought so many of those old wounds to the surface.

"I have to get some things out of my car," Caitlyn said when they passed the vehicle she'd left parked near his house.

"I'll have one of the ranch hands do it." There were plenty of trees and shrubs just across the road from her car, and he couldn't rule out that someone could hide there and take a shot at her.

He came to a stop in front of his house and was glad to see his brother Slade on his porch. Harlan was equally pleased to see the two armed ranch hands in the pasture between his place and the main house. That meant Slade had already taken some security measures.

There'd need to be more.

Seated in one of the white rocking chairs, Slade was armed with a rifle and his Glock in his waist holster. He looked like an Old West outlaw in his battered jeans, boots and black shirt.

"Harlan," Slade greeted when they got out of the car.

Then Slade's dark blue eyes landed on Caitlyn. No huggy welcome like the one Declan had given her. Slade wasn't the huggy type, and besides, like Harlan he was still pissed off about that article—which seemed close to being petty considering all the other crud that was going on now.

"Inside," Harlan instructed. And he didn't waste any time getting Caitlyn on the porch and through the already open front door. "Has the house already been processed for prints and evidence?"

Slade nodded. "Nothing so far, but it'll take the lab a while to work on everything they collected."

No doubt. Harlan was also betting they wouldn't find anything useful. He'd caught only a split-second glimpse of the man who'd used the Taser on them, but he was pretty sure the guy had been wearing gloves.

"All the ranch hands are armed," Slade continued. "And Wyatt's on his way back from the hospital with Kirby and Stella."

"The hospital?" Caitlyn and Harlan asked in unison.

"Kirby was just there for his cancer treatment, but as soon as they're back at the house, Wyatt will lock up and set the burglar alarm."

Good. Kirby was too weak to fight off a killer, and while Kirby's fiftysomething-year-old friend Stella was a decent shot, Harlan didn't want to test her marksmanship if someone managed to get onto the ranch. He considered taking Caitlyn to the main house as well, but he figured Kirby had already had enough upsets for the day.

"Stella?" Caitlyn asked. "The one who used to work at Rocky Creek?"

The very one. Harlan settled for a nod, but he saw that little flicker go through her eyes. Caitlyn had been pretty close to Stella in those days, but the bottom line was the woman was still a suspect as accessory to Webb's murder. Not in Harlan's mind. But apparently in everyone else's.

Including Caitlyn's.

"How long has Stella been here?" Caitlyn pressed.

"Not long." And this wasn't a subject he cared to discuss. Not with other things that needed to be done. "I want the road watched," Harlan told his brother, glancing back up at Caitlyn's car.

"Got two men heading out there now," Slade answered. "More will cover the back fence."

Yeah. Because that was the most vulnerable part of the ranch. The pastures had been designed to hold and feed livestock, not to ward off gunmen, and there were plenty of places where someone could climb the fence and gain access to the ranch.

"Any sign of our missing attacker?" Harlan asked, sweeping his gaze around the house and grounds.

Slade shook his head and opened his mouth, but he stopped when they saw an SUV approaching. A vehicle that Harlan recognized, thank God. It pulled to a stop in front of Harlan's house, and he spotted his brother Wyatt at the wheel. Stella was riding shotgun and a sickly-looking Kirby was slumped in the backseat.

Slade's phone rang, and he went out to the porch to take the call while Harlan went toward the SUV. So did Caitlyn, and before she even got there, Stella stepped out. The women greeted each other with open arms and squeals of delight.

"Girl, you are a sight for sore eyes," Stella declared.

"You, too. And you haven't changed a bit."

Stella touched her fingers to her graying auburn hair. "You and Wyatt could always lay on the sweet talk, but I'm a shallow woman and bent by flattery." She smiled at the joke, but the humor didn't quite make it to her weary eyes.

Caitlyn's attention landed on Kirby.

"Marshal Granger." Caitlyn's voice was clogged with emotion, probably because it looked as if the man was critically ill.

And hell, he might be.

One of Harlan's biggest fears was that Stella and Kirby were trying to keep the bad news about Kirby's prognosis to themselves.

"Caitlyn." Kirby managed a thin smile but didn't move from his position on the backseat. "Does this mean Harlan and you are back together?"

So no one had told him about the attack. Good. Harlan wasn't opposed to holding back some bad news, too, especially since it would only worry Kirby.

"Caitlyn's just visiting," Harlan settled for saying.

Kirby studied them both. Shook his head. "That's not a just-visiting kind of look on her face. Always thought you two were more suited for each other than you were willing to let on."

Harlan wasn't sure he liked this turn in the conversation, and he wanted to remind Kirby about the article Caitlyn had written, but behind them Slade cleared his throat and tapped his cell phone.

Oh, man. Not more bad news.

Harlan helped Stella back into the SUV. "You best get Kirby home."

Wyatt and Harlan exchanged a glance, and even though he'd call Wyatt to remind him about taking some extra security measures, his brother and he were no doubt on the same page.

"Was that call about Jay Farris?" Caitlyn asked Slade the second the SUV drove away.

Slade shook his head. "Don't know anything about Farris yet." He looked at Harlan. Then Caitlyn. "No. This bad news is about the two of you. The Rangers have sworn out a warrant for your arrests. They're on the way here now to take you both into custody."

CHAPTER SIX

CAITLYN STARED AT Slade and mentally repeated the bombshell he'd just dropped. It didn't get any more clear the second time it went through her head.

"Arrest us?" she asked. "Why?" And that was the real question, because none of this was making sense right now. "We were the ones who were nearly killed."

Slade's eyes were already an intense steely-blue, but that darkened them even more. "This doesn't have anything to do with the attack. At least I don't think it does. Someone anonymously sent the Rangers so-called *proof* that you two are responsible for the disappearance of Sherry Summers and the murder of Tiffany Brock."

A lot more things went through her head—including a *good God* or two. It had to be a joke that anyone would think she or Harlan had anything to do with what had happened to the two women, but Slade wasn't the joking type.

"Proof?" Harlan questioned.

Slade immediately shook his head. "The Rangers haven't shared it with the marshals, so I don't know what they have. All Ranger Morris would say was that you'd both be taken into custody. I've put out a few feelers, and maybe someone will know what's going on."

Harlan scrubbed his hand over his face. "Then I guess I'll have to see what Morris has when he arrives."

"Probably not a good idea for you to be here much longer," Slade warned. "As far as the Rangers are concerned, you've gone rogue and are on your way to being a full-fledged outlaw."

Caitlyn saw the slight flinch Harlan made, but she figured that reaction was just the tip of the iceberg. This had to cut him to the core, because if there was one thing he wasn't, it was a rogue lawman. She doubted Harlan had ever even had a parking ticket.

"And since they plan to charge you both with murder, there won't be bail," Slade continued. "They'll throw both your butts in jail."

Mercy. That didn't help Caitlyn deal with this. She tried to understand everything Slade had just told them, but it didn't make sense.

"First of all, there's no proof that Tiffany was even murdered," she said, trying to latch on to anything that would shed light on this. "I talked to her fiancé, Devin Mathis, and he said she died in a car accident."

"A suspicious one," Slade supplied.

And Caitlyn couldn't argue with that. Devin had indeed believed the accident had been staged, even though at that time the police hadn't been able to find any evidence to prove foul play. Maybe they'd found something now, but Caitlyn couldn't see how it would be linked back to Harlan and her. She hadn't seen or heard from Tiffany in years.

Then there was Sherry's disappearance. It fell into the suspicious category, too. In fact, it was Caitlyn's former roommates' circumstances that had made her believe Harlan—or someone else—could be trying to off residents of the Rocky Creek Children's Facility.

She was, of course, leaning to her *someone else* theory now.

"I also talked with Sherry's business partner, Curtis Newell," she continued. "And he doesn't think Sherry's away on some impromptu vacation. The hard drive on her computer has been wiped clean, and there's no money or clothes missing. Only her. He's thinking foul play, too. In fact, he hired a P.I. to try to find her."

Caitlyn turned to Harlan to get his take on this, but he just shook his head. "Whatever the Rangers have must be fake. We'll have to talk with them and sort it out."

Slade stepped in front of Harlan when he started to go inside. "Didn't you hear me? If you stay, they'll arrest you, and God knows how long it'll take to clear your names. It'd be a heck of a lot easier if you could figure out what's going on, and that won't happen if you're in Ranger custody."

Harlan didn't seem overly concerned with that, but Caitlyn sure was. She'd spent some time in jail before being transferred to juvenile hall and then reform school, and she didn't want to go back. Especially because someone had manufactured evidence against them.

"Can you talk to the Rangers again and try to find out what they have before they get here?" she asked Slade.

Harlan and Slade exchanged glances, and even though Slade didn't look too hopeful, he took out his phone and made a call. Harlan looked around the grounds again as if searching for bogeymen, and he nudged her inside. She had no idea how much time they had before the Rangers arrived, but they needed to make every second count.

"I need a phone," she insisted. Caitlyn glanced around but didn't see a landline or a cell. "I can try to track down Farris. He's the one who probably sent false evidence to the Rangers."

"Farris wasn't at Rocky Creek," Harlan reminded her. "And so far, everything seems to connect back to that." He paused, shook his head again. "And yet it doesn't connect at all."

"Unless Sherry or Tiffany saw something to do with Webb's murder." Caitlyn hadn't tossed that out there off-the-cuff. She'd had days to go over every single scenario, and that was one of them. "If they did, then maybe Sarah's confession brought this all back to the surface, and now her accomplice is trying to tie up loose ends."

Harlan didn't disagree. Nor did he make any move to give her a phone. "Maybe Farris is behind Tiffany's car accident and Sherry's disappearance. He could have done that as a way to draw you out."

Maybe. She had practically been in hiding prior to that. Always moving and working mainly from home. And the threats and suspicious activity had indeed brought her out into the open. It sickened her to think that Farris could have used her old childhood connections to do that.

"I need a phone," she repeated. "I can find out when Farris left the private institution."

But even the timing might not give him an alibi for these crimes. With his money, he could have hired someone to kill Tiffany and stage it to look like a car accident.

But that didn't make sense.

"If Farris had killed Tiffany to draw me out, he would have wanted me to know it was murder. It's the same for Sherry. A disappearance doesn't have the same emotional punch as murder."

Harlan made a sound of agreement, and he looked at her. Their gazes connected, but she hadn't needed that connection to know he was exhausted and frustrated. Just as she was. He forced out a long, weary breath and ran his fingers down the length of her arm.

It was far more comforting than it should have been.

So was the gentle grip he put on her wrist before his hand slipped into hers. Despite the mess they were in, she managed a weak smile.

And that was how Slade found them when he stepped into the entry with them. His expression stayed stony, but his eyebrows rose a fraction.

"Reliving the past?" he asked, and the tone of his voice wasn't friendly.

Caitlyn and Harlan moved away from each other. Not that they could go far. The entry was small, barely five feet across.

"I'm guessing you have something to tell us?" Harlan snapped at his brother.

"Yeah. Any chance either of you was near the site of Tiffany's car wreck?" Slade asked.

"No," Caitlyn and Harlan answered at the same time.

"Didn't figure you were, but someone sent the Rangers two eyewitness accounts that say otherwise."

"The eyewitnesses are lying." Which might be easy to prove if she and Harlan had solid alibis. Judging from Slade's expression, though, that wasn't all the news he had for them. "What else do the Rangers have?" she asked.

"My source says there are emails. Lots of them. From both of you to Sherry. And in those emails, you threaten her to stay quiet."

Despite the bone-weary fatigue, that sent a roar of anger through her. "Stay quiet about what?"

Slade shook his head. "Not sure, but I'm betting it has something to do with the Webb investigation."

Yeah, it almost certainly did. "But I didn't send any emails. In fact, the only reason I tried to contact Sherry was because of the threats I'd received."

"And I haven't been in touch with her at all," Harlan confirmed. "In fact, I didn't even know she was missing until Caitlyn showed up at my house in the middle of the night."

"I'll get someone on the emails," Slade explained. "And disproving those two eyewitnesses. Still, I think you should both lie low—away from the Rangers—because someone's clearly trying to frame you, and it's my guess they're doing that to take you out of commission."

So they couldn't investigate whatever the heck was happening to them.

She looked at Harlan to see what his take was, but his phone buzzed before he could say anything. "It's Sergeant Tinsley from Cross Creek."

Caitlyn immediately shifted her attention to the call, and she hoped like the devil that it was good news. Maybe they'd even managed to catch the ski-masked guy who'd shot at them.

"Marshal McKinney," Harlan answered, and she could hear the hope in his voice, too. They so needed a break.

But it wasn't exactly relief or good news that she saw in Harlan's body language. Caitlyn couldn't hear what Tinsley had said to make Harlan's forehead bunch up, but she figured it meant their attacker was still at large.

"Thanks for letting me know," Harlan said to Tinsley. "And call me the minute you find him." He ended the call and looked at her. "They got a print off the threatening note that was left on the steering wheel of the truck."

That was the last thing Caitlyn had expected, especially since Tinsley had already told them the cab of the truck was clean—no sign of anything they could use to confirm the identity of their attacker.

"The print belonged to Billy Webb," Harlan added.

Caitlyn didn't even try to stop the sound of surprise she made. Billy—Sarah and Jonah Webb's son. And a prime suspect as his mother's accomplice in the murder. Better yet, he was the one suspect the Rangers hadn't been able to find or interview.

"Billy," Slade repeated. "This is the first time he's surfaced since his father's body was found."

"First time he's surfaced in years," Harlan agreed. "He hasn't been using a credit card or bank account. No current driver's license either. Even his own mother claims she hasn't heard from him. The guy's been off the grid for years—so long in fact that I thought he might be dead."

Yes, and that was why the attack and the threats didn't make sense. "Why would he come after Harlan and me—especially like this?"

All three of them stayed quiet a moment, obviously giving that some thought. "Maybe he wants revenge," Slade finally suggested.

Harlan's gaze connected with hers, and she saw his *bingo!* moment.

"Maybe Billy didn't want his father dead," Harlan continued. "Maybe he's going after people he thinks could have helped his mother. Sarah's in a guarded room at the hospital," he quickly added.

Probably because he saw the alarm in her eyes. If this theory about Billy was true, then he would want his mother dead—and Sarah was in a coma, unable to protect herself.

There was no love lost between Caitlyn and Sarah. The woman had never lifted a finger to stop her husband from beating the kids at Rocky Creek. Caitlyn included. But truth was, Caitlyn owed Sarah a huge favor. If she hadn't knifed her own husband to death, then Harlan, his brothers and all the rest might have had to spend even more time in that hellhole.

"Why would Billy go after Sherry and Tiffany?" Slade asked—the very question that was on Caitlyn's mind. "They both had decent alibis for the night of the murder."

Decent but maybe not enough. "Billy might know something we don't," Caitlyn concluded. "There were a lot of people moving around the facility that night, and the window for Webb's murder is wide enough that anyone could have done it."

A chilling thought. Because maybe that meant Billy could be picking them off one by one. Still, Caitlyn wanted to know why he'd started with Tiffany. Maybe Sherry, too. And then moved on to her.

"Do you have a current photo of Billy?" she asked. "Because I wasn't able to find one."

Both Harlan and Slade shook their heads, and she

knew exactly what that meant. Yes, Sergeant Tinsley
and plenty of other cops would be looking for Billy,
but without a current photo, it would make that search
a whole lot more difficult—especially since, as Harlan
had already pointed out, Billy had been off the grid for
a while now.

Caitlyn heard the sound of a car engine, and all three
of them turned toward the road. She couldn't see the
ranch hands Slade had said would stand guard there.
But she did see the approaching bright red sports car.

Hardly the kind of vehicle a Texas Ranger would
drive.

"Someone you know?" Caitlyn immediately asked
Harlan and Slade.

They didn't answer but moved in front of her like
a curtain of solid muscle. Slade already had his rifle
ready, and Harlan drew his gun. Caitlyn didn't blame
them. If she'd had her weapon, she would have pulled,
too.

The car came to a noisy stop, the tires kicking up
gravel and dust from the road, and the driver didn't
waste a second before she heard the car door open. She
couldn't actually see it, because both men were block-
ing her view.

"You know him?" Harlan asked his brother.

Slade shook his head.

Caitlyn came up on her tiptoes and looked at their
visitor from over Harlan's shoulder.

God.

Her heart dropped to the floor.

"Caitlyn," the man said. Despite the wide smile
stretching his mouth, he lifted his hands in the air as if
surrendering. "Long time, no see."

"Who is he?" Harlan demanded.

Caitlyn opened her mouth, but it took several moments to get her throat unclamped so she could speak. "Jay Farris."

CHAPTER SEVEN

HARLAN AIMED HIS gun directly at the man walking toward his porch. Slade did the same, and he took up position on the other side of Caitlyn.

"Don't come a step closer," Harlan warned their visitor.

Farris came to a dead stop, but he kept smiling. Either this guy was truly nuts—a distinct possibility—or else he enjoyed unnerving everyone around him, because that smile was downright spooky. This darn sure wasn't a smiling kind of situation.

Harlan had never seen a photo of Farris and hadn't been sure what to expect, but he hadn't expected *this*. Farris wasn't the sort of man to blend into a crowd. Not with that stark bleached-blond hair and deep tan. In his cutoff khakis and white T-shirt he looked more like a rich beach bum than a would-be stalker.

Too bad Harlan couldn't say with 100 percent certainty that it'd been Farris wearing the ski mask at the motel. And now the waters were even muddier with Billy Webb's fingerprint that had been found on the latest threatening note. Still, Harlan wasn't about to dismiss blondie here as innocent just because Billy had resurfaced.

"Caitlyn," Farris repeated as if welcoming her to come closer.

Harlan didn't budge in case she intended to do just that, but Caitlyn didn't move either. One glance at her, and Harlan realized that was because she was frozen in place. She was too pale again, and she definitely wasn't smiling. He saw every bit of the fear in her eyes.

"What do you want?" she snapped at Farris. Her gaze was frozen as well on the madman who'd not only made her life a living hell, but also had tried to strangle her.

Yet here he was. Free as a bird.

Harlan would soon figure out what he could do about remedying that. The restraining order that Caitlyn had on Farris would have likely expired, but they could get a new one.

"I needed to see you," Farris said. If he was alarmed by the two guns trained on him, he didn't show it. "It's all over the news about your kidnapping. Someone took shots at you, they said, and when I saw Marshal McKinney's name, I did an internet search and found the address of the ranch. I thought you might be here."

Hell's bells. Of course it would be on the news. Harlan had forgotten about trying to suppress the story so it wouldn't clue in people like Farris that Caitlyn might be with him or any members of his family. Of course, if Farris was the person trying to kill them, he already knew about the attack anyway.

But there was something about this that just didn't fit.

If Farris had wanted Caitlyn dead, then why hadn't he killed her after he hit her with the Taser? He would have had the perfect opportunity, since she couldn't have fought back. Of course, sometimes crazy people didn't do logical things, and maybe he wanted a fight. Maybe he wanted to prolong her fear as long as possible.

"Are you okay?" Farris asked Caitlyn. "Were you hurt?"

She made a sound, a burst of laughter, but it wasn't from humor. "That's a strange question coming from you. The last time you were within reaching distance of me, you put your hands around my neck and tried to choke the life out of me."

It made Harlan's blood boil to hear that. Caitlyn wasn't a large woman by any means, and he hated that she'd come so close to dying. Back then and again today.

Finally Farris's smile dissolved. "Yes, *that,*" he mumbled. He scratched his eyebrow, then his head. "I was going through some bad stuff, but I got the help I needed, and I'm all better now."

"Forgive me if neither my neck nor I believe that," Caitlyn snapped.

Harlan wanted to cheer for her. It was hard to sound that gutsy when he could feel her trembling against his back.

"I can understand why you'd be skeptical," Farris went on as if discussing a parking ticket rather than a felony. "But, honestly, I'm just here to help."

"Help?" she repeated.

"How the hell can you help?" Harlan added. "And you'd better say it fast because you're not going to be anywhere near this ranch in a couple of minutes."

Despite his warning, Farris stayed unruffled, which only added to Harlan's opinion that this guy was crazier than a june bug. "I need to reach in my pocket and take out something. Please don't shoot me when I do it."

Harlan wasn't about to agree to that until he had more info. "What's in your pocket?"

"Something you both should see. It's a photo."

That got his attention. Apparently it got Caitlyn's, too. "What kind of photo?" she demanded.

"One of the marshal and you. Someone sent it to me early this morning."

Obviously as puzzled as he was, Caitlyn glanced at Harlan and shook her head.

"Take out the picture slowly, using just two fingers, and hold it up for us to see," Harlan ordered. "Don't come any closer."

Farris followed Harlan's orders to a tee, and he thrust the photo in their direction. Even though Farris was a good five yards away, Harlan could still make out Caitlyn and him. Her gasp let him know that she'd made it out, as well.

It was a shot of Caitlyn and him half-naked on the motel bed.

"Needless to say, I was shocked to get this," Farris went on. A muscle flickered in his jaw, and for the first time since his arrival, Harlan thought he might be seeing some real emotion on the man's face.

And that emotion was jealousy.

Great. Just what they needed. A jealous nut job of a stalker with homicidal tendencies.

"Who sent that to you?" Harlan asked.

"Don't know." Farris looked at the photo, and the jaw muscle got even tighter. "Someone rang my doorbell this morning, and when I answered it, no one was there. Just an envelope on the doorstep with this photo and a note inside." Farris's gaze snapped to Caitlyn. "I didn't know you were seeing your old flame."

"I'm not," she insisted.

Farris studied the picture again, made a sound of disagreement. "You're in bed with him."

"Not voluntarily," Harlan supplied. "Someone drugged us and handcuffed us together."

That caused Farris to pull back his shoulders, and without taking his attention off the photo, he shook his head again. "I don't see any handcuffs."

"They were there." Harlan held up his left hand so that Farris would see the reddish circular bruise on his wrist. "Now, what did the note say?"

It took a moment for Farris to answer, and while he could be faking, he seemed genuinely surprised with the handcuff revelation. "The note was typed, and it said you were in room 109 at the Starlight Inn in Cross Creek."

"God," Caitlyn murmured.

Harlan hadn't thought it possible, but he felt her muscles tense even more, and she put her hand on the small of his back. Probably because her legs weren't so steady. With her still fighting off the effects of the drug and the near fatal shooting, a confrontation with her stalker was the last thing she needed, but Harlan saw this from the eyes of a lawman. That photo was evidence of a setup.

Well, it was if Farris was telling the truth.

Harlan had no plans to believe him any time soon.

"I'll bet you weren't happy when you saw that picture of Caitlyn and me," Harlan remarked, and he kept a close watch on the man's reaction.

"I wasn't." His gaze rifled to Harlan. "Wait a minute. You don't think I was so enraged when I saw this that I then tried to kill you?"

Harlan shrugged, but that was exactly the direction he was going. "You tell me. Is that what happened?"

"No." Farris cursed and denied it again. "I got help

for my mental problems. I'm not a violent person anymore."

"I don't believe you," Caitlyn said, and she cleared her throat and repeated it. "Because someone did come to that motel room and try to kill us."

"Well, that someone wasn't me," Farris practically shouted. But the fit of temper went as fast as it came, and he scrubbed his hand over his face. "Look, I came here because I wanted to make sure you were okay and because I thought you should know about this photo. Caitlyn, someone obviously wants to hurt you."

"Obviously," she said with a massive amount of sarcasm dripping from her voice. "But I didn't need you or the photo to convince me of that. The bullets convinced me just fine."

"I'm sure they did. But what's this all about?" Farris pressed. "Is this happening because of one of your articles?"

Harlan wished it were that simple. Heck, for that matter he wished he could just go ahead and arrest Farris on the spot and force him to confess to setting all this up.

But Billy's fingerprint didn't fit.

In fact, it was entirely possible that Billy had been the one to set it up and that he'd merely used Farris as a pawn. As unhinged as Farris seemed to be, he'd be easy to manipulate.

"This is Marshal Slade Becker," Harlan said, tipping his head to his brother. "And he's going to escort you into town, where you'll be tested for gunshot residue."

He waited for Farris to object, but the man only shrugged. "I didn't fire a gun."

"Then you have nothing to be concerned about, do you?" Harlan answered.

Farris glanced at his car. Then the road. And Harlan braced himself for the man to make a run for it. He didn't. Farris turned back to them and nodded.

"Hope the test won't take long," Farris said. "I have a therapy appointment in two hours."

"I'll make it fast," Slade growled. "I'll follow you to the marshals' building on Main Street in town, and don't think about ditching me because I *will* chase you down."

Coming from Slade, that was a formidable threat, and Harlan mumbled a thanks to his brother.

"My advice," Slade whispered to Harlan. "Don't wait around for Ranger Morris to arrive and arrest you. We need to be able to clear your name in case this bleached-blond piece of work doesn't pan out." He went down the porch steps to his truck.

"I'll be in touch, Caitlyn," Farris called out to her as if this had been some kind of social visit. The man was an idiot.

Or else he was very smart.

And that was what worried Harlan most.

"What happens if there's gunshot residue?" Caitlyn asked. "Will that be enough to arrest him?"

Harlan watched them drive away. "Enough to hold him for a while."

He took her by the arm and led her back inside. Partly because he didn't want Farris gawking at her in his rearview mirror. But the main reason was there could still be another attack.

Right away he noticed the open drawers on his TV cabinet. Things had been moved around but not trashed even though there was fingerprint powder on just about every visible hard surface. His brothers had no doubt sent an entire team of CSIs out to his place once they'd realized he was missing.

Caitlyn pulled in a weary breath and sank onto his sofa. "What are we going to do about those warrants for our arrest?"

Harlan wasn't sure she was going to like this. Or even if it was the right thing to do, but he was going to listen to Slade on this. "We should leave."

She'd already started to ease the back of her head onto the sofa, but that stopped her. Harlan figured she'd at least question that decision.

Caitlyn didn't.

She got up and looked down at the scrubs she was still wearing. "At least let me get my overnight bag from my car so I can change clothes."

He nodded, locked the door. "I need to do the same." He'd stick out like a sore thumb in the green scrubs because he didn't come close to looking like a medic. "I won't be long, and if you hear a car drive up, stay away from the windows."

Harlan headed to his bedroom and grabbed a pair of jeans. His bed was unmade and things had been tossed around. A reminder that whoever had shot them with a Taser had probably ransacked the place.

But looking for what?

More proof that he and Caitlyn were sleeping together? Something to do with Webb's murder?

He pulled on his jeans and was in midzip when he heard the movement, and he automatically grabbed his gun and whirled in that direction.

However, it was only Caitlyn.

"Yeah, I'm jumpy, too," she muttered. She bracketed her hands on the jamb. "But I was thinking of something. Whoever orchestrated this attack didn't make any mistakes—"

When her explanation came to a fast halt, Harlan followed her gaze to his body. To his bare chest. Maybe even his open zipper.

"Sorry," she mumbled.

"Not to worry. I think we got an eyeful of each other when we woke up in that bed this morning." An eyeful he shouldn't be remembering with everything else on his mind, but Harlan was sure he wouldn't be able to forget it any time soon.

The past sixteen years had settled nicely on her body.

She cleared her throat, anchored her attention to the floor. "As I was saying…" But it took her several more seconds to continue. During that time, Harlan zipped up and grabbed a shirt. "Our attacker drew me out, waited until we were together and used that Taser before either of us could fight."

Harlan nodded. "He wasn't sloppy. So why leave a fingerprint on the threatening note in the truck?"

She nodded, too. "Are you thinking Farris might have planted Billy's print there?"

"Yeah." That was exactly what he was thinking. Too bad it would be a bear to prove, but it all started with finding Billy and getting his side of the story.

Harlan finished dressing and yanked open his nightstand drawer. His backup Glock was still there—yet another piece of this weird puzzle. Why hadn't their attacker taken it? He grabbed both it and his badge and some extra ammo.

But not the condoms.

Too much temptation, and he and Caitlyn already had enough of that without adding condoms to the mix.

"Where are we going?" Caitlyn stepped back when he approached the door. Purposely putting some distance between them.

And he knew why.

Despite his fatigue and stress, that old attraction was still there, rearing its head. Good thing Caitlyn knew it'd be stupid and reckless for them to act on it. But not acting on it would test them to the limits.

Because they were going to be attached at the hip, so to speak.

He opened his mouth to tell her they were heading to a place that Declan owned, but then he stopped and glanced around the room. Their attacker had clearly had some time to look for whatever he'd been looking for, but he'd also had time to plant a listening device. That was a long shot, of course, since the person probably thought he and Caitlyn wouldn't live long enough to return to his house, but it was a chance Harlan didn't want to take.

"I'll tell you when we're out of here," he whispered.

Caitlyn's eyes widened, and she, too, made a sweeping glance around the room. That also got her moving pretty darn fast, and they made it to the door before his phone buzzed.

"Please tell me there's not a problem with Farris," Caitlyn mumbled.

Harlan shook his head and stared at the caller's name on the screen. It was a name he recognized, but barely. "It's Curtis Newell."

The business partner of the missing woman, Sherry Summers.

"I didn't know you knew him," Caitlyn said, looking at the screen.

"I don't." Harlan hit the answer button. "Marshal McKinney."

"Marshal." The man sounded relieved or something. "I got your number from the Marshals Service because I'm trying to get in touch with Caitlyn Barnes. I heard about the shooting."

Harlan groaned. God knew how many people had heard and how many welfare-check calls like this there'd be. He didn't have time for them.

"Caitlyn's okay," Harlan assured the man.

"That's good, but it's not why I'm calling." Curtis said it so quickly that his words ran together. "I really need to speak with her."

Okay. Not a welfare check. In fact, this guy sounded frantic.

Harlan glanced at her, and she motioned for him to put the call on speaker. He did.

"I'm here, Curtis," Caitlyn said. "What's wrong? Have you found Sherry?"

"No, we haven't found her. But there's plenty wrong. God, Caitlyn, what the hell's going on?"

Harlan didn't like the sound of that, and judging from the way Caitlyn pulled in her breath, neither did she. "What happened?" she asked.

"I went over to Sherry's condo to check her mail and see if there were any messages on her answering machine. I've been doing that since she went missing. Someone had trashed the place and left her a threatening note."

Great day in the morning. If these were connected, then their attacker had been very busy. "What did the threat say?"

He heard Curtis's hard, quick breaths. "'This isn't over. You're a dead woman.'"

Caitlyn pressed her fingers to her mouth, but it didn't stop the soft gasp she made. That was because it was the identical threat that had been left for her in the truck.

"But that's not all," Curtis went on. "I just got a call from Devin Mathis. You know who he is?"

Yet another name that was familiar to Harlan, but he didn't know why.

"He was engaged to Tiffany Brock, a former resident at Rocky Creek who died in a car accident."

"Devin says she was murdered," Curtis corrected. "And he got a note, too. Someone left it on his car this morning. Not a threat exactly—the note was just one word. *Dead.*"

As a lawman, Harlan forced himself to look at the logistics of this. He and Caitlyn had been in Cross Creek, but if he remembered correctly, Sherry's condo and business were in Houston. So that meant their attacker likely had an accomplice. Or else had hired someone to do his dirty work. Because that was too much ground for one person to cover in that short period of time.

"Did the cops get any prints?" Caitlyn asked Curtis. Her voice was shaking as much as her hands were.

"Two—they were both on the notes that were sent to Devin and the one left in Sherry's condo. That's why I had to talk to you. I have to know what's going on."

"I don't know what's happening," she answered. "Was it Billy Webb's prints on the threat?"

"No." His breath seemed to shudder. "Caitlyn, it was yours and Marshal McKinney's. Did you two do something to Sherry? Are you trying to silence her?"

Oh, man. That hit him hard.

"No," Harlan and Caitlyn answered in unison. She looked at him, shook her head. "How could that have happened?"

Harlan didn't have any more answers for her than he did Curtis Newell. That was bad enough, but then he heard the sound of an approaching vehicle. One glance out the window, and he saw it was Ranger Morris. Not alone either. There were two other Rangers with him— and they'd likely come to arrest Caitlyn and him.

This was all a setup, of course, and the evidence was growing. Harlan seriously doubted that the cops who'd found the prints on those notes had withheld that evidence. If the Rangers hadn't heard it, they soon would.

"We'll have to call you back," Harlan said to Curtis.

"No—" Curtis insisted.

But Harlan ended the call anyway. "Come on." Harlan took Caitlyn by the arm and headed for the back door. "We have to leave now."

CHAPTER EIGHT

CAITLYN DIDN'T EVEN ask Harlan where they were going as he maneuvered the truck along the sharp curves on the rural road. But she hoped and prayed it was somewhere safe. Away from the person trying to kill them.

Away from the Rangers, too.

With everything else going on, it could be downright dangerous for them to be arrested, since it was clear now that someone was playing a cat-and-mouse game. Why, she didn't know. But here were notes left for both Devin and Curtis with Harlan's and her fingerprints and the so-called evidence someone had sent to the Rangers. No matter how many times she tossed it around in her head, she kept coming back to one place.

Rocky Creek.

And one specific event: Jonah Webb's murder.

Harlan had grabbed a laptop and some supplies from his family's main ranch house while they were making their *escape,* and she hoped she got a chance to use the computer to do some research.

"Never been a fugitive from justice before," Harlan grumbled. He finished off the last bite of the fast-food burger they'd stopped for along the way after they'd gotten out of Maverick Springs.

Caitlyn shrugged. "I have. When I was fourteen, I got into a car with some friends. Didn't know the car was stolen until the cops spotted us, and we ran. Don't worry—you'll do better with your fugitive status once you get past the sick-to-your-stomach stage."

He looked at her from the corner of his eye. She certainly wasn't making light of it—she was scared, tired and frustrated. But in the grand scheme of things, the Rangers seemed like the least of their worries.

And complicating things even more was the old attraction between them.

But for some reason, it was both of those things that felt like dead weight on her shoulders. The Rangers—that was understandable. The attraction not so much. Well, except for Harlan's hot body and the way that hot body filled out his jeans and T-shirt. He wasn't a bad boy, but he looked the part. She knew just how gentle he could be.

Even for a girl's first time.

She'd had a few lovers since then, but Caitlyn had never had a man treat her like priceless crystal while taking her breath away with pleasure. Ironic. That her first time had been her best, and she hadn't even known what she was doing. Thank goodness Harlan had.

"What you thinking about?" Harlan asked.

Her gaze slashed to his as she wondered what had prompted that question. Oh. Her fast breathing. Flushed cheeks. And though those things were nonverbal, judging from the heated, puzzled look in Harlan's eyes, he was picking up on it.

His breath kicked up the pace, too. No flushed cheeks, but the pulse on his throat did a little gallop. His lips parted. Probably to say something to her. But it was a reminder that the man's kisses were orgasmic.

Mercy.

Enough of this.

"Um, I keep thinking that I'm responsible for nearly getting us killed." It wasn't exactly a lie. She *had* thought this over and over again in the past few hours.

He blinked. Frowned. But didn't challenge her.

She crammed most of her burger into the bag. No appetite. "If I hadn't suspected you, I wouldn't have come to your house—"

"He would have found another way to get us together."

That was probably true, but if she hadn't come to Harlan, she suspected they wouldn't be dealing with the Rangers and definitely not the heat.

Harlan checked the rearview mirror again. Something they'd both been doing during the entire drive, but there was no one behind or ahead of them. He turned onto another road, more rugged than the previous one, and drove another mile. He brought the truck to a stop in front of a log house. This wasn't a cabin. It looked more like a vacation home nestled in the woods.

"Declan owns it." Harlan got out and grabbed the bags that they'd hastily packed at the ranch.

Talk about a surprise—for several reasons. For one thing, she'd always thought of Declan as a rolling stone. Not really the home-owner type. But that was just an observation, not her real concern.

Her real concern was security.

Harlan had already switched phones to a prepaid cell and had left word with his brothers to transfer any calls to the number. He'd also made sure they weren't followed. Still, there was the obvious five-hundred-pound gorilla in the room.

"What if the Rangers look for us here?" she asked. "Declan is, after all, your foster brother."

"They won't look here. The place isn't actually in his name. About two years ago, a distant relative of his from Ireland left it to him in his estate."

During their many chats, Declan had told her he was from Ireland. He still had a trace of the brogue, but it seemed odd that an Irish relative would buy a place like this in the middle of Nowhere, Texas, and then leave it to Declan.

"Why didn't this relative come forward when Declan was placed in Rocky Creek?" Because she knew his time there had been hell for him, and almost any family would have been better than what he'd had to face at the orphanage.

"Don't know," Harlan replied. He pressed in some numbers on the keypad by the door to unlock it. "Let's just say Declan has some secrets and leave it at that."

That only made her uneasy feeling even more uneasy. "Not secrets about Rocky Creek?" And more specifically, about Webb's murder?

But Harlan only shrugged, opened the door and punched in yet more numbers to disarm the security system before it started to beep. Obviously he wasn't planning to spill anything else about his kid brother, but that didn't mean Caitlyn couldn't do some digging. Right now, everyone was a suspect.

Well, except Harlan.

She seriously doubted he'd screw himself over like this if he was trying to hide his guilt about anything. Of course, he seemed genuinely close to his brothers, so they probably wouldn't put him through this either.

Now, she was a different story.

With the exception of Declan and maybe Stella, Harlan, his foster brothers and foster father might love to see her squirming on the end of a hook. That was why Kirby's words back at the ranch had surprised her. Something about her and Harlan being suited for each other. Well, he was wrong about that.

Despite the attraction, of course.

In that one area, she and Harlan seemed way too suited, and that didn't please either of them.

Harlan reset the alarm when he closed the door, and they put the bags on a foyer table and looked around. It looked like a place out of a glossy magazine, with its wood floors, leather furniture and massive stone fireplace. Even a work desk with a computer in the corner.

"There's a stocked freezer," Harlan said, leading her into the kitchen. "And canned goods. Just in case we're here longer than tonight. The bedrooms are upstairs."

"Two of them?" She hadn't intended to sound so concerned, but she did.

"Two," he verified, giving her a flat look. It would have worked—she might have believed the offended/uninterested act—if she hadn't seen the pulse at his throat begin to throb.

Jeez Louise.

It was bad enough that she was battling her hormones, but Harlan needed to stay sane. And unaroused.

"Why don't you go ahead and get some rest?" he mumbled.

She took a deep breath, hoping for a clear head. Didn't happen. "I'd rather get a little work done. And change my clothes," she said, looking down at the scrubs she was still wearing.

Harlan looked about to argue, but his phone buzzed. "It's Slade."

Which likely meant this might be news of the investigation. However, Harlan didn't put the call on speaker. Maybe because he wanted to buffer any more bad news they might get.

While he was occupied with that, Caitlyn went to the computer in the corner desk and turned it on. The perfect thing to get kisses and arousing thoughts out of her mind was to work. She logged on to her email account to the dozens of unanswered emails, including several from her boss, Jeb Parker, asking about the two articles she was supposed to be writing.

That caused her stomach to knot.

She hadn't forgotten about the articles, but nearly being killed had put them way on the back burner.

The first was a piece she needed to do about a captured fugitive who'd murdered his entire family and then fled. Caitlyn had managed to be in the news station's helicopter during the chase, and even though she'd already given Jeb several eyewitness articles, he wanted a follow-up. Not just a written one, but a TV appearance so they could run the footage of the helicopter chase. It would be an easy paycheck for her once she got around to it.

There was nothing easy about the second one.

Caitlyn opened the latest version of the second story that she'd put in secure cyber storage, and the headline she'd given it caused the knot in her stomach to get significantly worse.

"Trouble?" she heard someone ask.

Her own gasp echoed through the room. She'd been so caught up in what was on the screen, she hadn't heard anyone come up behind her, and she whirled around, automatically bringing up her hands to defend herself. But no defense was necessary. Because it was Harlan.

"Wired up much?" he murmured. "You really need to rest." Then he tipped his head to the screen. "Bad news?"

Caitlyn shook her head and stepped in front of it. "I'm just getting behind at work." Then she noticed his expression. "Did you get bad news?" she repeated.

Harlan lifted his shoulder. "Disappointing news," he corrected. "Slade tested Farris, but there was no gunshot residue on him."

She groaned. "So no arrest."

"No arrest," he confirmed. "But that doesn't mean he's innocent. It could mean he had on latex gloves when he fired those shots."

Caitlyn couldn't remember seeing gloves, but their attacker could have been wearing them. "What about an alibi for the shooting? Does Farris even have one?"

"Says he was alone at his parents' house, but claims one of the maids might be able to verify it."

"Or lie about it," Caitlyn muttered. If Farris had tested positive, it would have at least gotten him off the streets so Harlan and she could try to build a case against him.

"Farris turned over the photo and the note to Slade," Harlan went on. "The lab might be able to get some prints."

"Our prints," she supplied. "Like the ones on the threats that Devin and Curtis got."

Another shrug. "I figure when we were knocked out cold, it would have been easy to put our fingerprints on just about anything."

That sent a chill through her. Heaven knew what other *evidence* was going to surface. "But why is the person doing this? Why try to set us up?"

"Maybe to take the fall for Webb's murder." He paused, huffed. "But I'm pretty sure we were supposed to die in that motel room."

Caitlyn had already come to the same conclusion, but it was a whole new level of fear to hear it spoken aloud. Now the thoughts came at her nonstop. Billy had perhaps set them up and then sent Farris that photo, figuring the crazed stalker would do the killing for him.

And he'd come darn close to succeeding.

"Yeah," Caitlyn mumbled.

He was examining her face. Her eyes. And he no doubt knew what this was doing to her, because it was doing the same thing to him. Maybe worse. He had family to protect, and it didn't matter that his brothers were marshals and could take care of themselves. He never wanted to put them in danger, period.

"What about the motel?" she asked. "Were there any eyewitnesses who can help get us a better description of the shooter?"

"None. There was a traffic camera on the interstate, but it wasn't aimed in the direction of the motel."

And it was probably why their attacker had chosen to put them there.

"No sign of Billy yet," Harlan went on. "But the initial lab results are back, and it appears you and I were drugged with etorphine hydrochloride."

"The drug used on animals," she immediately supplied. "I did an article on it a while back." She snapped her fingers, trying to recall some details. "Only veterinarians have access to it, so maybe that's a way to trace our attacker."

Harlan was already shaking his head before she finished. "A large supply of it went missing a couple of months ago, and it's been showing up in black markets all over the country. Anyone with enough cash could have bought it, and I doubt we'll find a drug dealer willing to rat out a customer."

No. And besides, if it was Billy or Farris, they probably would have just hired someone to buy the drug for them so they could stay a step removed from any possible evidence.

"Do you have *any* good news?" she asked. And yes, there was frustration in her voice.

"Maybe. Slade is setting up meetings with both Curtis Newell and Devin Mathis. We'll see them in the morning."

Sherry's business partner and Tiffany's fiancé. Both had received threats and both might have information about who was behind the attacks. *Might*.

"Please tell me we're not meeting them here?" Caitlyn asked.

"No. And we obviously can't go to the marshals' building. Slade's making arrangements for someplace safe." He took her by the arm again. "Now rest."

God, she needed it. Every one of her muscles was stiff and sore. And rest would give her stupid body a chance to cool down from Harlan fantasies. She might have gotten her feet moving toward the stairs if Harlan hadn't flexed the grip on her forearm, sliding his fingers down, down, down. To her wrist. Then to her hand.

There was nothing sexual about it. Hand-holding. But he might as well have touched her in the most intimate of places, because her body turned warm and melty.

Harlan had started it with the hand-holding foreplay, but Caitlyn escalated things. Couldn't stop herself. That mouth was right there in front her. Mesmerizing. Filled with the hottest memories. So she leaned in. Pressed her lips to his.

Oh, mercy.

Big mistake. The contact hit her like a lightning bolt. All the heat, fire and intensity zapped her. Not just her either. Harlan made a sound. That male rumble in his chest and throat, and he dragged her to him. The press of their lips became a full-fledged kiss. French and everything.

Especially *everything*.

His arms were strong. She knew that. But knowing and experiencing it were two different things. Those strong arms drew her in until she was against his body. Not that she needed a punch of heat, but it made the kisses even better.

Mercy, he was good at this.

Gentle and rough at the same time. His hand went into her hair, to the back of her head so he could control the movement, angle and pressure. He already controlled everything else, so Caitlyn didn't even try to resist.

He tasted good. Like something familiar but forbidden. That was Harlan. A contradiction. Their bodies pressed closer. Until she could feel all those muscles on his chest.

His zipper, too.

No cooldown for her. Just the opposite. While her head yelled for her to back away, Caitlyn let her fingers and mouth play with fire. She slid her hand between them and touched. That incredible chest. His stomach— hard and tight.

She wanted to go lower. Actually, she wanted sex, and clearly Harlan wanted that, too, because his stomach wasn't the only part of him that was hard.

Without breaking the kiss, he moved her, turned her, until her bottom was pressed against the edge of the desk. A good angle for sex. Not so good for cashing in on some willpower. The new position put him right between her legs.

Everything aligned.

Only the blasted clothes were in the way. And as hot as the kisses had made her, clothing removal was just one touch away.

Or not.

Harlan stepped back.

Not easily. And she wasn't sure he wouldn't just dive right back at her again.

Harlan stood there. Breathing hard. Smelling like the sex she wanted to have with him. His hands tightened into fists. Finally one of them had acted like a responsible adult, but Caitlyn was having a hard time remembering why that was important.

Oh, because they had other things to do. Like clear their names and catch a killer.

So why did *this* suddenly seem more important than anything else?

"We need to agree that was a mistake," he insisted.

She glanced at the erection straining the zipper of his jeans. Then at her own nipples, puckered and very visible since she wasn't wearing a bra.

"A compromise," she murmured. "Let's just agree that it was mutual…and really, really good."

He laughed. The sound was so unexpected that it took Caitlyn a moment to shake off the tension and smile. Not because there was anything to smile about, but it was impossible to stay in sex-land with that laugh. And that smile. Mercy, the man had some big weapons in his male arsenal, and that smile was one of them. Except the smile didn't last. It dissolved in the blink of an eye, and the look on his face definitely wasn't that of a happy man.

"What the hell is that?" he snapped.

A jolt of fear went through her. God, she couldn't take any more bad news.

Afraid of what she might see, Caitlyn followed his gaze to the laptop screen. The scalding kiss had numbed her brain, because she'd forgotten *that* was on the screen. The working headline said it all.

U.S. Marshals' Cover-Up of Jonah Webb's Murder?

The question mark was there for a reason, because she wasn't at all sure there'd been a cover-up, but Harlan likely wouldn't even notice it. That was because his attention was nailed to the first paragraph and the other question she'd posed.

With his foster sons' help, did retired marshal Kirby Granger get away with murder?

"I can explain." But she couldn't. There was no explanation she could give Harlan that would undo the fury she now saw in his eyes.

"Save it," Harlan growled. He grabbed his bag and stormed upstairs.

CHAPTER NINE

"REALLY?" CAITLYN GRUMBLED. "You couldn't come up with a better meeting place?"

For once in the past fourteen hours or so, Harlan agreed with her, but he didn't mimic the huff she made when Slade turned onto the road at the weathered sign.

Rocky Creek Children's Facility.

Apparently they were headed back for another trip down memory lane. Harlan was more than a little fed up with those—especially the ones that involved Caitlyn. And her apparent need to screw over his family any chance she got.

"I figured this is the last place the Rangers would look for you," Slade explained. Except he always sounded as if he were picking a fight when he spoke. "Besides, it's vacant, and Joelle gave me the keys."

Joelle, their sister-in-law who'd once honchoed the investigation when it was still in the inquiry stage. That was why Joelle had the keys in the first place. Well, it sure as heck was past that inquiry stage now with the Rangers trying to arrest Caitlyn and him.

"Rudy Simmons, the caretaker, is away on a trip," Slade added. "So we'll have the place to ourselves."

"Jeez." Caitlyn forced out several breaths and pressed her hand over her heart. "If I'd known we were coming here, I would have had a shot of tequila or something."

Again Harlan agreed. The redbrick building was practically pristine. Grounds, too. Ironic that it looked so welcoming, but if someone had asked him to paint a picture of hell, it'd be Rocky Creek.

"It doesn't exactly have good memories for any of us," Harlan mumbled. Slade added a grunt of agreement.

Caitlyn mimicked that grunt. "You never did tell me how you ended up here," she added, glancing at Harlan.

"Bad luck." That was Harlan's usual answer when it came up in conversation. Which wasn't very often. But Caitlyn already knew that bad luck had played into everyone's stay at the hellhole. "My mom cut out when I was three, and I lived with my grandmother until she passed away."

"How old were you?" She sounded truly interested or maybe she just wanted the distraction. Harlan wouldn't have minded one either, but he also didn't want conversation to distract him from keeping them safe.

"Twelve." He looked around, trying to see if there were any threats. "By then I was a big kid, and I think that intimidated any potential foster parents. Guess they figured I'd beat them to a pulp or something."

"Yeah." She hesitated, nibbled some more on her bottom lip. "I got the same attitude. The piercings and hair color didn't help."

"All those fights probably didn't either," Slade growled, and Caitlyn mumbled an agreement. His phone dinged, and he glanced at the screen before he passed it to Harlan.

"The background checks on Curtis and Devin," Harlan relayed.

That got the worried look off Caitlyn's face, and she

scooted closer to him so she could see. Not that she had to scoot far. They were all sharing the single seat in Slade's truck and were already way too close. The maneuver put them hip to hip.

Harlan ignored it.

Okay, he tried.

And he focused on the summary that his brother Clayton had done on Curtis Newell. The basics were all there. Age thirty-seven, no criminal history. He had an MBA, and from the looks of it, he'd sunk nearly every penny of his inheritance from his grandmother into the private equity business that he and Sherry had started three years earlier.

No red flags.

The business wasn't exactly thriving, but there were no signs that it was about to go bust either. The only thing that seemed marginally suspect was that even before Sherry's disappearance, Curtis had been making the bulk of the business decisions despite the fact that she was the majority owner. That could be explained simply because Sherry had delegated that responsibility to him. Of course, it could also mean that Curtis had a lot to gain if Sherry died. He would become the sole owner of their company. People had murdered for a lot less.

Harlan moved on to the next report, for Devin Mathis.

"Whoa," Caitlyn said just seconds into the record.

Definitely a whoa. "According to the San Antonio cops, Devin initially was a suspect in Tiffany's car *accident*," Harlan said so that Slade would be in on this. "Several of Tiffany's friends have come forward to say the relationship had soured and that she was about to break off the engagement."

He mulled that over, and yes, it was a possible motive for Tiffany's murder. Love gone wrong always was. But that didn't explain Sherry's disappearance and the other things happening to Caitlyn and him.

"Wait." Caitlyn pointed toward the next line of the report. "Devin *was* a suspect, but he has a decent alibi. He was out of town for two days prior to the accident, and witnesses report that Tiffany drove the vehicle during that time."

"That only means Devin didn't tamper with the brakes or anything," Harlan pointed out. "He could have hired someone to do it for him."

Her sound of agreement was laced with frustration, and Harlan knew why. They still didn't have the answers they needed to make an arrest, and essentially both men had motive. What was missing was any kind of proof.

Slade pulled his truck to a stop in front of the building, and if he was having any kind of reaction to the place, he didn't show it.

"Curtis should be here any minute." Slade checked his watch and tossed Harlan the key for the front door. "He's bringing a P.I. friend with him. More like a bodyguard if you ask me. The guy's scared."

Yeah, because of the fingerprints found on the threatening notes. Harlan's and Caitlyn's. He didn't blame the man for not trusting them.

"I'll drive back down and wait at the end of the road so I can keep watch," Slade continued. "Devin Mathis is supposed to be checking into a hotel in town soon. When he arrives, he's to give me a call, and I'll let you know. Didn't figure you'd want to talk to Curtis and Devin together."

He didn't. Harlan wanted to hear what each man had to say about the threats and this entire mess of a situation. Of course, that might be harder because of the whole distrust issue.

"Thanks, Slade. For everything," Harlan added. Yeah, he wasn't exactly comfortable being here, but he was grateful that his brother had been able to set it all up.

Slade drove away, leaving both Caitlyn and him looking up at the building. "Let's get in there," she said under her breath, "and exorcize a few demons and ghosts."

Maybe because their kissing session was still hot on his mind, that comment didn't sound as shaky as her reaction when she'd first realized this was their meeting place. The building had the demons, all right. Probably ghosts, too, and not all bad. After all, this was also where he and Caitlyn had done the deed sixteen years ago.

They'd been the least likely couple to get together— ever. Her with her reform-school background, goth-girl attitude, piercings and weekly hair-color change. He'd been the Boy Scout. Not literally. No opportunity for that, but he'd never considered himself a bad boy. Still, he and Caitlyn had found their way together.

And they'd found each other again with that mistake of a kissing session.

Opposites attract, right?

But in their case, opposites had to stop attracting. If he could just figure out how.

"I'm sorry about the article," she said out of the blue.

Harlan didn't look at her. He unlocked the door and pushed it open. "Sorry I found out or sorry you wrote it?"

"Both." She paused. "It was a knee-jerk reaction to those threats. I figured if you were sending them to me, I wanted some kind of insurance. You know, something for the world to read if I ended up dead in a suspicious car accident?"

Now he looked at her. "When are you going to send it to your boss?"

"I won't. I deleted it this morning before we left to come here."

It wasn't the answer he'd expected. "That won't hurt your *career?*" And yeah, it was a jab at her earlier excuse for writing the article that had burned him. Except to her it probably wasn't an excuse.

And he hated that he could see it from her side.

"My boss owes me a boatload of favors," she answered. "So no, pulling one article won't burn too many bridges."

Too many, but it would burn some.

"Why'd you kill the article?" he asked, not sure he wanted to hear this.

"The kiss," she readily admitted.

Harlan cursed. Yeah, that kiss was pretty darn potent, but he didn't think for one minute that it had changed her mind.

Had it?

"Look, you're not trying to kill me, and I'm not trying to screw you." She winced at her word choice. "Correction—I'm not trying to get you or your family in judicial hot water."

Good to hear. Not sure he totally believed it. "So, you think Kirby's innocent?"

"No." Not a second of hesitation either. "But if he's guilty, if he did help kill Webb, then I'd rather give him a medal than write one word that might put him behind bars."

Harlan figured that was probably the truth, or close enough to it, but he wasn't about to let go of his anger just yet. The point was—she had written the article. Maybe just days ago. And it was still too recent to have him forgive and forget.

His phone buzzed, and when he answered it, Harlan heard Slade's voice. "Curtis Newell's driving up to the building now."

Showtime. Or rather interview time. Harlan put his phone away and popped the snap holder over his gun in his holster. "Just a precaution," he mumbled when Caitlyn made a sound of surprise.

Maybe it hadn't occurred to her that someone could have followed Curtis. Someone who could try to get past Slade. Plus, Harlan didn't know this man, and he wasn't going to blindly trust him. Curtis would be in the same mind-set.

Both he and Caitlyn drew in long breaths at the same time, and they looked out at the car that came to a stop directly in front of the steps. Earlier, Harlan had seen photos of Curtis, so he instantly recognized the stocky ginger-haired man who got out. He was wearing a dark blue suit more appropriate for a business meeting than an abandoned orphanage.

The second man was tall and bulky, and the jacket he was wearing no doubt concealed a weapon. He didn't come inside but rather stood in the doorway after his employer entered.

"Thanks for coming," Harlan greeted Curtis.

He gave an uneasy nod, barely sparing Harlan a glance before his gaze settled on Caitlyn. "I need to hear you say you didn't have anything to do with Sherry's disappearance."

"I didn't," she answered without hesitation. "And we didn't send her any threatening emails to warn her to shut up."

"The authorities think otherwise," Curtis reminded her.

"It doesn't mean it happened. Someone drugged and kidnapped Harlan and me, and we think the person got our prints on those notes when we were out cold."

Curtis kept staring at her. There were dark circles under his eyes—which were bloodshot. He looked like a man in need of sleep. "Then who's doing this?" he pressed.

"We don't know. But the person tried to kill us."

"Did he kill Sherry, too?" His voice cracked.

Now it was Harlan's turn to say, "We don't know."

Curtis made an unmanly-sounding moan. "I'm in love with her. And no, she didn't feel the same way about me, but I couldn't turn it off. The heart wants what it wants, you know?"

Harlan glanced at Caitlyn at the same moment she glanced at him. He frowned. She lifted her shoulder. The heart wasn't in on his attraction—well, hopefully not anyway—but Harlan could substitute heart for body, and it would describe the feeling he was trying to fight.

"I'm doing everything to find Sherry," Curtis went

on. "But the cops have no leads. It's like she just vanished."

Harlan wanted to give the man some hope, but he didn't intend to lie. "I think everything that's happening is linked to this place and Jonah Webb's murder. Did Sherry ever say she'd seen anything the night Webb disappeared?"

Curtis started shaking his head but stopped, paused. "She let something slip about four months ago, on the day that Webb's remains were discovered."

A day that Harlan remembered well. A crew working on the power lines had found what was left of Webb's body in a shallow grave about a mile from the Rocky Creek facility. Harlan had always figured the man was dead, but it hadn't been confirmed until that day.

"Sherry seemed worried," Curtis went on, "and when I asked why, she said she might have been in the wrong place at the wrong time that night."

Harlan and Caitlyn exchanged another puzzled glance. "I called Sherry just days after that, and she didn't mention anything to me. Any idea what she meant?" Caitlyn asked.

"No. But I can tell you that she was scared." His gaze went to Harlan. "Of you and your family. But others, too. She said she didn't think she could trust anyone from Rocky Creek."

Judging from the slight sound Caitlyn made, that was news to her. To Harlan, too. And he was reasonably sure that Sherry hadn't said anything to the Rangers investigating the case. Certainly not to Joelle either when she'd been interviewing possible witnesses and suspects.

"Once when Sherry was on the phone, I heard her

talking about Rocky Creek," Curtis continued. "She was scribbling down something, and later when I looked, I saw it was five names." He reached into his pocket, extracted a piece of paper. "I kept it."

Harlan took the paper that Curtis thrust at him, and Caitlyn moved closer. The names had indeed been scrawled along with some doodles, but they were still legible: Tiffany Brock, Caitlyn Barnes, Kirby Granger and Harlan McKinney. There was one other name on the list.

Billy Webb.

"I looked him up on the internet," Curtis said, "and I know it was his father who was murdered. I also found out he attempted suicide. I think Sherry was actually talking to him when she wrote down those names."

"What makes you say that?" Caitlyn asked.

"Just a gut feel." He shook his head. "I know you want more. I want more, too, because we need information to find Sherry. What if this crazy man is holding her captive somewhere?" Curtis grimaced. "What if he's torturing her?"

Harlan's stomach twisted, but that wasn't the worst-case scenario. No. The torturing could already be over, and Sherry could be dead.

Harlan's phone buzzed. Slade again. "Devin Mathis made it into town," his brother informed him. "Should I tell him where we are and have him drive out here?"

Curtis glanced behind him at the end of the road where the sleek car had come to a stop. "You have other people to see. I'll be going."

"You can go ahead and tell him to come out," Harlan said to his brother, and he purposely didn't mention Devin's name.

On the surface there didn't seem to be a direct connection between Devin and Curtis, and Harlan wanted to keep it that way. He didn't want the two teaming up to try to find the culprit for their loved ones' ill fates. Especially since they'd probably team up against Caitlyn and him.

Curtis looked at the note. "Could I please have that back? I want to keep it."

Harlan returned it and started to insist that the man give it to the authorities. That would be the legal thing to do, but it would be yet even more dirt against Caitlyn, Kirby and him. And besides, it might not even be important. Maybe Sherry was just jotting down names from her past.

Or setting them up.

"What?" Caitlyn whispered to him.

But Harlan didn't answer until Curtis had walked away and was out of earshot. "Curtis didn't mention one possibility—what if Sherry's alive and behind all of this?"

Caitlyn looked ready to dismiss that, but she didn't. "Maybe she helped Sarah kill Webb, and now she's trying to eliminate anyone who could prove it."

It was a stretch, and it only complicated things to add another suspect, but Harlan wanted to consider all the angles. Farris could be doing this to get his version of revenge against Caitlyn. Or Farris could be Billy's pawn.

And then there was Curtis.

He could have killed Sherry simply because she'd rejected him or because of a disagreement with their business—especially since Sherry was technically his boss since she owned the majority of their company.

Of course, that didn't make all the other pieces fit, but that only meant Harlan had to look harder in case that connection was there.

His phone buzzed, and Harlan answered it, figuring it was Slade, who'd tell them that Devin would be arriving soon.

"Harlan?" With just that one word, he could hear the trouble in his brother's voice. "I'm coming your way. We need to get the heck out of here fast."

"Why? What happened?" Harlan didn't wait. He took Caitlyn by the arm and got them out the door, running toward Slade's truck barreling up the road toward them.

"Someone alerted the Rangers that you're here. Don't know who, but I just got a call from a friend who's also a dispatcher."

Even though the call wasn't on speaker, Caitlyn must have heard anyway because she cursed. Slade braked to a stop in front of them, and he and Caitlyn jumped inside. Slade didn't wait even a second before he sped away.

"Who made the call?" Caitlyn fumbled with her seat belt and finally got it on.

"Don't know, but you gotta figure it was Curtis," Slade answered. "The call was made just seconds after he walked out of the meeting."

Hell, Harlan should have seen this one coming, but he'd figured that Curtis just wanted answers, too.

But maybe not.

"Curtis might have set us up," Harlan speculated. But he had to rethink that. If Curtis had simply wanted them arrested, he could have made the call before the meeting. In fact, he could have made it the moment he knew their location.

"Maybe Curtis wanted to find out what we knew." Caitlyn tossed out the words. "So he could either find Sherry or try to cover his tracks."

It was downright spooky how often they seemed to be on the same wavelength.

"So if Curtis is behind the attacks, then how does Tiffany's accident fit into all of this?" Slade asked.

"Maybe it doesn't fit, but Curtis could have used it," Harlan said and Caitlyn murmured an agreement. "Curtis would have known about the accident, and manufactured the threats and such to make it seem as if the two are connected."

In his experience people were often willing to do any-and everything to cover their tracks when a death was involved. But Harlan didn't want to start pointing the finger at Curtis simply because he'd called the authorities on them. And besides, maybe he hadn't.

Maybe it was Devin.

Before Harlan could even voice that, Slade's phone buzzed again. "Devin Mathis," he announced, and handed the phone to Harlan. Probably because Slade was practically flying down the country road.

"Marshal McKinney," Harlan answered, and he put it on speaker so Slade and Caitlyn could hear. "We're going to have to reschedule our meeting—"

"Maybe not," Devin answered. "In fact, I don't think we can reschedule. I'm still in town at the hotel and was on my way out the door for our meeting when I got a visitor."

Probably the Texas Rangers. It wouldn't be that much of a stretch for them to put a tail on Devin on the off chance that he could lead them to Caitlyn and him.

"He says it's important," Devin went on, "that he

needs to talk to you right away. And he doesn't want to go out to Rocky Creek to do it."

Surprise went through Caitlyn's eyes. "Is the guy's name Ranger Griffin Morris?"

"No," Devin immediately answered. "This guy's not a lawman. Says his name is Billy Webb."

Of all the names Harlan had expected Devin to say, that wasn't one of them. Half the state seemed to be looking for Billy, and here he'd shown up on Devin's doorstep.

"Why is he there, and what does he want?" Harlan asked.

"He won't tell me, but he says if you get here within thirty minutes, he can tell you everything he knows about what happened to his father."

CHAPTER TEN

CAITLYN BRACED HERSELF for Harlan to nix this meeting with Devin and Billy. He was operating on adrenaline now, making nonstop calls to set everything up. He clearly had a need to get whatever information Billy might have, but she figured any second Harlan would remember that she was in the truck with them and that it might not be *safe* for her to go face-to-face with Billy. And then Harlan would backtrack.

She hoped he didn't.

Because she was as anxious as Harlan and Slade to figure out what was going on. Maybe the info that Billy wanted to share with them wouldn't come with a huge price tag.

Harlan finished his latest call to Dallas, made a sweeping glance on both sides of the road leading into Rocky Creek. No one was following them, but the town was just ahead. Rocky Creek wasn't a big town, but there'd be people and traffic, both of which would make this trip hard on the nerves. Still, it had to be done.

"Dallas is on the way," he relayed to them. "I'll call the sheriff if things don't look right at the hotel."

"If you call him, he'll have to arrest us." The reminder wasn't necessary, but she said it anyway. Caitlyn didn't want to end up behind bars—that would put an end to this meeting in the worst way possible.

Well, one of the worst.

If Billy was a killer, then an arrest might be the least of their worries.

"Why the hell would Billy go to Devin?" Slade asked. He took the turn onto Main Street and drove toward the town center.

Caitlyn had already asked herself that question. Harlan, no doubt, too. "It only makes sense if he's connected to Tiffany or her car accident."

Harlan looked at her then, and she saw the trouble brewing in his eyes. "You'll wait in the truck with Slade. I'll go in and talk to Devin and Billy." And it wasn't exactly a suggestion.

"Billy might say things to me that he won't tell you," she fired back.

"Then those are things I won't get to hear, because you're not going anywhere near him."

So, this was the nixing that she'd braced herself for. Caitlyn tried to figure out a way around it—she really wanted to confront Billy face-to-face. But Harlan wasn't going to budge, and considering that Slade's expression was even steelier than usual, he was backing up Harlan on this.

"At least use your cell to call Slade, and then keep the phone on so I can listen that way."

If Harlan heard her suggestion, he didn't acknowledge it. He had his attention nailed to the hotel. During her days at the orphanage, the building had once been a private residence, but now it had been converted into a cozy bed-and-breakfast called the Bluebonnet Inn.

Slade came to a stop, not directly in front of the place but yards away. No sign of either Devin or Billy, but there were other vehicles parked on the street and two in the small heavily treed area on the far side of the inn. There was also a trickle of traffic in front of and behind them.

Too many places for someone to hide and wait to attack.

"Get down on the seat," Harlan warned her, and he eased his hand over his Glock before he opened the door.

"Be careful," she warned him right back.

But Harlan barely made it a step when the front door to the inn flew open, and Caitlyn saw a man run onto the porch. Not Billy, but Devin. She'd never actually met the man, but she'd seen plenty of photos, and he lived up to his rich preppy image in his khakis and white shirt. However, his expression wasn't preppy or rich but rather that of a concerned man.

"Billy left out back." Devin's voice wasn't a shout exactly, but it was close, and he pointed in the direction of the two vehicles beneath the sprawling oaks in the inn's parking lot. "That's his car."

Not exactly the economy vehicle she'd expected, but rather a Mercedes. Maybe Billy had come up in the world.

With his gun drawn, Slade stepped from the truck. "I'll go after him," he said to Harlan. "You wait here with Caitlyn."

Slade jumped the picket fence and hurried across the perfectly manicured lawn toward the cars, but Devin didn't follow him. He came down the steps and made a beeline for Harlan and her.

"Why did Billy leave?" Harlan asked. His tone wasn't friendly, and he, too, had his gun drawn.

Devin shook his head. His breath was gusting, and

his forehead was bunched up. "He got a call, and it must have spooked him or something. He didn't even say anything. He just started running."

Maybe a phone call from the person he was working with—or trying to set Billy up. Maybe even Farris.

Harlan volleyed his attention between Devin and Slade, all the while maneuvering himself so that he was in front of her. Protecting her. Caitlyn wasn't much of a damsel in distress, and she especially didn't like it when Harlan put himself in even more danger for her. She opened the glove compartment and found exactly what she expected to find there.

Slade's backup weapon.

She took it and got out, but she didn't move into the open. She might not be a damsel in distress, but she wasn't stupid either.

Harlan shot her a *get back in* glare, but she ignored it. "What did Billy plan to tell us?" she asked Devin.

She figured Devin would just shake his head, but he didn't. "He said he was being set up," Devin answered without taking his attention off the parking lot where Slade had now disappeared from sight. "He said someone planted his fingerprints on the threatening note left for you."

Caitlyn knew what that felt like, since someone had done the same to Harlan and her, but that didn't make Billy innocent. "How'd the person get his prints so he could do that?"

"He told me it could have even been something he actually touched. He remembers a waiter at a restaurant handing him a menu that had a piece of paper on the back of it to cover up some dishes that the waiter claimed were no longer available."

"Someone posed as a waiter to get his fingerprints?" Harlan didn't sound any more convinced than she was.

Devin nodded. "Billy said he took the menu, but after the waiter took his order, he didn't come back. He figured it was just lousy service and left, but now he's not so sure. He thinks it was a setup."

"Who did he say set him up?" Harlan asked.

Now Devin's gaze shifted to them. "You two. He thinks one of you helped his mother kill his father and now you're trying to cover your tracks."

Harlan mumbled the exact profanity that Caitlyn was thinking. "We're not the ones doing the setting up. We're on the receiving end of a scheme to make us look guilty as sin. We're not."

"Well, someone's behind this," Devin insisted. "And that someone likely murdered Tiffany."

Devin made it clear with his glare that he thought that the *someone* was Harlan and/or her. And Harlan made it clear with his glare that he was tired of being accused of something they hadn't done.

"I understand Tiffany and you didn't have an ideal engagement?" Harlan tossed out the words.

That put some starch in Devin's posture. "Are you accusing me of something?"

"Just asking a simple question. Generally I like simple answers to them."

"No, what you're looking for is a scapegoat." Devin stabbed his index finger toward Harlan's chest. "If you tie me to Tiffany's accident, then you can try and tie me to everything else that's happening. But I have no motive."

"Sure you do," Caitlyn challenged. "Tiffany was about to break off the engagement. It would have hu-

miliated you in front of your friends and family." That
was a stretch of the truth, but judging from the way
Devin's eyes narrowed, it hit a nerve.

His breath was gusting even harder now, and it took
Devin a moment to speak. "Let's just say for the sake
of argument that I did it. How the hell could that possibly connect to Billy Webb or the disappearance of this
other woman?"

Harlan shrugged. "Maybe you want to muddy the
waters."

"That doesn't make sense."

"It does if you manage to get suspicion off yourself
and onto someone else."

Devin opened his mouth, no doubt to return verbal
fire or at least deny it, but Slade came back into view.
He touched his hand to the hood of the Mercedes, said
something and hurried toward them.

"No sign of Billy," Slade grumbled, and he turned to
Devin. "How long ago did you say he arrived?"

"Right before I called you."

Slade shook his head. "Then something's not right,
because if Billy arrived fifteen minutes ago like you
said, the hood of his car should be hotter from the engine running."

That narrowed Devin's eyes again. "I'm sick and
tired of being accused of lying. For all I know Billy
could have been sitting out there for a while before he
came inside."

Harlan took a step closer to Devin. "And why would
he do that?"

"I don't know and I don't care. I came here to try to
help, but all of this has just convinced me that you or
one of your lawmen brothers left that threatening mes-

sage." Devin turned and headed for the inn. "If you want to speak to me about anything else, you can call my lawyer." He went inside and slammed the door behind him.

"That went well," Caitlyn mumbled. She glanced at Harlan and Slade. Then at the silver Mercedes. "You think Devin set all of this up, that maybe Billy was never even here?"

"It's possible." Harlan answered so quickly that he'd probably already come to the same conclusion. "It's also possible that Devin's calling the Rangers if he hasn't already. We need to leave now."

Harlan didn't wait. He took her by the arm, pushing her back into the truck. "If Devin is still here when Dallas arrives, he'll take him in for questioning."

That was something at least, but it didn't seem nearly enough.

Harlan had already started to get in when Caitlyn caught a movement by the Mercedes. A blur of motion.

"Is it Billy?" she asked.

Harlan didn't have time to answer because the blur of motion became a lot clearer. Someone wearing a ski mask. And that someone was armed.

He took aim at them and fired.

HARLAN'S HEART SLAMMED against his chest, and he threw himself onto the seat and in front of Caitlyn. It wasn't a second too soon, because the bullet blasted into the passenger's side window where he'd just been standing.

"Get us out of here!" Harlan told Slade.

His brother started the truck and threw it into gear just as a spray of bullets crashed through the front windshield. Slade had no choice but to get down. Harlan had to as well, and then a jolt knocked him forward, slamming his shoulder and head hard into the dash.

"What the heck was that?" Caitlyn hadn't collided with just the dash, but with Harlan, too.

Harlan's head was spinning from the impact, but from what he could tell, someone had crashed into their rear bumper. "Is it a second gunman?"

Slade sat up enough to look in his side mirror. "Don't think so. Looks like the driver got shot and lost control of the vehicle."

Hell. Just what they didn't need. An innocent bystander in this dangerous mix. It was bad enough that Caitlyn was here, but God knew how many people could be hurt. One way or another, Harlan had to stop the shooter.

Whoever he was.

From the glimpse he'd gotten of the man—and it was definitely a man—it could be any of their suspects: Curtis, Farris, Billy. Even Devin. He'd definitely had time to go back inside the inn, don a ski mask and head to the parking lot to fire those shots. Yeah, it'd be risky because someone inside could have seen him, but maybe Devin was desperate enough to try to cover his tracks.

With bullets, and lots of them.

Some of those bullets tore through the car on the street behind them again, and each shot echoed through him. Mercy. He hated that Caitlyn, he and now Slade were right in the middle of danger again.

"The sheriff will be here any second." Caitlyn was shaking and had a death grip on the gun she was holding.

But Harlan knew the fear wasn't just for the shooter.

It was also for the sheriff's arrival. Once he was on the scene, he'd have to arrest them.

The sound of sirens pierced through the gunfire. So did the shouts and screams of people nearby. People who'd hopefully taken cover. He didn't want anyone else hurt today, and the best way to make sure that happened for them was to get out of there. Without them, the shooter would have no targets. No reason to fire.

"Hold on," Slade warned them a split second before he hit the accelerator.

His brother stayed low in the seat, probably barely able to see over the dash. The truck lurched forward and plowed through the white picket fence that surrounded the inn, but it jarred to a stop because the tires bogged down in the soft ground and grass.

Oh, hell.

Now they were sitting ducks.

The shots didn't stop. In fact, they seemed to come at them even faster, each of them tearing through into the truck. Any one of the bullets could be lethal, and the only thing Harlan could do was keep his body over Caitlyn's to protect her as much as possible. If he lifted his head to return fire, he'd be shot and that would leave Slade to fight this battle on his own.

The sirens got closer, but Slade ignored them and kept pumping the gas to get them out of the bog. He gave the steering wheel a sharp turn to the left. The truck tore through yet more of the fence. Gate, too. But he managed to get even clearance from the vehicle that had collided with them. Slade peeled out onto the street and floored it.

The shooter gave them one last parting shot. A bullet slammed through the back window and sent a spray of safety glass onto them. Then, nothing. The rain of bullets finally stopped.

Harlan lifted his head enough to look out the side mirror. Thankfully, it was still intact, and he saw the swirling lights of a police cruiser headed right for the scene.

But he also saw something else.

A man running up the sidewalk away from the inn. Not a jog either. A full out-and-out run. Away from the truck and directly toward the police cruiser. The guy wasn't wearing a ski mask and wasn't carrying a gun, so Harlan couldn't tell if this was their shooter or not. The shooter could have easily ditched both ski mask and weapon to make himself look innocent.

Harlan wanted to turn around and go back to haul this guy in for questioning, but the sheriff must have had the same idea. The cruiser braked to a loud stop, the tires kicking up smoke on the asphalt, and Harlan caught just a glimpse of the two officers spilling out of the car and heading for the runner.

Slade didn't stop. Didn't slow down. He sped away. Of course, that didn't mean they were out of the woods. The sheriff had probably seen them leaving the scene. And if not, Devin or some other eyewitness would give him enough details so that he'd know exactly whom to arrest.

That ate away at Harlan.

He'd hoped this meeting would give them information to help their cause, but now it was just another note in their fugitive status. Worse, he'd entangled Slade in this now.

"We'll have to ditch the truck as soon as we can," Slade reminded them.

Just hearing the words hurt, too. Worse than any gunshot wound he'd ever had. Heck, they were acting like criminals, and even though an arrest would be bad, it couldn't be as bad as this.

Harlan glanced back in the mirror. "Turn around."

Caitlyn lifted her head, stared at him. "Have you lost your mind?"

"No. I've regained it. We'll just have to conduct the rest of this investigation behind bars. I want to go back, tell the sheriff what happened and check on the by-stander who might have been shot."

"Turn around," Harlan repeated when Slade kept staring at him, too.

Cursing, mumbling and sounding generally displeased with this notion, Slade hit the brakes and did a screeching U-turn in the road. "You'd better know what the hell you're doing," he added.

He did. It was the right thing. And no, it wouldn't be justice, since he and Caitlyn had been framed, but it was the only way he could live with himself.

Caitlyn huffed, sat up and pushed her hair from her face. "Always knew you were a Boy Scout." And it didn't sound like a compliment. Except after another huff, she leaned over, kissed his cheek. "I never was good at this running-from-the-law stuff either. Last time I did it, I ended up in reform school."

"Ditto," Slade growled. But unlike Caitlyn, he didn't seem nearly convinced that this was what they should be doing.

Harlan's phone buzzed, and he put the call on speaker when he saw Dallas's name on the screen. "We have a problem." Harlan greeted his brother.

"Yeah, I just heard. Someone tried to kill you. Wyatt's monitoring everything on the police radio, and I'm listening to it as it's happening," Dallas added. "I'm on my way to Rocky Creek now, not far out, so I should have some more details in the next half hour."

Good. They would need someone on their side at the police station. "We're on our way back, too."

Dallas didn't say anything for several moments. "Hold off on that and let me handle this. Caitlyn and you should go somewhere and wait."

"I don't want Slade in trouble for this," Harlan protested.

"He won't be. If someone sees the shot-up truck and reports it, I'll just tell the sheriff that I ordered Slade to get Caitlyn away from the scene. She's a civilian and doesn't need to be in the middle of a gunfight. I'll also convince the sheriff you went with them so Slade would have some backup in case Caitlyn was attacked again."

Harlan could hear the chatter from the police radio in the background. "Ranger Morris is calling in as we speak," Dallas continued, "and I want to find out what he has to say."

"But someone was shot at the scene," Harlan argued.

More radio chatter. "Yeah, and the sheriff is taking someone into custody."

The guy running from the scene, no doubt.

Caitlyn pulled in a hard breath. "Is it Devin Mathis?"

"No," Dallas answered. "According to the man's ID, it's Billy Webb."

CHAPTER ELEVEN

CAITLYN SANK ONTO the far end of the sofa at Declan's cabin and tried to focus on the lanky dark-haired man on the laptop screen.

Billy Webb.

Maybe he had the answers that would help them clear all of this up. Of course, he might only give them more questions, and that didn't help steady her any.

The cup of tea she'd just made herself was too strong and bitter, but she drank it anyway for the caffeine hit. She needed to be alert.

The wait and watch could go on for hours.

Maybe she wouldn't fall apart during that wait, but the odds weren't good. She already felt like one big raw nerve, and the images of the shooting just wouldn't stop. Hopefully, those images would end with their wait, and she could find some way to keep herself from losing it.

Some way that didn't involve leaning on Harlan's shoulders.

He hadn't offered his shoulder, and Caitlyn hadn't pushed. It would have been nice to be able to come unglued in his strong arms—even if that would only make things worse in the long run. Harlan didn't need her boo-hooing all over the place, and she didn't need to think of his arms as anything other than off-limits.

Despite the mental pep talk and her attempts to stop

it, Caitlyn felt tears burn her eyes, and she blinked them back, praying they didn't spill onto her cheeks. But they did, and when she went to swipe them away, Harlan looked at her.

"I'm okay," she quickly lied. He knew it was a lie, too, but he stayed put on his end of the sofa and fastened his attention back on the computer screen.

Thanks to Dallas, who was at the Rocky Creek sheriff's office, she and Harlan had not only visual but audio, as well. Ditto for his brothers back at the Maverick County marshals' office. All of them, including Slade, were tuned to it to see what Billy Webb had to say.

Or rather not say.

Because the only talking Billy had done was to ask for a lawyer.

Dallas hadn't mentioned to Sheriff Bruce Sheldon that the computer feed was also going to the cabin for Harlan and her to view. Probably for the best, since there was still a warrant out for their arrests. Though Harlan obviously didn't agree with her *for the best*.

His mood had been past the surly stage since Slade had dropped them off so he could head back to Rocky Creek and see if he could help. Like Harlan, Slade was a lawman to the core, and it was eating away at Harlan that the only thing he could do was sit, watch and stew. The only thing she could do was sit, watch and fight back tears.

"If we'd stayed, the gunman probably would have started firing more shots," she reminded him—again. "More people could have been hurt."

Or dead. They'd gotten lucky. According to Dallas,

there was only one wounded bystander, and he'd already been treated and released.

Harlan made a sound, sort of a grunt of disagreement.

He glanced at his phone. No messages or calls since the last time he'd checked a few minutes earlier, and he got up and went to the front window.

"If Billy moves, let me know," he grumbled.

But Billy didn't move. He sat at the table in the interview room, not looking especially concerned about anything. In fact, nothing about him was what Caitlyn had expected. The boy she remembered had been scared of his own shadow, but this Billy was, well, poised. The expensive-looking gray suit helped. So did the fashionable haircut. Definitely not the appearance of a man with mental issues or someone who'd been in hiding and off the grid.

And that in itself posed yet more questions.

Maybe Dallas would soon have some answers for them when he got back the results of the background check. Answers to questions like where had Billy been all this time. Why was he dressed like a business executive?

And had he been the one to shoot them?

He'd already submitted to a gunshot-residue test, and it had come back negative. That wasn't the only thing working in his favor of innocence. Dallas had already relayed to them that Billy had had no weapon on him when the sheriff had taken him into custody. Plus, there'd been no evidence in his car to prove he'd been the shooter or even part of the attack.

Maybe he wasn't. It was possible someone had set him up just as they'd done to Harlan and her.

Harlan did another phone check, huffed and leaned against the window frame. He was no doubt as exhausted as she was, but he didn't have the same weary look that Caitlyn was sure she had. He just looked, well, rumpled in his jeans and shirt. Of course, Harlan had a way of taking rumpled to a whole new level.

What the devil was she going to do about him?

They couldn't get within five feet of each other without touching or kissing. Good kissing, too. The kind that reminded her that she only wanted more from him, and more was something she was reasonably sure Harlan couldn't and wouldn't give her. Beneath all the rumpled hotness was still a nice guy who probably thought it best not to start something with her that he couldn't finish.

"I don't suppose it'd do any good if you tried to rest?" she suggested. "Might be a while before Billy's lawyer shows."

"Rest?" His left eyebrow rose.

Uh-oh. Did he think she meant *that* kind of rest? Maybe. Despite her teary red eyes, she was probably giving off weird vibes that his very male body had no trouble detecting.

"Could you rest?" And it sounded like a challenge coming from him. So, not *that* after all. He was just pointing out that neither of them would get much resting done until Billy did some talking.

Yes, it was going to be a long wait.

Or maybe not.

Harlan's phone finally buzzed, and he answered it so fast that it bobbled in his hand. "Dallas," he answered, and put the call on speaker.

Caitlyn set her tea aside and turned the laptop monitor in Harlan's direction so they wouldn't miss anything if Billy's lawyer showed. However, she also didn't want to miss any of this phone conversation, so she hurried closer to Harlan.

"Got the initial background check on Billy," Dallas started. "The clothes and car aren't an act. About ten years ago his paternal grandparents let him tap into a huge trust fund they'd set up for him, and he's been paying with cash this whole time. He's also been living in a house that's still in his grandmother's maiden name."

"Why didn't Billy's mother know any of this?" Harlan immediately asked. But he didn't wait for an answer. "Maybe she did and just didn't say."

Bingo. Of course, they couldn't ask her now because Sarah Webb was in a coma and might never wake up.

"Sarah could have lied about his whereabouts because she didn't want him to have to answer questions about that night," Dallas went on, "especially if he had anything to do with his father's murder."

Caitlyn tried not to huff, but she'd wanted more. Something that pointed the finger at Billy or else excluded him as a suspect. "Is there anything in Billy's background to indicate why he'd go after Harlan, me, Tiffany or Sherry?"

"Nothing." Dallas's sigh was louder than hers had been. "The fingerprint could have been gotten without his knowledge, as you two well know. And with no GSR on his hands and no solid evidence to point to him, I doubt the sheriff can hold Billy long. Heck, even Devin is saying he doesn't think Billy's the shooter, and he probably got the best look at the guy."

Interesting. Devin didn't seem like the good-hearted type to remove suspicion from a man he hardly knew.

Unless he did know him.

"Is it possible Devin and Billy were working together?" Caitlyn asked. "Because there was something...private in the threats I received."

She looked at Harlan at the same moment he looked at her. *You'll always be my first, Caitlyn.* Yes, definitely private and intimate. Too bad just the reminder brought back other recollections. Of that night. Of the recent kisses. Memories of everything she shouldn't be remembering.

Great. Her body reacted. The heat swirled through her. Slow and easy.

"Private?" Dallas questioned.

No way would she spell it out for him, so Caitlyn settled for an explanation that wouldn't make Harlan and her squirm. "Something that could have possibly been overheard by someone at Rocky Creek and then told to the person who's trying to kill us."

Dallas made a sound of agreement. "Someone like Billy. I'll look into that, but again, I doubt it'll be enough to hold him. I'll call you as soon as I have anything."

Harlan clicked the end-call button, and even though he didn't say anything, Caitlyn felt his frustration. It helped her a little because it kept her tears at bay. Tears and crying would only add to his frustration. Hers, too.

He made another of those sounds, part huff and part groan, and his gaze met hers. Her gaze of him was a little distorted, however, because she was literally seeing him through tear-speckled lashes. She didn't dare wipe her eyes again because it would only draw attention to something she didn't want him to notice.

"You should really think about getting some rest," he said. "You heard what Dallas said. Even when Billy's lawyer shows, it'll probably be just to get him released."

"And maybe a rightful release," she muttered.

He lifted his shoulder but didn't break the stare they had locked on each other. He did move, though. He reached up and brushed the pad of his thumb over those tears. "All those bad times at Rocky Creek, I never saw you cry."

"I'd rather have eaten glass. Tears are a sign of weakness."

Another shrug. "They're normal in situations like these."

"You aren't crying," she pointed out.

The corner of his mouth lifted just a fraction. "Wouldn't go with my image."

The corner of her mouth rose, too. Not a smile exactly. The fear and emotion from the shooting were too close to the surface for that, but it felt good to share a moment like this with Harlan. A moment that didn't involve her crying on his shoulder.

But the moment changed when he didn't pull back his hand. He kept it there. His fingers rested on her cheek while his heavy-lidded gaze melted all over her. Okay, the melting was her interpretation. Harlan certainly didn't look on the verge of kissing her again.

"Why me?" he asked.

Caitlyn blinked, shook her head.

"Why did you really give yourself to me at Rocky Creek?"

Oh. *That.* She didn't miss the *really* part of his question. After all, she'd already told him she had offered up her virginity because he was a good guy. That was true, but it was more than that.

"Why not Wyatt?" Harlan pushed. "He had the hots for you."

Caitlyn couldn't pretend that she hadn't noticed Wyatt's attention. She had. "Wyatt certainly had the looks," she confessed. "But you were the total package."

Ouch. That seemed way too relationship-y, and Harlan got that deer-caught-in-the-headlights look. Time to put this right back on him.

"Why me?" she fired back.

His hand moved from her cheek to her chin. So near her mouth. And his touch felt so good that she wanted to move into it. And maybe would have, but coming on the heels of her *total package* slip, the timing sucked.

He shook his head. "Doesn't work that way for a guy. You offered, and I accepted."

Now it was her turn to give him the skeptical eye. "Plenty of girls offered, not just at Rocky Creek but at the high school, too. The gossip mill worked pretty well in those days, so if you took up anyone else's offer other than Amy Simpson and that cute cross-country runner with the big boobs, I didn't hear about it."

And Caitlyn would almost certainly have heard, because she hadn't exactly hidden her feelings for Harlan. Also, since she was somewhat of a pariah, people would have loved to have thrown in her face the fact that Harlan was into someone else.

This time, the sound he made was of agreement. "Old water," he mumbled. "Old bridge."

"Yes, except this old water still feels…a little warm," she settled for saying.

The corner of his mouth lifted even higher, and while they truly had nothing to smile about, that helped with her raw nerves, too.

She figured that would do it. No way would Harlan keep touching her and staring at her after that comment.

Things were no doubt getting too *trip down memory lane* for him. But he surprised her—and judging from the profanity he mumbled, surprised himself—when he leaned in and put his mouth to hers.

That brief jolt of surprise vanished. Tears, too. In fact, it was as if his mouth took her on a supersonic ride to another place, another time.

Of course, it didn't stay just a kiss. They were stupid and weak when it came to each other. Caitlyn wrapped her arms around him, moved in closer and bam! She got what she'd been fantasying about but knowing it shouldn't happen. She got Harlan's shoulder, arms and chest.

Oh, and pretty much everything else, too.

Now body to body, they deepened the kiss, and the ache it created felt just as necessary as air.

The feeling only got worse when Harlan ran his hand between them, touching parts of her that were begging for attention. She remembered this touch. This raging insane need that he could create inside her.

Thank goodness oxygen soon became an issue, because they had to break the kiss and gulp in deep breaths. During those brief seconds their gazes met again, and Caitlyn was sure Harlan would realize the mistake they were making.

But nope.

They went right back to each other, the kiss even more intense. The touching harder and crazier. They grappled to get closer and knocked each other off balance. Harlan's shoulder slammed into the wall, but that still didn't loosen the grip they had on each other.

Or the precise alignment.

Harlan's beefcake chest gave her breasts some mind-blowing pressure. Ditto for the rest of him. Every part of them aligned so that his sex was against her. Yes, there were clothes between them, but she could still feel every last inch of him.

There was a serious problem with their being former lovers. Her body was trying to convince the rest of her that a round of quick sex with Harlan would be good for both of them.

Very good.

But afterward…well, afterward would be awkward and would likely put some distance between them. She didn't need distance when they were essentially fighting for their lives.

Caitlyn reminded herself of all that. Three times. And even though it took every ounce of willpower, she gripped him by the shoulders and pushed herself away from him.

Oh, mercy.

She instantly felt the loss, and regret of a different kind. The realization, too, that she was just as attracted to Harlan now as she had been sixteen years ago.

Caitlyn groaned. Stepped back even farther.

"I need to apologize," he mumbled.

She shook her head. "It's not that. I'm just trying to keep myself from going back for another round. Because we both know where this will lead if we keep kissing."

He stayed quiet a moment, giving that some thought, and giving her the look. The one that had melted her too many times to count. Caitlyn felt the tug, as if they were connected by a big rubber band that might snap her back to him at any second. And it probably would have.

If Harlan's phone hadn't buzzed.

Neither of them seemed relieved by the sound, but Caitlyn thought that later—when her body had cooled down some—they might be thankful for the interruption.

Might.

Harlan took out the phone. "It's Slade." And like the other call, he put this one on speaker.

"Hope you're sitting down," Slade immediately said, "because you're not going to believe what's just happened."

Caitlyn automatically groaned. Slade's tone always sounded the same to her—drenched in a gallon of gloom and doom—so she braced herself for more bad news.

"The Rangers killed the warrants for your arrest," Slade announced.

Harlan and she stared at each other, and even though it wasn't much to process, just one sentence, it didn't seem to make sense.

"Why?" they asked in unison.

"Still digging for the details, but whatever evidence they thought they had, it was discredited."

She shook her head. "How?"

"By someone unexpected. Farris."

That was the last name on earth she'd expected Slade to say. "How?" she repeated.

"Don't know all the facts there either, but what I do know is that Farris claims he sent those threatening emails to Sherry."

The surprise caused her stomach to flip-flop. Not that she'd thought for one second that Farris was innocent in all of this. Nope. But the surprise was that he would admit any wrongdoing.

And why would he?

"What does Farris want?" Caitlyn had meant the question more for herself than Slade.

"Who knows, but he's here at the Rocky Creek sheriff's office, and he's talking," Slade told her. "My advice? Since the law's not after you, both of you should get down here now and hear what this little viper has to say."

CHAPTER TWELVE

EVEN THOUGH CAITLYN and he were walking into the Rocky Creek sheriff's office, Harlan didn't exactly feel safe.

For a darn good reason.

They'd been shot at less than two miles from here.

Plus, they were about to face down two of the men who could be responsible for the shooting. Harlan wanted Caitlyn far from here, tucked away someplace safe. But someplace safe might not exist, and right now his best bet was to keep her by his side. He hoped like the devil that his decision didn't have anything to do with their recent kissing session.

But it probably did. And that riled him to the core. Attraction and kisses shouldn't be playing into any decision about her safety.

He got Caitlyn inside the building and immediately came face-to-face with not just Sheriff Sheldon but three uniformed deputies. Normally the uniforms wouldn't have made Harlan uneasy, but it had been less than a half hour since the Rangers had dropped the charges against Caitlyn and him. It might be a while before he trusted anyone with a badge unless it was one of his brothers.

And speaking of family, both Slade and Declan came up the side hall toward the reception area. Slade greeted them with his usual no-greeting that included zero change in his expression, but Declan's forehead bunched up, showing his concern.

"You two okay?" Declan asked, but his question seemed more for Caitlyn than Harlan.

Or maybe that was just Harlan's overactive imagination. He was still nursing a twinge of jealousy over the whispered conversation that Declan and she had had back at the hospital.

"Fine," Caitlyn lied, and she repeated it, sounding less of a lie when Declan gave her arm a gentle pat.

Harlan felt a rumble of jealousy over that, too, and wondered if he should just hit himself in the head with a big rock. It might knock some sense into him.

"Billy Webb's in the first room down the hall," Sheriff Sheldon informed them. "With his lawyer. That's my way of saying he's probably not gonna be talking much, but it doesn't matter, I guess, since we got nothing to hold him. He said he'd be leaving as soon as he spoke to you."

Well, at least Billy had waited around. Harlan didn't know if that proved his innocence or if he just didn't want to look guilty. "And what about Farris?"

The sheriff tipped his head toward the hall again. "He's in the room next to Billy Webb. No lawyer yet, but he's got a couple on the way. I figure he won't be leaving any time soon. It's gonna take us a while to sort through all of this, and the Rangers want to talk to him, too."

No surprise there. "I want to question Farris. You got any problems with that?"

Sheldon shook his head. "If you get him to confess to firing those shots, I want to know about it. Rocky

Creek ain't the wild, wild West, and I don't want any-body thinking they can come in here and start shoot-ing up the place."

Harlan doubted Farris would confess to anything that serious. In fact, this could all be part of the cat-and-mouse game he was playing with Caitlyn. Still, some-times people spilled things they didn't intend.

"There's a camera in the interview room," the sher-iff added. "Already turned on. I read Farris his rights, told him everything was on the record, so whatever he says I can and will use against him."

Harlan thanked Sheldon and considered asking Cait-lyn to wait with Slade or Declan. It would save her from facing down Farris again, but before Harlan could even make the suggestion, she was already walking in the direction of the interview rooms.

Harlan caught up with her, and they stopped in the doorway of the first room. The moment Billy spotted them he got to his feet.

"Caitlyn, Harlan," Billy greeted, and he came to them and shook their hands. His lawyer, a bald bulky man, got up, too, and stood behind him. "Wish this was under better circumstances," Billy added.

There was no trace of the stutter that Billy had once had. No trace of the painfully shy kid who'd kept to himself. Heck, he was wearing a Rolex, for heaven's sake, and from the looks of it, he'd had a recent mani-cure.

Yeah, he'd come up in the world, all right.

But Harlan knew that money didn't make a man in-nocent.

"You think Devin Mathis set up the shooting?" Billy came right out and asked.

Harlan had to shrug. "Who set up the meeting—you or Devin?"

"I did, but he'd been trying to find me for weeks. Even hired a P.I. So did Sherry's business partner, Curtis Newell." Billy looked at Caitlyn then. "And you."

She confirmed that with a nod. "A lot of people have been looking for you, especially me. Any reason you didn't want to be found?"

"I have a new life now," he said without hesitation. "I didn't want to get caught up in the old memories and a past I'd rather just forget."

"But something changed your mind," Harlan pointed out.

"Yes." He gave a weary sigh. "I started reading about the investigation of my father's death. About Tiffany's car accident and Sherry's disappearance. I didn't think it was a coincidence that those things were happening so soon after my mother's…incident at your family's ranch."

The *incident* had nearly killed Harlan's brother Dallas and Dallas's wife, Joelle. Sarah Webb had hired armed men to make sure no one uncovered the fact that she'd murdered her husband. Sarah had been seriously injured in the attack that she'd orchestrated and had lapsed into a coma before she could name her accomplice.

Was Harlan now looking at that accomplice?

"Who helped your mother kill your father?" Harlan asked.

"I honestly don't know, but it wasn't me." Again Billy didn't hesitate. "If you remember correctly, I didn't have much of a backbone in those days."

Caitlyn stared at him. "Or maybe you did. Webb was

beating your mother nearly every time his temper blew, and from what I remember, it happened often. You must have wanted to see him get his due."

Billy shrugged. "I didn't say I didn't have motive. I did. Just like the rest of you. My father had gotten approval to keep Rocky Creek open, and none of you wanted that—especially Kirby. Plus, Declan had been on the receiving end of Dad's fists that day. Joelle, too, if I remember correctly. All of that is motive for wanting him dead."

Harlan couldn't argue with any of it. Joelle had been a resident at Rocky Creek, and Webb had slapped her for some piddly infraction. Dallas and Joelle were just teenagers then, like the rest of his foster brothers, but they'd also been lovers. And Dallas was beyond protective of her, giving him a big reason to go after Webb.

But Harlan figured someone beat Dallas to it and put that knife in Webb.

The only thing Harlan was certain of was he hadn't killed the headmaster, and he was sure Caitlyn hadn't been involved either. For argument's sake, if he ruled out members of his family—and he intended to do that whether he should or not—that left Billy, Devin and Curtis.

Maybe Sherry, too, if she'd faked her disappearance.

Harlan took a business card from his wallet and wrote down the number for the prepaid cell he was still using. "Call me if you find out anything."

"I will." Billy took out a card, too. "And I ask you to do the same for me." He pulled in a long breath. "My father was a despicable man and deserved to die, but I've spent a decade and a half getting away from the muck that he caused in my life and others'. I don't want to be pulled back into it. That's why it's important that *I* find whoever's behind these attacks so my name will be cleared."

"I?" Harlan challenged. He didn't like the sound of that. "What are you planning to do?"

"Something that should have been done years ago. I intend to find the person responsible for my father's death."

Billy didn't wait for Harlan to respond to that. He eased past them, barely sparing them a glance, and he and his lawyer walked away.

"You believe him?" Caitlyn asked before they were even out of earshot.

Harlan had to shake his head. Billy was the obvious suspect in his father's death, and that made him the obvious suspect in any cover-up.

If that was what was going on.

But Billy wasn't the one who'd confessed to any wrongdoing. That honor fell to Jay Farris.

"I'm going in there," Caitlyn said before Harlan could offer to do the interview alone. She leaned in, lowered her voice to a whisper. "I can't let him know how much he still scares me."

Oh, man. Harlan gave her arm a rub as Declan had done, but when that didn't work, he dropped a kiss on her cheek. The fear was in her eyes again, probably because she hadn't had time to recover from the last attack. Now here she was about to face down someone who'd tried to kill her.

Maybe more than once.

"Besides," she added, "if Farris tries to strangle me again, I fully expect you to beat the living daylights out of him. Yes, I know that sounds sexist, but you're bigger than I am and can do a lot more damage. Promise me, if it comes down to it, you'll do *damage*."

He couldn't help it. He smiled. "I promise." In fact, Harlan almost welcomed it. He had a lot of dangerous energy boiling inside him, and he figured Farris better not push any of his buttons or he'd be on the receiving end of that energy.

Harlan opened the interview-room door, and unlike Billy, Farris didn't jump to his feet. He sat there, his face buried in his hands. "I'm so sorry, Caitlyn."

Harlan wasn't interested in an apology, and apparently neither was Caitlyn. She folded her arms over her chest. "Start talking, and explain the threatening notes and how you were able to discredit that so-called evidence."

Taking his time, Farris lowered his hands. "You should probably sit down."

"Start talking," she repeated. It wasn't a suggestion either.

Farris reached inside his pants pocket and pulled out a handful of paper. Not neatly folded—it looked as if he'd crammed it in there.

"My instructions," Farris explained, which didn't explain anything.

Harlan went closer and looked at the first note, which was handwritten in block letters. *Leave this for Caitlyn to find.*

"There was a note attached to it," Farris went on, "the one that warned her if she talked to the Rangers she'd be sorry." He fished out another note. "This one was attached to the one that said she'd die if she talked to them."

Harlan riffled through the others. If he followed Farris's explanation, then one of them would have been attached to the note that included the very private sentence—*you'll always be my first.*

"I didn't know where Caitlyn was, but this person knew—one of the notes had her address. Still, I didn't want to leave those threats for her to find," Farris went on. "I knew they'd upset her."

Caitlyn gave him a flat look. "And you expect me to believe that my being upset would bother you?"

Farris opened his mouth, but then his attention landed on Harlan, specifically how close he was standing to Caitlyn. Farris's gaze darted away but not before he swallowed hard. "It would have bothered me. Whether you believe it or not, I didn't want to torment you."

"But you did," she fired back.

"Only because I got that note." Farris jabbed his index finger at the papers.

Harlan didn't need to ask for clarification as to which note Farris meant, because it had already caught Harlan's attention. "'Do as I say, or you and Caitlyn will both die.'"

Farris nodded. "And with everything else going on, I didn't think it was a bluff."

"Who sent these to you?" Harlan didn't bother to sound as if he believed Farris. Because he didn't. Farris could have written all the notes himself and could have hired someone to find Caitlyn.

"I don't know who sent them, but whoever it was killed my dog, slashed my tires and vandalized my place. Then I got this note." He plucked another one from the stash. "It said if I didn't do as I was told, then the order releasing me from the institution would be revoked and I'd have to go back in. He—or she—said that's where they'd kill me."

Harlan studied his body language. It was right for someone who was genuinely upset, but Farris was likely a nutcase, which meant he could probably lie and not have any of the telltale signs.

"Ranger Morris will want to see all those notes," Harlan reminded Farris. If the man objected to that, he didn't show it either. "For now, talk to us about the evidence that you supposedly refuted."

"I disproved it," Farris corrected. Another gaze dodge. In Harlan's experience, that wasn't a good sign. "One of the notes said to hack into Sherry's computer and make it appear that Caitlyn and you had done it."

Caitlyn made a sound of surprise. "How'd you do that?"

"I'm good with computers." Farris's tone was somewhat defensive now, but he still didn't make direct eye contact. "Good at hacking," he mumbled. "My family owns a software business, and I've always helped. And as for setting you up, I just used your own personal computers."

"How?" Harlan demanded. "And if you say you broke into my house—"

"I didn't. Not yours anyway, but I did break into Caitlyn's once I had her address, and I used her computer so it could be traced back to her."

Harlan saw the goose bumps riffled over her arms. Yeah, that was a major creep factor to have her stalker, the SOB who'd tried to strangle her, break into her home.

"I didn't think it'd be easy or wise to get into your place." Farris glanced at Harlan. "So I made it look as if I'd used your computer. It was good enough to fool the Rangers anyway."

Caitlyn muttered some profanity and shifted her position so that she was even closer to him. Harlan figured it would just rile Farris even further or set him off, but after all the violations Farris had just confessed to, that seemed like a plus. So Harlan slid his arm around Caitlyn's waist and eased her to him. Until they were side by side, facing down this SOB who'd made their lives miserable.

"If I hadn't told the Rangers what I'd done, they'd still be after you." And Farris's eyes narrowed when he said that.

"If you hadn't lied in the first place, the Rangers would have had no reason to suspect us." Harlan didn't intend to give this guy any credit for clearing up something he'd helped set up.

"Did this note writer ever contact you personally?" Harlan asked.

"No. Just through the notes." Farris hesitated. "But I figured it was one of you. Or maybe Devin or Curtis. I don't have a motive to kill Tiffany in a fake car accident."

"You didn't have a motive to set me up," Harlan reminded him. "Other than the so-called threats you received. But you did it anyway."

"Wait a minute." Farris jumped to his feet. "You think I killed Tiffany? I didn't," he insisted before Harlan could answer. "I figure she was a pawn, just like I was."

Harlan gave that pawn theory some thought. Not Farris as a pawn but Tiffany as one. Maybe she had been if her fiancé, Devin, had murdered her and then tried to fix it so that it appeared connected to Rocky Creek.

"What about Sherry?" Caitlyn pressed. "Is she a pawn, too?"

"I don't know." With his mini fit of temper apparently exhausted, Farris sank back onto the chair. "But I found some strange things when I hacked into her computer."

"Like what?" And Harlan hoped whatever it was, Farris had kept copies, because Curtis had already told them that Sherry's hard drive had been wiped clean.

"She had notes, like a computer diary or something." Eyes still narrowed, he looked at Caitlyn. "Sherry wrote that she'd overheard you and Harlan that night in the basement."

Harlan felt the muscles in her body jerk. His probably did, too. *"That night?"* But he already knew what Farris meant.

"She said she was looking for a place to have a smoke, and she heard what you said to Caitlyn. Afterward. The line you said about her being your first."

Not a line, but Harlan had no intention of correcting him. At least now they knew who at Rocky Creek had overheard them. So did that mean Sherry had written those threatening notes? Harlan glanced at Caitlyn and saw the same question in her eyes.

"What else was in Sherry's files?" Caitlyn asked.

"That's just it—nothing that I would expect to find there. No files about her business or anyone else personal in her life. It was all about Tiffany's car accident and how she wondered if it was connected to Webb's murder."

Yeah, that was suspicious. Unless Sherry really was guilty and had done that to cover her tracks.

Harlan heard the rapidly approaching footsteps and automatically stepped in front of Caitlyn. He also put his hand over his weapon. But it was a false alarm of sorts.

"We're Jay Farris's attorneys," the man in the lead said. "And this interview ends now."

Farris only shrugged and tipped his head to the camera mounted in the corner. "That'll need to be turned off, too." His eyes were certainly no longer narrowed, and he seemed in complete control. In fact, he had the smug look of a man who'd accomplished his mission.

Whatever the hell that was.

Had all of this been some kind of act?

"Harlan can't protect you, you know." Farris had his attention pinned to Caitlyn now. "That's why I told you all about the notes and everything this person has made me do. I believe him when he says he'll kill you. And if you stay with Harlan, you'll both end up dead."

Harlan walked closer, stared down at Farris. "Is that a threat?"

"A warning." Farris lowered his voice to a whisper. "Whoever's behind this is smart, and if he or she can't use me to deliver threats and hack into computers, then they'll find someone else. Probably already has."

Harlan would have liked to dispute that, but he was afraid it was the truth. And that meant he had to get to the bottom of this fast—especially if Farris couldn't be connected to any of the violent things that had happened. If the Rangers could tie him only to the notes and the computer hacking, then he'd be released on bond. *Soon.*

One of the lawyers made an impatient sound and

motioned for Caitlyn and him to leave. Harlan obliged. Caitlyn was trembling, and the sooner he got her away from Farris, the better. He didn't want her to have to face the sheriff and the others while she was still composing herself, so Harlan led her into the now empty interview room where they'd talked with Billy.

"I'm a mess." Caitlyn swiped away a tear that slid down her cheek. "I'm scared. I can't think straight." Her gaze whipped to his. "And I really wanted an excuse for you to beat Farris to a pulp."

"The day's not over." He meant that to try to move things in a lighter direction, but it didn't work.

Harlan made a mental note to pick a fight with Farris first chance he got. No, it wasn't very lawman-like, but he hated seeing Caitlyn like this and wanted to do whatever it took to ease that tension from her body and face.

That caused him to freeze.

Oh, hell. He wasn't thinking straight either, and he knew exactly what was to blame. "Maybe we should just have sex and get it over with."

Okay. He clearly hadn't thought that through and should have kept that little suggestion to himself. Caitlyn stared at him. Blinked.

Then she smiled.

So maybe it had been worth sticking his foot in his mouth after all.

"We should have sex here?" Her mouth quivered again, and she slipped into his arms.

He made a show of looking at the hard tiled floor and table. It was to be part of the joke, but Harlan felt his body tense. Oh, man. Sexual jokes were never a good idea when it came to Caitlyn.

"Sorry, didn't mean to interrupt...anything," Declan said.

Harlan and she practically flew apart, and both cursed. No doubt because neither of them had heard anyone step into the doorway of the room. A big reminder that he should be thinking with his head.

"What do you want?" Harlan snapped.

"Probably not the same thing you do." Declan winked at Caitlyn. "Just have to tell you that I'm heading back to Maverick Springs." He tipped his fingers to the brim of his Stetson in a mock salute and strolled away.

That dangerous energy inside him hadn't lessened much, and for reasons he didn't want to explore, this whole winking and whispering with Declan was getting to him.

Okay, he did want to explore it.

"What's going on between Declan and you?" Yet another thing he should have thought through before opening his mouth.

"What do you mean?" And it sounded like a genuine question.

Too bad, because Harlan figured it'd make him sound like a jealous fool when he clarified it. "The whispering in the hospital parking lot."

"Oh, that." She shrugged but generally looked uncomfortable. "It's just an old bad joke."

And again she didn't offer to share it.

Probably for the best, especially since his phone buzzed. He didn't want to talk to anyone right now. Not until he saw the name on the screen.

Billy.

Harlan immediately got a bad feeling about this. "Anything wrong?" he greeted Billy. He didn't put the call on speaker, but Caitlyn moved her ear close enough to hear.

"Plenty. You need to get out to the Rocky Creek facility now." Billy's words raced together. "There's been another murder."

CHAPTER THIRTEEN

CAITLYN HADN'T THOUGHT this day could possibly get any worse, but she'd obviously been wrong.

"Who's been murdered?" Harlan asked Billy.

No answer.

Harlan got the same result when he tried again. Either Billy had hung up or the call had dropped. Of course, there was a third possibility. The worst of the scenarios.

Maybe Billy wasn't in any shape to answer.

Harlan hung up and jabbed the redial button. Caitlyn moved even closer to him, until they were breath to breath, but there was nothing to hear except for the call going to voice mail.

Mercy. She hoped Billy was okay, and while she was hoping, she added the hope that the man wasn't lying. She didn't know why he would, but with all the other crazy things happening, anything was possible.

Harlan hurried back into the main area of the sheriff's office. "Billy Webb just called and said someone was murdered out at Rocky Creek."

"You can ride out with me," Slade offered, and then headed outside, toward his truck that was parked just ahead of Harlan's. This one didn't have any bullet damage, so Slade must have traded out vehicles after the attack.

Declan had already left, but the sheriff and one of the deputies grabbed their hats and hurried to a cruiser in the side parking lot.

Harlan opened the passenger door of Slade's truck, but then stopped and looked at her. "This could be dangerous."

"I know." She climbed onto the seat anyway. "But I'd rather risk going to Rocky Creek with you than stay here at the sheriff's office with Farris."

No way could he argue with that. Besides, from what she could tell, there was only one deputy left to keep watch over Farris.

Yeah, the odds were much better with Harlan.

She slid over, and Harlan got in so that Slade could start the engine and speed away. Harlan tried Billy's number again but still no answer.

The sun had already started to dip low in the sky, and the twilight and darkness wouldn't make this trip easier—especially if the lawmen had to chase down a killer.

Slade sped over the country road, the sheriff's cruiser with the lights and siren going right behind them. Caitlyn was so caught up in the tenseness of the moment that she nearly jumped out of her skin when she felt someone touch her.

But it was Harlan.

A reassuring touch, too. He slid his hand over hers. It instantly made things better. And worse. Because this attraction going on between them was getting just as complicated as the investigation.

Caitlyn groaned. "You asked what the whispering between Declan and me was about. Well, I told you it was nothing, and it was. But I don't think you believed me."

Harlan looked at her if she'd lost it. Heck, maybe she had, but telling him that embarrassing inside joke was better than thinking about all the other things that were making her crazy. Like wondering who'd been murdered and why Billy wasn't answering his phone.

"Declan knew how I felt about you and used to tease me," she continued before Harlan said anything. "He'd come up to me at random places and times and whisper in my ear, 'Are you still crushing on Harlan?' My answer was always the same—'Am I still breathing?'"

Harlan's wide eyes took on a poleaxed expression that even the meager light couldn't cover.

Slade cleared his throat. "I can't exactly step out while you two talk," he complained. "And I really don't want to hear this."

Fair enough. It was on the personal side, even if it happened to be the silly musings of a teenage girl. It was right up there with the boy-band magazines she'd read so many times she'd memorized them.

"Why are you telling me this now?" Harlan demanded. "Do you think we're about to die or something?"

"Maybe," she admitted. That wasn't something they could totally dismiss. After all, someone had already tried to kill them twice, and as Harlan had pointed out, the day wasn't quite over yet. "But I also didn't want you to think I was keeping secrets."

"Like the article you were writing on Kirby," Slade challenged.

"Caitlyn axed that article," Harlan tossed out just as fast.

It had cost him to defend her and Caitlyn appreciated it. However, she knew it was motivated by the attraction. But even a strong attraction wasn't going to smooth over the differences between Harlan and her.

Would that stop them from landing in bed?

No.

But it would basically ensure that she'd get a broken heart out of this. In the grand scheme of things that was better than dying, but it was a sad day in a woman's life when it came down to those two options.

Slade turned onto the road toward Rocky Creek. Not cloaked in darkness, thank goodness. There were plenty of security lights blazing, and when the building came into view, Caitlyn immediately spotted not one car but two. One of them belonged to Billy, and she recognized another as Curtis's.

"What the hell is going on?" Harlan mumbled, and he tried Billy's phone again. Still no answer.

Before Slade and the cruiser even pulled to a stop, Curtis got out. Not alone either. He had his bodyguard with him—the same man who'd been with him when he'd visited Harlan and her.

But Billy wasn't in his vehicle.

It was empty, and the driver's door was wide-open. Worse, the repeated beeping sound let her know that the key was still in the ignition. Headlights on, too. Whatever had gone on here, it appeared that Billy had made a hasty exit.

And not a voluntary one.

"What happened?" Harlan asked Curtis the moment he got out. He drew his gun just as the sheriff and deputy did when they hurried from the cruiser. "Where's Billy Webb? And who was murdered?"

"Murdered?" Curtis repeated. The shock in his voice

made it seem as if he was hearing this for the first time. And maybe he was.

"Billy didn't say anything about anyone being murdered." Curtis was trying to catch his breath, and he motioned for his bodyguard to move closer to him. "Billy called me about a half hour ago and asked me to meet him here."

Caitlyn got out of the truck as well, but when she tried to go closer to the men, Harlan blocked her path. He scanned the area and positioned himself in front of her like a sentry.

"And you came because Billy asked?" Caitlyn didn't know if he was lying or just plain stupid. "There's a killer on the loose." Heck, maybe Curtis himself, and if so that would explain why he hadn't been afraid that he might die out here.

Of course, the same could be said for Billy.

"Where's Billy?" Harlan demanded.

"Don't know. We just got here a few minutes ago, and we found his car like this. He's not answering his phone either."

"How in the name of heaven did Billy convince you to come out here?" she asked.

Curtis cursed, but not at them. He cursed himself. "Billy said he was meeting someone who had answers about Sherry's disappearance. I need answers, and he sounded as if he had them. Besides, Sherry always said she liked Billy, that he was a good kid. I thought I could trust him."

"My advice? Don't trust anyone," Harlan warned. He looked back at her. "Stay put, and if anything goes wrong, get inside the truck."

She nodded, only because she didn't want an argument to distract him from finding the person Billy claimed had been murdered. Still, she didn't want Harlan headed into those woods.

But that was exactly the direction he went.

Slade stayed with her, taking over protection detail, but Harlan looked at the ground around Billy's car and started walking toward a thick cluster of trees on the east side of the property. Thankfully, he didn't go alone. Both Sheriff Sheldon and the deputy followed.

"I want a gun," she whispered to Slade. She figured he had some kind of backup on him. He stared at her, debating what to do, and finally reached into the back waist of his jeans and pulled out a small pistol.

"I was wrong to trust Billy, wasn't I?" But Curtis didn't wait for an answer. "Is he a killer? Is he the one behind all these bad things that have been happening?"

"I don't know." But considering that Billy wasn't answering his phone and was nowhere in sight, it was just as likely that Billy had been the victim of foul play.

Curtis hitched his thumb to the building. "Can we at least go inside and wait? I feel like a sitting duck out here."

"The door's got a lock on it," his bodyguard observed.

Harlan had a key, or at least he'd had one for their earlier visit. But then Caitlyn remembered that he hadn't locked it when they'd run out of there after someone—maybe Curtis—had called the Rangers on them.

"So who locked it?" She glanced back at Slade.

But Slade just lifted his shoulder. "Not me. Maybe the groundskeeper, Rudy Simmons, is back from his trip."

Caitlyn remembered the man, but he hadn't been there during their earlier visit. However, he could be the one Billy had called about. Maybe Billy had found the man's body, but that didn't answer the question of where Billy had gone.

And had he been forced to make a hasty exit from his vehicle?

Her heart began to bang against her chest when Harlan and the other lawmen disappeared into the woods. After the past two days of nothing but danger and chaos, she should have been numb to it by now, but Harlan and numb didn't go together.

There was no sound, no warning, but the security lights suddenly went out. Before Caitlyn could even react, Slade latched on to her, swinging her between him and the truck seat, and raised his gun.

"Harlan?" she shouted.

No answer. She braced herself for the sound of shots. For anything. But nothing happened.

Her heart was past the pounding stage now, and everything inside her screamed for her to run and help Harlan, but Slade kept her pinned in place.

Her eyes adjusted to the pitchy darkness, and thanks to the lights from Billy's car, she had no trouble seeing Curtis and his bodyguard. Both had weapons drawn, too. But the one person she couldn't see was Harlan.

"He could be ambushed." Her voice didn't have much sound, but Slade must have heard it.

"Harlan?" Slade called.

The moments crawled by, and Caitlyn hadn't thought that silence could terrify her any more than she already was, but it did. She couldn't just stand there if Harlan was in some kind of danger.

"I have to go," she told Slade, and she made sure it didn't sound like a suggestion.

That earned her another glare from him. Some profanity, too. But he started moving along with her. "Stay behind me and try not to get killed."

Not exactly a friendly invitation, but she'd take what she could get. Caitlyn stayed right with Slade as he made his way to the woods. Not a speedy trip, though, because he kept looking back at Curtis and his bodyguard. Caitlyn did, too, but neither man made an attempt to follow them. In fact, they got back inside their car.

Each step seemed to take a lifetime, but Slade didn't run. He inched along, his gaze snapping all around them. Caitlyn kept watch, too, but by the time she made it to the trees, the worst-case scenarios were starting to smother her.

Until she heard Harlan.

He whispered something she didn't understand, and before she actually saw him, his hand snaked out from the tree and he jerked her toward him. It was too dark for her to see his expression, but he put his mouth to her ear.

"Shhh." And Harlan tipped his head toward their right.

Caitlyn followed his gaze and saw a faint light in the distance. Maybe a flashlight, but if so, it was on the ground, and if someone was holding it, the person didn't seem to be moving.

Was it Billy?

And if he wasn't moving, did that mean he'd been hurt or even killed?

Harlan motioned for Slade to move behind her. He did, and along with the sheriff and deputy, they began to make their way toward the light. Above them a breeze was rattling the leaves just enough that it made it harder for Caitlyn to hear. Maybe those leaves and the breeze wouldn't mask the footsteps of anyone trying to sneak up on them.

They were still a good ten yards away from the light when Harlan's phone buzzed. Mumbling some profanity about the bad timing, he took out his cell, the screen like a beacon in the darkness.

"It's Billy," Harlan relayed to them in a whisper. He didn't put the call on speaker but Caitlyn stayed close enough to hear.

"Someone tried to kill me," Billy blurted out.

Mercy. That was not what she wanted to hear. It meant the killer was still out here in these woods.

"Where are you?" Harlan asked. He got them moving again.

"By the creek. Right after I talked to you, someone fired a shot at me. That's when I ran."

Caitlyn couldn't be sure, but she thought she actually heard the rushing creek water in the background. She certainly heard the fear in Billy's voice.

"I dropped my flashlight in the woods." Billy moaned. "By the body."

"Whose body?" Harlan demanded.

Billy made another sound as if he'd sucked in his breath. "I hear footsteps."

And with that, the call ended.

"Head to the creek," Harlan told Slade. "Take the deputy with you."

Slade didn't question his brother's order and neither did the deputy. As she watched them hurry away, however, Caitlyn had a sickening thought.

What if Billy had set all of this up?

What if he'd done this to separate them so he could pick them off one by one?

Maybe there'd been no murder—only the ones that Billy was planning now. Their murders. But Caitlyn wouldn't just let Billy or anyone else kill them without a fight. Thank God she'd gotten the gun from Slade.

Harlan pushed aside a low-hanging tree branch, and from over his shoulder Caitlyn spotted the flashlight on the ground amid some weeds. The lines of light sprayed out like fingers and moved with each new brush from the breeze.

Then Caitlyn saw the body.

There went her theory about no murder. The person was in a heap facedown.

The three of them moved forward in unison. Not much they could tell, though, because the person was wearing a raincoat and slicker-style hat.

"Keep watch," Harlan reminded them, and he stooped to touch his fingers to the person's neck.

Almost immediately he drew back his hand. "Dead."

Caitlyn's breath swooshed out. She'd hoped this was a false alarm, but no such luck. And she seriously doubted that it was the killer dead on the ground.

No.

This was another victim.

Harlan didn't touch the rest of the body or the flashlight, but he pushed the button on his phone to illuminate the screen so he could lower it to the face.

Even with the angle and the hat, Caitlyn could see the person's features, and she staggered back.

God.

Sherry Summers was no longer missing. She was dead.

CHAPTER FOURTEEN

HARLAN WAS GLAD it was close to midnight, because that meant this hellish day would soon be over.

Finally.

There was no way of knowing if tomorrow would be equally hellish, but anything short of death and serious injury would be an improvement.

"Anything new?" Caitlyn asked. She stood in the doorway of his home office sipping a longneck beer that she'd snagged from his fridge.

Nothing new that he wanted to relay to her, so he settled for a grunt that could have meant anything.

She'd showered. He caught a whiff of his soap. Shampoo, too. But they seemed to smell a lot better on her than they'd ever smelled on him.

"It's my last change of clothes," she mumbled, glancing down at her jeans and white camisole.

It took Harlan a moment to realize why she'd volunteered that. Because he was looking her over from head to toe. Actually, he was past the looking stage and had progressed to gawking, so he forced himself to glance away. Not that it would help. Her image was branded in his head. Her taste, too.

Heck, plain and simple, he was just branded all over when it came to Caitlyn.

That wasn't a news flash to either of them. She had

yet to step into his office since they'd arrived back at his house. In fact, she'd pretty much avoided getting anywhere near him.

Maybe because she felt as he did. If they touched, the hellish day might come crashing down on them.

Harlan wasn't sure what the result of the crashing might be—maybe sex or a good falling apart—but the latter seemed a lot to risk with the exhaustion already closing in.

Even though every bone and muscle in his body was yelling for him to get some sleep, he continued to scroll through the reports and emails he was getting about the investigation. Everyone seemed to be in on it. The marshals. Rangers. The locals from Rocky Creek. The governor was even asking questions, because Sherry's body had been found on state-owned property. So Harlan read them all, not liking much of what he was reading.

Farris was already out of jail on bond. Lots of money and good lawyers could manage that even for a man who should be locked away for life.

Billy was in hospital being treated for a gunshot wound to the arm. It wasn't serious, but the man had been so shaken up that he'd required some sedation. However, he'd be released soon.

Devin was nowhere to be found, and Curtis had had a major meltdown when he'd seen Sherry's body. According to his lawyer, Curtis was so distraught, he wouldn't be able to answer questions for a while.

Caitlyn cleared her throat, grabbing his attention again. "How'd Sherry die?"

Oh, it was going to hurt to say this and hurt even more for her to hear it. "She'd been strangled."

Caitlyn clamped her teeth over her bottom lip, but

not before she made a helpless little sound. Harlan could almost see the memories of Farris's attack zooming through her head.

"Farris could have done it," she choked out.

Yeah, Farris could have indeed killed Sherry, and his motive might be all mixed together with his obsession with Caitlyn. "We won't know for a while, but the ME thinks Sherry could have been dead for days."

Hell, maybe even weeks, because when Harlan had touched her, she'd felt ice-cold, as if her body had been frozen and then partially thawed. That meant any of their suspects could have killed her at any time, and their alibis were out the window.

"Did Billy happen to say how he knew the body was there?" Still holding the nearly full bottle of beer in her hand, Caitlyn reached down, pulled off her shoes and rubbed her feet. It seemed, well, normal except her hands were trembling.

"He said, but it didn't make a lot of sense." Harlan was hoping he could blame that on the sedative Billy had been given. "He claims he was out at Rocky Creek just to look around and maybe talk to the groundskeeper, and then he heard something in the woods and went to have a look. That's when he found the body."

"*Claims?* You don't believe him."

Harlan had to shrug. "As far as I'm concerned, he's still a suspect."

"Along with Devin, Curtis and Farris." The next sound she made was one of pure frustration.

She bobbled, nearly lost her footing and Harlan stood to catch her. However, Caitlyn waved him off and slid down to a sitting position on the floor. "I'd love to lean on you tonight, but we both know it'd lead straight to the bed."

Since it had already crossed his mind—many times—he hadn't expected her *stating the obvious* comment to hit him like a sucker punch. But he actually lost his breath for a moment. Not a very manly reaction, which was weird, because everything else about his reaction was manly times a thousand. His body sure wasn't going to let him forget that if he pushed this, just a little, he could have Caitlyn in his bed.

Or on his office floor.

The corner of her mouth lifted. "Face it, we're too tired for sex anyway."

"No such thing."

She laughed. It was smoky and thick and laced with the fatigue that had obviously made them both punchy. "What we need is to catch the killer, get some rest and then…go out to dinner or something."

"I'd prefer the sex. But dinner's a good start."

He stood there, watching her and wondering how long it was going to take him to get on the floor with her. But a thought stopped him, and he mentally repeated what she'd just said.

Catch the killer.

The only way that was going to happen was to flush him out.

Caitlyn tilted her head, studied him. "That doesn't seem like a foreplay kind of look in your eyes."

"It's not." And while it hurt to say that, he saw a glimmer of hope. A way of maybe ending the danger so that he and Caitlyn could, well, *have dinner.*

"What are you doing?" she asked when he took out his phone.

"Putting out some bait."

He called the marshals' office, and Slade answered. Obviously, Caitlyn and he weren't the only ones not getting any sleep tonight.

"Nothing to update," Slade immediately volunteered. "How about you?"

"No, and that's why I want to shake things up. I need something leaked, but I want it to come from the marshals so it looks official."

"I can send it from my work computer. What you want leaked?"

"A lie," Harlan readily admitted. "You okay with that?"

Slade just grunted. "What's the lie?"

"That the ME found something on Sherry's body. A partial fingerprint on the back of her neck that's consistent with the ligature marks from the strangulation that caused her death. And I want you to say that the Rangers are sending someone to the morgue first thing in the morning so the print can be retrieved and processed."

Slade stayed quiet a moment. "Most people know that it's hard as hell to retrieve a fingerprint from a body."

"Hard but not impossible. All I need is for Sherry's killer to have enough concern that he'll try to do something to cover up that print."

And not something that involved Caitlyn and him either. Nor anyone in his family.

"Guess this means you'll want someone watching the morgue?" Slade clarified.

"Oh, yeah. And I don't want the ME or anyone else in the building."

"No one's over there anyway this time of night. Not even a security guard, but they do have an alarm."

"Keep it on and have someone in place to watch all entrances and exits before you send out the leak. You got the manpower for that?"

"I can find it." Slade didn't hesitate. "I'll call you when I have something."

Caitlyn got to her feet and scrubbed her hand down the side of her jeans. "If it's Farris, he'll hire someone to destroy the evidence."

Harlan agreed. Billy likely would, too. And that left Devin and Curtis. He didn't know them well, but if they were behind these deaths, he doubted either would want evidence to convict them.

Of course, even if they managed to make an arrest, it still meant unraveling all the threatening notes, Farris's computer-hacking adventures, Tiffany's car accident, their own kidnapping and the shootings.

"What now?" Caitlyn asked.

"Now we wait." Harlan checked the time. "You should get some rest," he reminded her again. Reminded himself, too.

But he didn't move. Couldn't. And he swore that someone had cemented his feet to the floor.

"Do we really want to do this?" she asked, her voice all warm and breathy.

Since he was a guy, his body wasn't going to let him think long and hard about a question like that. So he just jumped right into the mistake they'd be making no matter how much thought he gave it.

Harlan reached out, hooked his arm around her waist and pulled her to him. The problem was she didn't even put up a token resistance or offer any other questions

that might force him to think. Then he kissed her and
forgot all about questions and common sense. Forgot
all about the other things he should be doing.

Hell, he forgot how to breathe.

Everything hit him at once. The feel of her in his
arms. The way she fit against his body. Her taste. Yeah,
especially that. Some women just tasted good, and Caitlyn tasted better than good.

She made a little purring sound deep in her throat
that stalled his breath, and she coiled her arms around
him. Soon they were plastered against each other. Until
his body started to remind him just how much better
this kiss would be if he stripped off Caitlyn's clothes
and kissed every inch of her body.

Caitlyn clearly had the same idea, because she went
after his shirt. And she wasn't very good at it. She
tugged, pulled, catching his chest hair. It didn't cool
him down one bit, and he finally let go of her for just
a second so he could shuck the shirt off over his head.

Her eyes lit up, she smiled and she looked at his chest
as if she planned to have him for dinner. Harlan figured
he was looking at her the same darn way.

While she kissed his chest, touched him and generally made him hot and crazy, Harlan rid her of her
own top. Her bra was lace and white. Barely there. But
it was too much between them, so he quickly rid her of
it and did some payback. He dropped lower and kissed
her breasts.

A lot.

"Yes," she mumbled. "And so help me, you'd better
not call this off when your conscience kicks in."

He lifted his head so he could give her a flat look,

took her hand and pressed it to the front of his jeans. "Does it feel like I'll call it off?"

Her next smile had a touch of the devil in it. "No." She shoved down his zipper and put her hand inside. Not just inside his jeans either. She might have fumbled with the shirt, but she found her way into his boxers without a problem and latched on to his erection.

Harlan was sure his eyes crossed.

"Hell," he muttered. And while he could still walk, he scooped her up and headed for his bedroom.

"Not up for sex on the floor?" she teased. Tormented, too, because while his hands were occupied with carrying her, she kept touching him. Kept driving him crazy. Until he dropped her onto the bed, yanked off his boots and settled on top of her.

Harlan grabbed her jeans and pulled them off. Panties, too. He saw the tiny white scars on her belly and some letters tattooed on her left hip.

She followed his gaze to what had snagged his attention. "I had navel rings. Relics from my wild-child days."

Now all hidden away for him to rediscover. That sent a rush of fire through him, but he stopped when he looked at the letters again.

H. M.

"Harlan McKinney," she provided.

"You had my initials tattooed on your body?" He felt his mouth drop open.

"Hey, a girl's first time is a big deal, and I didn't have enough money to put your whole name there."

He was touched. And sad that she'd obviously thought so much of him.

"No trips down memory lane," she insisted, and

kissed him so hard and deep that memory lane vanished.

Harlan kissed her right back. Not just her mouth either. But her breasts again. Her belly. Yeah, the tat. Before he went even lower and kissed her in the hottest, wettest part of her body.

"We didn't do this at Rocky Creek." She made a sound of pleasure and wound one hand into his hair. Her other hand clamped onto the bedding as if she was trying to anchor herself.

"We didn't do a lot of things."

Like go back for seconds, something that Harlan thought he might like to do tonight, especially since it was clear that this wasn't going to last nearly as long as he wanted.

"I want you naked," he heard her say a split second before she gave his hair a yank.

That got him moving up her body again. Caitlyn used her hands and feet to slide off his jeans and boxers, and even with all that moving around and adjusting, she still managed to get in some pretty potent kisses. She also pulled him on top of her.

Exactly where he wanted to be.

But thankfully all his common sense wasn't gone, because he fumbled in the nightstand drawer, located a condom and somehow managed to get the darn thing on even with Caitlyn pulling and tugging at him.

"No virgin surprises this time," he heard her whisper.

But the jolt was still there when he pushed inside her. Pure pleasure. There went his breath again, and he didn't care if he ever got it back. The only thing that mattered now was moving inside her and finding the release for the powder keg of pressure roaring through every inch of him.

Caitlyn was clearly on the same page when it came to pressure and release. She lifted her hips. Dug her fingers into his back. And met him thrust for thrust.

He felt the climax ripple through her body. Saw it, too, in the depths of her crystal-blue eyes. Heard it in her uneven breath. She mumbled something.

His name, he realized.

With his name still shaping her lips, she pulled him down to her. And kissed him.

Harlan returned the kiss. Hard and deep. And with Caitlyn's taste in his mouth, he let her take him to the only place he wanted to go.

CAITLYN WONDERED WHY she was still so wide-awake when she desperately needed sleep. She'd dozed on and off, but that was about it.

Her body was slack from the great sex, and she had a nice little sexual buzz still going on. Plus, she was in Harlan's bed snuggled in his arms while he snoozed away.

It should have been a perfect recipe for sleep.

If she could only turn off her mind.

For the first time in days, it wasn't the investigation that was weighing her down. Nor was it the sex or the anticipation of it. It was the consequences of sex that troubled her now. Harlan would regret it. Not the act itself, but he would likely feel as if he owed her something.

Like dinner.

Or dates.

He knew that she wouldn't expect anything from

him. After all, she hadn't so much as whimpered when they'd parted company sixteen years ago.

Well, she hadn't whimpered in front of him anyway.

But she had spent plenty of nights sobbing her eyes out for a boy she thought was so far above her that she would only pull him down into the gutter with her. But now there was no bad-girl gutter, just the massive differences in their chosen careers.

But after sex, even that didn't feel like an obstacle.

And that was why even if Harlan knew he didn't owe her, he would feel as if he did. Because he was a good man to the very core. She'd known that sixteen years ago, and she certainly knew it now.

"Don't you ever stop thinking?" he mumbled.

She looked down at him as he peeked out at her from one partially opened eye. "You can hear me think?"

"Pretty much." He hauled her closer, chest to chest, and tucked her head beneath his chin. "Other than your navel, what else did you have pierced?"

Caitlyn couldn't help it—she smiled. "You don't want to know."

Harlan pulled back, met her gaze. "Now I really want to know."

Mercy, he was even hotter post-sex with that rumpled black hair and sleepy gray bedroom eyes.

"I had my nose pierced." Caitlyn touched the spot that had long since healed. "My eyebrow." Also healed. "And my earlobes." She still had double sets of those, but once there had been a quadruple line of piercings.

He stared at her, obviously waiting. "Nothing else?"

"Sorry to ruin your erotic fantasies."

"Nothing's ruined." He ran his thumb over her bottom lip. "So, what were you thinking so hard about?"

Uh-oh.

Here it came. The dreaded relationship conversation. Caitlyn figured Harlan wasn't any better at this than she was. She also figured it was a conversation he didn't even want to have. She sure didn't.

"I was planning our wedding." And she didn't crack a smile when she said it.

That got his eyes wide-open.

Now she smiled. "Wait. Did I say wedding? I meant our next round of this." She slid her hand between them and touched, touched, touched. "Actually, I was thinking you've gotten really good at sex."

"So have you." Harlan pulled her back to him for a kiss, and just like that she was all hot again.

Sheez.

She wasn't a teenager, but she was acting and feeling like one.

The kissing continued. Not fast and frantic like before. But slow and lazy. Oh, yes. This time there'd be foreplay, and even though she'd just had Harlan, she wanted him and the foreplay all over again.

"Do I owe you an apology? A heart-to-heart talk?" Even with his mouth on hers, she could feel his smile. "Or an engagement ring?"

She smiled, too. "I'll settle for what you're doing right now."

But the last word had barely left her mouth when Harlan's phone buzzed.

He cursed, got up and located his jeans on the floor. Not easy to do, since every item of their clothing was scattered around. Still naked, he took out the phone and jabbed the button to answer it.

Harlan's back was to her, but Caitlyn could see the

anger over the interruption drain from his body. He turned and met her gaze, and she saw that the anger had been replaced by serious concern.

"Who?" Harlan snapped. But he obviously didn't get an answer, because he repeated it until he was practically shouting into the phone.

That got Caitlyn moving, and while she tried to hear what was going on, she snatched up her clothes and started dressing. "What happened?" she asked the second Harlan ended the call. He, too, put on his jeans.

"That was Billy. He said someone's kidnapped him. The person dragged him from his car and took him to Rocky Creek."

Her stomach went to her knees. Not only because she was concerned for Billy but because she knew this meant Harlan had to respond.

"Who did this?" she asked.

But Harlan shook his head and tugged on his boots. "Billy said it was someone wearing a ski mask."

Which told them nothing, because it could be any of their suspects.

Including Billy himself.

"Billy said if I brought anyone else to Rocky Creek, the kidnapper warned him that he'd start shooting." Harlan pressed a button on his phone, sandwiched the cell between his shoulder and ear and kept dressing at a frantic pace. As if every second counted.

And it probably did.

"It could be a trap." But she knew Harlan had no doubt already considered that.

"I'm sure of it, but I have no choice. I have to go."

It was his job, yes, but Caitlyn wanted to grab him and make him stay put.

"Slade," Harlan said when his brother came on the line. "We got a huge problem. Someone's kidnapped Billy. And Declan."

"Declan?" Caitlyn said on a gasp. Oh, God.

"Yeah, Declan," Harlan verified and went back to his phone conversation with Slade. "We have to get out to Rocky Creek right away."

CHAPTER FIFTEEN

EVERYTHING INSIDE HARLAN was racing—the bad thoughts and the fear for his brother's life. But he forced himself to think. He couldn't go off half-cocked when all of this could be a trap. One that could get Caitlyn, Declan, Billy, him and God knew who else killed.

First things first. He tried to call Declan, hanging on to the hope that this was all a hoax, that Declan would answer and assure him that he hadn't been kidnapped.

But the call went straight to voice mail.

Next up, he tried the number Billy had just used to call him. No answer there either.

That got Harlan moving even faster, and he grabbed some extra ammunition from the top shelf of his closet. An extra weapon, too, so he'd have a backup.

"Declan's really been taken?" Caitlyn asked. There was little color in her face now, and her hands were trembling.

"Probably." And Harlan could blame himself for that. "I shouldn't have planted the lie about the fingerprint."

Her shoulders went back. "You had no idea this monster would go after Declan."

No, but he should have anticipated it. He'd counted heavily on the guy trying to destroy the so-called fingerprint evidence. And maybe that was still the plan. The killer could be using Declan as a distraction.

Harlan made another call—this time to Slade. "Make sure you keep someone at the morgue."

Slade assured him that he would, and Harlan quickly ended the call so he could head out. "I'll take you to stay with Kirby and Stella—"

"I can help."

He took her by the arm and got her moving. "You can also get killed. Don't argue, because this isn't up for discussion. You'll stay with Stella, Kirby and Wyatt. The ranch hands will be around, too, and all of them know how to shoot."

"You really think the killer would come here?"

No. He didn't. And that was why Harlan had come up with this plan to leave her here. There were a dozen ranch hands plus Wyatt. The main house had a brand-new security system, something that just about everyone in town was talking about. The killer would know this wasn't the place for a showdown. Besides, killing them wouldn't destroy the evidence.

Unless the killer knew the fingerprint was fake.

That put a hard knot in his gut, but Harlan didn't back down on his plan. He led Caitlyn through his house and to the front door. His truck was parked just on the other side of the fence. Just a few yards away. But he didn't go barreling out into the darkness. He took a few precious seconds to look around. He didn't see anyone lurking in the shadows, but that didn't mean someone wasn't there.

"Wait here," he ordered and hurried out the door.

He braced himself for shots. For anything. But nothing happened, thank God.

Harlan jumped into his truck, started it and backed up enough so he could drive through the fence. The wood pickets went flying, and he stopped directly in front of the steps. He threw open the passenger door.

Even though Caitlyn was visibly shaken, she got moving when he motioned for her to get in. The second she was on the seat, she slammed the door, and he sped away. Toward the main house that was about a quarter of a mile away.

He took out his phone again to call Stella and tell her what was going on, but before he could press in her number, his cell buzzed, and he saw Billy's number on the screen. That didn't help the knot in his stomach. Yeah, he needed to talk to Billy, but he hoped like the devil that the man wasn't about to deliver some bad news.

"The kidnapper gave me a written message to pass on to you," Billy said.

"Who is he, and why the hell doesn't he tell me himself?" Harlan fired back.

"I don't know who he is, but I think he wants me to talk to you so you won't hear his voice. He says you have to bring Caitlyn with you."

Harlan didn't even have to think about it. "No way."

"If you don't, he'll kill Declan."

It was a good thing he'd reached the ranch house and could come to a stop. "Tell the kidnapper to let me talk to Declan," Harlan insisted. Because even though it wasn't something he could accept, he had to know if his brother was still alive. "Now!" he added when he didn't get an immediate response.

There were some sounds of the phone being moved around, and the seconds crawled by. Caitlyn sucked in her breath and scrambled across the seat until her ear was pressed right to his.

"Harlan," he finally heard Declan say.

Relief flooded through him. Fear, too. His brother was alive, and now he had to figure out how to keep it that way. "What happened?"

"I'm sorry. So sorry." Declan sounded drunk. Or rather drugged. "I was in the parking lot at work and someone hit me with a Taser."

Just as the killer had done to Caitlyn and him. "Are you okay?" And now it was Harlan's turn to hold his breath.

"He gave me something, some kind of drug, and I don't even think I can stand up."

Harlan knew the exact feeling. "Who took you?"

"None of our suspects. This guy's a hired gun, and the person who hired him is staying out of the picture."

Or maybe was elsewhere so he could attack. After all, Declan wasn't the primary target. Now the question was—had the killer used Declan to draw them out to Rocky Creek, or was this some kind of distraction to launch another attack? Or maybe a break-in at the morgue?

"I'll kill him." From the other end of the line, the voice tore through the silence, and it wasn't Declan or Billy. In fact, Harlan didn't think he'd ever heard that voice before.

"Who are you?" Harlan demanded.

"Someone who's going to kill your kid brother if you don't do as I say. And I'll keep killing until Caitlyn and you are out here. You've got forty-five minutes."

His heart dropped. "Not enough time." And Harlan didn't mean just distancewise either. It wasn't enough time for him to think up a way around this.

"Then you'll have to hurry, won't you?" the man

taunted. "And remember, don't bring anyone with you or the bullets start flying. Just Caitlyn and you."

"Wait." Harlan tried to think. "It'd be suicide for me to take Caitlyn in there. What kind of assurance do I have that you won't just kill us all?"

"None," the man readily answered. "But if you don't come, people are going to start dying."

Harlan had no trouble recognizing the next sound. The blast of a gunshot. Even though the sound came through the phone, it was still deafening, and it rocketed through him.

"Declan?" he shouted.

But Harlan was talking to himself, because the line went dead.

CAITLYN HAD TO make Harlan understand what needed to happen here. "There's no way I'll let you sacrifice Declan for me."

Even though her voice was shaking like the rest of her, she left no room for argument. Still, she saw the argument in Harlan's eyes.

"Declan's a lawman." He sounded as if he was trying to convince himself along with her. "I can figure a way out of this."

"And if you show up without me, you could all be dead before you have time to think of it." In fact, someone might already be dead.

That possibility twisted everything inside her.

She tried to reassure herself that the kidnapper wouldn't kill Declan, because he was the bait. The bargaining tool, as well. But it was possible that Billy had been shot or was already dead.

Unless, of course, Billy was behind this.

"We're wasting precious time," Caitlyn reminded him. "Start driving to Rocky Creek."

But he didn't. Harlan sat there, his attention volleying between her and the ranch house, where he'd intended to leave her.

"Look, we'll work out the details as we drive," she added. "And if by the time we get there you don't think you can make it safe, then you can drop me off at the sheriff's office in Rocky Creek."

That caused him to belt out some really bad profanity, but he threw the truck into gear and started driving. Thank God. Caitlyn certainly wasn't eager to rush to a showdown with this monster who'd made their lives hell, but she couldn't live with herself if she got Declan killed.

Harlan took out his phone and sped down the dark country road away from the ranch. "Slade," he said when his brother answered. "There's been a change of plans. Caitlyn and I are driving to the Rocky Creek Children's Facility."

She couldn't hear Slade's response.

"No, it's probably not a good idea," Harlan added to whatever Slade said, "but if I leave Caitlyn at the ranch, she'll try to follow."

She would, no doubt about it, and it was scary that Harlan knew her so well.

"Keep someone on the morgue," Harlan continued, "but we'll need backup. *Quiet* backup," he amended. "You remember how to get to Rocky Creek from that old ranch road?" He paused. "Good. Take that route and try to come up from behind. I don't know where they're holding Declan, but it's probably either inside the main building or close to it."

He finished that call and immediately made another to Dallas so he could ask about how tight the security was at the ranch. "Just a precaution," Harlan said to her when he no doubt saw the renewed concern in her eyes.

The next call was to his brother Clayton. After Harlan gave him a quick update, he asked him to do a quiet approach to the facility using the east side of the property. The woods where Sherry's body had been found. Harlan also reminded Clayton that Slade would be nearby, probably so they wouldn't accidentally shoot each other.

There was a lot of potential for things to go wrong.

"What about me? What do you need me to do?" she asked the moment he ended the call with Clayton.

But Harlan didn't answer. He kept driving and punched in another number. This time he put the call on speaker. However, the person who answered didn't say anything either.

"Billy?" Harlan greeted. "Are you there?" Nothing. But Caitlyn thought she could hear someone breathing on the other end of the line. "Billy, I need to talk to the man who kidnapped Declan."

"What the hell do you want?" The man's voice was so loud that Caitlyn jumped before she could stop herself. And it wasn't Billy. It was Declan's kidnapper.

"I need to work out some kind of deal," Harlan said.

"The only deal you're going to get is the one I already gave you. You and Caitlyn need to get out here and come alone. Nothing about that needs to be worked out."

"But it does." Harlan glanced at her, and even though he didn't say anything to her, he shook his head. "Caitlyn's sick, throwing up all over the place. I don't even think she can stand up."

That explained the headshake. He didn't want her jumping to say that she'd be there. Still, Caitlyn doubted the lie would work, especially since this guy likely had plans to kill them.

"She's pregnant," Harlan added. "We started seeing each other a couple of months ago. In secret. I didn't want to tell my family or anyone else because of this Webb investigation hanging over us. Talk to your boss, because I don't think he'd want to put a pregnant woman in the middle of a mess like this."

She figured the guy would just laugh that off, but he stayed quiet for several moments. "I'll get back to you on that."

Harlan punched the end-call button. "If he agrees, you're going to the sheriff's office." He mumbled something she didn't catch. "And if he doesn't agree, then it's probably Farris who's behind this."

Oh, yes. Because a pregnancy would only make Farris want to kill her even more. But if it was Billy, Devin or Curtis, why did they even want Harlan and her?

"Why would the killer want us dead if he still believes there's an incriminating fingerprint on Sherry's body?" she asked.

Harlan shook his head. "I'm not sure how any of this fits. Or if it fits at all. It could be just Farris playing a sick game."

For a moment Caitlyn thought she might indeed throw up. Her stomach was churning. "And if so, then you just made yourself a target, because Farris will think you fathered this make-believe baby. He'll be so enraged that he'll want to tear you apart."

"Hopefully. Anything to make him come after me and not Declan and you."

That turned her blood to ice. No way did she want Harlan to take the brunt of this, but how could she stop it?

How?

Maybe if she had a chance to speak to Farris, she could bargain with him. Maybe even make him believe that she'd go with him if he'd just call off this stupid plan. Of course, she couldn't go with him because he'd likely just kill her the first chance he got. But she might be able to buy them some time so that Harlan could rescue Declan, and maybe even Billy.

Harlan swore and looked at the phone screen as if trying to will the kidnapper to call back. The minutes and miles were just dissolving, and Harlan's mood got worse when the headlights landed on the sign ahead of them.

Rocky Creek Children's Facility.

He took the turn, but he switched off his headlights.

"I want a gun," Caitlyn insisted.

Harlan tipped his head to the glove compartment. "There's one in there."

Caitlyn opened it and pushed aside some plastic handcuffs and papers so she could grab the .38. She prayed she wouldn't have to use it, especially since she wasn't that good a shot. If it came down to her having to take out the killer and the kidnapper, then she and Harlan would be in deeper trouble than they already were.

Harlan pressed the redial button on his phone and again put the call on speaker.

"No deal," the kidnapper said the moment he answered. "You bring Caitlyn here with you."

Thanks to the moonlight, she got a glimpse of Harlan's jaw muscles that had turned to steel. "I want to talk to your boss, and I'm not taking no for an answer."

Harlan took the final turn, and ahead Caitlyn could see the silhouette of the sprawling facility. It looked even more menacing in the dark, and even though she didn't have second thoughts about coming here, Harlan apparently did.

He stopped the truck.

"You'll have to take no for an answer," the kidnapper insisted. "My boss is, well, indisposed right now."

Maybe because he was at the morgue trying to destroy evidence that didn't exist. If so, it was possible that whoever Slade had watching the place would capture him. And if not, that meant someone had to nab this kidnapper and get him to confess the name of the person who'd hired him.

Not exactly an easy night's work.

"Call him," Harlan insisted. "Tell him I'm not bringing Caitlyn unless he speaks to me." With that line drawn in the sand, Harlan hung up.

And the waiting began.

So did Caitlyn's renewed attempts to get Harlan to budge. "Stating the obvious here, but I don't want you to risk Declan's life for me. Besides, Farris won't just kill me once I step from the truck. He'll want…some time with me," Caitlyn settled for saying.

There went her stomach again. Another lurch. Mercy, she didn't want Farris within a hundred miles of her, but using herself as bait was the only way to reason with him.

"And if it's not Farris?" Harlan's question hung in the air, and he turned his head so their gazes met. "This person could want us dead simply because he thinks we've uncovered something that'll incriminate him as Webb's killer."

Yes, she'd considered that, but she could almost feel Farris nearby. It didn't make sense, and she wasn't the sort to rely on gut feelings or intuition, but she couldn't dismiss the feeling that Farris had some part in this.

She checked the time on the dash clock. Time was almost up. Well, it was if they were to believe the kidnapper's ultimatum that they had to arrive within forty-five minutes.

"What happens if he doesn't call back?" she asked.

Harlan opened his mouth to answer, but then he stopped. His gaze slashed to her side of the truck. Except his attention didn't land on her, but outside the window.

"Get down!" he shouted, and he drew his gun.

He didn't wait for her to move. Harlan caught the back of her neck and shoved her down onto the seat.

CHAPTER SIXTEEN

HARLAN BRACED HIMSELF for an attack, for bullets to come bashing through the truck. He kept his gun aimed and ready while he pinned Caitlyn beneath him.

But nothing happened.

It was hard to hear over his own pulse pounding in his ears and Caitlyn's ragged breathing, but he damn sure didn't hear any bullets. He lifted his head so he could try to get a better look at the shadowy figure that he'd seen just seconds earlier.

"Stay down." Caitlyn latched on to him and tried to pull him back onto the seat with her.

"I think he's gone," Harlan let her know.

"Who was it?"

He had to shake his head, but it wouldn't have been Slade or Clayton. If they'd somehow managed to get out here ahead of him, they wouldn't be in this area of the grounds. Maybe it hadn't been the kidnapper either, because there was a huge possibility that the killer had hired more than one henchman. God knew how many hired guns Caitlyn and he would have to face, and that was the biggest reason of all for him to throw the truck into gear and haul her butt to the sheriff's office. It had been a huge mistake bringing her here.

"Declan," she reminded him.

He wasn't about to let his kid brother die, but he was

pretty sure Declan and he were of a like mind on this. Neither would want to sacrifice Caitlyn to save themselves. Of course, Caitlyn was insisting the same thing about them.

Harlan waited, and the seconds seemed to be flying by. He took out his phone again to call the kidnapper, but he also moved off Caitlyn so he could put the truck in gear. He spared her a glance to see how she was holding up—not well—but then he kept his attention pinned to their surroundings. Hard to do with the moon creating some eerie shadows over the trees and shrubs.

He pushed the redial button. And waited. Waited some more. Until he thought his heart might beat out of his chest. Everything inside him yelled for him to get Caitlyn out of there, so he threw the truck into Reverse. Maybe the kidnapper would see that he was leaving and answer the damn call.

Or not.

Harlan had barely touched his foot to the accelerator when the blast came. He didn't see the shooter, but he felt the impact, all right. The bullet slammed into the front windshield, taking out the safety glass and zinging past his head.

Caitlyn screamed for him to get down, and he did. Harlan also gunned the engine and tried to put some distance between them and the shooter.

More shots came.

Not just one either, but bullets began to pelt the truck. Whoever was shooting at them was almost directly ahead, maybe behind one of the trees that was close to the road.

Since Harlan couldn't lift his head enough to see where he was going, he tried to do the best he could to keep the truck on the road. He also fired a blind shot in the direction of the shooter in the hopes that he'd get lucky. Or at least get the guy to duck behind cover.

It didn't work.

The shots didn't slow down one bit, and it didn't take long before the truck jolted. And Harlan knew why. The gunman had shot out the front tire. Maybe both of them. Harlan lost what little control he had of the steering wheel, and they slammed into the ditch.

With the impact, both Caitlyn and he flew into the dash. His shoulder hit the steering wheel, and by some miracle he managed to hang on to his gun. However, Caitlyn wasn't so lucky. He heard the heavy jolt her body took, and even though she immediately tried to scramble to get her gun, Harlan didn't think it would be easy to find in the darkness and with all hell breaking loose.

More bullets came, and even though he tried to steer the truck, things went from bad to worse when he realized they couldn't move. They'd landed in a ditch filled with several inches of water. Just enough to bog down the tires on the driver's side of the truck.

A bullet crashed through the passenger's window, and even though Caitlyn was still searching for her gun, the sheet of safety glass crashed against her head.

Hell. The shooter had moved, maybe closing in on them from the right. He couldn't just sit there while they were gunned down. The metal exterior of the truck wouldn't keep them safe much longer. Maybe his brothers would arrive soon, hear the shots and give him some backup.

Harlan fired a shot in the direction of the shooter, and in the same motion he threw open his door. Not easy, because he had to push the bottom of the door through the boggy ditch. However, he finally got it open wide enough that he could get Caitlyn out of there.

"This way." He reached across the seat and hauled her closer.

Caitlyn continued to fumble for the gun and grabbed it just before Harlan dragged her out with him. Both of them stepped into the ditch. Definitely not dry. It was filled with stagnant water and clotted mud, and he sank all the way to his knees.

He used the door for cover and kept track of the angle of the bullets. They were still coming from the other side of the truck. Good. Maybe they'd stay that way at least for a few more seconds.

"Move fast," Harlan warned her, and he stepped out of the ditch, pulling her along with him.

He didn't even try to stay on his feet, because it would make them too easy a target. With Caitlyn in tow, Harlan dove behind the nearest tree. They hit the ground hard, and he landed right on the same shoulder that had slammed into the dash. The pain shot through him, but he ignored it and came up ready to fire.

Harlan pulled the trigger, the bullet landing somewhere in the direction of the shooter. He waited to see if the guy would move and come after them.

But nothing.

No more shots.

Harlan drew Caitlyn even closer until he had her pressed against the tree. She, too, had her gun aimed across the road where the shooter had fired his last shot, but all that either of them could do was keep their aim ready and listen for any sound of movement.

Nothing.

Where the devil was this guy?

Harlan glanced up the road at the building. Still no sign of anyone there, not even any vehicles. Not that he'd expected the kidnapper to have Declan in plain sight, but he hoped that his brother wasn't anywhere in the line of fire.

Caitlyn was trembling now, and her breath was gusting to the point that he was worried she might hyperventilate. He didn't want to say anything out loud for fear it would help the shooter pinpoint them, but Harlan did brush his lips on her temple. It wasn't much, but it was the best he could offer for now. Once he got her out of this, though, he'd owe her a huge apology for nearly getting her killed.

That thought had no sooner crossed his mind when he finally heard something. Definitely not a shot.

But footsteps.

Not coming from the front of the truck either, but from the back.

Harlan moved again, pushing Caitlyn behind him so he could face the person making those footsteps. The person wasn't exactly skulking and was coming at them fast. Maybe it was one of his brothers trying to make enough noise so that Harlan wouldn't shoot first.

Even though Harlan couldn't actually see Caitlyn, he felt her adjust, and she moved her gun into position, too. They waited, breaths held.

They didn't have to wait long.

The person came out from the back of the truck. Running. Harlan couldn't make out who the guy was before he launched himself at Caitlyn and him.

BEFORE CAITLYN COULD get out of the way, the man plowed into them, knocking Harlan, her and himself to the ground. Once again she lost the grip on the gun and it went flying. Too bad she couldn't have flown with it, because both men crashed right down onto her.

Suddenly she was fighting for her breath. She couldn't move, but mercy, she could feel. She felt as if she'd been hit by a couple of Mack trucks.

Harlan latched on to the guy and shoved both himself and the man off her. Thank God. Still fighting for breath, Caitlyn rolled to the side and tried to pick through the darkness to see who'd done this. She seriously doubted it was Clayton or Slade, because they probably would have said something before launching an attack.

And there was no doubt about it—this was an attack.

The man threw a punch at Harlan, and it connected, but it glanced right off his jaw as if he hadn't even felt it. Maybe because the blow hadn't been that hard, but also because Harlan had to be operating on pure adrenaline.

Caitlyn certainly was.

Despite the crushing pain in her chest, she groped around on the ground, searching for the gun she'd dropped. Harlan might need her as backup if something went wrong with this fight.

A shot blasted through the air.

Sending her heart to her knees.

Despite the other shots, the sound was still unexpected, and deafening. And it robbed her of her breath again.

"Harlan?" she shouted. But she couldn't tell if he'd been hit or if he'd even been the one to fire that shot.

The scuffle continued with fists flying and with the men tangled around each other in the fight. They stumbled backward and would have crashed into her again if Caitlyn hadn't scrambled out of the way just in the nick of time.

Harlan's back bashed into the tree. She heard the sound of pain he made. His profanity, too. And despite that pain he came up fighting. He drew back his gun and knocked the guy upside the head.

Still the man didn't stop.

Caitlyn saw the weapon he had clutched in his hand. He made a feral sound. More animal than human. And though she didn't recognize his voice, there was something about that sound, some raw emotion in it that she did recognize.

"Farris?" she called out.

The man stopped. For just a fraction of a second. And he turned toward her as if he were trying to launch himself at her.

Harlan didn't let that happen.

He grabbed Farris by the throat and slung him to the ground. Unlike her, however, Farris held on to his gun, and even though he was on the ground, he pointed the weapon directly at her.

Caitlyn froze.

"Marshal, if you pull the trigger, I'll pull mine," Farris warned. "And Caitlyn will die."

God. This was exactly what she'd spent months trying to avoid. Yes, Harlan was armed, and he had his gun pointed at Farris, but Farris could get off a shot, kill her and then turn that gun on Harlan.

She had to do something to stop this.

"You have no reason to kill Harlan." She tried to keep her voice level. Hard to do, since she was shaking from head to toe.

"Yeah, I do." Farris was shaking, too, and she prayed

he didn't pull that trigger before she could talk him out of it. "I know you're pregnant, and I know it's his kid."

She shook her head. "No. I'm not pregnant."

"You're lying. I heard Harlan when he said it, and he was practically gloating."

So Farris had been listening in on that call. No surprise there, since it was his hired gun they'd been talking to. The person had likely kidnapped Declan and Billy, too, because Farris wouldn't have wanted to get his hands dirty like that.

But he'd saved his fight to come after her.

"How could you have gone to his bed?" Farris spat out the words, and without taking his eyes or gun off her, he got to his feet. Less than a yard away from Harlan.

"I didn't," she lied. She shook her head when Harlan inched closer to Farris. Probably because he was planning to knock that gun from his hand.

Or try.

But Caitlyn was hoping it wouldn't come to that.

"Harlan hates me," Caitlyn said, "because I'm writing an article about his foster father. I'm spilling all the details of how the marshals are covering up his involvement in Jonah Webb's murder."

Farris glanced at Harlan. Maybe to see if he could tell if that was true. Harlan didn't jump to defend her, thank God, but there must have been something about Harlan's expression that made Farris's mouth twist into a snarl.

"Don't you know that I see you've been with him?" Farris fired back.

Yeah, she could see that, and she could argue it until she was blue in the face, but Farris wasn't going to believe her. It was time to go with plan two.

"I'll go with you," she told Farris.

Now Harlan protested. First with some vicious profanity. And while he didn't exactly look at her, she could feel every muscle in his body reacting to that. "You're not going anywhere with this nutcase."

"That's not your decision to make," Farris fired back. Though he still didn't sound convinced that she was telling the truth.

And she wasn't.

No way would she leave with him. Heaven knew what kind of sick ways he could come up with to torture her before he killed her. And he would kill her. His obsession and rage wouldn't allow him to keep her alive. But Caitlyn was counting heavily on Harlan being able to stop a getaway. All she needed to do was give Farris enough distraction for Harlan to get the jump on him.

She took a step closer to Farris, hoping that it was distraction enough.

It snagged Farris's attention, all right. His split-second glances turned just slightly longer each time his gaze swung in her direction. He was obviously trying to figure out if he could trust her. Or at least trying to figure out how to get her out of there while neutralizing Harlan.

"I'll go with him," she said to Harlan.

Like Farris, Harlan gave her only a quick glance, but in that simple glance something passed between them. She saw his silent assurance that he was not going to let her die.

Too bad that Farris must have seen it, too.

A strangled groan tore from Farris's throat. "You're in love with him. You bitch!"

And that was the only warning she got before Farris launched himself at her. He didn't reach her.

Thanks to Harlan.

Before Farris could get to her, Harlan tackled him, and again both men crashed to the ground. This time, though, she saw Farris's gun go flying, and Caitlyn knew this fight was pretty much over. Harlan not only outsized him, he'd been trained how to fight.

Still, Farris fought like a wildcat, all the while yelling and flailing his arms around. One punch from Harlan, however, and Farris's head flopped back.

Caitlyn reached for Farris's gun so that he wouldn't be able to snatch it up, but reaching for it was as far as she got.

Someone hooked an arm around her neck, and her body snapped back. She landed right against his chest. And before she could make a sound, someone shoved a gun to her head.

CHAPTER SEVENTEEN

HARLAN HAD TO restrain himself, but part of him wished that Farris was dead so the man could no longer torment Caitlyn.

But he wasn't about to murder an unarmed man.

Especially one he could restrain. He grabbed Farris and hauled him to his feet so he could drag him to the truck and get a pair of plastic handcuffs from the glove compartment.

Harlan stopped when he caught a movement from the corner of his eye, and without loosening his grip on Farris, he whirled in Caitlyn's direction.

Everything inside him came crashing down.

No, hell, no. This couldn't be happening. But it was. Caitlyn was standing there, white as a ghost in the pale moonlight, and someone had a gun on her.

"I didn't see him in time," she whispered.

That felt like a fist around his heart. She was apologizing for being put in another life-and-death situation. One not of her own making. It was Farris's making.

Or maybe not.

Harlan had to amend that theory when he caught a glimpse of the man's face. Not some hired gun. He knew this man.

Curtis.

"You said I could have Caitlyn," Farris practically shouted. "You said you wouldn't hurt her."

"There's been a change of plans." Curtis's voice was eerily calm, and unlike Farris, his hand wasn't shaking.

The mark of a cold-blooded killer.

"Marshal McKinney, you need to put down your gun and step away from Farris," Curtis ordered.

Harlan didn't budge, but Farris struggled, fighting to get away from him. However, Harlan held on. He didn't want Farris going after Caitlyn. Not with that gun right at her head. Even if Curtis didn't have plans to shoot her, the gun might accidentally go off.

"This guy isn't dealing with a full deck," Harlan said, tipping his head to Farris. "If I let him go, he might try to kill all of us."

"He won't." And there didn't appear to be a shred of doubt in Curtis's tone, which meant they'd worked out some kind of sick deal.

Caitlyn didn't say a word. Didn't take her gaze off Harlan, and he cursed when he realized that she was still giving him an apologetic look.

"Your gun," Curtis reminded Harlan. "And let go of Farris so he can leave."

Farris made another of those outraged sounds. "I'm not leaving without her." Again he tried to tear himself away from Harlan, but Curtis shifted the gun toward Harlan and him.

"My advice—cooperate." And coming from Curtis, it didn't sound like a suggestion. "If things work out as planned, you might be able to have Caitlyn after all." Curtis's mouth tightened. "Though why you'd want a woman in love with another man, I don't know."

It was twice in one night that someone had accused

her of being in love with him, and if Harlan hadn't been between this rock and a hard place, he might have given it some thought. However, the only thoughts he had right now were how to get out of this.

Caitlyn muttered something and shifted her body weight as if she might drop to the ground. Curtis hooked his arm around her neck, snapped her to him and pointed the gun at her again.

As bad as it was to see that gun right on her—and it was bad—Harlan had to look at the bigger picture here. He had to keep Curtis's mind off the fact that Harlan was still armed. The longer he could hang on to his gun, the better.

"Where's Declan?" Harlan wanted to know the answer to that, but he wasn't sure he'd get the truth from Curtis. Still, the conversation might distract him until Harlan could figure out a way to get that gun from his hand.

"He'll join us soon. At gunpoint, of course."

Harlan didn't doubt the gunpoint part. In fact, there might be several hired guns in on this. But why was he bringing Declan here?

"You plan to use Declan for more leverage?" Harlan asked. But he already had the ultimate leverage with Caitlyn.

"You don't need Declan or Harlan down here if you have me," Caitlyn volunteered. "You can let them go."

Curtis made a sound of disagreement. "I need you both, actually. You and Harlan," he clarified, aiming a glare at Farris. "Temporarily. Just hold on to your sanity a moment or two longer, and you might get what you want from this."

Because Harlan still had a grip on Farris, he felt the

man's muscle tense. "I paid big money to get her," Farris shouted. "Hell, I funded this entire operation for one reason. *Her.*"

So that explained, well, pretty much nothing. Farris had the money to pay for an attack like this, but Harlan still didn't know the reason Curtis would plan their capture and murder.

But he could guess why.

"It's your fingerprint they'll find on Sherry's neck," Harlan challenged.

Curtis didn't jump to deny it. "There'll be no fingerprint to find, because right about now someone's blowing up the morgue."

Harlan had no idea if that was true, but at that exact moment his phone buzzed. He couldn't take his attention off Curtis to see who was calling and why. But maybe if someone had tried to set an explosive at the morgue, then the person watching the place had managed to stop it.

He could hope anyway.

Curtis obviously hoped the opposite because he smiled. For a moment or two anyway. Then he glanced down at his watch and cursed.

Was this profanity for Declan because he hadn't arrived yet? Or was something else going on? Either way, Harlan hoped he had his own backup in the area. Certainly by now Slade and/or Clayton should be nearby, and he hoped like the devil it didn't take them too long to get here.

"This is the third time I've asked you to put down that gun," Curtis warned Harlan. "If I have to ask again, I start shooting, and Caitlyn will get the first bullet."

Now Harlan cursed. Because he knew time for distraction was over. He couldn't risk Caitlyn's life, so he dropped his gun on the ground. Right by his feet. Maybe he'd be able to get to it in a hurry if things turned bad.

And he was afraid *bad* was just getting started.

"You murdered Sherry," Caitlyn concluded, obviously trying to make her own distraction. "And now you're trying to cover it up by using us." Despite the gun at her head, she tossed Curtis a glare. "Did you kill Tiffany, too?"

"I had to. I'd already killed Sherry and needed a way to cover it up." Curtis lifted his shoulder. "I figured if the Rangers would try to link Tiffany's death to Webb's murder, then they'd try to link Sherry's, too."

"And you wanted Sherry dead because she was asking questions about some of your shady business investments." Plain and simple, it was a guess, but judging from the way Curtis's eyes narrowed, Harlan had hit pay dirt. "So you sent out those threatening notes to make everyone believe her disappearance was connected to Rocky Creek."

"I sent those notes," Farris piped up.

Curtis huffed as if dealing with an annoying insect. "Because I told him to do it. Farris isn't much of a self-starter when it comes to detailed plans like this one. All that psychosis gets in the way."

Taunting a crazy man wasn't how Harlan would have gone about this. However, it was obvious Curtis wasn't pleased with the man who'd paid to cover up a murder, all so he could get his hands on Caitlyn.

"I'm guessing that Curtis promised he'd draw out Caitlyn for you," Harlan asked Farris.

"He promised more than that," Farris confirmed. "He contacted me out of the blue and said he could draw her out. He told me I could do whatever I wanted and that I wouldn't have to go back to that place."

To the institution, no doubt.

Curtis checked his watch again. Cursed some more. The man was obviously unaware or just didn't care that Farris was about to snap.

"Henry?" Curtis called out. Probably to the man who'd kidnapped Declan.

No answer.

And that only made Curtis's profanity even worse.

"You think Curtis will keep his promise to you?" Caitlyn asked, her attention nailed to Farris now. "You really believe he'll let you out of this alive? Not a chance. No way would he let a loon like you go so you could spill to every lawman in the state."

Farris stopped struggling, his gaze locked with Caitlyn's. Hell. She was baiting him. The very thing Harlan didn't want her to do, even if she was trying to get Farris to go after Curtis and not her.

"Don't listen to her," Curtis snapped.

"He doesn't want you to listen because he knows I'll tell you that you've been duped. All that money you spent, and he has no intention of following through on his promises." She paused, managed a syrupy smile. "Because he intends to keep me for himself."

Farris froze. Unlike Caitlyn, Harlan couldn't see the man's expression, but he didn't need to see it to feel the rage roar through Farris's body.

Before Harlan could stop him, Farris ripped out of Harlan's grip and, screaming, lunged for Caitlyn.

Just as a shot blasted the night air.

THE SHOT CAME so close to Caitlyn's right ear that she felt the heat from the bullet. And the deafening noise. God, it was awful. The pain stabbed through her head, and she would have fallen to her knees if Curtis hadn't kept a death grip choke hold around her neck.

But Farris was the one who dropped to his knees.

With his gaze frozen on her, he slipped to the ground. "I'll always love you," Farris said.

Even though the pain made everything sound like a roar, she somehow managed to hear the words. Sickening words from a sick man.

Farris reached out as if he might try to touch her, but Curtis kicked at him, his boot connecting with Farris's hand. Grunting in pain, Farris pulled back his hand and clutched it to his chest.

Where the bullet had slammed into him.

"Goodbye, Caitlyn," Farris mumbled, and he slumped into a heap.

Caitlyn didn't have to feel his pulse to know he was dead. She could see it on his now lifeless face. There was no way she could feel sorry for him. Not after everything he'd done, but she was also painfully aware that the biggest threat wasn't Farris.

But rather Curtis.

Now that he'd killed Farris and confessed to Sherry's murder, there was no way he'd let them walk out of there alive. Of course, there was no way she and Harlan would just stand by while he shot them either. But Curtis was the one with the gun.

There was a rustling sound to her left, and while keeping her firmly in his grip, Curtis pivoted in that direction. Harlan moved, too. Toward his gun on the ground next to Farris.

"If you pick it up, she dies," Curtis warned him.

Harlan stopped, but the rustling sound didn't.

"Henry?" Curtis called out.

"Not Henry," the person answered.

Slade.

Caitlyn felt instant relief followed by instant fear. Slade sounded close. Very close. And that meant he could be hurt. It was bad enough that she and Harlan were in danger—Declan, too—but she didn't want to add any more of Harlan's family members to the mix.

"Who are you?" Curtis demanded.

"Marshal Slade Becker. And I'm guessing you're about to be dead."

That didn't help with her fear. Yes, Slade was likely a good shot, but Curtis's gun was still pressed right to her head. Worse, at any second he could turn that gun on Harlan.

Curtis dragged her toward a tree until his back was right up against it. That would make it much harder for Slade to get off a shot.

And that meant this was likely a standoff.

"Where's Declan?" Harlan called out to his brother. He didn't take his attention off her, and his body was in a position as if he was primed and ready for a fight.

"Safe and with Clayton. He's a little groggy from being drugged, but he'll be okay. We've cuffed the kidnapper."

Caitlyn had no idea if that was true, but prayed it was, because it meant Curtis had no backup.

Curtis reacted to what Slade had said by cursing and digging the gun barrel into the side of her head. She felt the skin break and the sting of pain. Felt the warm blood, too.

But the worst was seeing Harlan's reaction.

Anger seemed to jolt through his entire body, and she shook her head, praying he wouldn't do anything that would get him killed.

"They found a guy at the morgue, and he had a bag of explosives with him," Slade continued, his voice calm as if discussing the weather. "I'm guessing so he could blow up the place with Sherry's body inside. The sheriff called in a SWAT team and they have him surrounded."

"Shut up!" Curtis yelled. He cursed and shoved her forward. "Caitlyn's coming with me, and you'll both back off because if you don't, she dies."

This couldn't play out in her favor. Either Harlan would get shot trying to stop Curtis, or if Curtis did manage to take her, she wouldn't live long. She, Harlan and now Slade were the ultimate loose ends.

Maybe even Declan, too.

She had to do something to stop this from becoming worse than it already was. But what? Hard to do much of anything when she didn't have a weapon and Curtis was bigger and stronger than she was.

"I'll go with him." She kept her gaze pinned to Harlan when she said that and hoped he would get out of the way when Curtis started shooting.

And he *would* shoot.

Maybe in the next second or two. He was probably counting on the shots to draw out Slade, since Harlan's brother wouldn't be able to return fire as long as she was Curtis's human shield.

"I'm going to hold you to that dinner date," Caitlyn added.

She saw surprise flash through Harlan's eyes, and she also felt Curtis move the gun away from her head.

Mercy.

He was taking aim at Harlan.

Harlan reacted, already moving down and to the side. Or rather trying to do that so he could scoop up his gun. But she knew there wasn't enough time, because Curtis already had him in his sights.

Caitlyn screamed at the top of her lungs and twisted her body so that she could shove her side against Curtis. It didn't knock him down, but it did cause his hand to move at the exact moment that he pulled the trigger.

The bullet flew past Harlan and smacked into the tree next to him.

Harlan didn't waste any time, and he didn't stoop to pick up his gun. He came right at them, looking very much like a linebacker going after an opposing player. Caitlyn tried to grab Curtis's hand to stop him from firing again.

But she failed.

Curtis pulled the trigger not once but twice, both shots blasting so close to her ear that it drowned out all other sounds. Including whatever Harlan said to her. While he ran toward them, she saw his mouth moving, almost as if he were speaking in slow motion, but she couldn't make out a word.

But she sure felt the impact of Harlan tackling Curtis.

Harlan was a big man, and all those solid muscles plowed right into them. All three went to the ground so hard that Caitlyn could have sworn she saw stars. The pain would have been well worth it.

If Curtis hadn't managed to get off another shot.

Caitlyn couldn't see where the bullet landed, but she prayed it hadn't hit Harlan.

She rammed her elbow into Curtis's stomach and felt

the small victory when he yelped in pain. But her victory was short-lived, because he fired again.

And then he bashed the gun against the side of her head.

It was as if her brain exploded, and Caitlyn had no choice but to quit fighting. The only thing she could do was try to get out of the mix so she'd have a better chance of grabbing that gun from Curtis.

She twisted and turned. Tried to maneuver her body to the side. But she was pinned between them, and she caught the blows coming from both men's fists. It was obvious that Harlan was trying to fight around her, but Curtis kept shoving her right at Harlan's fist.

Caitlyn felt a hard jolt, and for a moment she thought she'd been punched again. But this was no punch. Someone took her by the shoulder, his grip hard and bruising, and he yanked her from the middle of the fight. She caught a glimpse of Slade's face before he slung her on the ground behind him and went after Curtis.

Not that Harlan needed his help.

With her out of the way, Harlan clamped on to Curtis's right wrist and slammed his hand against the tree. The gun finally went flying. But before it even fell, Harlan landed a crushing blow to Curtis's jaw. His head flopped back and his body went limp.

Caitlyn's vision was still blurred from the punches she'd taken. Her hearing sucked, too, because of the bullets fired so close to her ear. But she could see and hear enough to know that this fight was over. Farris was dead and Harlan hauled Curtis to his feet and bashed him into the tree.

Slade pulled a pair of plastic cuffs from his pocket and used them to restrain the man.

"I'll transport him in my vehicle and call the sheriff to see if they have the situation at the morgue contained," Slade volunteered. He looked back at her. "You okay?"

"Fine," she lied. She tried to get up, but her legs were just too wobbly. Caitlyn decided to sit there for a few seconds and catch her breath.

The danger had passed, yes, but it would take a lifetime or two to forget how close they'd all come to dying tonight.

"You should probably run her by the hospital," Slade suggested to Harlan.

Harlan's gaze snapped to her, and she could have sworn the color drained from his face. She must have looked pretty bad for him to have that reaction, and he hurried to help her to her feet.

"Were you shot?" But he didn't wait for her to answer. He shoved her hair from her face and looked her over.

"Not shot," she assured him. However, her panic soon mimicked his when she saw the blood trickling down the side of his head. "Were you?"

He shook his head, snapped her to him and hugged her. It was a little too hard, considering that every part of her was hurting, but Caitlyn didn't pull away. That hug was exactly what she needed.

"This isn't over," Curtis snarled. The look he gave them all could have frozen Hades.

"Sure looks like it's over to me," Harlan snarled right back.

Slade grabbed Curtis and got him moving.

"If you arrest me, he dies," Curtis shouted over his shoulder.

That stopped Slade in his tracks, and he turned and stared at the man. "What the hell does that mean?"

Harlan moved closer, and because he still had her in his grip, Caitlyn got her legs working so she could move, too. This was probably some last-ditch ploy from Curtis to get them to release him, but Caitlyn was positive that wasn't going to happen. Curtis had killed at least two people and had attempted to kill them. The only place he was going was to jail.

But still Curtis smiled.

Definitely not the expression she'd expected, and an icy chill went through her that was bone deep.

"I have an insurance policy." Curtis's smile widened. "If you arrest me, he dies."

No. That icy chill got significantly worse. "Who dies?" Caitlyn managed to ask.

"Kirby, of course. Must have forgotten to mention that I sent a hired gun to the ranch." Curtis met Harlan's stare head-on. "And if he doesn't get a call from me in the next few minutes, his orders are to start shooting."

CHAPTER EIGHTEEN

HARLAN COULDN'T GET his body to move fast enough. He whipped out his phone and punched in the number of the ranch office. The chief hand, Cutter, should have answered the landline, but it rang several times before the answering machine kicked in.

Hell.

He tried Wyatt's cell next because his brother was supposed to be inside the ranch house with Kirby and Stella. But again it rang only once and then went to voice mail.

There could have been a dozen reasons for Wyatt and Cutter not to answer, but Harlan could think of only one very bad one.

The ranch was under attack. His family could need immediate help, and here he was a good forty-five minutes out.

"I'll phone Sheriff Geary," Slade volunteered. He kept a firm grip on Curtis and made the call so he could get some backup out to the ranch. Still, it would take the sheriff at least twenty minutes to arrive.

"My hired gun will be mighty hard to see in the dark," Curtis bragged. "No telling how many places he could hide on a ranch and wait to ambush any- and everyone. You can get all the lawmen you know out there on foot, and it won't save Kirby because you can't kill what you can't see."

It took every ounce of Harlan's restraint not to knock this guy's teeth down his throat. "Call off your man," Harlan demanded.

"Not a chance." Any sign of gloating disappeared, and the eyes of a killer stared back at Harlan. "If I have to rot in a jail cell, then it'll help knowing that you've lost someone you love."

That did it. Harlan caught Curtis's shoulder and bashed him into a tree. "Call off your man," he repeated, and to get his point across he gave Curtis another hard knock.

Curtis laughed. "You think I can file charges for brutality? Heck, might even get the case thrown out because you beat a confession out of me."

Not a chance, and while he would like to add more bruises and maybe a broken bone or two to Curtis's injuries, it was clear this conversation was getting them nowhere fast.

"The sheriff's on his way out to the ranch," Slade relayed to Harlan. "He'll try to contact Wyatt and the others, too."

It was a good start, but not nearly good enough. Harlan needed a vehicle, and unfortunately his truck was literally in a bog.

"What about a chopper?" Caitlyn asked. "Do the marshals have one?"

Harlan shook his head. "The nearest one is in San Antonio, and the sheriff doesn't have one either." They were looking at an hour, maybe longer because it would take an approval higher than Saul to get a chopper in the air.

Kirby, Stella and God knew who else could be dead by then.

Caitlyn snapped her fingers, took his phone and started punching in numbers. "I'm calling my old boss" was all she said.

Harlan wasn't sure she'd get anywhere with this call, but one thing good came out of it. For the first time since his arrest, Curtis actually looked concerned that his plan might not work.

"No time to explain," Caitlyn said the moment her boss answered. She was talking so fast that her words ran together. "But you know all those favors you owe me—well, I'm cashing in. I need the news chopper in the air *now.* Get it out to the Blue Creek Ranch near Maverick Springs." She paused. "Yes, that's the place. Put on the search-and-find lights. There's a gunman on the loose out there, and people are in danger."

Harlan hadn't realized he was holding his breath until she hit the end-call button and handed him back his phone. "He's on the way out there."

Good. Though a reporter probably wouldn't have a way to take out the gunman, at least the lights might help pinpoint the guy's location.

"My truck's that way, parked just up the road," Slade said, tipping his head in that direction and tossing Harlan his keys. "Take Caitlyn with you and leave now. Clayton, Declan and I will take this piece of slime and catch up with you."

Harlan didn't refuse his brother's offer, and even though Caitlyn didn't appear to be in any shape to run, he didn't want to leave her alone there with Farris's body. And he damn sure didn't want her having to ride back to Maverick Springs with the man who'd just tried to murder her.

"Curtis could be lying," Caitlyn said when he caught her hand and got them moving.

Yeah. And Harlan had to remind himself that a lone hired gun would be seriously outnumbered by Wyatt and the other ranch hands. Plus, the security system would have alerted them that they had an intruder trying to break into the house.

Well, unless Curtis had somehow managed to take that out, too.

But Harlan didn't allow himself to go there. He just ran, and when it was clear that Caitlyn wasn't going to be able to keep up with him, he scooped her up in his arms and ran as fast as he could.

His lungs were burning when he finally reached Slade's truck, and he practically shoved Caitlyn inside. She clearly had injuries on her face and arms, and he prayed he wasn't making things worse with his rough treatment.

"Give me your phone," she insisted. "I'll keep calling while you drive." But she didn't wait for him to hand her the phone—she yanked it from his pocket.

"Try Dallas first. His number should be in there because I called him earlier." He started the engine and drove out of there fast.

Thank God there was no traffic at this hour. No rain or fog either. Of course, he'd be driving like a crazy man, so that created more than enough obstacles in their path.

Every passing second seemed to take hours, and with each of those seconds, his worries skyrocketed. Even if Caitlyn and he got there before the gunman could start shooting, that would only put her right back in danger. He couldn't do that to her, but he had to help his family.

Caitlyn scrolled through the recently called numbers, located Dallas's and pressed the button. Harlan heard the call go to voice mail. His nerves were already shot, and that sure didn't help.

"Who should I try next?" she asked.

Harlan mentally went through the possibilities. "Try the house's landline," he finally said, and he rattled off the number.

He heard the rings from the other end of the line. And he prayed and waited. He stopped counting at five rings and was ready to tell her to hang up and call someone else. But then Harlan heard a voice.

Stella.

"Who's there?" Stella demanded.

Caitlyn hit the button to put the call on speaker. "It's me, Harlan. What's going on?"

"Maybe some trouble," the woman immediately answered. Her voice was a whisper. "Somebody set off that new security alarm, and Cutter, Dallas and Wyatt are out there trying to figure who it is."

So unless this was a horrible coincidence, Curtis hadn't been bluffing. He had indeed sent someone. Even though he was already speeding, Harlan went even faster, and prayed the miles would disappear between him and the ranch.

"It's a gunman hired by Curtis Newell," Harlan told her, "and he has orders to shoot up the place."

"Great day in the morning." Stella also mumbled something he didn't catch. "I doubt Wyatt and the others will answer their phones. Probably got the ringers off. What should I do, Harlan? It's dark out there, and trying to find a gunman would be like looking for a needle in a haystack."

Yeah, and the guy could just hide until he had an easy kill shot. "A helicopter's on the way. It might help. In the meantime stay down and stay quiet. Kirby, too," Harlan added. "I don't want either of you taking any chances."

"But if someone could get hurt—"

"Wyatt and Dallas know how to handle this," he said, cutting off any protest. No way did he want Stella out there facing down a hired killer. "Sheriff Geary should be out there any minute now. Call him and tell him what's going on so he doesn't walk into an ambush."

"I will, but get here as fast as you can."

Oh, he would do that. He damn sure didn't want Curtis claiming any more victims. It was bad enough that he'd gotten his hands on Caitlyn.

Harlan glanced at her, but it took more than several glances to take it all in, and what he saw turned his stomach. Even in the thin moonlight, he could see the blood. Not just one spot either but multiple places, including a line running from her eyebrow to her chin.

He'd lost count of how many punches she'd taken while in the middle of his fight with Curtis. Too many, that was for sure.

Harlan cursed, shook his head. "Look what that SOB did to you."

"That bad, huh?" She leaned over and looked in the rearview mirror. "Yeah, that bad."

Caitlyn used the back of her hand to swipe at the blood. Since there was blood on her hand, that didn't work very well, so she grabbed some tissues from his glove compartment. But she didn't dab at her face. She dabbed at his, and even though Harlan tried not to react, he winced when she hit a sore spot.

"Look what that SOB did to you," she repeated.

Harlan didn't want to do a mirror check, but he could feel some of his injuries. Maybe even a cracked rib or two. Still, he'd gotten off lucky.

Because Caitlyn was alive.

The realization of that miracle hit him so hard that he hooked his arm around her and pulled her closer to him. He needed to feel her next to him. Needed to know that she was somehow going to forgive him for not doing a better job of protecting her.

"I'm sorry." He kept his eyes on the road, but he brushed a very gentle kiss on her injured cheek.

She pulled back, looked at him. "For what?"

"For not living up to that complete-package notion you had about me."

That earned him a scowl. "I would give you an elbow jab for that, but I don't want to add to the bruises." She settled against him as if that was exactly where she belonged. "You lived up to the *notion* just fine."

Harlan kept his attention fastened on the road, but he couldn't push the other thoughts out of his head. Thoughts of Caitlyn. Not just of all the bad things that had gone wrong since she'd come back into his life. But of the things that had gone right, too.

Like this moment with her next to him. Making love to her. Hell, just being with her.

"Look." Her head whipped up from his shoulder, and she pointed to the night sky.

Even with just a quick glance, Harlan saw the light in the distance. The helicopter had arrived and had a giant spotlight aimed at the ranch.

He hadn't thought it possible, but time seemed to go even slower, and he could have sworn it took him an hour to drive those last two miles. However, the closer he got, the brighter the light was from the helicopter.

Harlan flew past his place and drove the last leg to the main house. When he took the final curve, he saw someone. And not just someone but a man holding a rifle. His heart went to his knees until he realized that someone was Wyatt.

And he wasn't alone.

Dallas and Cutter were there. The sheriff, too, and they all had weapons pointed at a man kneeling on the ground.

Harlan slammed on the brakes and jumped out. Caitlyn did, too, and she hurried to his side. Just in case things weren't as under control as he thought, Harlan stepped in front of her.

"You're a little late," Wyatt greeted him. "Thanks to the chopper, we found this moron about two minutes ago. Don't worry. Everyone's okay. He didn't get off a shot."

The relief was instant. A lot of prayers had been answered tonight. "You can thank Caitlyn for the chopper," Harlan let his brother know.

"Well, thank you, darlin'." It was Wyatt's usual charming tone, and he aimed that rock-star grin at Caitlyn. A grin that dissolved right away when his gaze landed on them.

"Sheez, you two look like hell," Wyatt mumbled at the same time Dallas said, "How many fights did you lose tonight?" Dallas didn't wait for an answer, because his phone buzzed.

"We won the important one," Harlan insisted.

Well, the important one against Curtis anyway. Harlan figured there was another battle he had left to fight, and this one was just as important as life and death. He put his arm around Caitlyn and pulled her closer to him.

"I'll get this guy into town," the sheriff volunteered.

"I want a plea deal," the man grumbled as Sheriff Geary led him to the cruiser parked just a few yards away. "I'll tell you whatever you want to know. I've got proof that Sherry found out Curtis was laundering money. I stashed away some emails and notes. I'll give 'em to you for a plea deal."

"The only way that deal will happen is if you also have proof that Curtis killed her," Harlan argued.

"Got that, too. He killed her himself. Strangled her right there in her office and then he had me help him cram the body into a freezer at my hunting cabin. I'll show you where it all happened if I get that plea deal."

Harlan wasn't about to refuse the information, but it wouldn't be needed to convict Curtis. Not only did they have his confession, he'd murdered Farris in front of them.

"Clayton, Slade and Declan are on their way to the jail with Curtis," Dallas relayed when he ended his call. "And I just let the chopper crew know the threat was over so they could leave."

Good. One less thing to worry about. Next on his list was getting Caitlyn checked out by the doctor. Well, the next to the next thing. He had something he had to get off his mind first, and it wouldn't wait.

"I don't want just a dinner date with you," Harlan told her.

Caitlyn blinked, and thanks to the chopper he had no trouble seeing her surprised expression. He braced himself for some comeback that would dismiss everything they'd found together.

She shook her head. "And I don't want just sex with you."

Dallas cleared his throat and muttered something about needing to check on Kirby and Stella. Wyatt mumbled something about them finding a bed—soon.

Harlan ignored them both and kissed her. He tried to keep it gentle because they were cut in all the wrong places, but he wanted it to be hot and deep enough to cloud her head a little. Or maybe just to make her remember that they had something special here.

The sheriff's cruiser drove past them. The chopper turned and whirled away, taking the clopping noise with it. But Harlan didn't break the kiss until breathing became an issue.

He pulled back, gathered his breath so he could say what he needed to say.

"I'm in love with you."

Except he wasn't the one to say it. Caitlyn did. She took the words right out of his mouth.

"Run for cover if you feel the need," she continued. "But I've been in love with you since I was sixteen. And though I'm sure you'd like me to feel differently, I'm still in love with you."

He smiled. Winced. Smiled again. "I want you in love with me because I'm in love with you."

Now she smiled. Slow and easy. She grabbed a handful of his shirt and snapped him to her. Yeah, they both winced, but Harlan was sure the heat and love overpowered the pain.

"Marry me," he said. Harlan made sure it wasn't

exactly a question. Because he couldn't take no for an answer.

Caitlyn had been in his life for a long time, and now he wanted her in his heart for even longer.

For a lifetime.

She nodded. "Yes, and if I could say it any faster, I would, because I don't want you to change your mind."

He had no intention of changing his mind and showed her with another kiss.

"Caitlyn, you'll always be my first," he said with his lips touching hers. "And my last."

She smiled. "Even better." Caitlyn kissed him to show him how much she meant it.

* * * * *

We hope you enjoyed reading

AGAINST THE FIRE
by *New York Times* bestselling author
KAT MARTIN
and
OUTLAW LAWMAN
by *USA TODAY* bestselling author
DELORES FOSSEN

Both were originally Harlequin® Series and
MIRA Books stories!

You crave excitement!
Harlequin® Intrigue stories deal in serious
romantic suspense, keeping you on the edge
of your seat as resourceful, true-to-life women
and strong, fearless men fight for survival.

INTRIGUE

**EDGE-OF-YOUR-SEAT INTRIGUE,
FEARLESS ROMANCE.**

Look for six *new* romances every month from
Harlequin Intrigue!

Available wherever books and ebooks are sold.

Something wasn't right.

US marshal Holden Ryland didn't have to rely on his lawman's instincts to know that. The Craftsman-style house was pitch-dark except for a single dim light in the front room. The home owner, Nicky Hart, hated the dark, and whenever she was home, every light was usually blazing.

So, either she'd skipped out on their little chat, or... Holden decided to go with the skipping-out theory because at the moment it was the lesser of two evils. After all, there was a reason why they needed to talk.

A bad one.

Holden slid his hand over the gun in his holster and got out of his truck. He'd barely made it a few steps when her white cat came darting out from beneath the porch. It headed right toward him, coiling around his leg and meowing.

Another sign that something was wrong.

Nicky didn't let the cat outside—ever.

Was Nicky inside? And if so, had something happened to her? Holden cursed himself for not having done a silent approach. That way, he could have parked up the street, slipped around to the side of the house and looked in the windows. It might have alerted her neighbors, but that was better than dealing with some of the bad scenarios going through his head. Still, he hadn't taken that precaution because he hadn't figured he would run into any kind of immediate trouble.

Well, no trouble other than an argument with Nicky.

When he'd called Nicky an hour earlier and told her that he was on his way to their hometown of Silver Creek to talk to her, she hadn't said a word about anything being wrong. In fact, she sounded as if she'd been expecting his call. But then she'd sent a text just a few minutes later, saying she wouldn't be available after all.

Right.

Holden wasn't about to believe that lie. She was dodging him. And not doing a very good job of it, either, because her garage door was up, and he could see her car. That meant she was probably inside and that there was a good explanation for no lights on and the cat being outside. He hoped there was a good explanation anyway.

He kept watch around him, kept watch of the house, too, and made his way to the porch. However, before Holden could even ring the bell, the front door flew open, and he braced himself for what he might see.

INTRIGUE

EDGE-OF-YOUR-SEAT INTRIGUE, FEARLESS ROMANCE.

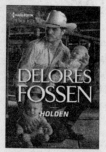

Save $1.00

on the purchase of ANY Harlequin® Intrigue book.

Available wherever books are sold, including most bookstores, supermarkets, drugstores and discount stores.

Save $1.00

on the purchase of any Harlequin® Intrigue book.

Coupon valid until April 30, 2017.
Redeemable at participating outlets in the U.S. and Canada only.
Not redeemable at Barnes & Noble stores. Limit one coupon per customer.

If you enjoyed this story by
New York Times bestselling author

KAT MARTIN

be sure to check out her next high-stakes suspense

AGAINST THE LAW

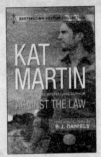

Available April 2017 wherever
Harlequin® Bestselling Author Collection
books and ebooks are sold.

Connect with us on Harlequin.com for info on our
new releases, access to exclusive offers, free online
reads and much more!

Other ways to keep in touch:

Harlequin.com/Newsletters

 Facebook.com/HarlequinBooks

Twitter.com/HarlequinBooks

HarlequinBlog.com

HBACKM0217

THE WORLD IS BETTER WITH

Romance

Harlequin has everything from contemporary, passionate and heartwarming to suspenseful and inspirational stories.

Whatever your mood, we have romance when you need it, wherever you are!

HARLEQUIN®

A *Romance* FOR EVERY MOOD™

www.Harlequin.com

#RomanceWhenYouNeedIt

Reading Has Its Rewards
Earn **FREE BOOKS!**

Register at **Harlequin My Rewards** and submit your Harlequin purchases from wherever you shop to earn points for free books and other exclusive rewards.

Join for FREE today at **www.HarlequinMyRewards.com**.

HSHMYBPA2016